Weber's debut novel is a tour de force! A story of guts, angst, bolcranes, word fights, and storms beyond imagining. Her heroine, a lightning-wielding young woman of immense power and a soft, questioning heart, captures you from word one and holds tight until the final line. Unwilling to let the journey go, I eagerly await Weber's (and Nym's) next adventure."

—KATHERINE REAY, AUTHOR OF DEAR MR. KNIGHTLEY, FOR STORM SIREN

"Mary Weber has created a fascinating, twisted world. Storm Siren sucked me in from page one—I couldn't stop reading! This is a definite must-read, the kind of book that kept me up late into the night turning the pages!"

—LINDSAY CUMMINGS, AUTHOR OF THE MURDER COMPLEX

"Don't miss this one!"

—SERENA CHASE, USATODAY.COM, FOR STORM SIREN

"Readers who enjoyed Marissa Meyer's Cinder series will enjoy this fast-paced fantasy which combines an intriguing storyline with as many twists and turns as a chapter of Game of Thrones!"

—DODIE OWENS, EDITOR, SCHOOL LIBRARY JOURNAL TEEN, FOR STORM SIREN

"Readers will easily find themselves captivated. The breathtaking surprise ending is nothing short of horrific, promising even more dark and bizarre adventures to come in the Storm Siren trilogy."

—RT BOOK REVIEWS, 4 STARS

"Fantasy readers will feel at home in Weber's first novel. . . . A detailed backdrop and large cast bring vividness to the story."

—PUBLISHERS WEEKLY, FOR STORM SIREN

"Weber builds a fascinating and believable fantasy world."

—KIRKUS REVIEWS, FOR STORM SIREN

ACCLAIM FOR MARY WEBER

"A touching and empowering testament to the power of tru[
knowing who you are, *Siren's Fury* is a solid, slightly steamp[
up to the fantasy-driven first book that will leave you with a[
craving for the next volume in the series."

—USA[

"There are few things more exciting to discover than a debut n[
with powerful storytelling and beautiful language. *Storm Sire*[
those rarities. I'll read anything Mary Weber writes. More, plea[

—JAY ASHER, *NEW YORK TIMES* BE[

AUTHOR OF *THIRTEEN REA*[

"*Storm Siren* is a riveting tale from start to finish. Between th[
ing romance, the rich and inventive fantasy world, and one seri[
dropping finale, readers will clamor for the next book—and I'll[
front of the line!"

—MARISSA MEYER, *NEW YORK TIMES* BES[

AUTHOR OF *CINDER* AND THE LUNAR CHR[

"Intense and intriguing. Fans of high stakes fantasy won't be able[
down."

—C.J. REDWINE, AUTHOR OF *DEFIANCE*, FOR *STOR*[

"A riveting read! Mary Weber's rich world and heartbreaking heroi[
me from page one. You're going to fall in love with this love story."

—JOSEPHINE ANGELINI, INTERNATIONALLY BESTS[

AUTHOR OF THE *STARCROSSED* TRILOGY, FOR *STORM*[

"Elegant prose and intricate world-building twist into a breathless cy[
of a story that will constantly keep you guessing. More, please!"

—SHANNON MESSENGER, AUTHOR O[

SKY FALL SERIES, FOR *STORM S*[

"This adventure, in the vein of 1980s fantasy films, has readers rooting for the heroes to smite the wicked baddies. Buy where fantasy flies."

—DANIELLE SERRA, *SCHOOL LIBRARY JOURNAL*, FOR *STORM SIREN*

"Mary Weber's debut novel reflects an author sensitive to her audience, a stellar imagination, and a killer ability with smart and savvy prose."

—RELZ REVIEWZ, FOR *STORM SIREN*

"Between the beautiful words used to create this fairy-tale world, to the amazing power of the Elementals, to the aspects of slavery and war, I'd say this book is a must-read for any fantasy lover. It's powerful and will keep you turning pages faster than you thought possible. I can't believe this is Mary Weber's debut novel. Congratulations!"

—GOOD CHOICE READING BLOG, FOR *STORM SIREN*

SIREN'S SONG

Other Books by Mary Weber

Storm Siren
Siren's Fury

SIREN'S SONG

Book Three in the Storm Siren Trilogy

MARY WEBER

Thomas Nelson
Since 1798

Published in Nashville, Tennessee, by Thomas Nelson. Thomas Nelson is a registered trademark of HarperCollins Christian Publishing, Inc.

Author is represented by the literary agency of Alive Communications, Inc., 7680 Goddard Street, Suite 200, Colorado Springs, CO 80920, www. alivecommunications.com.

Map by Tom Gaddis

Thomas Nelson titles may be purchased in bulk for educational, business, fund-raising, or sales promotional use. For information, please e-mail SpecialMarkets@ThomasNelson.com.

Publisher's Note: This novel is a work of fiction. Names, characters, places, and incidents are either products of the author's imagination or used fictitiously. All characters are fictional, and any similarity to people living or dead is purely coincidental.

Library of Congress Cataloging-in-Publication Data

Names: Weber, Mary (Mary Christine) author.
Title: Siren's song / Mary Weber.
Description: Nashville : Thomas Nelson, [2016] | Series: The storm siren trilogy
Identifiers: LCCN 2015036284 | ISBN 9781401690403 (hardback)
Subjects: LCSH: Fantasy fiction.
Classification: LCC PS3623.E3946 S63 2016 | DDC 813/.6--dc23 LC record available at http://lccn.loc.gov/2015036284

Printed in the United States of America

16 17 18 19 20 RRD 6 5 4 3 2

For Jeanette Morris, who is the queen
of helping me find my voice
in my writing and, even more so, in my soul.

And for Allen Arnold,
(aka Allen the Fabler, Travelling Baronet).
For stepping into my Story and changing it forever.
And for providing big brother laughter
and heart along the way.

For my shield this day I call:
strong power . . .
in the glorious company
of the holy and risen ones,
in the prayers of the fathers,
in visions prophetic
and commands apostolic,
in the annals of witness,
in virginal innocence,
in the deeds of steadfast men.

—FROM SAINT PATRICK'S BREASTPLATE

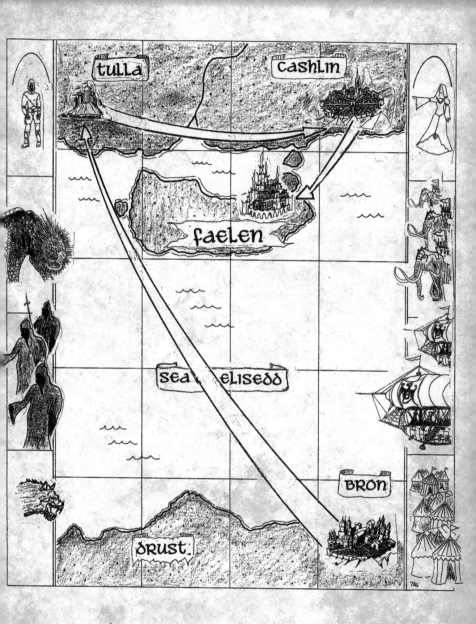

SEVENTEEN YEARS AGO

S HORT MEWING SOUNDS RIPPLE THE NIGHT AIR inside the thin wooden shack. The whimpers are soft and brand new, like the baby emitting them, and hardly muted by blankets the mum's using to swaddle the tiny child against her chest.

"Thank the Creator it's a girl," a man's voice breathes. "Let me see her."

"She's too chilled. Wait until morning."

"Helena." His voice is gentle, coaxing. "Let me see our child."

The woman clings tighter, attaching the babe to her breast so the suckling takes the place of the cries.

"Helena," he says again, but this time his tone is laced with suspicion. "What's wrong?"

"Nothing. Just let us wait until—"

A slight brush of cold as the blanket is pulled back from the babe's head. It's followed by an exclamation—both from the suddenly cold child and the surprised man.

"She's . . . she's . . ."

"She's like you," the mum murmurs.

"Impossible." But the man's tone is more astonishment than annoyance. "What do you think it means?"

"It means she's the miracle."

"She's Elemental."

"She's the one we have been waiting for. From the prophecy." Her firm tone falls desperate. "She *must be* the one."

The man lets the blanket drop back over the babe's head with a surprised grunt. "But she's from us."

"Aye. And what's wrong with us?"

A soft chuckle. "A lowly common-house maid living in an internment camp because she made the mistake of marrying an Elemental. And a half-crippled one at that." He lifts the blanket again. "We can't keep her. Our time here is already limited, and if they find her, she'll be—"

"I know."

"I'll call for Delaney," the man muses. "She'll know what to do."

"She'll send her away."

"Better that than the alternative."

The woman pulls the babe from her breast enough to peer down at the snowy-white fuzz on her head and sea-blue eyes. "And if she doesn't survive?"

"She's not even supposed to exist. Whatever choice we make, she may not survive. So hold it all lightly, my love."

The crying starts up again, soft and mewing.

For a moment it sounds like the notes of a lament coming from the babe's mouth.

The babe who was never supposed to exist.

The babe who is not meant to survive.

CHAPTER 1

I PULL HARDER ON THE AIR CURRENTS WHILE STARING at the broad-shouldered black man beside me. I still can't keep my focus off him—off the fact that he's real and alive and truly here with me—feet planted firmly on the airship's deck as he surveys the Tullan earth flying by beneath our small war-shredded fleet. The red dirt and rocks have long since changed with the landscape below to brown and green shadows, blending together like a muddy painting as the airship vibrates and the sound of the droning engine competes with his soldiers' shouts.

Eogan doesn't move to give orders or shout back. Just stands there in his torn red Bron suit in the same stance he's been in ever since finishing his kingly duty of checking on his men and assessing the full extent of our losses. And, if my suspicions are correct, interrogating Lady Isobel and Lord Myles in the dining room where they're being detained.

His handsome face barely shows the strain.

Even his skin and clothes, stained with the blood of wraiths and men from the battle we're fleeing, only serve to make his twenty-two-year-old self look fierce as hulls.

I bite my lip and steady my legs, weakened from my aching chest wounds. And keep my gaze level on him. This king who spent the past few months as my trainer, stealing every bent piece of my bleeding soul only to break those pieces with his own confessions—before resetting them.

He is the choice I made over this world and the Tullan people.

He is the chance I took. *And I'd take it again in a heartbeat.*

For the hundredth time in the past four hours, the thought emerges that I don't know if that makes me selfish or weak or daftly insane, but there is the bittersweet truth of it.

∞

FOUR HOURS EARLIER

I reach up and push fingers into Eogan's jagged black hair, then pull him closer as he studies me with a gaze that says he knows how unsure my heart is. And how heavily it's breaking. For Colin's homeland of Tulla and its people we've just abandoned to Draewulf. For the entire Hidden Lands.

The airship we're being whisked away on lurches, then rises higher as Eogan's green eyes pierce mine, and suddenly I swear he's pulling back the lid on my soul, and in the process he's accidentally exposing *his* soul. Which, if the flash of grief is any indication, is aching just as bad as mine. Even if he still doesn't know how to acknowledge it—or what to do with it.

Next thing I know his mouth is present against mine, his lips searing, burning my bones, setting my soul to crash into his earthen heart like sea storms in winter. Bringing with it a hint of his calm to flow through my sliced-open, bleeding chest where I'd clawed my flesh open in my attempt to get the dark ability out. Willing me the belief that love can fix a multitude of worlds and souls and wounds—and promising to send my hope soaring for what goodness our world can still produce. And for the hundredth time around this man I am completely undone.

Blast him.

I have to resist turning back to survey the burnt sky and red rocks of Tulla, or look for Draewulf's ships amid the smoke. *Are they pursuing us?* "What happens if Draewulf reaches Cashlin first?" I whisper.

"He'll take over the queen and her Luminescent ability."

"And then what—he'll come for Faelen's King Sedric?" *Will his Dark Army come?*

"Then he'll come for me," Eogan says.

My hand flutters to find his against the cold metal. "I won't let him. We'll hide you."

His smile is soft as he shakes his head. "I've been hiding the past four years and it didn't do any good. The only way to defeat him now is to fight."

"And if he kills you next time?"

He falls silent. Enough so that I look up at him. "If he kills me, then he'll come to Faelen," he says quietly. "But not for King Sedric."

I frown. "But the prophecy—"

"The right to rule was given to five Uathúils—five monarchs. And the line of Faelen's royal blood was always the strongest. A lineage that belonged to the original rulers of Faelen." He pauses and softens his gaze, reaching his words deep into my soul. "Sedric's ancestors weren't Uathúils, nor were they the original kings. The Elementals were."

The airship shudders, and the sensation is answered by a matching quiver beneath my skin. In my veins. In my chest's torn-open flesh that is threatening to make me feel woozy. I blink and frown harder at him. And swallow as the voice of the witch who was Draewulf's wife rattles in my chest. *"And whatever you do, don't let him take the final one."*

When I look down, my left hand is twisting even tighter into the crippled stump owner number fourteen made of it. As it squeezes, a tiny black line emerges through the vein beneath its skin, and for a fleeting second the feeling of dark hunger edges my lungs.

Like the distinct imitation of a spider testing my sinew before beginning to reweave her web.

Eogan's voice emerges again through the wind and sea salt and snowcapped air. "When he comes to Faelen, it'll be for you. Because you're last in line, Nym."

∽

PRESENT

I inhale and open my mouth. Then shut it.

Eogan's gaze shifts to study mine before it falls to my shaky fist. "How is it?"

I swallow and glance away and crush my fingers to give a fresh burst of wind. "It's weak, but the power's definitely there. It's growing."

"That's not what I meant." He nods at my chest.

"Still hurts, but it'll be fine." *I hope.* I haven't looked at it since the sight of the shredded skin nearly made me vomit hours ago.

He slips a hand over my arm as if to test to see if I'm lying, because clearly he knows me too well. The span of a heartbeat goes by before I feel his soothing ability wash over me, and this time I welcome it, embrace it, allow my body to rest in it a moment.

His face turns the slightest bit gray and weary. "And without the dark ability, how is it?"

"Better. Calmer." I allow a smile. "More myself."

He snorts. "So, ornery as hulls then. Lovely."

6

I'm debating smacking the arrogance off his face, except he glances away—so quick I almost miss his expression in the dying sun. It's thick with tension and hope and something suggestive of attraction.

I smirk. Until two seconds later when I nearly jump out of my skin as the nearby airships sound their horns.

One,

two,

five airships altogether, counting ours. The captains alerting each other we're all here. We're all okay, and we're all flying as fast as possible through the icy air to the strange kingdom of Cashlin, which we've never seen, to rescue a Luminescent queen we've never met. In hopes we'll reach her before Draewulf is done ravaging the land of Tulla we've left only hours ago.

I peer down at my own blood-hardened, torn red dress. Just like earlier, I don't have to look behind us to know the black smoke from the battle is still climbing. I feel it billowing up and clawing at the sky. Like spirits from the grave. Moving over the mountains along our right—to reach beyond them to Faelen and the Elisedd Sea.

Suddenly my stomach is twisting again over what those wraiths are doing to the people we left behind in Tulla. What they're doing to Rasha, Cashlin's princess and my friend. If only we'd acted faster, stronger—if only I'd been more decisive and moved against Draewulf on the flight there from the kingdom of Bron—

Eogan's lips flicker sad. "Don't."

"What?"

He raises a perfect brow at me. "I know you're thinking it again, and *don't*."

"Really? Because I was thinking how very much like a bolcrane you—"

The airship beneath our feet lurches and drops down on the currents, wobbling so hard I have to grab the deck railing to keep my balance this time. *Litches.*

"We'll get Rasha back, I swear. And like I said, I was wrong about you being able to kill Draewulf. Once you'd destroyed me, he wouldn't have had my block to contain him and would've succeeded sooner. So stop skinning yourself over it. Better to focus on asking me your questions, don't you think?"

I frown at his daft piercing gaze. The conceited stare that says he knows what else I've been thinking and is simply waiting for me to get around to it while he stands here. *Blasted oaf.* The questions come flooding back anyway, though—about me being Draewulf's final target. About my Elemental heritage. About what I am and what my parents must have been.

I snort, purse all hint of amusement from my lips, and don't ask anything.

His short laugh catches in the breeze, and next thing I know the sound has sent my lungs running for air—my aches and attitude melting with it. Because it's the rich chuckle that's his and his alone. Draewulf could never mimic or claim it even when he possessed Eogan's body—and how no one recognized it was the shape-shifter wearing Eogan's skin based on that missing clue is ridiculous.

Even so, I allow a barrage of ice flecks to impale his jagged black bangs swagged across his left cheek. He pushes a hand through them, which only succeeds in making them stand up like a rooster tail, making me chuckle too.

And just like that, the air is thick with it again. He doesn't even feign differently, just swerves his admiring gaze across my messy-haired, tattered-dress figure and reaches for me. He tows me close until I can feel his warm breath fighting the wind for the right to snag my hair.

For less than three seconds I actually pretend to bat him away before giving in to the comfort of his arms and skin and uniformed chest. Because whatever I regret about having to leave the Terrenes and their people to fend for themselves, I *will not* regret this. *Him.*

"I missed you," I whisper.

"I rather missed me too."

I pinch his bicep and he yelps—before I fold in tighter between his arms and try as hard as hulls to hear his heart beat beat beating over the airship's droning. I'm answered with another surge of calm that flows through my skin to coat the very lining of my veins and rib cage.

"I'm glad you're you again," he murmurs into my hair.

"Are you just going to repeat everything I'm thinking? Because I was about to say the same for you."

He laughs, although it's weaker this time. "To be honest, I'd rather erase everything you're thinking." He tugs my chin up until my eyes connect with his. "Except for this." He presses his lips to my forehead. Where they stay.

Where *we* stay for what feels like hours.

Until a soldier's shrill voice rips apart the moment. "Look ahead! To the mountain peaks."

We're almost there.

I feel Eogan swallow and sigh before he releases me and turns to the soldiers assembling across the deck. There's a new weariness in his stance.

"I should help them. Except . . ." Except his gaze says he's not about to leave my side any more than he's already had to.

"I'll help too."

He nods toward those soldiers who are shoving aside the ignored wraith bodies from Draewulf's Dark Army piled outside the dining room wall. Or what's left of the bodies. Apparently the living dead can only be stopped by dismemberment beyond recognition, which means the pieces are still leaking greasy black blood all over the deck.

It calls a shiver up my spine. Because even their blood still feels alive. As if the sorcery that made them is still here, still feeding off their flesh.

Still hunting us.

My skin prickles and the sensation of Draewulf's presence suddenly rushes across the distance to slither inside my blood and just about bowls me over. *"I'm coming for it,"* I feel him murmur. *"For all of it. I'm coming for you."*

What the—? I gasp and fog spurts up past us as the ship dips. I peer behind us through the misty dim at the Tullan black smoke.

Eogan pauses. "Nym?"

I shake my head. "It's nothing. I just—"

A muffled boom shakes the metal beneath our feet, and the next second a blast of air attacks my face and body and sends the ship shuddering.

What in blazes?

I look over in time to see one of the four nearby airships plunge down. The resounding boom is followed by a terrible shredding that's loud enough to drown out the roar of our own engines. *Oh hulls no.* I lean over the railing and watch as the neighboring ship begins spinning below us, slowly at first, until it picks up speed and twists in the air.

I glance up at Eogan, then around at the faces of the soldiers as they rush to the railing. My gut swirls in horror right along with that ship.

"Is it Draewulf?" someone shouts.

"Or the Cashlins? Are they targeting us?"

Eogan's fingers move almost instinctively from my waist to my arm, and I tighten my left hand's deformed fingers into a fist. We're rewarded by a flash of light igniting the dark sky, followed by a ripple of thunder that is still weak and weary sounding, but at least my abilities are coming back.

Eogan presses down on my wrist—not to will me his calm but to ignite my power. I lift my hand and let the air currents slide over it, cold and smooth like ocean tides on white sand. And beg the Elemental in my blood to stir faster, stronger. To shiver alive and recuperate quicker.

One heartpulse.

Two heartpulses.

The nearby ship keeps lilting and falling in spurts.

Three.

"It's not working." *Oh litches, it's not working.*

I turn to Eogan. And pause. Because suddenly it's not just me—something's wrong with him too. Eogan is weakening. Whatever energy he's giving out, it's draining him and his skin is turning ashen.

I pull my arm away and grapple for control of the wind beneath the dropping airship, but it's nearly impossible, especially without interfering with the flight of the one we're on or the three farther out. The wind around us begins wailing, the atmosphere growing violent. I cling with one hand to the rail while my other works to steady the air.

Until the failing airship below us tilts up midspin and exposes the source of the shredding: the ship has a gaping hole in its side.

The soldier closest to me gasps. "Sabotage."

"No, it was weakened during the battle, and the force of the wind at our speed has taken its toll." Eogan points to where the airship's metal sheeting has peeled back. "That's not man or magic caused. It's a design flaw."

The soldier respectfully looks away. Eogan would know such a thing better than anyone. He's the one who created them.

It doesn't matter now though because the ship just keeps spinning faster. Like a child's pinwheel.

Another boom rocks the air from my chest as one of the metal planks peels off the ship's side and flies up to rupture the balloon.

The moment freezes.

Every soldier lining the deck near us freezes.

As if we all know the horror that is to come for the soldiers and child captains on board that airboat.

It drops like a rock from the space nearby.

CHAPTER 2

B LEEDING HULLS," EOGAN BELLOWS.

Pieces of the ship's balloon rip and tear off and flail up wildly past us as the thing falls, sinking down down down. Like one of the paper boat-kites I used to take out to fly in storms when owner number three wasn't looking. Those ships always sank as soon as the rain hit them.

Oh please, no.

My prayers are too late. My stomach clenches and ignites as a burst of flames and heat billows up through the dark, announcing that the ship and its occupants have hit what appears to be a thickly forested ground.

Suddenly my insides are lurching and my nausea is twisting into fear as a loud tearing sound rips through the space above me. This time it's closer. Louder.

Without looking up, I know it's our ship.

Eogan's large guard, Kenan, swears, and I glance up at the giant balloon overhead to where the Bron soldiers have used metal ropes and tethered themselves to posts as they scamper about. A few minutes ago they were almost done repairing the rip Draewulf put in the balloon.

Not anymore.

The hole has just split wider with the shifting winds and a spike of metal from the other ship's hull that flew up and impaled it.

Eogan grabs for me, pulling me against him, and yells for the men to hit the deck or tie onto something. The airship lilts and drops, and I swear bile comes up my throat.

From somewhere nearby, Kenan yells, "Tell the captains to go faster."

"We've just passed over the river separating Tulla from Cashlin," Eogan says. "Any faster and this ship will shred apart like the one we just lost. Have the fuelers open the vents all the way to keep the balloon filled, and have the men who're roped on clear the rest of the bodies from the deck."

Kenan nods. "You, you, you." He points to three soldiers. "Get these wraith corpses overboard now." Then he roars across the ship, "Flood the vents! And fix the bleeding hole!"

"Not enough wire-weave to cover it!" comes a shout from above.

"Then bleeding get some more!"

I clench my left hand and pull up a surge of wind, as feeble as it is, to steady the ship for the men above as the guards begin picking up the wraith bodies and shoving them overboard.

Eogan releases me to touch my shoulder. "I'm going to help the captains. Come with me."

Kenan's giant black hands are on Eogan's chest in a heartbeat. "You look like hulls, Your Majesty, and you're not tied on." Kenan keeps his palm there but glances up and yells, "What of the other airships?"

"They're holding up," the lookout calls back.

Eogan swipes Kenan's hand away. "The captains will need help navigating this, and I'm the best person for it if we're going to make it." He wobbles as he points past the black shadows of the peaks and forests we're heading over to the glittering city in the distance. The soldiers shove off the last of the wraiths and the airship pulls up higher—just in time, too, from what I can see of the jagged, white-tipped mountaintops poking from the dark. "The other ships will have to follow or figure out the terrain on their own."

I catch Kenan's glance at the second-story quarters where the two child captains are. *Kel.* He's probably scared out of his wits. Poor boy.

"Your Majesty, I think you and Nym should—"

Too late. We're descending faster. The stars become clearer, freckling the sky with their light as we make it over the range. I shut my eyes and reach up and will the spark in my Elemental veins to connect with the atmosphere. To strengthen enough to hold us up until the captains find a place to land.

Except next thing I know we're slowly turning in a circle on the winds.

Litches.

"The fuel is running out," Eogan says.

I open my eyes and look at him as his fingers squeeze mine. "Arguing about my health or safety won't make a difference if we're dropping too fast," he says. "Tell the engine room to find every last ounce of fuel. And, engineers, engage the air-fins!"

I start to follow. "I'm coming."

Except neither of us is going anywhere because a rush of air blasts my lungs and rocks the ship harder. And suddenly the world drops out from underneath us and we are falling . . .

falling . . .

falling.

Kenan points toward flickering fires lighting up a forest's edge and lights farther out illuminating what appears to be a city made completely of glass that's swirling in and out of sight as we spin. The glow is growing brighter.

One of the soldiers behind us yells, "Hold on to something, boys, and pray our captains steer us well!"

Out of the dim, Eogan's arms clamp around either side of me, then his hands latch onto the railing as he shoves us both down. I wrap around his body, which is abruptly shivering, and grip my good hand onto the metal beam. And curl my other against his chest.

We spin faster and metal shrieks as we're jolted and jostled against treetops and then thrown free from the rail to skid across the cold deck amid groans from the soldiers. The airship bumps and we're aloft again, only to come down harder with a loud crunching noise and metal screaming and pieces breaking off because all hulls has broken loose.

It lasts mere seconds.

It lasts a lifetime.

Jostling and spinning and bumping.

Then we're crashing as the ship plows through what sounds like metal and glass breaking and material ripping.

Things are flying past us—thunking the deck and bending the rail—until my body's ripped free from Eogan's grip and I'm shoved against the opposite side of the ship.

My head hits. My back hits. My chest hurts.

The ship comes to a stop with a jerk, and everything slows, until with one final squeal the whole thing lists to the side so the deck is now slanted toward me and my hips are against the lower railing.

Silence falls except for the sputtering, whirring hum of the engine.

The taste of blood travels the back of my throat from my nose. I cough, sit up, and rub my head as I look around for Eogan.

He's a few paces away already getting to his feet and heading across the slanted deck. Beyond him, surrounding us, are what appear to be tall, lit-up glass towers sparkling in starry-night reflection.

I blink and wave Eogan off. He nods and flips around to his men. "Everyone survive?"

Mutters of "here, here, here" fill the air.

"Good." He looks toward the captains' room. "Kenan, see to your son and the other captain, then the prisoners. You two soldiers there—ensure that no one gets within five paces of Nym while I demand to see the queen."

"I'll speak to the queen," I say, pulling myself up. "You men see that King Eogan gets a physician."

It may be dark, but the expression on Eogan's face when he turns is quite clear. *Like hulls.*

Not that it matters because the next second we're doused in torchlight—hundreds of flickering beams igniting the dark and splaying out beyond the airship. Shouts surround us—sharp and angry above the noise of the broken, whining engine.

There's a sound of scraping and bumping, and something's being shoved up against the ship's side while the furious voices beyond only grow louder.

"Halt where you stand!"

The man's accent is odd. Like Princess Rasha's.

Tramping feet draw closer as a head appears above us, from the ship's side that's tilting upward.

"We're refugees come from today's battle in Tulla," Eogan calls out in a weakened yet somehow still king-like tone. "I demand to see Queen Laiha."

A commotion beyond the man grows and suddenly he moves aside, and the boarding plank he came up on is swarming with guards dressed in the same purple colors I've seen Rasha wear so often.

Eogan raises his arms. "I'm Eogan, king of Bron, elder brother to the once-king and now-deceased Odion whom I slew in battle. I have urgent news for your queen regarding Princess Rasha and the monster Draewulf."

His next words are lower, muttered, and it's not until a few heart-pulses go by that I realize they're intended for me. "Do not react."

Because two seconds later a scuffle erupts and I'm watching what looks to be a black bag shoved over his head just before one comes down on my own.

And everything is dark.

CHAPTER 3

THE SKY OVERHEAD BARKS LOUD.

Fingers grab the collar at my throat and yank me forward while others grip my wrists and in three seconds bind them before feeling down the outside of my dress skirt.

I wrench forward and kick out, but my foot connects with only air as the hold on my neck tightens and forces me still. They're searching for weapons, not pleasure.

When the hands reach my ankles, the owner grunts. He's found my knives. The groping fingers confiscate them, and the hand at my throat yanks me forward to walk up the sloping deck. I feel out the grooves in the metal boards beneath my leather boots to help me shuffle the unreasonable number of paces before my toes bump into the plank.

The hand tugs again and I step up onto the wood—and it's all I can do to blindly focus on my footing while the blasted guard leads me by my dress down from the ship. Like a heifer for auction.

It sparks sickly recollections of being led to auction five, ten, fifteen times from the age of six until my final selling two months ago in the autumn of my seventeenth year. Except the hoods I wore then were used to hide my waist-length, stark-white Elemental hair, not to hinder me from seeing where I was headed.

I always knew where I was headed.

I let the sky crack another angry growl. I'm tempted to be done with this and light up wherever we are with a burst of energy, but Eogan's caution moments ago rings in my ears. *"Do not react."*

Fine. I purse my lips—only to have my feet stumble when I reach the plank's base. My boots barely stop me from tripping onto what feels like slick stone slabs beneath them.

The fingers at my neck stiffen and snag the edge of the hood over my face. Rather than yank it off though, they wrap into it and tighten until the cloth is clamped and sticking to the blood on my nose. Every inhale pulls the material into my mouth, and I jerk backward and twist my hands behind me. But again I touch nothing. Just like I can't hear anything other than the hurried tramp tramp tramping of boots and stifled voices speaking to each other.

Slow down, Nym. Inhale through the cloth.

"This one claims . . . of Bron . . ."

"Take these . . . rest . . ."

"The girl's with me and . . . *stays* with me. So are . . . two boys," Eogan's muffled voice says from somewhere on my left. "Touch them . . . I'll rip . . ."

"She'll want them . . ."

I whip my head this way and that, but the cloak mutes any clarity. *What are they saying?* A soft hand pushes me forward again, to move faster, until I'm bumping against stairs now.

We climb through the cold and wind.

I stagger.

Suddenly someone's shoving me through a door into a room or corridor where the air is much warmer. And the smell . . .

Even through the bloody hooded material, the smell is that of a dead body left on ice too long.

Footsteps on tile.

My arm is grabbed and I'm jerked to a halt.

Harried breath and odd accents.

A *clip clip clipping* as boots move away before the hood is yanked off, and my eyes are blinking because the light in here is blinding.

It's as if every surface is a mirror reflecting the glow.

I squint for a moment until my eyes adjust—it's not mirrors but glass the light is bouncing off of. The walls and room edges are cut in such a way as to give the impression that we are standing inside a giant jewel. And draped from every glass beam and surface above us are tapestries of orange, red, gold, and purple. They drip from the ceiling like rainbowed teardrops. The room is exquisite and delicate, and I swear if anyone steps too hard or speaks too loud, the whole place will crack and shatter around us.

Including the people who are standing before us like majestically silent statues. They look just like chess pieces.

I raise a brow. Rasha never mentioned this gaudy side of her people.

I glare at them and their white robes and try to ignore their stares and the awareness that my chest is slightly exposed through my torn dress. If they notice, they don't react—they just stand watching, at least forty of them, some with blank faces, while others have eyes that are flickering a red glow almost as bright as the candles on the giant stands. It makes patterns on the white-and-opaque-checkered floor.

Oh . . .

We *are* on a chessboard.

I peer closer at the squares. Some of the people are actually standing on them in a pattern. I glance up and around, from one to another, and absorb their blank eyes. Their oddly shiny faces and glossy bodies. The chiseled way they're standing.

Oh hulls.

They're real. But they're not.

They're people who were once alive but are now encased in glass, their faces permanently stilled in unfocused attention.

My stomach turns. No wonder it smells like death in here . . .

"Checkmate," a woman's voice rings out.

CHAPTER 4

I PEER THROUGH THE ASSORTMENT OF GLASS AND real bodies to a woman seated in front of an enormous fireplace, whose red eyes are glowing so bright they're illuminating her face like a sunburst. She's reading our intentions, just like Rasha does. The woman nods at a group of Luminescents who must've been the ones playing against her, and they promptly begin clearing the glass-encased dead people off the checkered floor. I shudder.

Rasha's mum. Has to be.

Her deep skin tone and rich, earthen, auburn hair match Rasha's, as does her wispy garment style. Only her body is different. Where Rasha has curves, this woman used to, but they've rounded out to blend together. Something about her body looks matronly and kind, unlike her icy expression.

My stomach goes from nauseated to wanting to vomit all over her pretty glass floor.

"Well, if this isn't cozy." Eogan eyes the woman. And despite the fact he's keeping his shoulders straight and his head lifted proud, I note the foreign weakness in his tone.

I frown and, beyond him, Kenan tips his almost-shaved black head of hair as if to let me know he's sensed Eogan's weariness too.

A shuffling draws our attention behind us, and before we can speak further, Lord Myles and Lady Isobel are escorted to stand on the far side of Kenan in front of a host of live, purple-clothed Cashlin guards who reassemble themselves to block us in. As if we could run anywhere.

"Bleeding hulls, the oaf still livesss." Myles leans forward and flashes his silver tooth. *You're welcome, sweetheart*, he mouths and tilts his head toward Eogan.

Apparently he was still knocked out when Eogan went to speak with him and Isobel on the airship.

"Perhaps we can trade Lord Myles for whatever they're asking," I mutter.

Eogan's lips twitch and Kenan actually chuckles, even as both their gazes stay on the man across the room in front of us, dressed in brown leggings and a tunic and wearing a prickly robe that looks to be made from actual dead fir needles. He's leaning to address the queen.

"Well, this should go fabulous," Lady Isobel murmurs.

The dead-fir-robed man moves behind the woman and pushes against her chair, which I only now realize is on wheels. Then the whole thing is moving and I'm watching in fascination. I've never seen such a thing, but know of many who would envy one.

He moves her a good few paces toward us until she nods. "That's enough."

"Queen Laiha." Eogan drops to one knee, and Kenan and Myles follow suit, so I slip down too. But I keep my gaze fixed on the woman.

"King Eogan," she says, and it's uncanny how much like Rasha her voice sounds. "You have come from the war in Tulla."

Eogan nods and she twitches her chin for us to rise. I sneak a peek at Lady Isobel, who's not moved from her stance—neither to bow nor to acknowledge anyone in this room other than the queen, at whom she's glaring.

24

I'm grateful she no longer has her Mortisfaire ability of turning hearts to physical stone. Something tells me there are not enough guards in this room if Isobel decided Queen Laiha would be the first to go.

"We've rushed here to warn you not only that Draewulf has your daughter," Eogan says, "but if he's not already on his way, he will be shortly."

The flash in the queen's crimson gaze would be imperceptible if her face didn't pale from its rich brown to a light ash, like Rasha's when she gets upset. "So I've seen." Her eyes burn red and her tone is cold. "And yet you left her with him."

"I beg forgiveness, Your Majesty, but the circumstances necessitated we do so. If there had been another choice, we would have taken it. Unfortunately, I have not exactly been myself of late."

She snorts, as if she knows exactly what he's been recently, and for an instant I swear he flinches. "And now you have come to try and what? Protect me? Forgive me if I do not see the need for it. I am perfectly capable of caring for my people myself." She swipes her gaze over all of us. "You've wasted your time."

I bite back a dry laugh. Coming from a woman who, thus far, has not moved any of her limbs aside from her neck and head, I can't help but admire her spunk. Even if she's an idiot.

Her gaze snaps to mine. "You think I'm a fool? That I need your help because I do not understand the danger heading this direction? I assure you I have known of Draewulf's continued existence for some time now. That is partly why I sent my child down to Faelen, as I'm sure Rasha told you."

"If that's so, then I wonder how you don't understand the danger your daughter is in."

"Draewulf will not harm her while I am still alive."

"True. But if you perish without him shifting into you, he'll consume her instead. Which, as King Eogan said, is why we've come. To prevent both those events from happening."

Her eyes blaze like the furnace behind her. "I thank you for flying this way to bring your warning; however, I fear you may just as well have hurried the attack. Because I assure you, from where I sit, I see a king whose broken body has barely survived housing a shape-shifter for the past two weeks and whose kingdom is currently under siege by the very army following him to my door. And you"—she keeps her gaze steady on me—"have just survived consuming a power that nearly destroyed all of Tulla."

She flicks a glance at Lord Myles, who's looking more put out about the state of his clothing than anything to do with the queen at the moment. He keeps lifting his cravat and sniffing it. Then smoothing a pale, long-fingered hand over his black hair.

"A power that has now been absorbed by this one." She's staring disgustedly at him.

I peer from her to Myles's thin, handsome face, and back. Something in her expression says she's not just repulsed by his consumption of the power.

Oh.

Oh.

She's seeing him as the half-bred product of a Luminescent mother's affair with his royal Faelen father. *She knows what he is.* Just like Rasha knew.

My heart moves toward him. For the queen's disdain. For the visions I've seen of his childhood that said such reactions were the cloak he's been smothered by all his life.

I turn back to Her Majesty.

Focus, Nym. If Queen Laiha could see all this just since we've been in this room with her, what else could she know? I glance at

Lady Isobel and catch the hint of discomfort in her glare. I swallow. Isobel must see it—how much better the queen is at perceiving intentions and plans than even Rasha. What could Her Highness get out of Draewulf's daughter if given a few minutes?

I'm tempted to ask.

"Your Highness, we are not here to argue those facts," Eogan says firmly. "Nor are we in any position to defend what we have recently done and been through. We are, however, concerned not only for you and your people's safety but also for that of the entire five kingdoms within the Hidden Lands. As you know, we haven't *led* Draewulf to your door. He would be coming with or without us. Our hope in coming is that we might persuade you to join us— to come to Faelen where we can shield you and mount a defense."

She actually lets out a laugh. "Not led him to my door? You've brought his daughter here as collateral!" Her eyes slash to Lady Isobel. "You think he won't come for her? With her you will draw him to us, and what would he find? The group of us—the final components he needs to consume—all together in one place. We might as well do Draewulf's work for him. As I said, no thank you, I'll stand with my people."

"Even though the protection we can offer is more than what you have here?"

"Protection? You mean your small band of Bron soldiers and a weakly king?"

The Elemental in my blood bristles. Overhead the hint of a rumble snaps and fills the outside air. "Are you saying we're too weak to stop Draewulf?"

Queen Laiha clamps her mouth shut.

After a moment her gaze drifts to the checkered crystalline floor at our feet. As if she's looking at it but seeing something else.

Like the old woman neighbor of owner number seven who would rattle bones in a bag and stare into a milk stone in an attempt to see the future.

"Will we stop Draewulf?" I growl. Does she know? Can she already see?

"That I will not answer. Much depends on choices made."

"Pardon my bluntness, Highness," Eogan interrupts. "But doesn't that include *your* choice? Join us! Defend the Hidden Lands with us—not just your own people."

Her tone cuts the air. "Young man, I've lived a very long time. And the one thing I know is that the best protection is not to run to another's war, but to defend my borders and people as is my responsibility. And they in turn will defend me. Now"—she nods to the guards standing nearby—"lock them up. Except for him." She tips her chin to Eogan. "The Bron king will come with me to my chambers."

"What?" I blurt out. "We have to get to Faelen. And what about Tulla? Those people are separated from you by a river and a few mountain peaks—they're your neighbors. And they're dying even as we speak."

"They are not as helpless as you believe, I assure you. They'll have dug underground chambers and will mount—"

"Your Majesty, their king is dead. Taken by Draewulf."

At least she has the consideration to allow a look of sadness across her face when she turns her eyes on Eogan. "Yes. But they will survive awhile longer. Now, we are not a people of war, but as it seems we currently have little choice, I have defenses to prepare. I thank you for the concern, but I'm not interested." With that she veers a hard stare at me. "And neither should you be, considering you'll need to hurry if you want to save him."

Save him?

Save who? What's that supposed to mean? I peer over at Eogan.

Then past him to Lord Myles, who's given up on his cravat and is staring at his arm as if it's itching.

Litches. The poison is working its way in.

Before I can demand further explanation, Queen Laiha turns her gaze on her guards. "Take them. And see if the other airships have landed anywhere. If they have, confiscate them and bring their soldiers in." She dips her head to the man behind her who promptly grips her chair and wheels her away from us.

"Your Majesty, I ask you to—"

A guard moves in to cut Eogan off, resulting in Kenan's fist suddenly swinging at her. The female Luminescent ducks before he's barely begun, and it's only then it occurs to me that the majority of the guards are women. And a few have remnants of red in their eyes. Another guard thrusts a hand into Kenan's back, then his neck, followed by his side, crippling him almost without moving.

"Kenan, don't," Eogan murmurs, but my peal of thunder is already ricocheting through the hall. Except I don't even get my hand up before another of the red-eyed guards grabs my wrist and shakes her head. Kenan falls to his knees, frowning in seeming confusion while my eyes widen with clarity.

I recall Rasha talking of the Luminescents in the palace. Of how quiet it is here since most of them have no need for speaking. They just read each other's intentions.

Just like they read Kenan's to throw a punch. Just like they read mine before my own fist went up to bring down more than thunder.

They could see it coming.

CHAPTER 5

ARE YOU JESTING US?" MYLES YELLS. "WE'RE TRY-
ing to help you foolsss! Eogan, you're the woman's blasted
equal. Tell them!"

"You should be more concerned about what I'm going to tell *you*
when I get back," Eogan rumbles. He flicks me a look, then strides
away between four guards, toward where the queen just exited.

"Oh, get off your blasted horse." Myles yanks his arm free to
veer toward me as Lady Isobel slinks ahead with the guards leading us out of the crystal hall. Abruptly he is crowding my face and
lowering his voice. "That fool won't listen—fine. But you should.
Because I'm telling you, get usss out of here, or *I will*."

"You lied and used me to get at that power," I snarl. "So threatening me with it is *far* from in your best interest right now."

Lady Isobel snorts. "Who cares how he got the power? Do you
really want someone as inexperienced as he is to actually try to
use it?"

I narrow my gaze. "Maybe he'll knock himself out."

"Listen here, you little—" She turns to glower at me. "That
power he absorbed—"

"Won't be effective for a while longer. And if he *does* use it, I
will see to it his family heirlooms are damaged. Permanently."

Myles's appalled curse brings what is clearly an unwilling smile to her face.

"Say what you will," he says, "but you owe me for freeing Eogan from Draewulf'sss grip, my dear girl."

Is he being serious? He didn't help. He . . . *Oh.* He doesn't know. He was already knocked out when Draewulf pulled free of Eogan's body. "You didn't help me free him. You nearly had me kill everyone."

"Funny how quickly you turn to blaming when you were initially the one *begging for it.*"

"Myles, shut up."

"All I'm saying—"

"All I'm saying is, you will shut up until I can murder you. And if you have to be near me beforehand, then make yourself useful and figure out what the queen wants with Eogan and how to get us out of here."

His expression sours as he straightens and slicks a hand over his shiny black hair. "How should I know what the woman wantsss? She's as unstable as her daughter. Only a fool would make enemies of us while an entire army is headed for her gatesss."

"I'd say you're all bleeding fools if you think insulting their queen right now will help our situation," Kenan growls behind us.

I ignore him and look up at the female guard leading the way. "There was a man on our ship by the name of Lord Wellimton. What happened to him?"

"Anyone putting up a fight was kept bound."

"And the two boys in the captains' room?"

"I . . . believe they were taken with the others."

A throaty sound tells me Kenan's listening.

I slow and put my hand on his arm. "If either of those boys is harmed, I will take it more personally than you desire," I say in a tight tone to the guard.

The woman says nothing. Just turns us down another glass corner to face a long flight of glistening stairs. They give the illusion they're leading up to the night sky due to the clear domed ceiling over us with the stars filtering through. Like little solar flares.

Rasha probably spent her childhood studying those stars from this same spot.

That sudden thought nearly bowls me over. *Bleeding hulls, I miss her.* I blink hard and refuse to imagine where she is right now, what they're doing to her. *Just find a way to escape and rescue her, Nym.*

Three flights of those shiny stairs deposit us just beneath that glass dome and at the top of one of the three corner crystal towers I glimpsed before our airship crashed. The short hallway is shaped like a square and empty of people or doors except for an opening at the end. It's a room—the only one up here as far as I can tell—and while not by any means dungeon quality, it carries vague reminders of my slave quarters at owners' numbers seven and nine. Two sparse beds. Three candle lanterns. And a cold floor to be shared by too many of us.

Except it is beyond impeccably clean, and three of the walls are made of see-through glass.

I sway a moment as I enter at the sense of dizziness it brings— being this high up and able to look out on the lit-up crystal city below from multiple angles at once is overwhelming. Only the wall with the door I'm stepping through is made of wood. The rest are peering over the courtyards and lights and outer ramparts and giant-statued gates that lead to the massive forest beyond.

I frown as I steady myself and move closer for a clearer look at the night-shadowed landscape. Is it me or does something seem off about those gates?

Before I can figure out what, Myles's swearing draws me back to the room. A male Cashlin guard and two female Luminescents who've prodded Myles through the doorway have ruffled his suit in the process. They say nothing about his insults—just deposit him in the room's center before they shut the door and then line up against the wall.

"That's it?" Lady Isobel scoffs at the Cashlin male guard and two ladies with us before she slinks down onto one of the cushioned cots. She spreads her voluptuous self out like a fox, so even with her hands still tied behind her back she looks powerful.

I watch the way she sizes up the guard and shake my head. What are they thinking, leaving only three soldiers alone with all of us? Leaving them alone with *her*?

I glance over at the male guard. With a slight build and blond hair, he reminds me of the Faelen schoolchildren I played with my eighth year, albeit with a far less innocent glint in his eye. He's about nineteen, I'd guess, and he's smirking back at Isobel.

"Oh-good-father-of-Bron, this confinement better not take long," Kenan mutters beside me.

"How about removing these binders?" Lady Isobel holds out her wrists to the male guard and slides a smile across her face that I suspect is the same one she used to seduce Eogan when they were younger.

My stomach sours. She and Eogan may be the same age and same height and have been raised near-inseparably for years, but that's where the similarities end.

The guard switches to a charming smile of his own but doesn't move.

"Humph. I see where your Princess Rasha gets her manners," Isobel says.

The besotted one glances at the Luminescent nearest me. I catch a cautious look between them.

"Do you know her?" I ask them casually. "Princess Rasha? You're all about her age, I suspect."

The male guard shoots another look at his Luminescent counterpart before he turns to say firmly, "The princess is a friend to all her people."

Liar. She had few friends, as I recall. I stare straight at him. But maybe he could've been one of them. I wonder . . .

The Luminescent close by ruffles her purple flowing robe and clears her throat. When I turn to look, she's glaring at me. *Interesting.* I scan the ceiling with its clear glass surface, then peer out the window again at the gates below.

"She believed in this cause," I say.

"Except I seem to recall her suggesting her dear queen mum wanted Draewulf alive as much as I did." Myles's voice snakes over from where he's plopped himself down on the other bed opposite Isobel. He prances his long fingers across the cover. "Which isss rather odd when you think about it. Now, why would Queen Laiha want the shape-shifter alive, do you suppose? And be willing to possibly sacrifice her own daughter now?"

The guard's face shadows, and I swear it's like a red filter snaps down over the Luminescents' pupils. One makes a clicking noise with her tongue while their male counterpart refuses to answer.

I glare at Myles. *Thanks a lot.*

He shrugs and smiles acidly as if to say it's true.

"Nice try, Elemental, but he wouldn't have given you any information anyway." Lady Isobel rolls over on her bed. She yawns and scans their Luminescent faces before flipping her raven-black hair away from her high cheekbones. "The people of this culture are not encouraged to think for themselves. No wonder their princess wanted out."

"You should not say such things," the male guard says. But the tightening of his jaw indicates Lady Isobel's words struck something. I turn to Eogan's former fiancée and catch her watching me. She tips her head and simpers cleverly, "They study intentions. I study emotions."

"So you'll know which one to hit first when you turn his heart to stone," Myles says.

Except I can't tell whether he's insulting or admiring her. Or trying to get a rise out of the guards. My guess is the latter two.

I turn back to the male Cashlin. "All I'm saying is Rasha and a whole lot of people could use our help right now. Especially if your queen dies."

The guard ignores me, and the second Luminescent speaks for the first time. "Are any of you in here the airship's captains?"

What?

Myles snorts and peers away.

"They did not survive," Kenan says quickly, not looking at any of us. His gaze flickers down, and instantly the Luminescent's eyes flash red. I've been around Rasha long enough to know that in that one movement of Kenan's gaze dropping, the Luminescent saw what she needed.

None of us are the captains.

Kenan's son is.

"We will inform the Inters."

"The Inters?" Myles sits up. "Now that'sss interesting."

"Who are they?" Kenan demands.

Myles hardly even looks at him, just turns to stare strangely at the gates. I follow his eyes to the large lantern-lit crystal sides topped with the two enormous carved statues. Does he see what's off about them? I scan the whole section briefly and frown again because I still can't place my finger on it. I go back to listening for what in hulls Inters are.

"Questioners. Seekersss. The Cashlin version of an interrogator, I believe."

The female Luminescents move to the door and, after saying something to the male guard, stride out. He follows to shut it behind them before turning to face Kenan's large body that is suddenly lunging for him with a bellow. The guard holds out a slender wrist and slaps Kenan on the side of the neck, and the giant man slumps to the floor.

The Cashlin then flips around and slips toward the bed Lady Isobel's on. She barely has time to sit up before he touches her. Lady Isobel's smile stays frozen in place as her body goes limp on the bed.

What the—?

The guard turns and presses the same wrist onto Myles's neck, causing him to drop from his half-risen state.

His movements are graceful. Delicate and quick. Like a dancer.

An evil dancer.

I lurch backward just as he comes for me too, jumping away toward the far glass wall.

He slides a foot toward me and lifts his hand. "Oh, come now, it won't be that bad."

"What'd you do to them?"

"Just keeping all of you from being any more disruptive."

He dances closer.

Too close. I kick him in the family jewels, yank down a weak bolt of lightning over the glass in warning, and flip toward the wall by the door. "Is that how you people keep the peace? Drugging? Killing?"

His hand pauses in midair.

"Do you like to use it on Rasha as well?" I say, my breath coming fast.

"We would never . . ." His face goes blank before it crinkles into a frown. "How well did you know the princess?"

"Didn't you hear your queen? Her daughter and I are friends." I eye his hand and notice the tiny, almost imperceptible glass circle on his wrist. Keeping my distance, I tip my head toward it. "What are you doing to us?"

"This?" He hardly glances at the wristlet. "It knocks you out."

"I gathered that." *But I'd much prefer to stay conscious, thank you.* "How long will its effect last on them?" I jut my head toward the three he's attacked.

"Long enough. But that doesn't matter. What are you planning to do about the princess?"

"Rescue her. Which is more than I can say for her own mother." I keep my stare on that wristlet catching the candlelight and refracting it on the wall. "So how about you don't use that on me and we discuss what Rasha would rather you and I be doing to save her."

He shrugs. "The Luminescents in the hall will know if I've not used it. Besides, it'll be better this way. Less painful."

I choke. "What will be less painful?"

He doesn't answer, just lashes forward as I clench my hand into a fist and call down the nighttime sky. A crack of lightning goes off somewhere nearby and I start toward the window, but next thing I know I'm sliding to the floor in front of it as the awareness hits that the skin on my neck feels prickly.

Firelights flicker in the distance, illuminating the dark kingdom beyond the window and Castle. *Such lovely lights*, I think. *Like fireflies. Like the firefly trees at home in Faelen . . .*

The lights in the room seem to be dimming. The yellow glow from candles fading odd-like, and the guard is standing over me.

"What . . . do with us?" My lips feel thick as my head hits the floor.

"Interrogate you," he says just as a door opens and the red hue of the Luminescents' glowing eyes fills the hall.

CHAPTER 6

DRIP DROP GOES THE SNOW, LIKE LITTLE LACE BUDS TWIRLING ONTO THE garden. The wind is swirling, humming, scattering the puffs beyond the breath-fogged window. "Look at the flakes, Father."

"Aye." He ducks his head near mine. "Lady Weather's jealous. She's trying to match your hair. Just like she's tryin' to match your harmonious voice." He tweaks a white lock near my ear, and I glance up at his pockmarked face and dark curls cut short by Mum's dainty hands.

I frown. "But I don't want it white. I want hair the same as yours."

He pauses, then pulls me onto his lap. It's the first time I've mentioned such a thing, even though I've tried to stain my long locks dark with Fendres dirt many times when he and Mum weren't looking. "Now, why'd you want to have a plain mess like this?" He brushes his curls up so they frizz out over his head like a burberry bush. "You want to look like a bolcrane? Is that it?" And before I can move, he's curling his hands into pretend claws and tickling my sides. I scream and jump away to find my small wooden sword carved by those hands.

"All right, then! If I can't eat *you*, I'll go after your mum!" he roars, scampering on all fours toward the soft-faced angel currently knitting a Solstice gift in front of the fire.

He snarls until she bats him back with her needle. "Tegan! You'll make me drop a stitch and then the poor child will catch cold." She laughs.

"It's all right. I'll save you, Mum." I plant myself in front of her to face my father.

"Save her? Impossible! You can't defeat me!" He swipes the air with his taut, thick arms.

"I don't want to defeat you!" I giggle and toss my blade aside to throw my hands around his neck. "I want to tame you so I can ride on your back!"

He stops and stares at me a moment before leveling his face to mine. And plants a kiss on my pale nose. "That's my girl," he whispers, scooping me into the rich scent of his earthen skin. "Never destroy what simply needs taming, Nymia. Mercy grows hearts more than bitterness." He presses his hand against my heart. "Like this one in here."

I pucker my lips. "How do you know, Father?"

"How? Because I have you. My gift of mercy who's grown this old heart right big. Good thing, too, 'cuz your mum's cooking isn't much for growing the stomach."

"I heard that," Mum murmurs.

"A gift?" I frown.

"Sure." He tucks back another lock of my hair and settles a stare at me. "When you were born, you survived, though you weren't supposed to." His smile is soft. "I like to believe it was for your mum and me. For our hearts." He sits up straight and clears his throat. "Now, how 'bout we sing something beautiful for your mum, eh?"

Except . . .

Except three hours later I open my eyes to discover that he was wrong because mercy cares little for the heart of a five-year-old girl. Nor does it do anything to douse the fires or death screams of her parents as she rouses to the awareness that she's standing out in the blood-drenched snow, watching her home cave in. In the freezing mist, and ash, and horrific dark.

Always that dark. Even more terrifying than any of the nights with the human monsters that would follow.

Deep. Freezing.

Suffocating the song voice I'd all but forgotten.

Always whispering, "You survived. Even when you weren't supposed to."

I survived.

But wasn't supposed to.

I gasp awake, only to choke and reach for my face—and find tears there at the ache of a memory long forgotten. My dad's face. My mum's hands. Our last night together as a family before their deaths.

Except we weren't a real family according to Eogan. Not by blood relation, anyway.

I cough and wince at the red lights splitting through the fog of my mind. And overhead—that sound of rain. It's hitting the glossed-over glass walls and ceiling with a harsh *tap tap tapping*.

I curl my fingers to force it to stop, but it just keeps going. Harder, louder than before. Pounding into my brain as if it can punch holes to get in through my skull and gain access.

Access to what?

Images of my owners, one, two, three, flash before my eyes. I blink as the memories of beatings and mocking voices play in fast increments through my head. *"You'll do as I say or Draewulf will come to eat your brains."* My first owner's words flip around, drawing up recollections of washing his clothes. Then his son's.

I shudder, and somewhere within my chest a cry pushes up and out at these faces I cannot bear. These people who destroyed me.

These people whom I then destroyed.

"Make it stop. I don't want to remember," I hear my voice gasping over and over. "Please make it stop."

Something pricks my neck and the drumming raindrop voices fade, along with my mind.

I'M IN EOGAN'S BRON CASTLE NOW, SPEAKING WITH SIR GOWON. EXCEPT he's not listening to me. He's refusing to understand that Eogan has been taken over by Draewulf. I reach my fingers for his waist-shirt and twist. "What does the Elegy 96 say?"

He grips a hand over mine. "You'll kindly unhand me."

I step closer. Squeeze harder. The hissing from the wraiths outside the room grows louder. "What does it say?" I demand. "What does Eogan think has begun?" Suddenly my arms are crawling and my veins, my chest . . .

"Nym, stop!" Rasha says.

"Read his intentions. What do you see?"

Her hand tugs at me. "You're going to kill him! We'll find it another way. We'll ask Isobel! You can't do—"

Can't I? I stare at her as the heat from my fury floods the ice in my blood. I am beyond finished with this man's uncaring for the world going to the pit of hulls all around him while he stays in his comfortable fool ignorance. I pull, yanking the energy from his chest bones. Like marrow I can taste.

Sir Gowon wheezes and stumbles forward. He opens his mouth and I sense it—the words on the tip of his confused, tormented mind. I will make him speak or else—

Then he gasps:

> "When shadows are sewn to sinew and bone, and
> darkness rules the land,

Let storms collide and Elisedd's hope arise,
Before the beast forces fate's hand.
Just as from one it came and to five was entrusted, to
only one it can go, to rule or to seek justice.
If his demise is to be Elemental,
Interrupt the blood of kings in each land."

I stare.

"Elegy 96 is a prophecy," he slurs. "Handed down for generations of Bron kings. It's a foretelling of what is to come."

Twenty seconds go by as every vein in my body is curling up like roots around my chest.

And then my mind is flashing backward to the witch's house. "He's taking the blood in order," Draewulf's wife says. "He needed Eogan first. Interrupt the blood of kings, and whatever you do, don't let him take the final one."

Come on, Nym. Wake up.
I try to pry my eyes open but they're too heavy.
And now my memories are moving forward to Eogan.

ON THE AIRSHIP, HE'S STARING AT ME, TALKING TO ME BECAUSE AN Elemental will be Draewulf's downfall.

The airship shudders, and the sensation is answered by a matching shiver beneath my skin, in my veins, as Eogan's voice emerges again through the wind and sea salt and snowcapped air. "When Draewulf comes to Faelen, it'll be for you. Because your Elemental ancestors were the original rulers of Faelen. And you're last in line, Nym."

The red raindrops are back, pounding my head again. I try to duck. To get out of the way, but their piercing glow follows me.

"The prophecy," one of the red drops says.

"The queen knows of the prophecy," another answers. "Reach back further. To the beginning."

"I don't want to go back," I tell it. "I need to move forward." Always forward.

"We need the past," the hammering drops say. "To help see the future."

What future? "There is no future if he can't be stopped." Doesn't the bloody rain know this?

"Exactly."

STICK WALLS. SLATTED LIGHT. HEAT AND STENCH AND SWEAT COATING the air, coating my lungs, which can barely breathe. I'm gasping as if they don't know how to work yet. They squish and ache and, oh, my body aches. I sneeze and blink and suddenly I'm staring up at a face that is brown.

A pair of stormy gray eyes blink back. I smile. They smile. Then drop water on my cheeks—and I wail because it's startling and frightening and I don't want to see this woman cry. This woman I don't know but somehow I must be a part of. Must have come from.

And from the man hovering behind her.

Why does he look so sad too? With that white hair and those sea-blue eyes that are beautiful.

Are they mad?

Footsteps outside. Tromping. Making angry sounds. And more cries are coming from somewhere.

Why are they so angry? Is that what's making this couple sad?

"It's time," a whisper says.

The woman holds me closer, and I can feel how small I am. She squeezes me to her breast, and suddenly I want to stay here. With her. I want to nuzzle against her and sleep.

"If we're going to get her out, it has to be now," the blue-eyed hovering man says.

"I know, I just . . ."

The lovely woman is crying again. Then she's handing me to an old lady in a scratchy cloth that makes me want to wail. Before I can, she pops a thumb in my mouth and swishes us out a small door while the sad lady stands, watching and crying, and the man holds her.

The angry footsteps are growing closer.

The old woman runs faster, weaving around hovels and trees.

"Hurry," a male voice says.

And suddenly I'm being shoved through a tiny dirt hole beneath a tall stone fence that looks made to keep people in permanently. "Poor child," the old lady mutters. "May the Creator spare her."

"Halt!" a voice yells, but it's too late because the new male hands that have taken me from the woman and already strapped me to their chest are working to mount a horse to take me away.

"To the Fendres Mountains," the male whispers. "I know a man and his wife you'll be safe with there, far from this blasted internment camp."

I lean forward and blink and try to catch my breath, but what the hulls was that?

It's no use, though. I can't find the air. I don't know if I ever will. I need to cough. I need to inhale and escape these memories and these red pelting raindrops that are abruptly fading fading fading.

I choke and squint and stare around me as the darkness lifts and the raindrops slow.

Not raindrops. Voices. Questions.

Red Luminescent eyes dull around me at the same moment the throbbing in my head stops.

I frown. *What in—?* "What have you done?" I demand of the three Luminescents in front of me.

They don't answer.
They don't have to.
They are the Inters.
And now they're finished.

CHAPTER 7

A CREAKING SOUND ERUPTS BEHIND ME through the red-illuminated dark and someone's poking my shoulder. "This way."

A door opens, sending in a candlelit glow over my shoulder to light up the heavily curtained room and the three elderly Luminescents all seated in a row. They're so old it appears as if their skin is decaying. I cough, and it's as if I'm inhaling that scent of dead bodies on ice again. I gag and shove off from the freezing chair I've been sitting on. I am done with this place.

Out of the dim, the dancing Cashlin guard's hand reaches for me. I shift away before he can prick me again, but he just says, "If you behave, I won't use it now that they're finished."

Is he jesting? I look from him to my interrogators. "You invaded my mind without my permission. You invaded my memories!"

"Memories you could not have given us if we'd simply asked," they say in unison.

"You had no right." I'm shaking now. And my hand is flexing. A lightning bolt streaks down and I barely stop it from slamming into the ceiling. I reach my hand out where I feel it itching beneath the skin—and sense the Inter's Luminescent strength beating through their blood. For the slightest moment it calls to me. *Take it.*

"And you had no right to crash into our home," their three

voices ring. "We simply wanted to ensure you were who we thought and had no ulterior motives."

I shove the subtle dark thirst aside and squeeze my fist until the sky rumbles and crashes, then breaks open into rain. Real rain. "You had no right."

"We needed more about you. Specifically, what Draewulf's designs are upon you."

"And?"

"It is as you believe. Just as the Creator gave power to the five original bloodlines, the beast will take those powers to rule all. Including you, who are Elisedd's hope." The three women look behind me as if one entity and tip their heads. "He will take you last as the final piece to secure his immortality."

"He *will* take me?"

"You are now dismissed."

The Cashlin male guard slips beside me and holds out a hand.

I glare at the Luminescents, then turn and stride for the door. To hulls with all of them.

As I step out and the door swings shut, I call down one more lightning strike. Its aim is slick and true, and the crashing of glass rocks the ceiling of the room we just came from. Not enough to kill them by my estimation. But enough to interrupt their abilities for a time.

The male guard looks at me but says nothing. Just keeps leading us away with what I'd say is a hint of respect in the firm set of his jaw.

"I didn't harm them detrimentally."

"And you didn't hear a complaint from me."

I frown.

He shrugs and continues his stride. "The Inters would've seen you intended to cause such damage and could've stopped you. They saw fit not to. Which means it is not my responsibility."

Interesting. "In that case, I need to reach Eogan. I need to get our people out of here."

He blinks again but doesn't reply as we walk down one, two, three opaque glass hallways through this palace that I swear is like a womb. Warm and pulsing with rhythms and heartbeats of life through the walls and floors and atmosphere, even though it's completely void of voices or other patrons. It's creepy. It takes a moment to realize I keep looking for more glass-encased dead people as if it's *their* rhythms and heartbeats I'm sensing.

"Where are all the people?"

He glances over. "Only a few live here, mainly the Luminescents. Having too many people around sets off their abilities constantly and tires them." He leads me through an archway and into a clear sort of tunnel with a see-through floor—and abruptly we're walking high above the city where the morning dawn is just beginning to hit. "Thus, the majority of our people live outside the Castle. Along there." He points below toward the shadowed city walls.

One section of the city's main wall is built into the forested mountainside like a hornet's nest. All patchworked and transparent and stacked up like catacombs. On the opposite side of us is a lower wall, dividing the inner Castle from the outer city. With the morning still gray, it's easy to see the breakfast fires illuminating the elegant houses carved out along that wall. Great glass porticos and columns, like something from one of Adora's historical picture books I used to browse through in her library. These styles are old and incredibly graceful.

My annoyance at the guard and his people abates slightly, if simply out of respect for the beauty and artistic heritage created by a people who are stubborn, yes, and even despicably wretched, but are that way from age and lack of contact with an outside world that has been changing too fast.

The tunnel we're walking through arches ahead of us. It must be over one hundred paces above the ground, and after a moment we're crossing over an entire section of the Castle's courtyard. I slow for a moment as the vastness of it all catches up with me, then pull my gaze up and keep walking.

"How does everything not break?" I say.

"It's stronger than you'd think."

"The glass?"

"Technically it's not glass. It's a combination of tree sap from our forests and the minerals we mine."

I eye the span of forest beyond the city that he's referring to. "And that's easier than simply using the wood?"

"Wood is useful for many things, but if you hadn't noticed, it tends to burn." He shifts his gaze to proudly scan the courtyard below. "This city has been standing longer than any other in the entire Hidden Lands. And, Creator willing, it will stand for many centuries to come."

"How did they make it?" I wave a hand around us at the crystal tunnel we're inside of. "I mean . . . look at this."

"Carefully and with lots of heat."

Heat? I shoot him a glance. *Could my abilities bring it down if I tried?*

"We erect molds and fill them with the molten liquid we melt the minerals down to, then add the sap extracted from the trees. Don't you have windows in Faelen?"

"Of course. At least in the nicer houses."

"Have you ever seen anyone make them?"

I frown.

"Exactly. *We* make and trade them. Or we did years ago."

"Now you just keep to yourselves and let the rest of the world destroy each other," I say and walk faster. A moment goes by before

I notice him tapping his circle wristlet. I shiver and edge away. "Do you make that too?"

He looks smug. "Among other potions. The herb farmers up in the Pass make it. It's harmless, odorless, and—"

"Allows your Luminescents inappropriate access to a person's mind."

He shrugs. "It's more humane than other forms of interrogation."

"So that's what your people appease themselves with in order to uphold their pacifist status?" I scowl at him, but if he notices, it doesn't matter because we're almost to the end of the glass tunnel and he's already indicating another part of the city. The giant gates fitted into a thick wall are sitting exposed toward Tulla. I squint and look again for that odd aspect that feels out of place. As if they've forgotten something and I just can't put my finger on it.

I stall. And stare harder.

Where are their archers? Where are their *soldiers*?

I peer around to count how many archers I can spot atop those walls. There aren't any. Then I glance around in search of some semblance of the Cashlin army barracks or soldier dwellings near those gates.

Nothing.

They have nothing. No protection.

Just elegant crystal houses with beautifully laid-out pathways and pale-green gardens that look half frozen in this chilly climate.

Oh, Rasha . . . what in litches are your people thinking?

I swallow and glance up at him. "What's your name?"

He slows and turns to me. An odd expression flickers across his features. He opens his mouth. Shuts it. "Doesn't matter."

The look disappears as quickly as it came, but it's replaced by an abrupt dawning within me that he's relishing the idea of his anonymity. *Probably doesn't get much of that around here with all the*

Luminescents. I smirk. "Well, 'Doesn't Matter,' where's your army? Where are your guards and soldiers?"

The pink that floods his face is a color of shame, or perhaps exasperation. "We've rarely needed them before, so we . . ."

"Just stopped having them?"

"No. We have them. Just not at the level we may have once had."

My stomach twists. "Your queen is insane. She suspected Draewulf was alive and yet let your defenses dwindle?"

"Stubborn perhaps, but not insane."

"But the barracks? The archers? The lookouts at your city gates—?"

"They are there," he says hurriedly. "Just hidden. The rest . . . we're gathering."

Oh litches.

Oh bleeding litches.

We truly have hastened these people's already-impending deaths. And there's not a bleeding thing we can do.

"I have to see Eogan," I whisper.

CHAPTER 8

S IR DOESN'T MATTER WALKS ME PAST THE WAITING row of Luminescents in the hallway and opens the door to the room in which he'd used his wristlet to prick me.

I hesitate before entering. The candles must've gone out—or been put out—leaving it hard to see, other than to tell that the space is wretchedly quiet and almost empty. Are the others still being interrogated by the Inters? I doubt it. I step in and, too late, the oaf shuts the door behind me and a second later I hear the sound of wood clicking into place, locking me in the dim. *Curse him.*

Before I turn to let loose on the door, the sound of snoring snags my gaze to Kenan. He's lying on one of the beds, his nose twitching as a splash of gray dawn ripples across his face. And seated in the shadows on the floor nearby him, less than ten paces from where I stand, watching me as if he's been waiting for hours . . .

"Eogan."

My soul stumbles.

He looks weary and beautiful and what I imagine coming home to be like. I stare at those brilliant green eyes and swear I can feel his heart beating all the way from where I'm paused. Steady. Quiet.

Safe.

Oh hulls, I want to climb inside that heart and never let go—just feel his rhythm steadying my soul as it drowns out the past and present and entire rest of the world.

"You survived," he says, still studying me.

I clear my throat and try to ignore the bloom of heat invading my cheeks. "As did you apparently. Did they hit you with that drug?"

He shakes his head, and something about it says it would've been more merciful if they had. "But three hours of questioning was enough for the queen to decide I wasn't a threat. How about you? Did it hurt? The interrogation?"

Yes. No. I won't say because it doesn't matter—his clearly hurt more.

I slip down to the floor so the weighted space between us narrows as I face him and those emerald eyes that are holding mine like clouds holding back a storm. I can feel the friction in them, fighting to repress the ache that's settling in here with us. "Are *you* all right?"

He flicks his hand as if to say it's no big deal. "Fine."

Liar. "What did she want?"

"A reading of Draewulf and Bron, and to know about Isobel and me. And you." He dips his head but doesn't drop his gaze, allowing it to burn through the dark as a shadow of hesitation flickers. A hint of pain. "She wanted to know what Draewulf had done through me, as well as my future intentions."

"And?"

He firms his chin. Watching. Waiting.

For what?

"What did you say?" I want to ask. *"About what you've done? About Isobel and you? About your past and your future?"*

"And what did she say about Draewulf and me?"

But that hesitation . . .

It asks if I really want to know.

I look away. To exhale. Inhale. To forget how blasted tired I am and try to focus on the fact that if we're going to even have a future at all, we need to escape.

He nods and straightens and leans back, nonchalant-like, against the bed. "Dare I inquire about yours?"

My gaze flashes up.

Until I realize he's not asking about my future intentions.

Oh. I shift my position. "I met the Inters and they're blasted eerie. I may have left them a bit put off."

"I imagine you did." His grin matches his tone. "And what did they find?"

"They asked about my past. They wanted the truth about who I am and who I was born as, which . . ." I study him beneath my lashes. "I was born in an internment camp, apparently."

He raises a brow.

And I was not supposed to survive.

"I saw my real parents. In my mind." I give him a pointed look. "Funny how it seems everyone's more informed of my past than I am."

His expression stills. In the lines and lips I've come to know all too well in the past few months.

It's his struggle to guard me from himself.

I look at my hands to hide the sudden tightness in my chest as a soft rain starts to drizzle on the glass ceiling. It falls into rhythm with my voice when I finally work up the courage to ask the question I've held on to since we left Tulla yesterday. "So how long have *you* known?"

"About?"

"My parents, or rather the fact that the ones you killed were *not* my birth parents. And that I would be the final piece. Or the fact that Draewulf needed me."

"I suspected it when I first realized you were true Elemental."

My voice hitches. "When?" If the weight of the room was already heavy, it's itching with static now. As if the storm I can sense building outside is working its way into this room. Into us.

"That day you nearly killed me and Colin out in the meadow because I'd angered you by asking about the redheaded girl."

"You knew *then*? That I was the heir? That I was Draewulf's endgame?"

"As I said, I suspected."

I snort and look away.

"The prophecy—the Elegy my people kept hidden," he says, as if in explanation.

I stride to the window and stare at those gates.

"I suspected because of the prophecy. If your people had known of it, they would've drawn the same conclusion."

"And you simply never found the time to mention it," I whisper.

"I wasn't sure until I saw Draewulf go for you at the battle in the Keep."

"Why didn't you say something at Adora's?"

"If I'd told you I suspected it at Adora's, or even a few weeks ago when Draewulf had shape-shifted into me, what would you have done?"

"I would've appreciated your honesty."

His chuckle is soft. Even as the next moment the tired tension etched through his countenance suddenly acknowledges where we are—and what we've been through—and it's as if the events of these past few weeks have just dropped into this room, and we are both staring it all in the face. "No. You would've scoffed and resented the pressure that kind of expectation put upon you. And back at Adora's, you would've run."

"I would not have run. I—"

He stares at me.

"Okay, fine. *If* I'd believed you. But your trust problems not-withstanding, the fact that you didn't tell me—"

His tone edges cold. "Tell you what? That your parents weren't really your parents and your royal blood makes you a final pawn in a madman's game? Not perhaps the best use of time while trying to earn a terrified girl's trust—particularly one whose emotions call down lightning on anyone who infuriates her."

"But neither was withholding it."

His expression narrows as he shifts against the bed. "In that case, I pray you'll forgive me for being an unbearably selfish person. Because I can say with all confidence you *never* would have trusted me, let alone spoken another word to me, if I'd told you then." His jaw flexes before he looks away and murmurs, "And that was some-thing I was wholly unwilling to induce."

Whatever my next words were going to be, they're shoved aside as his gaze slips self-consciously onto my lips, then my torn cloth-ing and hands. *He couldn't bear me not speaking to him?*

I swallow.

"Besides, it's not something either of us needs to worry about. I won't let Draewulf near you. And if there comes a more suitable time when you'd like to investigate your heritage, I will try to help as much as I'm able."

"I'm not sure you or I will have much control over how near Draewulf gets to us. But . . . thanks." I brush my fingers against my dress only to find them met by a light scratching in the veins of my wrist.

As if to remind me it's still there.

The poison. Diminished now by the Elemental song that's reclaimed my blood, but the dark power I ingested still exists too.

He frowns and leans forward so he's looking straight at me. "How are you? The rest of you—since the other abilities and the

Keep and . . . Colin." He tips his chin back just enough to truly examine my eyes.

I open my mouth to tell him that it's fine—that everything's fine now and I am fine too, but the grief that suddenly creases his softening green eyes stops me. And reminds me that we both feel it. I blink quickly, and he gives a single nod that says he hates the loss as much as I do.

His gaze falls and I scrutinize it, scrutinize his sallowing skin as I step away from the window. "I'd say I'm still better than you, I suspect."

He chuckles. "I'm all right." But something in that rich tone suggests he is lying. He's not all right. He's not been since Draewulf.

I slip over to drop beside him and touch his chest through his bloody shirt, feel for the bones covering his heart. "And this? How is it?"

His large fingers slide over my deformed ones and hold them in place on his chest. Even as I catch his glance toward the bed where Lady Isobel was splayed out only hours ago.

I don't know if it's the fact that Eogan spent so many years without the ability to feel for anyone but her or that he spent them in the throes of passion with her that makes me cringe more.

"Nymia," Eogan whispers.

I shake off that woman's presence as he presses my hand harder beneath his, as if to make me read his feelings aloud here and claim them forever. As if I could know how else to fix him internally along with his weakened body. I swallow back a choked sadness. For him. For me.

A heavy raindrop hits the roof.

It's followed by another, then another, as the drizzle turns to a downpour, lending to the weight of the atmosphere and magnifying it—matching his heartpulse that is picking up beneath his hand he's just slid beneath my chin. He lifts my face until my eyes meet his and allows me to see his soul for a brief moment. As if to declare it now beats fresh and free of Draewulf's control and Isobel's treachery.

His other thumb slides to my wrist and compresses so I can feel my own heart pulsing as well. A rhythm for a rhythm, like the storm descending on our ceiling. Out of sync but still in pattern. Full of harmonious beauty and cold and closeness.

Oh hulls.

That friction in the air becomes unbearable. Just like his eyes and his warm fingers against my hand, and his heart beat beat beating beneath my skin, burning my veins with tension.

Hunger.

Blast you, Eogan.

I swallow before my lungs come undone right in front of him. But it's too late because I can feel the ridge of bones over his heart expanding as he leans in closer, measuring the distance in inches between us so we are mere shadows of skin and sinew and breath. With an expression that says exactly what we are both hungry for.

I freeze. *Don't move, Nym. Don't breathe. Don't break this moment.* I just stare at this man who was strong enough to survive Draewulf. Who was strong enough to survive me and all I've done.

Who was humble enough to survive his own history.

His gaze moves to my throat, then stalls on my mouth and stays there. And in it I see the same look I've come to know so well, the thing that means more to me than any notion of desire ever could.

His respect.

My insides dissolve to match the rain coming down overhead as his breath catches. I hear it. I swear I hear it, except he doesn't lean in farther, doesn't press it as a shadow flits behind his gaze. As if he's been sitting in this room, waiting for this moment, and now he can't decide what to do with it. No—what he *should* do with it.

He glances toward the door. "Nym, I—"

That ache in his eyes becomes more pronounced.

I frown.

"When Draewulf was acting as me . . ."

What did the queen say to him? Because it had to be her who gave him caution—who made his hesitancy so raw.

"Were the things he did through me as bad as I imagine?"

Oh hulls.

I swallow. And now I am aching too.

My lack of answer leads him to nod. "I see."

"It wasn't you." Although I of all people know that doesn't appease the guilt.

"I know. I just keep thinking, what if there's—?"

I narrow my gaze. Not just at whatever he's implying but at whatever's been done to him. Because his words are interrupted by his coughing and his skin looks grayer than before.

I look closer.

Hulls. He really is ill.

"What'd the queen do when she interrogated you?"

He shakes his head. "I'm fi—"

"What did that woman do?"

"Nothing. It's not from her. It's from my blocking ability trying to ward off her questions. I'll be fine once my body gets rest."

I tug his arm to pull him down and myself up. Is he growing weaker? "Then rest while I go put a knife to her th—"

He smiles and stops me. "Believe me, I've spent the past many hours thinking I'd like to fall asleep next to you while you angrily wield knives. Sadly"—he brushes a strand of hair from my shoulder—"we have too much—"

A few feet away Kenan jerks into a sitting position, making me jump. "Bleeding hulls!" He grabs beneath his arm where he usually carries a blade. He swats at it a few times, then flips around to stare at us.

"Relax, Kenan," Eogan growls.

"What happened? What did they do to us?"

"Drugged you. You'll survive."

Kenan's scowl eases. He shifts position so he's off the bed and squatting on his haunches. "I guess that's more than I can say for them when I get—" He stops. And squints at Eogan's gray face. "You look like litches."

"So I hear."

"And he's refusing to rest," I say.

Eogan waves us off. "I slept a little when they brought me from the queen."

"And? What'd the old hag want? She going to let us go?"

"She's undecided."

Kenan scoffs. "Of course she is. What'd she get out of you, Highness?"

"A brief history of my life, my father's life, and every opinion I've ever had on the realm of Cashlin. Whatever she saw appeased her that I've no designs on taking her kingdom."

Kenan nods. "But we're getting out of here anyway, right?"

"Of course."

"About that." I look back and forth between the two men. "I saw their city for a few moments. Eogan, they have no defenses."

Footfalls sound beyond the door, coming down the hall. They fall in unison with the raindrops now thundering above our heads. Five, six, seven individuals by my estimation. Eogan is up and standing beside the door in a heartbeat, as is Kenan. I tighten my fist in preparation as Kenan steps back and the door opens. Myles and Isobel enter the room.

I pause at Myles's wide, sunken eyes. He looks terrible. There are gasps from Sir Doesn't Matter and Kenan as they both jump away from Eogan. *What the—?* Who for a moment is no longer Eogan but Draewulf, baring his teeth and rising to his taller, wolfish height.

Lady Isobel screeches and my hand goes out, but before I can react, I catch the shiver in the air around him.

The ripple of atmosphere . . .

It's an illusion created by Lord Myles.

"Stop!" I lunge for the guard who's lifting his wristlet and kick my leg out to clip Myles's knees. He stumbles forward and the vision of Draewulf dissipates.

"It's Myles's ability, not Eogan!" I turn to Eogan who's standing there, the rippling atmosphere gone, his normal form returned.

He's staring at me with a sickened expression.

Myles curses and wheels around, even as behind him the Luminescents concur, "It was an illusion." They must've seen, just like Princess Rasha, that Myles's power wouldn't work on their intuitive minds.

"What in hulls is wrong with you?" Lady Isobel snarls, smacking her hand across Myles's face. "Are you trying to get us all killed?"

"It wasn't his fault." I look at Myles, then back at Lady Isobel. "The poison's starting in."

"Oh, of all the—"

An odd moan cuts off Isobel's cursing, and Eogan stumbles against me. *What the—?* His face has gone white as a ferret-cat and his eyes are fading fading fading to the color of death.

"Eogan!"

Before Kenan or I can catch him, he slumps to the floor.

CHAPTER 9

B LOOD IS POOLING.

It's on the floor around Eogan's head and jagged hair and black skin that has gone completely ashen. I drop to the ground and loosen his cloak to seek out his pulse.

Weak.

Blasted hulls. With shaky fingers, I yank open his coat and choke back a cry. Blood has seeped down to cover the right half of his tunic. I work to unlace the side with my good hand as a blend of feet converge around us, and four Luminescents are suddenly bending over. "Help me," I growl.

Then Kenan's there too, kneeling to help loosen the tunic. When we pull it away, the young male guard overhead gasps. Bruising covers Eogan's ribs and extends up and around to where the blood's coming from—that slice on the back of his neck.

Oh please, no.

It's oozing deep red and glossy, and too fast for safety. I press my hands over the wound, but the amount of fluid slicking out onto the glassy floor makes me ill. How did this happen? He wasn't bleeding moments ago.

Kenan places a hand on top of mine on the cut to compress harder.

"Will he be all right?"

He doesn't answer.

I turn to the Luminescents. "What's happening to him?"

One of them invades my vision. "Miss, let us take him to another room."

"Can you help him?"

When the woman doesn't respond, I look to Kenan.

"They blasted well better help him." He presses me aside and slips his other arm beneath Eogan as two female guards ready their hands to assist him.

My fingers fall from the back of Eogan's neck as they pick up the king, only to feel warm blood surge. It gushes and falls in large droplets onto the shiny floor, but I don't have time to care because I'm stalking their heels as they rush him away.

We're halfway down the crystal hall when someone bumps my arm. Lady Isobel. She's accompanied by Lord Myles and the rest of the Luminescent guards. I frown and turn, but her hand on my arm slows me as she leans in with a look that has lost its amusement. "Turn yourself and Queen Laiha over to my father when he arrives," she hisses. "And he may be inclined to spare the rest of these people along with Faelen. If not . . ." She sneers. "They're all going to die because of you."

A crash of thunder rattles the crystalline ceiling and walls. It's the only sign I've heard her as I fling her hand off and rush after the Cashlins and Kenan carrying Eogan. Because whether or not Lady Isobel actually believes her own words, I'm not daft enough to.

The room they've taken Eogan to is less than thirty paces down the first staircase. Kenan releases Eogan to a third Cashlin right as I reach them at the doorway. We've just entered when a disturbance behind us catches Kenan's attention. He wheels around, causing me to nearly slam into him.

His expression narrows.

Is she jesting? I turn to tell Lady Isobel to go to—

"I'm told this one is yours." The guard striding toward us is oozing disapproval as he holds Kel by the collar of his black-and-red Bron airship captain's uniform. "He *insisted* on being brought to you after he'd been adequately questioned."

The tiny seven-year-old's giant, white-toothed grin and the guard's limp say Kel did more than insist.

"Thank you. I'll take him from here." When the man moves away, Kenan growls at his son, "I'm pleased you're alive, but you shouldn't have joined us."

"Yes, Father, but . . ."

I shove past them and head into the room, leaving them to sort out their family disagreement beneath the watchful eyes of the Luminescent guards hovering around them.

Crisp white and golden linens curtain the entire room, spreading over more glass walls and the room's single furniture item—a bed. Just like the rest of the palace, the scent of icy death permeates the air, causing my stomach to roll.

The guards place Eogan facedown on the small cot. *Oh litches.*

I hurry over to the foot of it and try to hold back my horror as the cut on Eogan's upper back oozes more blood in dark, ribboned streams across his shoulders and neck. It stains the impeccably bright bedsheets.

"Give me a rag," one of the Cashlins is saying, and when she glances up at her companions, her eyes are glowing red. "And a needle. And get the Prestere."

The room erupts into controlled chaos. One person moves to obey and another cuts off the rest of Eogan's cloak and tunic.

"Miss, we need you to leave."

I blink. *What?*

It's the young Cashlin male. I frown.

"We have to work on him, but in order to do so, we need as much room as possible. And as little . . ." He glances down at my hands that are somehow both clenched into fists, and I know he's sensing my fear. My anger. He's hearing the atmosphere outside rattling a storm bigger than anything they're used to.

I peer over at Kenan who's striding in with Kel. The boy looks subdued, but the expression on the large man's face says he'll tear anyone limb from limb if they try to remove him from his king.

"Miss . . ."

I turn back to the guard. "I'll stay out of the way, but I'm not leaving him."

I've been away from him too long, fought too hard to be banished from his side when we don't even know what's wrong or how in hulls to help him. I back against the wall as Kel shuffles over to join me. He stands very official and stiff-like with his little hands behind his back and his black-eyed gaze solemn.

The Cashlin purses his lips, then nods, and somehow we both know he understands and that there's not enough time to argue anyway. A moment longer and the Luminescents are huddling around Eogan, blocking my view while I'm striving to hear any hint of him breathing. *Is* he breathing? *Litches, Eogan, please be breathing.*

Beside me, Kel is speaking again to his father, conveying something that has his whole little face strained. "I tried, Father. I couldn't help him."

Kenan nods at me. "He speaks of the child Soren—the other captain. He's dead."

What? I glance at Kel. *I will unleash a hailstorm on every Luminescent in this wretched place if they killed a child.* "What happened?"

"When the ship crashed, it . . . it broke his neck, I think."

I sink beside him. "Kel, I'm—"

His onyx face blushes furiously and he scowls. "I'm not a baby."

I rise just as quickly. "Of course you're not. But I'm sad about this."

The furrowed lines in his brow ease slowly, until he nods once and slips his hand into mine while his father steps over to the bed.

One minute drags by.

Two minutes.

Five minutes of me standing there with bated lungs, swearing internally over the lives we've lost and at the life in front of us that I'm scared we're losing. *Blast, Eogan, fight this or I will kill you myself.*

Suddenly Queen Laiha's words float through my foggy head. *"You'll need to hurry if you want to save him."*

I squint. What exactly had she meant? I look up at the Luminescents surrounding him. Was she speaking of Eogan? Are we wasting our time?

Does she know how to save him?

Kenan emerges from the bustle of bodies and approaches. His onyx face has sallowed.

My heart deflates. "Is he—?"

A tight shake of his head. "He's still here. For now."

"I need to speak to the queen," I say in a low tone. "I'm going to find her. Don't leave his side until I return." I don't wait for his reply before releasing Kel and stepping toward the door. But I've not even tugged on the fancy etched glass when a man my height, dressed in a long purple robe and smelling of floral cinnamon, pushes it open and nearly collides into me.

"Pardon," I snap.

He ignores me and shuffles in, mumbling something incoherent and bringing me to frown as I turn to see the Luminescents and Cashlins moving away in order for the short purple man to stand solely over Eogan.

Still mumbling, he inspects Eogan, until after a moment I draw closer to inspect him too. The blood is cleaned up, but it only makes the bruising appear stronger, deeper, as if the bones in Eogan's back have been broken. My stomach turns to sand. Was he suffering while we were speaking earlier? Was that his hesitation? His nervousness?

"Can you help him?" I ask the purple man.

The mumbling fool ignores me and sets a basket on the bed, from which he pulls a clear glass jar filled with an orange substance. There's a slight popping sound as he lifts the lid, and then he swipes his fingers into the thick orange cream and spreads it along the length of the gash on the back of Eogan's neck. When the liquid touches the layers of torn muscle and skin, they sizzle and let off a sharp, acrid smell that fills the room.

I step forward. "What in hul—?" But Kenan is beside me, grabbing my arm.

"Wait," he says, even as his mouth stays in a snarl. He watches the proceedings like a hawk.

The foul scent continues to pervade the air, but the sizzling along Eogan's upper back settles down. The Luminescents seem just as entranced by the scene as I am, and while they're watching it, I slide my hand out and grab one of the smaller blades left on the edge of the bed. It still has blood on it and I slip it between my dress skirts.

Kenan eyes me with approval, and I promptly refocus my mind on Eogan in case any of the Luminescents happen to switch their attention to me and my thoughts.

As quickly as he started, the mumbling man stops and returns the jar to his basket while the guards collect their rags and sewing threads and cutting blades and silently stride past us to exit the room.

The man, whom I presume is the Prestere, or physician, is the last to step away for the door.

I plant myself in front of him. "I need to see the queen."

He doesn't acknowledge me, just brushes right past.

I grasp his purple robe. "Did you hear me? We can't save him here—I need to speak to the queen."

He murmurs something unintelligible and yanks open the door. He pauses midstep. Then he leans forward, picks something up from the floor, and straightens. The sound of rustling parchment says he's opening a slip of paper. He turns back to us and holds it up. "Did you drop this?" His voice is the sound of rough rocks clacking together.

In the entryway light, the paper looks the color of blood. Or perhaps to my overwrought mind everything looks like blood. I stroll over for a closer inspection, shaking my head as I draw near. "No."

For the first time the man's gaze sweeps up and holds my own. The intimation behind it stops me cold.

"What?"

He flips the thing over in his hands and sniffs it once. He peers at it again, eyes tightening into a glare.

"Good hulls, man, what is it?" Kenan says behind me.

In answer the man holds up the paper with its scrawled inscription for me to see.

I read it once, quietly. Then again, aloud so Kenan can hear, as my head implodes from anger. I shut my eyes to keep from tipping over in the spinning room. The message searing itself against the inside of my eyelids.

"I'll see you soon, pet."

It must have been on Eogan. I flip around to stare at him. Draewulf must have placed it in his overcoat pocket with the chance the shape-shifter would lose his hold and be forced from Eogan's body.

Which means . . . Draewulf *knew* he might lose his hold.

My attempt to follow the man who is leaving the room is interrupted by a soft groan. Kenan's already striding over to the bed. I cross the ten steps in half a second. Eogan's back is moving with shallow breathing, even if his uncloaked skin is marred with that bruising and stitching and odd-looking burn marks from the orange paste.

I rest fingertips from my good hand on his shoulder and glance up at Kenan, who's bending over the king's face to peer at his closed eyes and the pulsing of his neck.

Eogan's body jerks and stiffens. His hand jolts up and grasps Kenan's arm, causing me to screech. He squeezes it until his knuckles pop.

"It's just me, Eogan," the guard growls. "Relax."

The grip loosens immediately and Eogan's muscles slacken. His eyes open far enough to glare at the large guard. "Get Nym, you oaf. Make sure she's safe."

"She's right here. Now shut up and rest before you kill yourself."

Eogan's eyes close, although I highly doubt it's in obedience. His head lolls to the side again, and only the continued rapid rise and fall of his sewn-up upper back keeps me sane. I bite my tongue and gulp. *He's still alive.*

My hands tighten again into fists, and I'm rewarded by a responding peal of thunder.

Kenan looks over at me. "Not sure that's helping."

"It might," Kel's small voice pipes up. "Do it again!"

"Kel," Kenan barks.

"It's neat," Kel mumbles.

"You'll be silent or I will personally have the Luminescents lock you up again."

"Yes, Father."

I glance back at Kenan. "When do we know if he'll be all right?"

He doesn't answer, just shrugs and looks around until he finds a spot on the floor facing the door. He sits down, elbows on his knees with his bloody hands aloft, and rests his chin in the crook of his arm, the spirit of fatigue descending over him.

His eyes droop shut and a single drop of blood falls from his fingers to the glass tile, making a beaded design. I glance at Eogan, his lungs heaving his muscles up and down rhythmically. Then peer over at Kel who is silently watching his father.

"Your guess is as good as mine," Kenan says finally from the crook of his arm. "But from what I've gathered, whatever they've done won't be permanent. He's still dying."

My fears exactly.

"I'll be back," I whisper and stride out to find the queen.

CHAPTER 10

THE HALL IS DEAD SILENT. THE HOST OF Luminescents that was here minutes ago is gone and there's neither sound nor sign of anyone.

I tighten my grip on the confiscated blade at my side and peek back at Eogan's room. Then, straightening my shoulders, I slink down the crystal hall to slip quick and quiet around one corner, then another, taking the passages and stairs leading away from this glassy wing of the Castle. Things begin to look more familiar toward the throne room we were brought to last night.

My head pounds dull with the rain drumming on the high ceiling that's flickering rainbows and shadows in the candelabra lighting. Or maybe my head's pounding from a lack of sleep and the loss of blood from my own chest, I don't know—but whatever the cause, it's beating louder and harder the closer I get. Stressing that something is very wrong.

When I reach the giant, closed, crystal throne-room doors, I stop. After a moment of no one appearing, I skirt past them and around the curved wall to a small corridor shooting off from the right.

A horn blasts. It's distant and muffled, but in the silence it makes me jump. Two seconds later it repeats, and this time I'm already trying one door, two doors, three doors down the hall while shaking

72

off the awareness that Rasha has walked this hall and touched these doors before. That she should be here now.

C'mon, Nym, focus.

Unfortunately, the doors are locked. Between my time at Adora's house and Faelen's Castle, I've a suspicion all royal rooms tend to be located in a similar layout. *At least I hope they are.* I aim for the last one located at the far end.

The door is unlocked, and pressing it brings me onto a platform attached to an arched bridge that spans over a giant domed room. Or rather, a garden enclosed in a room, with plants and flowers edging the circular walls and dripping from boxes hung in mid-air throughout the humid space. In the center, directly beneath the bridge and domed glass ceiling, a pond ripples with what appear to be five real, live snake-swans. They float and glide upon the blue surface, their necks writhing up and around, listening for any movement their blind eyes are unable to detect. I inspect them as the heat in here crushes against my lungs.

It's suffocating. I pull my braid off my damp neck and, keeping my eye on those swans, cross the tiny arching bridge.

Not until I'm coming down the arch on the other side do I see the guard standing like a white statue. Blocking my way.

She assesses me with red-rimmed pupils.

"The queen," I say.

The woman opens an intricately etched gate attached to the bridge and extends her arm to usher me down onto a curling stairwell. "She's expecting you."

I raise a brow, ignore the shiver curling up my throat, and stride forward as the guard shuts it behind me, and abruptly I'm walking down a circle of steps to the garden.

We emerge beside the lake and come face-to-face with *her.*

Queen Laiha.

She's seated in the same wheeling chair as earlier, facing the lake, except this time the backdrop behind her is floral trees and an enormous window displaying a stormy landscape. Aside from the red glow emanating from her crimson eyes, she, along with the rest of the room, is bathed in a suffocating glare coming from the glass ceiling that tweaks the rain and sunlight as it shines in and magnifies it. Any other time I would've been mesmerized by such a trick.

Unfortunately for her, I don't give a bleeding litch.

"You *knew* he was dying, and you still kept us." My voice shakes in fury.

"Which is why I suggested in the throne room that you'd want to hurry."

Is she jesting? "You're the one who detained us and *interrogated* him." I point my blade at her. I don't care if she is Rasha's mum. "Now tell me how to fix him."

Behind me I hear a clink of metal and my skin pricks as the guard pulls her own blade and holds it to my back. I stiffen.

The queen clears her throat and stares at me with a face that is neither stern nor overly caring. Merely . . . patient. "The Bron king can't be fixed here." She glances to the window. "My members have worked to shore up what little life he has left, but you'll have to go quickly. Especially as even now the ships come. The horn has sounded."

I don't ask what ships because we both already know. "You tortured him while knowing he was dying."

She shrugs her lips. "He was dying anyway, through no fault of my own. You've no doubt seen from the injury on his neck, his internal wounds are from Draewulf. My interrogation may have sped up their progress, but it was his use of his ability that prevented them from mending in the first place."

What the blast is she talking about? Is she unhinged?

She lets out a tinkling laugh. "Most likely. But I did what I needed to for my people. Now I will allow you to do what you need to for yours. You are free to leave."

Just like that? Is she daft? "Lovely. How do I *save* him?"

"You know the answer."

I let the blade flash again and the one at my back pricks harder. I clench my teeth. "If I knew, I'd not be standing here asking."

"The Valley of Origin, of course. I suggest you take the fastest of your airships."

The Valley in Faelen?

"I assume you mean the ships you confiscated."

"The two that were not destroyed in your crash—which took down a bit of my Castle, I remind you—are ready and waiting for your departure."

I bite my lip. "You're saying there's someone in the Valley who can help him? Where will I find this person?"

"Not a person. Well, not in our definition of one, anyway." She stares at me meaningfully as if I'm to understand this.

I don't.

And I don't have time for her riddles. "Tell me what it is then—"

"It is not for me to say, only for you to find." She turns her head to gaze out the window as if she's heard something.

I open my mouth, then shut it. *I'm done with this.*

I turn to go, but her voice rises. "The internal bleeding set in around the torn organs and then, after my questioning of Eogan, the entry point on his neck. As I said, it may have even been able to heal given time for his ability to work. However . . ." Her eyes bore into my chest so profoundly that I follow her gaze down to my sliced, stained dress. "In gifting you his strength for healing on the airship, he became weakened past even what his power can fix."

I narrow my eyes and peel back a piece of the material to see what she's staring at.

It's only then I'm struck by the realization that my chest hasn't ached in hours, since just before we crashed the airship. Not only that, but somehow the wounds that oozed the blood are gone. I pull more of the cloth away from my chest and poke gently where only last night my flesh was torn open. It's smooth. It's soft. My skin is whole.

She nods.

"How—?"

"You assume his gift is blocking others' abilities. Considering you love him, I find it curious you know so little of him." She tilts her head and drifts her gaze over me.

Whatever words were in my mouth are sliding back into my throat. What is she talking about? "Is that what you told *him*?" My mind flashes to an hour ago in the room with Eogan, when he seemed so hesitant. "What did you say to him? What's his ability and what will help him?"

"What another asks of me is not for you to know. Nor is the answer given them. You should be less concerned with that and more with getting him to the Valley." Her head snaps to the window again. "Even now Draewulf draws closer."

I bat a hand toward the sky and light it up as if this is of little concern. "So come with us. Help me save Eogan, your people, and the Hidden Lands."

Her eyes harden. "I've already said I will not leave my people. Draewulf will try to take me, yes. And if he succeeds, that is my destiny."

"*If* he succeeds?" How can her Luminescent sight see so much and yet leave so much to fate? And how can she not know what he will do—what he's *capable* of? "I believe we make our own destiny. We make our own choices."

"Then you can choose to respect mine."

"Even though it will cost your daughter's life as well?"

She tips her head as if to shrug, but not before I see the tightening of her throat. "If she is meant to survive, then she will."

I give a harsh laugh as I pull away from the guard's knife that's now annoying me. "Are you insane? Of course she's meant to survive—we all are!"

"Then perhaps you should help her do so. But as I said, respect my decision."

"Respect your choice to endanger the entire Hidden Lands because you'll only protect your own people—but not your own daughter? Forgive me, but I've seen your defenses. You can't protect your city!"

The same irritation I had toward Rasha bubbles up into my mind before I can stop it. Was it destiny that caused the murder of my Elemental race? Or simply the decision on Cashlin's and Tulla's parts to care only about themselves?

Her gaze snaps. "We have our reasons."

"Yes, Rasha mentioned as much. Too bad she'd no idea how little care for her you have."

"Careful," the guard behind me growls.

"She does not always see eye to eye with those reasons," the queen says. "But the safety of our people has always come first."

I allow the words I spoke to Rasha not four days ago to emerge in my head—that my Elemental kind has spent the last hundred years being slaughtered while Cashlin has protected its own.

"Ah, but you did not know your people as I did. If so, you might feel differently. They were arrogant and too powerful for their own good. Lucky for your kingdom at the time, none of the Elementals were as powerful as you, nor could they bear working together—plus, there were other kinds of Uathúils to control them. Had your people been more unified, they might've overcome the Uathúils hired to confine them in their internment camps before those same Uathúils began to be hunted themselves."

I step toward her, my stomach churning and my hand clenching. The guard and her blade are right on my heels, but I don't care. "And that's your excuse for letting them die?"

"Oh, they put up a good fight and slaughtered their fair share of Faelenians. As I said, had they been more numerous and humble enough to combine forces, they would've succeeded. You should thank hulls they didn't."

I open my mouth just as her voice softens. "Nym, it is arrogance that brought them down just as much as Draewulf's truce. I know you often believe your Elemental ability is a curse, but they *used* it as one. And, for that matter, you should understand I have often believed the same of my ability. That it is a curse. Imagine knowing how almost every decision of those you come in contact with will likely result. It's a burden."

Her eyes moisten, and in that moment it's a kick of guilt to my chest. I've never thought of that. Either for her or for Rasha. Nearby, the lake water ripples, followed by the honk of a swan.

"Your kind made their own choice. Perhaps it was their destiny, or perhaps it was just foolhardy. However, just because I can see a possible ending doesn't mean I'm obligated to act upon it. Then or now."

I don't want to talk about this anymore. "You admit you could've seen what would happen to the Elementals. Just as I suspect you can see what will happen to us. So tell me—what *will* happen to us now?"

"I know you and my daughter are quite close, and I'm aware of the burden you carry for her and the Tullan people. While you may have hurried Draewulf to my door, it is neither your fault that he is on the move, nor that you could not defend all of them."

Why is she telling me this? "Just answer the question."

"I am. Because what I know is—this time, this path before the Hidden Lands is not mine to decide." The queen drops her voice. "It is yours."

"Mine?" I frown. "To decide what?"

"All of it," she whispers. And suddenly her eyes are hardening. As if willing me to make the right choice. As if assuming I know what in hulls she's referring to.

"Just as even now you still feel the effects of the poisoned power that will always scratch at you. Because the choices we make have lasting consequences. You were lucky with that one. Because what you decide for the future of Faelen will be a choice of such magnitude, the consequences are beyond imagining."

I glare at her. I have no idea what to do with this. "And what am I supposed to decide?"

Her lips twitch. "Come here, child."

I narrow my gaze even more and flip a look at the guard to make sure I'm not going to get a knife in my gut. Then I step near her. As I do, the scent of frozen death invades my nostrils, invoking a fear I didn't know was there. *Good hulls.*

She stares at my hand, as if curling her mind around my gimpy fingers, and it's all I can do not to yank away as her icy gaze cuts into me. She closes her eyes and waits. Until her breathing gets heavier and the only thing interrupting the silence is my heart beating and her breathing and the *honk honk honk* of those swans getting closer behind us.

"You have three choices in front of you." Her voice sounds old and thin now, like brittle blades on paper. "The first is to run with

Eogan to the Valley of Origin and hope you arrive in time. If he's healed, you'll escape with him to hide in Drust." Her eyes flare open and stare at me. How she knew this was on my mind scares me. I haven't even fully formed the thought of running and hiding with him yet, but now that she says it . . . "In which case you both will survive for a time."

"And the Hidden Lands?" I swallow. "Will they survive if Draewulf can't find me?"

"There is a chance he won't find you for a while but could continue to wage his war, morphing humanity into his wraiths. At least until there is hardly a world left to take over. Or . . . your second option is to leave now with Eogan for the Valley, then prepare for war in Faelen. In which case, I should warn you that whether Eogan survives long enough to be healed or not, you'll still need to get to the Valley of Origin if you wish to have a chance at beating the beast. As the last Elemental, it is your responsibility to call forth the rest."

"I'm sorry?"

"The other Uathúils. Faelen is *your* land, Nym. The Valley is your birthright."

She sighs and murmurs something about what they're teaching in Faelen these days.

"Just like each of the Uathúil kings' blood is tied to sacred spaces in their lands, yours is tied to the Valley. And that is where you will call them because your true capabilities are not just in controlling the weather, they are in calling what once was into existence again."

She suddenly twists her neck around to look at the sky. Then jerks her head back toward me. I see it. The moving lights in the distance that are too colorful and too fast. Draewulf's ships. The red in her eyes flares. "You need to leave."

I plant my feet firmly beside her chair and lean in. "Not until I know what you're talking about."

Her eyes snap and the guard behind me shifts. "Hope. And Uathúils. Both of which are the only chance at saving this world from Draewulf."

"And these Uathúils—how am I supposed to call them?"

"I cannot say."

I wave an arm in the air. "What in litches *can* you say?"

Her eyes flash red and harden.

I narrow mine. "In that case, what's the third option?"

She turns her head toward the lake and the swans that are getting closer.

I lift my knife and hear the slide of a footstep behind me. But the Luminescent guard must read my intentions because she doesn't cut me.

Queen Laiha's gaze swerves back to mine, however, and the spark there says if she could get up from her chair and slap me herself she would. Instead she tips her head toward the edge of the lake. "Touch it."

"Pardon?" I frown and turn. The water is crystal clear and rippling gently on the white-sand shore.

"Touch the water with your boot, and then back up."

I walk the four paces over and, scowling, tap my foot on the water.

There's an instant honking and commotion, and I barely have time to look up when the five snake-swans are charging toward me. I jump backward as they rush the shoreline, writhing their necks and pecking at the water as if I've thrown in food.

"Not food," the queen whispers behind me. "A threat. Before I took them in, they'd been abused by man. Because of that, they now sense any disturbance of their territory to be a threat. And to a certain degree they are right. You could be a danger to them if you wanted to."

The blind snake-swans are growing more and more agitated. Suddenly one lifts its head higher than the rest and throws itself on the sand. Flopping violently. *What the—?*

My gut twists in horror as the other four descend on it and rip into its wings with their razor teeth until the poor thing's shredded and bleeding and dying. It gives one final, feeble honk and the others race away to the center of the glittering lake.

"And yet," whispers the queen with a note of sadness, "these types of animals have such a bond that when all else fails in the face of danger, one will ultimately sacrifice itself for the sake of the others. If you truly had been a threat, you would've taken this one as an easy kill and left the others alone. In that way, the sacrifice of one may save the many."

I turn and stare at her and the guard.

Then peer back over at the limp swan as my throat tightens. What she's suggesting pricks my shoulder blades. "You're suggesting I sacrifice myself."

"That is the third option, yes. Because without your blood, Draewulf cannot ever fully succeed. He will stay mortal and thus can eventually be killed."

"By an Elemental who no longer exists because I'm the last of my race."

"Maybe. Or perhaps in sacrificing yourself, you will destroy him too."

"Well, which is it?"

She shakes her head.

"Are you saying I should kill myself?"

"Not in the least—I would never condone such a thing. I'm saying you can run or fight, but when the time comes—and it will—you may have to fall at the hand of another before Draewulf takes you. No one escapes this life, nor do they escape war, unscathed. And in this case you are the piece that will make all the difference. So *hold it all lightly, Nym.*"

The words from the Inters slip through my head: *I wasn't supposed to survive.*

A sharp throat clearing comes from the Cashlin guard. "Your Majesty, three of Draewulf's airships are nearly here."

My legs are frozen, my head is frozen, and my voice has gone to litches. Eogan's dying and this is all a hull's nest.

"Your Majesty," the female guard says, more insistent.

"Just tell me." I swallow. "If it comes down to such a thing, will my sacrifice guarantee Draewulf's defeat and my people's freedom?"

The queen's face grows gray. "I cannot answer that other than to say freedom comes in many forms. But it *always* comes at a price."

"And what if I run? Will that at least slow his defeat?"

"It will."

"In that case, if the people will die no matter what, then why spend their last few weeks leading them to a violent end?"

"I think the question is, can you justify not trying to defeat him?"

"I can if you're wrong."

The guard slips her hand onto my arm.

"Again, I cannot tell you for certain."

"Because you don't *know*, or you refuse?"

"As I said, ultimately the choice is yours to make. Now leave. The time has drawn short for Eogan, and his death will be at your feet if you willingly stay."

The drone of an airship rattles the domed glass ceiling as I stare at her. Knowing that what I choose now will set the course for not just the Hidden Lands' destiny, but her destiny as well.

And that is a weight I don't want anything to do with.

She nods at me, as if already knowing what my choice will be.

"Take that there," she says calmly, and with a tip of her head indicates a letter slid into the Luminescent guard's pocket. "Give it to King Sedric." She pauses, then, as if on second thought, says, "Tell him from what I can see, you have roughly ten days."

"Until what?"

"Until Draewulf is finished with Cashlin."

Wait—*ten*? I grab the letter just as the Luminescent jumps toward the queen and grabs the handles on her chair.

"I must see to Her Majesty. Show yourself—" The guard's words are drowned out in an explosion that blasts just beyond the window behind the queen, sending the sound of shattering glass through the room as a burst of heat and fire and screams billows up from a section of city wall in the distance.

The bombing shakes the entire Castle. It's so violent and loud. I drop to a crouch while the guard hovers over the queen as we wait for the sky to fall. Except Queen Laiha's expression doesn't seem concerned, and after a moment the shaking stops and the garden room stays intact.

I rise and tuck King Sedric's letter into my dress top.

"Go!" the guard says.

"The sooner, the better," the queen adds. "For all of us."

I'm racing up the crystal stairs to the bridge when her voice calls after me, "You should know, though, that the one called Lord Myles stands on the edge of a decision as well. One choice will send him over a precipice and turn him into a lesser Draewulf. The other will most likely cost his life but will help the Hidden Lands survive. Help him if you can. But should he decide wrong, destroy him. And, Nym!"

I barely turn.

"If you can . . ." Her voice cracks, and for a second I hear my own mother's tone coming through. It's as if all her crazy, hardened veneer has just peeled off and exposed who she truly is—with the heart of a mother's love—behind it. "Help Rasha. She will need you and . . . you will need her if Draewulf truly takes me."

What in hulls? I swallow. She's finally mentioning that now? And then I don't care because I'm running for the door. With a final glance at the snake-swans, I push out of the room just as the queen's call of "Hold it lightly, Nym!" is cut off by another bomb and the sound ricochets through the palace.

CHAPTER 11

T HE PALACE STAYS STANDING AS I PLOW DOWN
the hallways and past frantically moving Cashlins who've
emerged from hulls knows where toward the room where
I left Eogan. I've almost reached it when the young male guard,
Kenan, Kel, and Eogan appear.

I stall for a half second as they head toward me.

"You're—"

"Whatever they did to me worked." Eogan steps forward, still
weak looking but coherent.

I frown at the bags beneath his eyes.

"We have to get out of here. Kenan said you went for Queen
Laiha."

"She's staying, but she's released us to take our airships and go."

"They're this way," the guard says. "Follow me."

"And the crews?" Kenan demands.

"Already aboard and waiting. The queen had me send two
Luminescents to escort your Lord Myles and Lady Isobel as well."
The guard's already turned down a corridor. "They'll be on the
ship in the West Courtyard. We need to reach it before Draewulf's
bombs do."

We're jogging to keep up with him now, and Kenan's got his
arm under Eogan's shoulder. "Your queen will *die* here, and then

her daughter as well," Eogan says quietly to him. "She must have seen this."

"I agree. But she has made her choice. Whether it is for the best or not. However, as far as Princess Rasha—"

Kenan shakes his head as if the guard's crazy. "But at the cost of how many lives? And because of some stubborn—"

"She asked us to rescue Rasha," I say.

The Cashlin guard's body slows until almost frozen mid-movement, and Eogan's eyes find mine.

"She believes we're going to need her. But beyond that, it's no use," I say. "The queen won't come, and we have to go." I tug Eogan's arm and push Kenan and the guard forward. "Eogan's still going to die unless we get him to the Valley. And if his body fails, Draewulf has enough of his blood that his power and land will transfer to the monster fully."

I keep my hand on Eogan's arm and peer up as another rumble shakes the crystal ceiling. "Now do you trust me or not?"

Another explosion.

Another shaking and shivering and shattering somewhere in the palace.

A long inhale of breath, as if from out of nowhere, and half the palace guards run past us.

"Kenan, we're leaving," Eogan growls. His throat clenches as he swallows and clasps my hand and pulls us forward into a run.

"How many bombs can each of Draewulf's ships hold?" I yell.

"Up to two."

Kenan tips his head. "Except back in Bron he loaded a number of the airships' cargo bays with bombs. So he has far more at his disposal."

"He'll likely have brought one of those ships then from Tulla. I assume this is his way of shaking us free before he drops wraiths on the city." Eogan looks at the Cashlin guard. "How many ships total did Draewulf bring to this capitol?"

"Five by our count."

"Meaning he thinks it'll be easy to take the city then."

Ahead of us the guard nods. "My thoughts as well."

"The queen said Cashlin will last ten days," I say over the noise.

The guard stops. Turns.

As do the others.

I swallow. "That's her estimation, anyway."

A moment longer and then the guard nods, turns, and pushes through a door to the West Courtyard where one of our airships is hovering in the center. Overhead, our other ship is flying low and as close to the mountain as possible. I twist my hand to pull up a shroud of thick fog to cloak them better from Draewulf's eyes as we break into a full run.

"Kenan, I need to be in the captains' room," Eogan says. "And I'll not accept an argument on it."

Kenan nods and eyes me. "Kel, you stay with Nym."

At the loading dock, Cashlin guards are waiting to wave us up the ramp. The young male with us doesn't stop. He ascends ahead of us, and as I near the top, I spot two red-eyed Luminescents already aboard amid our crew scurrying about the deck.

"You're coming with us then," Eogan says to him in a statement, not a question.

"If I may, Your Highness. As well as those two Luminescents. Queen Laiha sends us as a token of assistance to King Sedric."

Eogan pats his shoulder and moves past the man toward the captains' room. "Get us in the air," he yells as the fourth bomb hits. And this time a shatter of glass crashes from the palace ceiling onto the rooftop nearest us.

I duck even though we're instantly rising up up up into the fog-cloak, with only the smallest lights to reveal the location of the other ships. I peer over the railing onto the city and palace that have black holes and smoke emanating from four different vicinities. All those people.

Kel's chilly hand grabs mine. "Can't you stop them?"

My surge of thunder snaps and a thread of lightning ignites over the city. It illuminates Draewulf's five airships, eerily close, through the fog.

I clench my fist and drag another shred of lightning down to tear through one of those ships. It lights up like a furnace—all spark and flame and wisps of shredded balloon—and then it's falling from the sky onto one of the crystal streets.

The next moment the fog is darkening, like ink seeping into it. The thick, blackening wisps swirl up and around where the other ships are, blocking them from my vision.

I send in a gale wind to shove it away, but the darkness clings to the atmosphere like a plagued leech. Thick and unmoving.

I send in another shredded bolt, but it slices right through the black cloud and explodes a section of housing below it. *Litches.* Three more attempts end in the same result, and it occurs to me that the cloud is doing more than hiding them. It's acting as some sort of shield.

My curled fist lets the sky sizzle overhead but holds off sending any more. If I can't see them, I can't hit them. Suddenly my wrist aches, my lungs ache.

"What're you doing?" Kel yells. "Why are you shielding them?"

"I'm not. It's Draewulf. And my ability's still too weak to break through it." I pull my hand from the boy's and use both fists to shove a gust between us and those ships. Propelling us faster in the wind. Pushing us away from the city, away from that black cloud, and away from Draewulf.

"Is Princess Rasha on one of those ships?" The Luminescents' voices are eerily close.

My gut lurches. *Litch.* I shake my head; I don't know. But hulls, I hope not. I continue to force the gale to give us distance, then close my eyes as the sounds of Eogan shouting orders from the captains' room, and the airship's drone, and the crashing of glass and metal below swirl around me.

After a moment I can stand it no longer and beg the Elemental in my blood to at least bring forth rain like it did earlier.

It's barely a mist on my face when it begins. Water droplets sprinkling the air, carrying cool breath from the thickening clouds. As if this, a sigh of mercy on the earth, it is willing to give.

It immediately dims the smoke and fires that have flared up around the swiftly fading city.

The air whips around me just as the ship is moving beneath my boots, dragging us to another place and leaving in our wake another devastation.

I bend both hands now and I'm rewarded by a downpour. It patters and drops and slaps the balloon overhead and the deck railing and Kel's and my heads. Soon it's coming down so hard that the city and Draewulf's airships are dissolved into the storm. But if they're faring anything like our ships, Draewulf's captains are struggling to keep them aright as they weave and bob about on the wind.

Good.

I turn to look at the waterlogged Kel, and the guard, Sir Doesn't Matter, and the Cashlin Luminescents, and the soldiers assembling themselves into units on our ship's deck. Kel smiles a bright-white, toothy grin at me through giant drips falling from his nearly shaved black bangs before he looks back to the mountains we're climbing over.

I share his smile halfheartedly and lessen the rain. Then turn with him to face Faelen.

Ten days.

CHAPTER 12

THE RAIN KEEPS UP FOR HOURS, GUSHING, REFRESH-
ing, washing the blood and wraith smell from my skin and
off the ship as it pushes us forward through the afternoon
toward Faelen.

Eogan's doing his best to stay awake and rest while assisting the
captains, and Kenan's ensuring the prisoners are overly secured—
including Lord Wellimton, whom the soldiers put into a holding
cell with Myles and Isobel. Which makes me grin.

"He's an angry person." Kel wrinkles his nose as the wind whips
over the airship railing. "And not much for caring who knows it. He
says being confined with two traitors on 'a bleeding Bron king's
ship' is the worst offense, and that King Sedric will punish you all."

I raise a brow. "I'm sure he's saying it, but I'm more curious as
to how you *know* he's saying it."

"The air vents are all the same on these ships."

I eye him with what amusement I can muster. "I assume your
father still doesn't know about your escapade in Faelen using those
vents?"

"Nah. And don't you go telling him either."

"Or else what?"

"Not sure," he mumbles. "But I'll think of something." His big

92

dark eyes watch me from his black, rain-spattered face. "You going to come inside soon? You got goose bumps." He nods to my hands.

I look down at my wrists peeking out from the cuff sleeves that are overly long but still the shortest I could find. It took me half an hour to dig up this Bron uniform from a storage closet. "I like the rain." I close my eyes and inhale the air that has gradually gone from icy to only mildly cold the farther south we've flown over the Cashlin mountains. "If you concentrate, you can smell the salt in the wind. We've almost reached the sea."

"You think we're going to make it in time then?" Kel whispers.

"To save Eogan?"

He shrugs. "Just asking. 'Cuz he looks pretty all right to me, except . . ."

"Except what?"

He shakes his head.

"What?"

He furrows his brow. "I just think something's off with him, and not just 'cuz he's still ill."

I frown. "Want to explain that?"

His little lips purse together as he swerves his gaze to meet mine. So solemn. So intent. Finally, "It means nothing. And if it did—it's not my business to worry about. But . . . here he comes, so just don't kiss him or anything."

I ease my frown and follow Kel's gaze to where Eogan emerges from the captains' room. "Well, now you've ruined my plan. Because I was thinking I'd smack him a good one right in front of—"

Kel's gone before I can finish, scurrying past Eogan with an exaggerated gagging sound. I move to assist Eogan, but he waves me off even as his gaze catches mine and glimmers. "What was that about?"

"Nothing. I'm merely beginning to think it's a Bron curse for the men to talk in hints so as to keep the world confused," I say lighter than I feel. I eye him closer. *What did Kel mean?*

His eyes scan my cheeks. "Must've been quite the hint seeing as it's got you—"

Suddenly my face feels beyond warm. I narrow my brow and he clears his throat. "Easing the rain up."

I snort and look up. Yes, the rain softened right along with Kel's embarrassing kissing comment.

When I drop my gaze, Eogan is studying me with amusement. "Think we'll make it in time?"

"For?"

He swags a hand dramatically down his chest with a lopsided smile. "Survival, or whatever it was the queen told you."

"Funny, Kel was just asking the same thing," I say with forced casualness. "Maybe if you'd lie down and rest for once."

"I'm feeling much better, thank you."

"You don't look it." I move over to support him, but he shakes his head and leans against the railing. "Truly, I'm fine. Whatever they did—"

"Liar."

"So now I'm confusing *and* a liar? What have the Bron men ever done to deserve—"

I level a glare at him, prompting him to laugh and lift both hands in surrender.

"Fine. But when do I confuse you? Aside from the whole shapeshifter thing, which I'll remind you was completely beyond my fault."

I actually snort. Has he not spent the past few months living the same days as me? "You confuse people with your intentions. With your words and with what you hide and what you want. I'd think you'd know that, considering all the time I've spent yelling at you."

He straightens and smirks. "All right, another fair point. I'll give you that." He shoves a hand through his bangs and pauses as he eyes me. "The fact is, I think I've spent most of my life hiding things—initially from my father—and then when I came to Faelen, from everyone else. But these days . . ." His gaze turns sincere. "I think you'll find my intentions are quite clear."

They are?

Then what about his hesitation in the room this morning . . . ?

The old awareness that he's a king and I'm a newly emancipated slave slips over my shoulders like a scratchy shroud.

"Thank you for getting us out of Cashlin, by the way." He glances at the soldiers working the ship while their counterparts catch an hour's sleep in the hull.

"We all did."

"Maybe, but without your storm moving in, we wouldn't have made it."

"What did the queen say to you?" I ask, assessing his sallow complexion.

His expression flickers puzzled, then clears with apparent acceptance of the topic change. "I told you, she asked questions."

"But she also said things to you, I assume. Can I ask what?"

His brow goes up but he stays silent, studying me, as if he's trying to decide what to say or, perhaps, how to say it.

"She gave me options," he murmurs after a moment, his voice barely rising above the airship's drone. "She told me we could fight Draewulf, or we could run and hide and hope Draewulf never finds us. Or . . . we could separate, and I could put as much distance as possible between me and you to keep Draewulf from capturing us both. However, she could give no guarantee that any of those would work."

That's what she gave him? "That's it?"

He nods and continues staring at me. "Why?"

Something inside breathes a sigh of relief, releasing a tension I didn't even know was there. Perhaps because I know his beautiful face and soul well enough to understand if she had suggested the option of either him or me dying, he would've claimed it in a heart-pulse. He would've seen it as his responsibility to sacrifice for the good of everyone.

Including me.

But that's not how it's supposed to be. Because *I* am the one who was never supposed to survive.

And she didn't give him the option . . .

I smile in spite of his sincerity.

"Are you going to tell me what it is you're thinking?"

"Do you know what you're going to decide?"

His expression takes on the same hesitation I saw earlier today in the room with him, after he'd returned from the queen. "I'll not abandon you in hopes he'll not find us. But I'll not control you either. However, if we run . . ." He lifts his eyes and stares hard out at the peaks and the glimmer of Faelen just beyond them.

"We have no guarantee he won't destroy them just to draw us out," I whisper.

He nods as if this is exactly what he was thinking. "Which is why I still believe we must fight."

"I agree."

"Even though it could destroy all of them." His tone says he knows how heavily such a choice will weigh on me.

"I know."

"We will lead them to war, but ultimately it is their choice whether to follow. They still have the freedom to choose."

I snort. "Many of them have no idea what freedom even is."

"Then let's pray we introduce them to it."

I swallow and keep my eyes on the horizon just as white peaks come into view. And beneath them, a blue so deep it calls to my lungs and steals my breath, only to replace it with salted air and the smell of woods being lapped by lazuli waters.

The Elisedd Sea.

My blood snaps within my veins at the sight. And Faelen, the island of my birth and birthright. We're almost home.

My chest clenches at that reality—that this truly is my home, and these are my people.

A people I will endanger in an effort to bring them freedom, because I am willing to fight, yes. But if I can give them freedom easier—if I can circumvent Draewulf by allowing myself to be killed at the start of the battle . . . *"Hold it all lightly. You will have to sacrifice."*

I slip my hand over Eogan's and nod. Of course we will fight. Because it's the only choice we can in good conscience make. Anything beyond that . . .

"And may I ask what choices she gave *you*?"

"The queen? The same," I say without thinking.

His brow rises in surprise before furrowing. "And?"

"And that Rasha will need us as much as we need her to defeat Draewulf . . . *if* . . ."

"If the queen dies." He stares at me with a gaze that says we both know it's no longer a question of "if."

I nod.

"Your eyes still say she suggested more."

I drop my gaze back toward the Cashlin cliffs, now dropping away into the sea, and say nothing.

"What aren't you telling me?"

That you or I could die to keep Draewulf from succeeding. That no matter what, one of us will die in fighting him.

I steady my voice. "I'm not ready to speak of it because I'm still not quite sure what she meant."

The snort he utters reminds me why he was Bron's military general for so many years. He's no daft fool. He nods and waits.

I clear my throat. Then lighten my tone. "Tell me what it was like."

"What what was like?"

"Fighting Draewulf inside you. Tell me again how you survived. Perhaps there's something in it that can help us defeat him on a larger scale."

Eogan's green gaze enfolds mine. "It was like screaming inside the blackest night—not knowing where I was or where everyone else went. The times I erupted to the surface, it was like drowning at sea and fighting for air. And the times I sank back, it was . . . quiet." He stops.

The way he said it, I suspect he means more than quiet. He means lonely.

He leans heavily onto the railing and his hands shake slightly for a moment, and I swear his eyes are starting to look glassed over. Suddenly everything within me is cracking and becoming all fissures at the fact that he is so clearly fading—and at what he's not saying. About the years he's spent knowing true aloneness more than anyone else in this world. Hearing in his tone the understanding of what it means to be completely separated from love.

Except for the feeble amount offered as a sick perversion—a skinny lust so frail and weak and emaciated by the woman who couldn't bear, couldn't *trust*, to let him feel for anyone but herself.

From where the sensation emerges I don't know, but my heart is abruptly fluttering like a bird, confessing as I peer up into his eyes that I would give anything in this moment to offer it.

Life.

Love. At least what little I've learned from him and Colin and even Breck.

And to take what he's willing to give in return, in the hopes that I could grow the skinny love he's known, until it becomes full and whole and reaching. One that starts at your soles and reaches into your spirit and on up into your throat until you're pouring pouring pouring out the words and hopes and everything about yourself that you would give, without reservation, to another being.

That is what I want to promise him at this moment. That is what I want to ask of him.

And suddenly I know this is what I can give to him.

If I hadn't decided before, my soul is answering now—we will fight, yes. But if too many lives are in danger of being lost, then I will choose the biggest love I know to give. The thing that will keep the monster from ever consuming Eogan again or his life and land and soul. That will keep Draewulf from decimating our people.

I straighten my shoulders harder.

"What did the queen tell you, Nym?" he asks weakly, still staring toward Faelen.

I swallow and keep my gaze steady as he turns those questioning eyes to me. "I won't argue with you, and I know I have no right to demand any truth from you. But is it unfair of me to ask you to trust me?"

"You of all people should know that sometimes we keep our own counsel for a time," I whisper. I lift a hand, half draped in that too-large Bron coat, and press it to his face. Then stand on my tiptoes and place a kiss on his chin.

"Trust *me* this time," I murmur.

CHAPTER 13

*T*AP.

    Tap, tap.

    Tap.

"Your tapping the railing won't make us go any faster, you know."

Maybe. Maybe not. "Is it annoying you?"

Eogan tips his head to my crippled hand where my knuckles are rapping the metal so hard they've apparently begun bleeding. *Oh.* I pull them away and push them into my sides. And try not to stare at the bags beneath my trainer's eyes that have been growing grayer over the past two hours. Nor at the slight shivering that's taken hold of his body.

"We're going to make it in time," he says, and I almost laugh at the forced levity in his tone.

"Your Highness! Warboats off the starboard," a voice breaks in.

When I glance up, the lookout stationed on the skywalk is pointing frantically to the ocean—to the vessels crowding the channel between Tulla's cliffs and Faelen's shores. Five of the boats are flying Bron's silver-and-black-striped colors, with an airship floating above one of them, and the seven facing them are sporting Faelen's. Despite the wind and weather, the boats and ship are showing no movement from either side. It's a standoff.

"Well, that might come in handy." Eogan nods toward the airship.

I frown. That wasn't there a few days ago. Then I look at Eogan. Does he remember? "Draewulf brought them with us to attack Tulla."

His lips grow pale, but whether it's from illness or the recollection, I can't tell. He just nods. "Question is, are they full of his Dark Army or my men?" He turns. "Kenan."

The large guard is already striding toward us. "M'lord?"

Eogan raises his brow toward the boats.

"They mainly hold our men, Your Majesty, but I was told each contains wraiths as well. As far as their numbers, that I don't know."

"Lady Isobel will," I say, not taking my eyes off the floating airship below.

"And the men aboard? Where do they stand?"

"The soldiers are true to you, m'lord. Although I can't say the same about the Bron Assembly. I believe you will have your hands full with a couple of its members when you return."

"And Faelen's Council and King Sedric won't be the friendliest either." Eogan rubs a hand over his chin and looks back down at the standoff. "Although it appears they're staying their attack, which means confirmation hasn't reached them of Draewulf's actions yet. At least that's in our favor." He glances at me. "Shall we ask her?"

"She'll not be cooperative."

"Something that seems to be a trait among the women around here." He grins and pushes off to start walking toward the dining area just as I swipe a hand out to cuff his elbow. *Bolcrane.*

Kenan snorts and looks away, but the next moment Eogan lurches and I'm jumping over to slide my body beneath his arm just as his legs seem to stumble. I wrap my own arm around his back to steady him.

"I'm fine," he growls.

"Of course you are." But I wait for him to find his feet and make it inside the dining room before letting go.

We step through a guarded doorway into the midsize room where Lady Isobel appears to be asleep on the bed beneath the only window and Lord Wellimton is doing the same beside Lord Myles, who's sitting with wrists shackled to the cot they've claimed. Not surprisingly, Myles's clothing and hair still look somewhat respectably handsome, as if he spent the past few hours smoothing them.

"So at lassst you've come to visit, my dear." He flicks his gaze from me to Eogan and smirks. "Although you could've left the dying lover outside. Death is such a mood deflator."

"Unless you are, in fact, dead," Eogan says. "Perhaps we should experiment."

Myles's expression turns a leery shade of shock. As if he's unsure whether Eogan's jesting.

I move between them. "We need to know Draewulf's time frame and how many wraiths are on the warboats."

His expression sours to instant boredom and he bats a hand toward Lady Isobel. "Ask the monster's daughter. I was simply eye ornamentation for this whole adventure."

Right. "You're also a good spy. So spit it up."

He sniffs as if accepting a compliment and lifts his less-than-manicured nails. "As for the time frame, your guess is as good as mine."

"And the wraiths?"

He pauses. Long enough for Eogan to press me aside and hover over the poor, arrogant fool.

"I may have overheard the Cashlin Inters say they believed the crews were made up of mostly Bron soldiers and few wraiths."

The Inters?

"What else did they tell you?" Eogan growls.

"Nothing that concerns you."

Eogan leans down. "What else, Myles?"

The drop of his gaze to his hands is so quick, so miniscule, I almost miss the tiny black lines etching the skin of Myles's fists. I choke and pull back as his expression pains, then tightens.

"That poison won't slow down, you know," Eogan says.

"Oh, I very much hope not." Myles flexes a fist. "Imagine what I'll do with it before all this is over. I may even decide to help you eliminate Draewulf."

A shiver ripples through my own hands and up my arms where, without even peeking, I know the hint of black is still lightly visible in my veins. Stained into my forearms like a barren tree beneath the mugplant tattoos.

A laugh bursts forth from Lady Isobel. "I told you he couldn't handle it," she purrs from her cot beneath the window.

Eogan keeps his eyes on Myles, then sighs and rubs a hand through his black hair. After a moment he reaches for Myles's neck.

The oaf jerks away. "I'll thank you to keep your pawsss off me."

"Do you want help or not, you fool?" Eogan presses three fingers against the Lord Protectorate's skin.

What's he doing?

"Better yet, slit his throat," Lady Isobel says.

Two seconds later Eogan stands, but rather than pull entirely back, he sticks out his hand against the wall to steady himself. His eyes dull and his coloring fades to ash. But even as I go to help him, he's uttering, "I'm fine. It's nothing."

Like hulls it is.

"Sir." A soldier stands at the door. "Kenan needs assistance."

Eogan slips his hand into mine. "I'll be right back. Don't injure them while I'm gone." Then releases me and strides from the room.

"Seems lover boy isn't in the best shape, no? Perhapsss we should've acted sooner. I'd just hate to see you having gone through ingesting that to—"

"Shut up, Myles." I look at Lady Isobel curled like a ferret-cat on her bed. "How do I help him?"

"Eogan?"

"I assume you still have feelings for him, yes? How do I repair the damage your father did?"

"Not that telling you wouldn't be loads of fun, but I have other things on my mind at the moment." She turns over and faces the wall.

"Like your missing ability?" I step closer.

"Once I get those powers back, I'm going to rip your heart out before I turn it to stone."

"Maybe." I reach out and let my hand go frozen against her skin. "But I know the feeling of losing something so a part of you," I say softly. "It aches."

For the slightest second I feel her unease beneath my fingers. As if this admission is on her mind too. "Don't let us lose Eogan too."

She stiffens. And turns toward me with a hardening smile that is eerie and disgusting and exactly like her father's. "Your inability to purposefully harm people will always be your down-fall." She reaches up and grabs my icy hand with her warm one and presses it harder into her skin. "And because of that, my father will conquer more of your people. He'll take it slow—take Cashlin and let you build up your army of farmers and peasants and children in Faelen. And then just when you're confident you might have a bleeding chance in hulls, he'll swoop in and smear you all over the face of the land. And you'll be responsible for all those deaths."

I pull my hand away to keep from slapping her. She just laughs.

I glare at her, then at Myles, who's grinning and watching as if hoping for a fight.

Her voice goes seductive. "Too bad you didn't turn yourself over. He may have been inclined to spare the rest. But now?" She winks. "Now he'll come for you last. So what does it matter if Eogan survives this flight? If he does, Draewulf will take Eogan before your very eyes, and this time you'll hear him scream from the pain just before lover boy's skin is ripped to shreds."

I swallow and it takes everything within me not to shoot an ice pick through her face. I look away and snap, "What are you smiling about, Myles? You're going to die just like him if that poison stays." I tip my head toward his shaking hands, then turn again to Isobel. "If Eogan dies before we reach the Valley, I promise you will be quickly behind. Now, what is your father's plan?"

"I'm thrilled to say I honestly don't know. Depends on how fast the precious Terrenes and Cashlins die."

"And Rasha? Where will he keep her in the meantime?"

"Oh, as close to his heart as possible, I imagine."

"*Where?*"

"I don't know. Where would *you* keep such a prize?" she murmurs.

Without even trying, the thought pops into my head that I'd keep her in Tulla with the bulk of the wraith army, just in case things went wrong in Cashlin.

I don't let her see my widening eyes. I merely jut my chin at Myles. "How do I help him control the poison in him?"

"Again, how should I know?"

"Because your witch of a mother gave it to him," I snarl.

She shrugs. "I couldn't tell you. That's what it does to people not strong enough to contain it. They get a little bit"—Isobel leans toward me and whispers—"crazy."

"That's a lie."

She snorts. "Oh, have you met yourself, precious? Besides . . . if you want to know so badly, perhaps you should ask my mother."

It requires all my strength to stay my anger.

"Never destroy what simply needs taming, Nymia. Mercy grows hearts more than bitterness." My father's words slip unbidden through my thoughts and abruptly beg what little compassion I have for her to flow into my soul. When it does, the sight of her looking so stiff and snide wavers like a mask. Another moment and suddenly all I can see is a furious child who has perhaps lost just as much as I have. Maybe more.

My voice turns gentle. "There are many things I should very much like to ask her. Like why she and your father did this to you."

I don't mean it as a cut, but her eyes flash dark beneath her lashes. She jerks against her tethers and lets out a string of curses.

I swallow and then turn and leave her to her own twisted threats.

In the dining area Eogan and Kenan are speaking together while the guards look on. I eye Eogan—he's seated in a chair at least—then walk to the giant open window and stare out of it, allowing my blood to cool and my fears to calm as I note we've passed over the channel and are racing over the snowcapped, spiked Hythra Mountains. *Thank hulls.* I tighten my Bron coat and shiver from the icy wind, only to become aware that Eogan is shivering harder again too. And his face is glistening.

Frowning, I step closer and immediately feel it. The heat. He's burning up—the fever emanating from his skin is so hot it's making the air ripple. His breathing goes odd and his chest inflates the slightest bit, although from his expression he's trying to hide it as he keeps talking, saying something about the poison in Lord Myles.

"Eogan," I say.

He touches his lower neck, covered in stitches and that orange substance, and beneath his fingers I note the skin—how it's flaming red along the line of jagged thread. "It's nothing," he whispers without looking at me.

"Right. And you'd think the universe would give us a break."

He swerves his gaze to mine and tries to smile, but then his face is blanching and his breathing begins rattling, low and shallow.

"Oh, for bleeding sake." Kenan crouches and starts to tug Eogan's shoulder. "Help me get him up and onto a bed bef—"

"No, don't." I reach out my hand to push his away.

"But we have—"

"I think when he touched Myles to help him in there, he gave him a bit of his healing. And drained his ability." I study Eogan's gaze, which seems to be fading in and out. "If we touch him again, I fear . . ."

I glance up at the two guards. "Tell the captains that if they're not already going as fast as possible, they'd better be. And don't allow anyone to enter this room until we're ready to disembark. When we are, have a cot ready to carry him."

The soldiers look from me to Kenan, who nods. "Do as she says."

They click their heels and turn for the door, then close it behind them after they hurry out.

I watch the up and down of Eogan's torso. The side of his face. His eyes scanning now beneath closed lids. The neck muscles twitching at random. It matches the twitching and lurching of my heart.

A second later Eogan jerks and his eyes open. And then he blacks out again.

CHAPTER 14

T HERE," I SAY TO THE BOY CAPTAINS WHO, JUST like Kel and their counterparts on every other Bron ship, know their vessel like the palms of their own small hands.

They veer us to where I'm pointing, on the left along the Hythra Mountain range separating Faelen from the eastern Elisedd Sea, just as the afternoon sun is being hedged by gray clouds. I spot the glistening white-rock crown that is Faelen's Castle and the High Court and the peasant fields surrounding it. My chest squeezes. I imagine little children playing while their nursemaids scold them to get back indoors because it looks like rain.

More than rain—it looks like another storm. The air is edgy with my mood. I steady my tapping foot.

"Aim for the third valley on the far side of the Castle," I tell the boys. "Beyond those foothills."

The hills and shallow green valleys fly beneath us, bringing a homesickness for the only place I've ever truly known and for the time Eogan and Colin and I had that I can no longer get back. "To that field five terrameters off." I indicate it ahead of us.

"But, m'lady, there's a flat plane near the far end of the lake. Shouldn't we—?"

"We can't land in the Valley. It's sacred. Land there and the men and I will run the rest of the way."

He pulls back on a hand stick while working a pedal with his foot, prompting the ship to shudder hard. I curl a fist to pull in the winds, helping to slow us down and soften the landing, but it's still rough. There's a loud clunking noise beneath us, even through the hum of the airship.

"Anchor's dropped," one of the boys says.

The ship scrapes the treetops for a good two terrameters before it jerks to a halt and almost throws me off my feet. Then it's settling, floating at tree level above the ground as the men on deck toss ropes tethered to sacks of sand to hold us in place.

From the window I spot our second airship farther out.

"They'll hold until we give orders," the second boy captain says, but I'm already striding from the room and down the stairs.

"Lower the plank!" Kenan yells, and the soldiers let down a giant metal walk with thin rails on each side.

Ten of the men disembark one by one while I turn to the dining area. The two guards who'd been with us earlier are already stepping through the door, carrying a stretcher with Eogan, ashen-faced and unmoving, toward us.

"Leave the prisoners in place and double their guards," I say to Kenan. "Then bring two of the soldiers from below as well as these two here and follow me. We'll have to run."

He nods and beckons the larger group of soldiers. "You heard the lady. Assist His Majesty by watching the ship. We won't be long. You two—with me."

I trail the men and stretcher down, and as soon as we reach the grassy space, we begin to jog quickly toward the hill that is the only thing standing between us and the Valley of Origin. What in blazes we're supposed to find here I have no idea, but something in me says to head for the lake. For the hundredth time today I curse Queen Laiha and her daft elusiveness.

"Hurry," I snap at the men, even though it's unnecessary.

We head uphill and pass along linden bushes similar to those Eogan and I tramped through so recently on a hillside a terrameter or two from here. I try not to think about where we've been since that day last month. Or how we stood together in the rainbow mist with his lips so close to mine . . .

I clear my throat and push us toward the right, on a trail that should lead us through the forest line and down to the lake. The soldiers and Kenan aren't speaking, but I can feel their gazes on me. As if they're wondering it too—where we're going and how walking to some lake is supposed to help anything.

"I don't know," I almost tell them, but I move faster along the path. *Bleeding hulls, I don't know.*

Until the weight of silence becomes too much. "How is he?"

"Alive," is the response.

I nod just as we crest the hilltop and begin our descent. I'm already sweating at the pace we're going combined with the warm Bron coat I'm wearing.

A flicker through the trees shows the lake. Placid. Gray. Glittering as I remember it beneath the storm-soaked sky and deflating evening sun. For a moment I swear my blood ignites. Fiery. Alive. Calling to the ache in my chest and the song I once heard here in my soul. I move even quicker, aware that the spaces between the trees are thinning, allowing more glimpses through the trees and colorful branches to say we're getting closer.

"Miss," Kenan murmurs.

When I look over, he simply indicates Eogan.

I nod. *Litches.* And break us into a full run so that within minutes I'm not the only one coughing and gasping. Suddenly we're erupting from the tree line onto a grassy bank that shelves straight into the lake, and it is glorious, and beautiful, and just as magical as I remember it.

The scent of pine and age is unbelievable.

"Bring him here and set him down." I stumble to the water's edge.

They do and then look at me. As if somehow I should know what to do. I truly have no idea. "Bleeding vague Luminescents." I swear again.

I grab Eogan's hand to place it gently in the water because it's the only thing I can think of—it's the only element I feel in control of—and close my eyes and inhale, and hope to hulls the things I've experienced here before—and the things Eogan's experienced in this space even without me—will work again.

The feeling in my veins picks up immediately, that strumming and calling, and just as quickly, the poison in my wrist reacts. Scratching beneath my skin as if trying to get out. I open my eyes and utter a cry, but it just keeps burning, fighting, and for a moment I can hear the spider screaming.

Then that song from so long ago—that sensation that the melody of the ancients is here and moving—creeps over my skin. And it feels like home.

I breathe deep and will it upon Eogan.

Please, Creator of the Hidden Lands, if you exist, let this work.

The smooth surface of the lake ripples and sloughs. I inhale deeper, clenching my fist as the water begins lapping the shoreline. Then it's not just lapping, but moving in time to the melody within my soul. But something's stopping it from coming forth. From building into more. The burning in my arm begins itching, and I glance down at it to find the black in my veins vibrating.

The power I consumed is resisting the power here.

Abruptly the rippling turns to waves, rolling up from the center and heading our direction to break just before they reach us. The foam of the gray lake water sprinkles up into the air and now the atmosphere is full of it.

And I still have no idea what I'm supposed to do.

"Hold it all lightly, Nym." Queen Laiha's words slip into my mind.

I loosen my fists and do the same thing I've done here before. I shut my eyes tighter, place my hand on Eogan, and let forth my whisper. Another prayer to the Creator that if he truly does exist to let my Elemental blood rise and bring the crystal shield with it. That armor that is diamond and light and powerful enough to hold even Draewulf off for a few moments.

A muttered exclamation sounds behind me, and I open my eyes.

The waves have turned to spirals and are churning from the lake in giant pillars. Like hands reaching for the sky in twirls and snakes and columns ten times our height. Kenan and the four soldiers back up, uttering curses, as I feel Eogan's heartbeat beneath my fingertips.

I look down to see my crystalline shield stretch over Eogan, coating his skin like water, turning it to midnight skies covered in a million stars.

Oh, thank hulls.

Except . . .

I peer closer.

It's not doing anything else.

One, two, three, I count, willing his heartpulses to strengthen, to respond, as around us the air is sparkling with water droplets filling the atmosphere in rainbow hues of red and blue and orange. Set against the green backdrop of the forest and hills and mountains with white peaks. "Come on," I mutter. *C'mon.*

The atmosphere stirs round me—a hurricane blinding me—and

next thing I know it's yanking at the very veins inside me, as if pulling at my marrow and blood. There's a break in the tone—a prodding that's forcing me back from Eogan, forcing me to release him, as if the block or whatever his ability is within him is pressing me away. I gasp and the shield covering him is shivering, then cracking and dissolving off of him into the air, and then the world suddenly slips away.

Litches.

I can't see, can't feel, can't hear anything but that melody in my chest.

I shut my eyes. And wait.

One minute.

Two minutes.

Three minutes go by before I open my eyelids, but when I do, it's to find the lake has emptied half of itself out to touch the sky in millions of water drops, floating in the air, on my breath, on my skin. They sparkle and twist and bump each other in a dance that is both colorful and clear.

I blink and the watery fog begins to fade—enough so I can see again, and Eogan is somehow awake and seated in front of me, watching the beauty of it too. "Well, that's not something one sees every day," he murmurs.

I laugh, but it comes out a sob. *Is he all right?* "Are you—do you—?" But I don't even have to ask because I can feel it just as clearly as I see it. His color is returning, stronger, richer than before, and that wound on his neck is now just a scar and the bruising surrounding it has faded. And his face and eyes and hair . . .

His hair is standing straight up from all the static.

He catches my glance and I snicker.

"Yes, well, if mine's a mess, imagine what yours looks like right now." His lips twitch as I shove my hands to my white tresses—which are in fact also standing straight on end. "Seriously, I almost feel mortified for you," he continues with a wink.

I laugh a third time, and it carries louder and farther than intended across the waters. As if on cue, the dewdrops collect and condense and begin to collapse back into the lake's center, creating waves that crash around our ankles. Until my relief turns to another sob, and I slip my hand into his just to make sure he really is real this time. And that he really is fine.

"Remind me not to ever make you angry in a place like this," he whispers. "Because I don't mind admitting this is hands down the bleeding strangest thing I've been through." He tightens his large fingers around my shaking ones. His hand is warm.

"Better now?" I ask because I don't know what to say.

"You have no idea." He draws close and lingers his gaze on mine. "Although"—he clears his throat—"don't you need something here too?"

"The queen wasn't exactly clear on that point."

"Got it." He looks around at the still-rippling water. "Well, perhaps I should throw you in? Maybe you're supposed to become one with your element or something."

He starts to pick me up, but I'm already screeching and batting him away. "I'll figure it out on my own, thankyouverymuch." I turn to look at the guards, who're no longer there. They've backed up behind the tree line, looking scared or in awe. *Whatever.* I slip off my boots and allow the cool foam to continue its surge around me.

Nothing.

I wade in farther, until I'm up to my waist, followed by my chest and shoulders.

"Watch out for piranhas," Eogan calls.

I shoot him a very uncouth gesture before diving the hulls in. When I come up, I use my fists to bring up the water in more columns. And just like with Eogan, it's as if the Valley loses her breath and regains it all at once, and it's full of life and silence and more beauty than my head can comprehend.

But that's it.

After climbing from the water, I dry off over the grass. The Bron soldiers are staring at me as if I may be possessed, and I hear Eogan over there assuring them that yes, I am.

I grin and look toward the trees farther down, as if expecting Uathúils will emerge. But there's not a branch moving or a bird chirping that sounds out of place through the early evening dim.

What was I expecting? That my power would somehow call a horde of fighters down to help us? If they were hiding somewhere, they surely would've shown themselves by now. What had the queen said? That this was *one* possible solution, but if it didn't work . . .

Eogan looks over and peers square into my face. As if to assure me. "We *will* win the war, Nym. It's not all on you."

I blink and glance down because I'm pretty certain it is, in fact, up to me.

But before I can head toward him, the sound of a horn blasts through the entire Valley.

"Blasted litch," Eogan says.

CHAPTER 15

W E'RE RUNNING THROUGH THE TREES, TRIP-
ping over bracken and bushes in the dim when the
horn blows again.

I clench my fist. If this is to be the beginning of the fight, might
as well make it a good one. "Draewulf?" I toss out in Eogan's direction while rumbling the sky.

He glances up at the evening lights and shakes his head. "I hav-
en't heard a third airship."

How he could tell one droning sound from another is beyond
me—maybe it's the lack of bombs going off, but I don't ask. I just
keep my blood peaked and continue running beside him as that
horn blows a third time, until suddenly we're erupting from the
brush and forest into the meadow.

We stall.

Our airship is surrounded by Faelen soldiers and horses.

"You'll halt if you value your men," a familiar voice rings out.

I slow and squint through the torch-lit dim. *Rolf?*

King Sedric's Captain of the Guard is sitting atop his steed,
pointing a sword toward the Cashlin guard's throat.

"Rolf!" A crack of thunder rumbles overhead—partially in
relief and partially to let him know it's me. I step forward with my
hands up.

His fierce expression flickers. "M'lady?" He keeps the blade in place but peers closer. "What are you doing here?"

"We need to see King Sedric. There's war in Tulla and Cashlin, and it's headed this way."

"Reports from the waterway claim Tulla is under attack from Bron airships." He glances behind me up to where Eogan's standing. "Are the delegates with you as well?"

"A few. But Lady Gwen and Lord Percival stayed." I don't know how else to explain the fact that they're being held as hostages by Draewulf's wraith army. *If they haven't been turned into wraiths themselves.*

He furrows his brow and lowers his voice, glancing at Eogan. "The Bron king's airships were seen heading for Tulla three days ago, and there's been dust and smoke visible to the watchmen on our warboats. Do you know of this?"

"I do, and we've only barely escaped from there. Which is why we need to speak with King Sedric immediately." I tip my head toward the Cashlin guard. "That man and two Luminescents are with us as well. We brought them to assist in the fight."

Rolf's eyes cloud. He frowns at Eogan but his words are for me. "Fight against whom, miss?"

Litches.

I look around at his men. They don't know about Draewulf.

I start forward, but one of the Faelen guards steps beside me, as if to caution me to stop where I am, even as his gaze stays friendly. I peer insistently at the captain. "The Dark Army and Draewulf."

Rolf's expression shutters in confusion. "Draewulf? You'll forgive me, miss, but he is dead. You and I both saw it." But his sword sags away from the Cashlin guard before he extends it toward the soldier blocking me. He waves it to allow me through.

I stride up to the horse. "To explain right now would take more time than we have. I must see the king. I have a letter from Cashlin's Queen Laiha for him." I pull the correspondence from my tunic and hold it up. "And, Rolf," I add before he can argue. "We have Lady Isobel as prisoner aboard this ship."

His brow rises.

My lungs beat. My head beats. My legs and muscles ache, weary with the reality that I've hardly slept in two days and we barely made it in time for Eogan to survive. Yet somehow he did—*again*—and I've not even had time to process my relief or awe or whatever in litches I'm feeling about that. And now I'm trying to convince the king's Captain of the Guard that we're not the threat that's coming. Much like we tried to convince Queen Laiha.

I steady myself while I wait wait wait because he's taking too blasted long to decide and I am so very, very tired.

An eternity later . . .

"Fine, but one ship stays here along with half my men. And the other one that has Lady Isobel aboard"—he tilts his head—"flies behind us with some of my soldiers aboard as they check for bombs and weapons. It will stop exactly one terrameter from the High Court, and if it gets any closer, I will personally kill King Eogan. Is that clear?" he says louder.

"Quite," Eogan replies so his own men can hear.

"Then unit one, get aboard, leaving your horses here," Rolf says coldly. "The rest stay with the other. I'll send instructions when I've spoken with the king. And you four"—he beckons the Cashlin, Eogan, Kenan, and me—"you'll ride between my men with their swords aimed at your guts."

Further orders are given, and the airship is loaded with familiar-faced Faelen soldiers while we take their steeds. It's not until I've mounted that it dawns on me I've not ridden in weeks—not since the Keep and Colin and Haven.

Haven. My lungs cringe with a sudden need to see that warhorse. To smother my face in her mane and ride free from one side of Faelen to the other without a care in the world other than what to feed her massive meat-eating appetite.

"Head out!" Rolf calls a moment later, and the small company we're in starts for the Castle.

Even at our fastest pace, it's a good few hours' ride. As cautioned, the airship moves slowly behind us, keeping its distance while its droning hum through the night air probably disturbs any wildlife within two terrameters.

Beside me, the Cashlin guard gasps when we come over a ridge to see the city splayed out before us—its white stones glistening like a bone carcass beneath the full moon and black sky. Torchlights glimmer around it and along the High Court town streets that wind their way down from the hilltop it sits on to the base. Beyond that, utter darkness clothes the rest of the land that belongs to the Faelen peasantry, their homes and fields bathing in a cool wind and candle-less sleep.

I look past them to where Litchfell Forest lies and, above that, my home in the Fendres. Or what used to be my home. But even with the moon out, all I see is a mass of more black.

The closer we get to the High Court, with its pale stone streets and arches snaking up to the perfect Castle peaks atop its hill, the more homesickness invades me. Then Rolf's calling out orders for the airship to stop. "Have they found explosives?" he asks the nearest guard.

The soldier rides to the ship, and a shouting match ensues with the soldiers above, in which it's apparently determined the ship is out of weaponry aside from an assortment of swords and archery tools.

"Confiscate it all, then wait for my signal to move the ship into the Northern Wing's upper courtyard."

"May I suggest you keep Lord Myles and Lady Isobel locked on board until we've spoken to the king?" Eogan says to Rolf.

"Lord Myles is with her?" The captain gives him a startled look.

"He's ingested a poison that will soon render him a threat," I say.

Despite his skeptical air, the captain nods. "Fine. We'll address that with King Sedric as well. You five! Stay with the ship until it's secured. The rest continue on."

I follow his gaze toward the massive gateway that the main road butts into, and a shiver goes up my spine as I think of another night on these streets, a hundred years ago, when Draewulf took life after life of men, women, and children.

And the 130-year-old beast is close to doing it again . . .

"Just focus on the task at hand," Eogan murmurs, making me aware that my fists are clenched around my horse's reins and the sky above is growling. "And for hulls' sakes, if you unleash the rain and soak me after all I've been through . . ."

I smile at his attempt to soothe my mood. "You'll do what?" I whisper.

Through the dim he narrows the distance between us enough for me to catch the spark in his eye. He lets his humored gaze slide suggestively down my body. I hear his inhale before he clears his throat.

I grin, but abruptly a shadow has clouded his face and he looks away.

"What?"

"Nothing."

"Liar."

He doesn't pull his steed away but doesn't speak either.

Until I glance over and catch him studying me again. I frown.

"Did I . . . did he . . . ?"

I wait as the expression on his face hardens.

"Nym, I asked you what Draewulf did while in my body. But with you . . . did he . . . ? Did he *hurt* you by using me?"

"Like sexually?"

His jaw clenches and he gives a brief nod, his gaze burning through the night to search my eyes as if to gauge if I will lie to him.

I shake my head. "He only hurt me like he hurts everyone else. By stealing what we love and scarring our bodies."

One . . . two . . . three . . . I swear I can hear the pulses of Eogan's heartbeat as he assesses this answer. The next second his relief is tangible and he's releasing his breath and his shoulders ease. "Good," is all he says before kicking his heels into his horse's side to ride on a bit ahead.

The captain yells out again—for us to hurry this time—and the ship's hum begins to lessen as we gain distance and our horses' hooves hit the cobblestone streets.

We climb the winding road as, ahead of us, men are running through the courtyards with torches. Word has already reached here apparently.

Thirty palace guards stand waiting for us when we arrive at the final archway and emerge through the Castle's main gate.

"I'll escort the Elemental and King Eogan to His Highness," Rolf says to his men. "Detain the other two with whatever force necessary."

We dismount and step into the mass of soldiers watching us. I'm met by their polite nods and shining eyes as we pass through one of the four doors leading from the courtyard into the stone Castle, and as soon as we enter I find I'm inhaling. Because for all its uncomfortable luxuriousness, it is home. And the air inside, just like the weather outside, is filled with the scents of Faelen life and dirt and heart.

No one stops us. They just stare as Rolf leads the way down three lengthy hallways and a maze of stairs and corridors to the king's quarters. We enter what appears to be a set of private sitting rooms—they're filled with the smell of roasted meat and wine, and my stomach is instantly grumbling.

"Wait here," the captain says.

Food, I mouth to Eogan, who sends me a wink as Rolf goes to fetch the king.

"I dare you to steal some," he whispers.

I grab a roll and toss him one as well, and we've only finished them before the nineteen-year-old boy-king himself is standing in front of us, looking tired and disheveled and clearly having been awaiting us. His face is a mixture of concern and shock, even though his eyes have a better spark in them than I've seen at any point in the last three months of knowing him. I suspect it's due to the fact that the past week of sworn peace and Draewulf presumably dead has made for the most rest he's had in years. Even the lines under his eyes are hardly shadows.

I swallow a twinge of guilt that we're about to ruin it for him.

"Your Highness," he says, attempting to control his strained tone as he eyes Eogan. "Nym."

I drop into a deep curtsy and Eogan tips his head. "King Sedric."

Sedric frowns, as if my bowing is ridiculous. "Please. Don't. Just tell me the news. King Eogan, I've heard strange rumors this week . . ."

"Draewulf is alive," I say with enough thunderous effect that he'll think twice before doubting me. "He stole Eogan's airships and made war on Tulla. We've barely escaped with our lives. As it is . . ." I look over at Rolf, who's reentered the room. "Not everyone made it back with us."

King Sedric looks ready to laugh at the absurdity or kill something. I wouldn't blame him for either.

"I have a letter." I pull it out.

"I certainly hope it offers more explanation than the last letter you left for me, which merely attempted to excuse you sneaking off to Bron." He narrows his gaze at me.

Warmth attacks my cheeks. "My apologies, Your Highness." I shove it toward him. "This one is from the Cashlin queen, Laiha, Princess Rasha's mother."

"The Cashlin? Was she in Bron too?"

"Your Majesty," Eogan interrupts. "May I suggest a strong drink before we continue? I know I could go for a swig."

The king comes to life. "Yes, yes, of course." He snaps at Rolf to step into the shadows before leading us across the room to a set of very proper, very firm, blue tapestry chairs that match the wall hangings and carpet. He strides to a side table and pours our drinks and hands them out himself. Water for me. Ale for him and Eogan.

Then sits in one of the chairs.

Eogan and I follow suit as Sedric takes a long sip and eyes the letter in his hand. As if he knows his week of rest will be over the moment he opens it.

Eogan drinks and watches.

I wait and rub the itching black veins in my hand.

When King Sedric's glass is empty, he breaks the letter's seal and begins to read.

Five minutes. Eight minutes. Ten minutes pass while we sit in silence.

Until I can't take it anymore and shift in my seat. When I look over at Eogan, he's eyeing my water with a smirk.

"What?"

"Scared?" he murmurs in a tone referring to our conversation with Colin a few weeks ago.

I look away. And then smile even as the ache for Colin's loss flares fresh and alive. Within seconds Eogan's hand has slipped over mine. He gives a light squeeze and looks back to King Sedric.

"Your Majesty, I should tell you there are three individuals aboard the airship at this moment whom you'll be interested to see."

The king nods. "Lord Myles and Lady Isobel. She speaks of them in her letter. Of both their betrayals and Myles's added ability, and the loss of Isobel's."

"There is also the matter of Lord Wellimton," Eogan broaches. "He may believe I am trying to assert myself and wage war on Tulla and the Hidden Lands on behalf of Bron. Using Draewulf and Lady Isobel's Dark Army."

The king stares at both of us and chews his lip. "The queen's report here addresses the matter of Draewulf inhabiting your body for a time. Although"—he glances down at the paper seriously—"she assures me now you are completely yourself."

Eogan doesn't answer.

"Do you believe her?" I ask softly.

He looks at me. "I'm not sure I have a choice, considering the options in front of us. Although, will you also give *your* word, Nym, that Eogan is now in his proper mind and is in no way a threat?"

"I swear it."

He turns to Eogan. "May I ask you to confirm, then, how long Draewulf was in control of you?"

"Since the battle at the Keep, Your Highness."

"So the treaty I signed . . ."

"Was with him. Although I can assure you my commitment to peace with Faelen is far and above anything Draewulf agreed to on my behalf. As it is toward the entire Hidden Lands. Which is why I am here now."

"And yet you'll forgive me if I'm a bit leery."

"I would think less of you were you not."

Sedric nods and swirls his cup in his hand. "Nym, I'd like to hear a bit more about all this from you. Alone."

Eogan promptly rises and tips his head to us both and, before I can say anything, is escorted out by Rolf.

It's only after the door shuts that Sedric looks straight at me. "Was your sneaking aboard that airship due to your knowledge that Draewulf was in King Eogan's body?"

"It was."

"And you chose not to inform me."

I was prepared for his anger at this, but not for the look of disappointment that accompanies it. "Forgive me, sire, but I'd just found out. I knew telling you could endanger the entire Hidden Lands."

His brow goes up. "And not telling me didn't?"

"You would've been forced to execute him here on Faelen soil, which not only would've restarted our war with Bron, but with Lady Isobel and her wraith army as well. And it wouldn't have worked anyway. Draewulf cannot be killed by anything you or your men can do."

The brow stays up. "I assume you can back up that claim?"

"We've tried to kill him, yes. In the process, we've also found a supposed solution."

"I could have you jailed for treason—for allowing our greatest enemy to go free."

I decide against mentioning that my ability could get me out of any jail he put me in. "I defeated him once, Your Majesty. I was prepared to defeat him again. But without sacrificing you or the rest of the Faelen people."

He purses his mouth.

"And I assume the 'supposed solution' *can* destroy him?"

I stare him straight in the eye. Fierce and firm.

He nods. "I see."

He rubs his chin and looks up at the door Eogan was escorted through. "I think your romantic interest resulted in you delaying longer than I or anyone else would've deemed wise." He looks back at me. "However . . . 'the heart leads where even devils fear to tread.' Isn't that the saying?"

"I did try, Your Highness," I whisper.

The stalling of whatever he was going to say is an indication he gets the depth of what I'm trying to explain. That even if I know how to kill the shape-shifter, it's not a sure thing. "Now Draewulf is attempting to get at the Cashlin queen. After that, he'll be coming for Eogan and me."

"Due to the prophecy." He taps the letter.

I nod. "I believe we need to rescue Rasha if possible. As it stands now, if Draewulf consumes both her and her mum . . ."

He stands. "His powers will be near unstoppable."

I follow suit and decide not to mention that his powers already are.

"And what of my cousin, Lord Myles? What—?"

A loud pounding on the door erupts, and he's barely uttered, "Of all the— Come in," before the thing's burst wide open and a guard rushes in.

"The Dark Army, Your Majesty. Everywhere. They're crawling off the ships!"

CHAPTER 16

THE KING'S EYES NARROW AT ME.

"That's not possible," I say, and before he has a chance to move, I'm striding for the door. *Is it the airship from the channel?* I've just reached it when Sedric steps in front of me.

He flaps the letter, his expression as dark as his tone. "Tell me this wasn't a setup."

"I swear to you."

His nostrils twitch as he stares at me, then flips around and barks through the doorway at his men, "Rolf and you three, come with Nym and me. The others stay with King Eogan." He glances at him. "I'm certain you understand." And storms past.

Eogan nods as I go to follow Sedric, but his mouth is tight. Confused in the same way I am. How could they have followed so quickly without us seeing them? Unless Draewulf had already sent them from Tulla . . .

Oh hulls.

We're running down the hall, the soldiers' feet flagging behind us, turning corner after corner as I feel our dread rising.

Please don't let Draewulf be here yet.

We're not ready.

At the Eastern Courtyard's corridor a group of soldiers, swords drawn, are holding the door shut.

"Let us through."

"Your Majesty—"

"Now."

I recognize the guard, Tannin, as he opens the door. We're immediately bathed in the sounds of yelling and Faelen swords clanging against the courtyard flagstones beside a ship floating two feet from the ground. *What in—?* It's swarming with wraiths. Gray torn cloaks cover their emaciated half-dead human bodies, except for their feet and hands, which are mostly made from bolcrane claws, and their hollow faces that look like half-eaten skulls.

"Mother of—" Rolf utters. "What in curses are those?"

"Wraiths," I whisper. "Lady Isobel's Dark Army made from dead bodies and beasts."

They're crawling along the deck and railings and then dropping to the ground. Attacking the air like a chaotic cete of badgers.

The king steps forward as Tannin tries to stall me. "Miss, it's dangerous."

"Thank you, but let me through." I push past him and to the right of Sedric, who's got his blade lifted.

"Our weapons appear to have no effect on them, sire," Tannin says.

I raise my fist and the sky shudders and crackles a warning for the Faelen soldiers to move back, just like the air is sparking along my fingers as I feel the ice picks form midair.

I unleash the icy knives to puncture through the wraiths' skulls.

They plow through the clothing and faces—and the metal of the ship even—as if it's all corporeal. The images waver like vapor, then turn solid again. I raise a brow and narrow my focus, and one by one the wraiths dissipate in front of me at the same moment the awareness dawns that there's no smell. No scent of death or decay or plague.

I look harder at the ship and it disappears too.

"*Are you bleeding fooling with me?*" I yell.

I flip around to Rolf. "We told you not to bring him here. Where is he?" I swerve around in search of Myles but can't find him. The next moment I'm grabbing King Sedric's arm as he moves to rush forward into the frenzy. "Your Highness, they're not real. It's a mirage."

"*What?*" The king slows and looks down at my hand on his arm. I remove it, and he levels his gaze to mine.

"Lord Myles is creating a mirage. Watch." Before he can stop me, I stride to the closest apparition as it lunges. A few of the guards scramble to follow, but the wraith's claws have already swiped right through me without touching.

The men gasp. They pause their remounting attack as Rolf strides over and, sword in hand, holds it out against the wraith who, while fighting aggressively, is having no effect. Rolf stabs the thing but it just keeps attacking the empty space beside me.

"What in blazes?" The captain jumps forward to slice through another—only to find his blade jutting through the vaporous ship as well. He flips around, his eyes widening, and hisses to me, "What kind of magic is this?"

I peer up into the sky for the other ship.

There. In the distance. Hovering exactly where we left it, lights glowing in the night air, just beyond the High Court. I squint to assure myself it's real and that there are no others. "Is Myles still on the ship?"

"He is."

Impossible. He's using his abilities from that distance and for this long a period?

"It's coming from there." I point after a second. "I'm afraid Lord Myles has ingested a poison that is enhancing his ability— and this is a result of it."

"He's doing this intentionally?" King Sedric asks.

"That I don't know."

"From that far?" Rolf turns his disbelief toward the king.

"His ability is strong." Sedric's tone isn't as surprised as I'd expect. Neither is his gaze, which is watching the wraiths as they appear to be jumping from the airship. "They certainly look real."

"And from what I understand, his ability will become even stronger over the next few days."

He drops his gaze to me. "How do we stop it?"

"If I'm right about Eogan's ability, he should be able to slow Myles's. Although, in truth, my method would simply be to slap him."

Despite the chaos swirling around us, Sedric grins, then tips his head toward the airship in the distant sky. "That is the ship you came in on and that he is still being held hostage in, I presume."

"I told them to hold outside the High Court, Your Highness," Rolf says. "The second ship is by the large lake valley with another unit of men."

Sedric purses his lips and looks around at the Faelen soldiers still pouring into the courtyard—half of whom now look confused while the recent additions are attacking the visions with more fervor. "Captain, I don't envy you having to convince them their eyes are deceiving them, but have them stop before they accidentally kill each other. Do you know if we've lost any men in this?"

Without waiting I ignite the sky directly above us with three lightning flares set off in succession. Powerful enough to illuminate the courtyard and mirage in a wall of bright light for a moment and hopefully to override what the men think they're seeing.

The mirage in front of us flickers twice, then disappears.

When the thunder from the flares has died down, the space falls silent and empty except for confused tones and hushed questions. Rolf and Sedric turn their eyes on me.

I shrug. "Almost as good as slapping him."

Rolf tips his head and says, "Thank you," before calling to his men. "It was an illusion brought on by magic, nothing more! The beings you saw weren't real. You are hereby ordered to sheath your swords and stand guard, but do not engage anything further that appears unless my command is given."

The men obey as Rolf puts away his own blade. "Your Highness, what would you have me do with that airship and the Lord Protectorate?"

King Sedric frowns. "I assume you've searched it?"

"We have."

Sedric runs a hand along his youthful chin. "In that case, bring the ship in, lock Lady Isobel in the dungeon, and bring my cousin to me. And, Rolf, double your guard around the High Court."

"Yes, Your Majesty. But in regard to Lady Isobel—"

"According to the Cashlin queen, Lady Isobel's powers are gone for the time being." Sedric looks at me for confirmation and, when I give it, adds, "I'll be in the War Room. We'll convene in three hours." He nods to me. "My apologies for the shortness of time, especially as it appears you've had very little sleep. But still . . . I'll ask you to be there."

Tannin has hardly shut the door to my room before I drop onto the bed, fully clothed and wholly uncaring. Two seconds later I've drifted into a black sleep.

CHAPTER 17

THE FORESTED SWAMP AIR ATTACKS MY THROAT, FOLLOWED BY THE smell of something frightening. I gag and cough and suddenly my tiny body is shaking. I don't like this place. I want to go back to the woman who held me. The woman I came from.

But the animal galloping and jostling beneath us doesn't stop. He continues carrying us farther as the voice of the man holding me whispers, "Shh. They'll come for us if you cry." His tone prickles my skin, telling me he no longer means the bad men from the camp he took me from.

There is a new danger here.

I blink as the shadows descend too deep for me to see farther than my tiny hands that are reaching up to grab at his face just as a roar sounds in the distance.

"Litch," he mutters, and his rough arms squeeze me too close, too tight, until I cry.

"Almost there, child."

The animal carrying us jerks and swerves when the roar comes again. *What is the noise coming from? Make it stop.* But the roaring grows louder as my cries fill my ears until suddenly there's a break in the air, and the humidity and shadows fade to be replaced by cold.

We're going up.

A whinny, and then the jostling animal beneath us slows, then comes to a stop in front of another man. A large man. With a pock-marked face and a mess of curled hair and a kind smile.

He begins speaking, but I can't understand what's said.

There's a flash of silver, and suddenly the kind man turns danger-ous as he raises a sword and launches it toward us.

Not toward us, past us. The one holding me turns around just as a roar emerges and then is cut short by the sword.

A giant black, greasy beast with a sharp-toothed mouth falls to the ground with a *whump*.

"We'll take care of her, Nathan." The kind man strides forward to take me. He unfolds the swath of blankets and holds me lightly against his chest. Then grunts. "She's Elemental," he murmurs after a pause.

"Aye. Shouldn't even exist, let alone survive," the other man says. "But I figured that wouldn't matter much to your wife."

I squirm and whimper. My skin's getting cold and I'm hungry for my mum's milk.

"You thought right. And thank you."

There's an exchange of more words and then the man remounts his animal and rides away.

"Not supposed to exist, eh?" The big man pats my head. "Well, you do. So now we'll see if we can help you survive."

I blink and feel my chest settle as his rich, soothing voice coos a bit longer, then transitions to ripple forth in a lullaby song.

"Miss, they're ready for you."

I moan and roll over and refuse to release my dream. My *memory*.

My other father.

Whatever the Inters jogged open in me, it's a space I didn't even know existed. And now it's like an aching, leaking place that's terrifying and I want to curse them for it.

"We'll see if we can help you survive."

"Miss." Tannin's voice enters my head again as his hand on my shoulder shakes me.

I bat it away.

"Miss, please."

"Quit playing with your life, Tannin."

"Something I'm loath to do, I assure you—except the Council is assembled in the War Chamber. The king is waiting."

I peer out between protesting eyelids to find his brown hair is, as usual, sticking up like a thatched roof. "He said three hours."

"And that it's been, miss." His idolizing expression eases to pity. "I'd be happy to have them bring you a cup of tea to the Chamber if that would help."

I pull my sore body up and shift my scowl to the lush blankets. "Stop making me like you, Tannin. But yes, it would, thank you." After dragging my legs off the bed, I lean over the water bowl and splash my face. Then dab my skin dry before I attempt to pat my hair into some measure of decency until the kind guard reenters.

"I've summoned the maid to send tea."

I flick a hand at the door. "Then I'm yours to lead."

We reach the first bend in the hall. "How's your daughter, by the way?"

"Excellent. And it's kind of you to remember." He grins. "Although she keeps begging her mum to stain her hair white."

"I seem to recall wanting mine stained brown." I give him a rueful smile.

"She's also been attempting to re-create your battle at the Keep with her dolls. It's resulted in half the yard being drenched in water from the pump and her mum's stove having a permanent case of wet wood."

I snort.

He chuckles and opens a door to another passageway. "It's good for her to have a heroine. And I think it's mostly harmless." He shakes his head. "Although I may have told her that she's not getting any more dolls if she keeps ruining the garden."

I grin and look away as the memories brought back by the Inters of my own father surface—of his teasing smile and handmade swords and voice that used to sing full and throaty with mine. It's a moment of reprieve I'm grateful to Tannin for.

When we reach the chamber door, Tannin reaches down and, quick as lightning, squeezes my hand. "We're behind you, m'lady." Then he leads us both into the cherrywood-paneled room lined with bookshelves and two maps—no curtains or windows.

It's crowded with puffy-eyed counts and lords whose rumpled hair and clothing suggest no one dressed the old geezers upon bustling them from their beds. Most are wearing half-tucked tunics and wrinkled pants, and one appears to have simply pulled a cloak on over his nightshirt.

I bite back a grin. He and the others are familiar faces from Adora's parties—the men I spied on and sidled up to with Colin when gathering information on how he and I could best serve in the war. And now Adora is imprisoned somewhere beneath us for her traitorous acts, and they're eyeing me with a foreign look of reverence—the same that's been etched on everyone's face since the Keep—as I stride past.

"Gentlemen," I murmur even as my lungs give a slight squeeze and I glance around for Eogan.

He and Kenan are standing near King Sedric and four councilmen looking down at the war table taking up the room's center. I note the three guards hovering between Sedric and Eogan—as if to say Sedric may be moving ahead on his instincts to trust us, but that doesn't mean he's a fool. *Huh. Good for him.*

I also note the number of servants dotting the room, holding trays of steaming mead and bread, and if the councilmen's expressions toward me are of reverence, these slaves have a look of hunger. Of desperation.

They're not just hopeful I'll save us all. They need to believe it.

I glance away.

"I agree, Your Highness," Eogan's rich voice rumbles. "But a strong offense *will* be our best chance."

"But do we have the resources to provide such an offense?" Sedric peers at Rolf and the head councilman.

They begin muttering between themselves over the lumpy, clay-molded table. It appears to be a miniature representation of the entire Hidden Lands, in realistic proportions.

I raise a brow and step closer, and can't help but gawk at the magnificent detail. Even the kingdom of Tulla is crafted very near exact, with small, movable pawns painted black while others are red, to represent what I presume by their positions are Bron's airships and Draewulf's army. The only kingdom not well developed is Draewulf's land of Drust. Which more than anything says how eerily little we know of it.

Eogan glances up and gives me his beautiful half smile. I smile back, raising a brow at his hair that is sticking up with roguish abandon. Then discreetly ensure my own is in place as he goes to show Sedric what parts of Bron have been saturated by wraiths and whereabouts he suspects they'll be positioned soon in Cashlin.

Murmurs of the councilmen sink in around me, low conversations—whispers regarding Draewulf and the Dark Army. Whispers regarding me. My mouth stays shut and my stomach burns with old resentment for these men and their opulence paired with an utter lack of care for the farmers and soldiers they sent to the front lines while staying safely seated inside this room. Until something twitches to mix in with the resentment, as if forcibly budding inside me while I stand sifting through their words. *Hope.* For what they know and what they understand about war and strategy. Because without more Uathúils to fight, these men and their knowledge of war are sadly our main defense.

Oh hulls. These men, myself, and Eogan are our only hope.

A caustic laugh slips out. What a depressing thought.

Eogan lifts his gaze to meet mine again, his brow forming a question.

I shake my head and nod to King Sedric, who's straightened to look at me too.

"You're here." He smiles.

"As requested."

"I've already brought the men up to speed and they've argued the utter"—he glances at Eogan—"*strangeness* of this entire situation to their hearts' content. Now we can proceed." Sedric turns to Rolf, who promptly calls the room to order, while from my peripheral I catch the guards tighten around Eogan.

As soon as the place falls silent, Sedric pulls out the letter from Queen Laiha. "As we have all agreed to believe this information presented to us, we must act immediately to defend against this threat."

"Your Majesty, I am not intending disrespect to any parties present," a councilman pipes up. "But can't the Elemental do her trick again and save us the time and deaths?"

Eogan's watching me. I can feel his eyes on my face.

"Why didn't she and King Eogan simply kill Draewulf when they had the chance?" another councilman asks.

It's almost amusing how comfortable they are talking about Eogan and me as if we're not in the room. I snort. Such is the arrogance of these men. Everyone is a tool, a weapon, a pawn on their clay map. I peer around at their expectant faces and let a grumble of thunder roll over the Castle. "Is it not enough Eogan and I saved you once?" I say loud enough to cut off their voices. "Do you want to live or not? If so, we will proceed as King Sedric says. If not, then by all means continue wasting our time."

"Yes, but what good is a weapon if you're not going to use it?" someone mutters.

"She's not a weapon." Eogan's voice cuts through the room. "She's a woman who might be willing to help the people who enslaved her if they'd ask respectfully. And she'll not be able to kill him anyway—at least not without help."

"What does the monster want, anyway?"

I seek out Eogan's gaze. "It's my understanding that by using the abilities within the five original bloodlines, he can achieve immortality. And once he does, he'll have enough power both from the blood and from the land to rule unhindered." I clear my throat. "After that, the suspicion is he'll turn those subjects less than loyal to him into wraiths."

The councilman snorts. "Yes, we heard the prophecy from the queen's letter. But forgive me if I think the whole thing of bloodlines—"

"Is very specific," Eogan growls.

The councilman frowns. "Right. And according to the prophecy, the shape-shifter needs the queen's body and blood, has to finish you off, and then has to consume King Sedric to achieve immortality?"

"Not King Sedric."

Sedric raises his gaze to peer at Eogan. But Eogan's looking at me. I swallow.

"I believe it's Nym he needs," Sedric says softly.

I turn to the confused councilman. "He may need Lord Myles now as well. The dark essence he consumed is needed for the recipient to control all five Uathúil abilities within one body."

"He won't need Myles, actually." Eogan glances down at my curled hand. "Not since you still retain some of it."

"No offense intended to Your Majesties or Nym here," interrupts a thoughtful-looking gentleman standing near Tannin. "But wouldn't a simple solution be to . . . *eliminate* those with the abilities Draewulf needs?"

The man doesn't spell the rest out and he doesn't have to. His implication is clear even as he looks wholly guilty of broaching it.

Eogan nods. "It's a possibility I believe we've all considered," he adds without looking at me. "However, you'll need our abilities in order to defeat Draewulf."

"Ah." The man steps back. "So it's the water-and-bucket scenario. You need one to get the other. Unfortunately, on both sides in this case."

Eogan nods again. "And in that regard, I'm not certain it matters *what* the prophecy says or what we believe." He leans over the map. "As it is now, Faelen is the final kingdom standing. So no matter what Draewulf's ultimate goal is, we *must* prepare for war."

"How long do you believe we have before he moves on us?" a guard asks.

"Ten days," I say. "Roughly."

"King Sedric," Rolf interrupts. "Might I propose we at least start assembling scouting units?"

"Agreed. See that it's done by dawn. I believe it's safe to assume Draewulf will launch his first, if not main, attack on the northern waterway." He turns to Eogan. "And what of your warboats in the channel?"

He waves a hand over the map. "If we can use Your Highness's warboats and the two airships at my disposal, we might reclaim them fairly simply. And on that note, I believe it wise to continue the discussion about what type of offense Faelen is planning."

"Do you have something specific in mind?" King Sedric asks.

A number of low coughs go round the room, and Eogan meets them with a confidence grown from a man who knows what evil is capable of. What *he* was once capable of. Eogan points to a section of the map along Faelen's northern border. "Raiding parties. Scouting parties along the coast. And assembling encampments here in Faelen, particularly along Litchfell Forest."

He runs a finger from the northern waterway across the green that's edging Faelen's western border. "It's the ideal spot for Draewulf to accumulate and hide his wraiths, seeing as even the bolcranes will leave them alone."

The slightest hint of a chill enters the room. Either at the reality that we'll be fighting the dead—or at the fact that they're so horrific even the beasts they're partly made from will shirk them.

King Sedric rubs his chin and nods.

"But, sire, if I may—" The councilman nearest Sedric juts a hand out over the map. "I think the bigger concern is that we simply do not have the men needed, and the people we *do* have are weary of war."

"Can we impose a draft like before?" someone asks from the back. "Force the people to at least give us their slaves to bulk up the ranks?"

I nearly choke on my tongue, and, as if in unison, the servants in the room freeze.

"Are you jesting?" the count says. "Their slaves won't fight for Faelen. If anything they're likely to fight against us."

"And rightly so," I mutter.

Every gaze in the room turns. "And what do you suggest?" the councilman asks.

"They'll follow Nym," Eogan says quietly.

I glance at him and frown. I don't want to be the one to send them to their deaths.

His eyes soften at the corners. *A shield maiden for your people . . .* "Ask her to speak to them."

"Actually, sire, it could work," Rolf whispers to Sedric.

I glare at Eogan before turning to nod at Rolf and Sedric. "If you set up a track of speaking places for me, I could take a few soldiers and spread the word. If they respond to it, they'll come. If not . . ." I refuse to look at the servants in the room.

"Then we've lost nothing but a bit of time," Eogan says.

One by one the men begin uttering agreement.

"They do worship her," Rolf says.

"If she can't convince them, then we never could," the count adds.

"However." I lift my voice so it's loud and firm, not taking my eyes off Sedric as I feel my bones shore up within me. "I'll not be convincing them to join a draft. Because let's face it—it won't matter. They'll be dead. But at least they'll be dead right alongside you."

I peer around at every face as I swear the slightest gasp is uttered. Holding them just long enough to make them drop their gazes. "Because that will be my promise to them. That when they show up to fight this war they never asked for, you'll be fighting right there with them—not holed up in some room making choices with their lives. You'll be on the field too."

I look back to Sedric. "And when I ask the poor and enslaved to join you on that field, I'll also be promising them their freedom. Whether they choose to fight or not."

CHAPTER 18

I SWEAR IT'S LIKE A BLASTED BREEZE JUST WAFTED through with how loud and numerous the murmurs just became.

"She can't do that, can she?"

"Set the slaves free?"

"She'll crash our economy!"

"Your Highness—"

The reactions grow louder, taking over the atmosphere and my voice.

I stop talking and allow my skin to tingle with the weather as their words and tones roll off my back, much the way they used to at slave auctions when old men would haggle prices. The chattering builds quickly into an argument—except this time I can't tell who's on which side.

Until a hard chuckle echoes off the walls, causing the men to stall and turn.

"She's offering you a plan that will avoid a civil war and is the only chance you have of saving your nation, let alone your economy." Eogan scoffs. "Do you think the best weapon you have is not capable of being a voice of wisdom?"

"But to free them?" a councilman yells. "We'll have their peasant owners in an uprising and *they'll* refuse to fight! Better we call a draft."

A rush of tension ripples down my arms as the outside air crackles loud enough for them to hear it, just like I can feel it. "King Sedric," I say quietly. "Might I remind you of your word given to Colin and me at the Keep?" I can feel the heat in my face. In my blood. Daring him.

He opens his mouth. Shuts it. And, after a moment, tips his head to say that yes, he remembers.

"I'm assuming you still plan to honor that promise."

"Is she threatening the king?" someone whispers.

"Silence." Sedric's voice rings across the space, squelching the rising mutterings going on around us.

Eogan is watching me. I can feel his eyes as Sedric nods my way. "I do." Then looks up and around at the gathering. "We will go with Nym's suggestion. And I will hear no more about it."

He lifts a hand before the arguments can begin. "Now." He turns back to me, and I drop my gaze to help him save face from the gawking expressions that claim insult against the woman who just put the king in his place. "Do you have an opinion on how to bring unity among the peasants and their slaves in this plan of yours?"

"No," I answer honestly. "But I'll have one by the time I get to the first township."

Sedric nods and taps on the map to draw attention where it's due. "Then let us commence with discussing Draewulf's next move."

"It might help to know exactly *how* to defeat him," Kenan suggests.

Rolf moves a pawn on the map. "I thought that's what we're discussing."

"I believe he means we need to speak with Lady Isobel," King Sedric says.

"Use the Luminescents to ask her," I say.

"Or we could torture her," one of the councilman growls.

"She's used to pain. It would take too long." Eogan's tone is

143

matter-of-fact, but for whatever reason something in it snags at me. At the space in me that resents her and loathes her capabilities.

She's used to pain? The thought gives me pause—what sort of life has she been through that she could be familiar with such a thing?

Eogan catches me staring at him. I look away, but even so, the hint of compassion seeps up through my bones into my chest. Perhaps there's a reason Eogan used to love her beyond the fact it was the only emotion allowed him.

Sedric turns to his Captain of the Guard. "Have your men finished debriefing Lord Myles and the rest?"

"They have. The Lord Protectorate and others are now in the upper Northern Wing under guard, sire."

"Good. Bring us the Cashlins." Sedric looks at me.

I nod. "May I also request Rolf bring in Kenan's son, Kel, Your Highness? He's one of the airship captains and familiar with most of the passengers who came with us."

Kenan looks over at me as Sedric nods to Rolf. "Agreed."

When the War Chamber door shuts behind Rolf and his men, the room explodes in conversation. I listen and attempt to keep my suddenly drooping eyelids propped up.

Minutes later the chamber door opens again, and Rolf and his guard unit are ushering in the Cashlin guard and the two Luminescents along with Kel—all with hands tied beneath their backs.

"Kel." I reach out a hand and the guards release him to me.

"Ah, the young captain, I presume," Sedric says, and it's a credit to his years at High Court that his face shows not even a hint of shock at Kel's size or obvious age.

"One of them." Kel peers over at his father and Eogan. His hand tightens around mine.

"Welcome, then. And would you mind sticking around here a bit to share what you know with us? I think you'd be most valuable."

The little boy's face fills with pride and seriousness. "Would be my honor, sire."

"Very good." Sedric looks toward the Cashlin guard and two Luminescents.

"I am Mia and this is Mel." The shorter of the two women steps forward. They point to the guard, Sir Doesn't Matter. "This is Gilford. We were sent on behalf of our people to be deeper eyes and ears for you. My only regret is we could not send more."

"I'm grateful for whatever you can give us."

Mel nods.

I smirk at the Cashlin. *Gilford, huh?*

Eogan looks to the king, then to the other council members. "Your Highness, I believe if we can give Nym enough time and distract the rest of his army, she will be able to provide another advantage."

I will? "How?" I want to ask, but this is clearly not the time to instill doubt. Instead, I swallow and my hands curled against my sides begin to shake. I clench them until there's the slightest rumble of thunder in the distance that gives me away. The entire table turns toward me, but I just force a weak smile and say nothing as Kel nuzzles his shoulder against me. His eyelids are heavy too. Poor boy.

"She can bring forth the Uathúils—if there are any others hiding in Faelen," Eogan says.

"*Are* there more?" Sedric runs a hand over his boyish chin, only half-hiding his look of alarm.

I wither Eogan a look. "Supposedly."

"I see." Sedric follows my gaze. "I assume you know where they're hiding out, Your Highness?"

"Your Majesty," a councilman in the back says. "I must protest allowing this man to run around Faelen searching for Uathúils."

"Allow me to ease your mind, then, that I have no intention of going to find them. They've supposedly already been called forth."

Eogan nods toward me. "They will come when it's time. As for me, once we are through here tonight, my attentions need to be placed upon Bron."

"You think Draewulf's forces in Bron will attack us from the southern border in airships?"

"Doubtful. However—"

"And what of your forces under siege in Bron?"

"I'll be honest." Eogan peers at Sedric. "My commitment is to help Faelen win this war, because if it doesn't, the rest of the world will fall. However, I need to return home long enough to set events in motion that will assure the survival of my people as well."

I veer my gaze to him. He's returning home?

"Of course, I will need Your Highness's permission to do such a thing."

"Given," Sedric says. "Although the quicker you return, the better. For all our sakes."

"Agreed. I will leave as soon as we've finalized a plan."

I don't even realize I'm shaking my head until Kel pokes me in the side. My chest is suddenly sinking, as if there's not enough blood and tissue and sinew to hold the bones in place. Like a birdcage breaking because we did *not* just go through every impossible thing the past few days to have Eogan head straight back to the heart of the plague and army and death.

"Then it's decided," Sedric says. "Rolf, please take our Luminescent friends to begin their interview with Lady Isobel. The war generals and I will stay here. Tannin, when you've seen to the lady Nym's needs, please begin preparations for an Assembly here this evening—considering it's already morning—where we will make an announcement regarding what's been decided here."

He raises his voice. "At that time, I will ask everyone to join up with our efforts, especially those from the High Court, so Nym may use such as encouragement for the lower castes. We will reconvene later."

A few of the councilmen begin shuffling out. Others remain. They begin talking, but I'm not listening. Because all I can see are Eogan's eyes swerving onto mine with a firm expression that says he needs me to understand.

I give a slight shake of my head, swallow, and look back to King Sedric so my gaze won't burn a chasm in his head.

Because I understand only all too well.

I understand that he's signing his own death sentence if the wraiths there figure out who he is before the final attack has even begun.

CHAPTER 19

TAKE ME TO SEE HIM."

"Miss, I don't—"

"Is he in the same room as last week?" I continue walking as Tannin hurries to keep up.

"Miss, I know you've spent time with Bron's king, but considering he's here in a rather different capacity than your trainer now, taking you to his chambers lies outside protocol and I can assure you King Sedric will not approve. Not to mention that area is under tight security."

"Do I appear to care? Because I'm quite certain I don't. I need to speak with Eogan before he makes further plans, so you will please take me there *now*."

He begins to steer off toward a set of stairs. "Perhaps a hot bath would be better at this time, and while you do so, I'd be happy to inquire for—"

I flip around and allow a spark of friction to fill the hallway's air. He swallows.

"You may stay to ensure I return with you," I say, recalling last week when I promised something similar only to slip onto the ship and leave for Bron. "But I *will* speak to him immediately."

His face goes tight, but after a moment he nods. "I will stand *directly* outside the door."

"And I'll be grateful for it." My tone softens. "Thank you, Tannin."

He sniffs and shakes his head, then proceeds to turn us down two different corridors until we reach the same hallway I stood in last week that leads to Eogan's room. I falter a second as the air drains from my chest at the recollection of what he was in that room. At what he almost became.

The past ten days have been a bleeding nightmare.

I bite back the bile itching up my throat and stare stiff-like at Eogan's guards. "I'd like to speak with the king."

"He's not seeing anyone—"

A crash of thunder explodes so loud above the Castle even I jump. I lean in. "I don't care what he's *not* doing—let me in there."

"She's obtained a special request," Tannin says, not looking at me.

I file away a reminder that I owe him and his family something grand for such a smooth lie. Perhaps a bucket-case of dolls.

The larger guard hesitates. "We were not informed of such a request."

"Where is Kenan?" I demand, looking around. "Perhaps we should rouse him from—"

The guard knocks on the door, murmuring something about this being a wholly inappropriate time. I don't wait for a reply from within. I merely lean forward and pound on the door myself, then push it open and enter. "Eogan, I . . ."

Oh.

He's standing beside a water basin, pulling a drying cloth around himself.

His eyes widen a second before sparking with amused interest as he ties the cloth around his waist and legs. "May I help you?"

Behind me the door slowly swings shut. Did I push it or did one of the guards pull it? I don't know. I—

He lifts a brow and runs a hand over the back of his neck while his chest stares back at me. "I'm waiting to hear about the fire."

I frown.

"I assume that is why you've interrupted my bath, yes? The Castle's burning down? Although"—he waves a hand toward me—"you don't look much in a hurry."

I clear my throat and try to gather together the collapsing air in my lungs and force it into a coherent sentence. Or even a thought. *Yes, think a thought, Nym. And for bleeding's sake look away.*

"My face is up here."

I flick my gaze up to find a hint of entertainment in his. I scowl as his brow goes up and a funny look emerges in his eyes even as his jaw clenches.

I peel my gaze away and drop it to the floor, firming it once I remember why I'm standing in a half-naked man's room. "I came to ask why in bracken you're so willing to toss your life to hulls."

"Pardon?"

"You're going back to Bron."

"If I don't, my people will die either from plague or by the magic creating those wraiths. I have to give them the truth and a chance."

"And that justifies you going back? If you do you're as good as dead, either from your own people or from the wraiths when they discover you're no longer Draewulf."

"So you'd ask me to sacrifice my own people?" His voice has a touch of exasperation. Enough so that I glance up at his face.

"On the roof Myles and I heard Draewulf and Isobel say they are the ones whose magic can turn people to wraiths. I don't believe it can be done without them. Besides, he's coming for us now, not your people."

His expression flashes disgust. "I'm quite aware he created more last week in Bron—while using my body, thank you. But if anything, him not being there gives my people a fighting chance right now. And whether they're directly in harm's way at this moment or not, my people still need to be given the truth and courage to fight back against the beasts that have surrounded them."

"Blast it all, Eogan, can't you simply wait? At least until this war is fought? Because for all you know we *won't* win—and then it won't matter what in hulls you fix in Bron!"

He scoffs and pushes a hand through his wet hair. "So that's why you're barging into my private rooms right now? To ask me to be a coward to my own people, Nym?" He frowns. "What would you do if you were me?"

I snort. "Perhaps I see the benefit to barging in on you like this! Maybe it's the only way I feel you'll actually listen to me."

Any earlier hint of humor falls away, leaving the set look of arrogance. "Oh, I'm listening to you. I just don't happen to agree with you on this one. Now, if you don't mind—"

I let out a laugh. "You don't listen to anyone. And you're not the only one at stake here—or have you forgotten that Draewulf is coming to our borders, not Bron's? He's already been to your kingdom and guess what? He left them alive! Which is more than I can say he's going to do here with my people or with Cashlin, not to mention Rasha right now." My cheeks burn and I look down to mutter, "And could you put some clothes on, please?"

He gives a sharp snort. "I thought you wanted me at my most vulnerable. Or is this how you imagine—?"

"No, I don't imagine." *I refuse to imagine. Stop imagining, Nym.* "Just put some bleeding clothes on." I toss him a tunic and pants that've been laid out across the bed in obvious preparation. Then turn around and tap my foot and keep my thoughts on how very nice the stone tiles in his room look. They have lovely, raw hand-cut patterns that look nothing like the cut of Eogan's chest with or without a shirt on.

"And hurry up," I grumble after a moment. "I'm not done discussing this."

I swear he utters what sounds like a curse word under his breath. "Is that what you call it? I thought you were yelling and lecturing."

"I wouldn't have to if you had any half-litched sense of self-preservation." I listen to him pull on his clothing behind the screen in the corner.

"Done."

When I turn around, he's standing closer than I expected, his broad shoulders taking up the majority of the space in front of me as he repeatedly pushes a hand through his still-damp hair, sending my skin flushing hot all over again. Blast him. "And if you want to talk about danger," he murmurs, "how about we talk about you? Perhaps you should tell me about the scouting excursions you're planning to take while you're rousing support for the war."

What? I frown.

He gives that hard laugh again. "Because I know you, Nym. I'm not a bleeding idiot." He strides over to one of two chairs near the window and rests his hand on it while staring out over the black landscape beyond.

I follow. And stop when I see what he's looking at. His two lit-up airships crawling with men preparing them.

"You'll do what you think is best and I'll do what I believe in. Whether either of us agrees with the other or not."

"But you are playing with your life and I didn't work this hard—I didn't take on a litched other power—just to have you throw everything away!"

"I didn't ask you to take on that power. In fact, I clearly warned you against it."

"Who bleeding cares? I don't need you going off and getting yourself killed! Not when we're this close! Not when Draewulf is breathing at our front door." My breath is coming faster now. More furious. For what he's throwing away. For what will likely happen to him. For his complete lack of seeing the bigger picture. The sky rumbles my frustration. "You said you wouldn't abandon me."

The slight flinch of his eyes says my comment hit home. But the next second he's leaning in until only inches separate our lips. "If I were abandoning you, I'd return to my people and stay there. I'm not. I'm simply trying to do the best I can for everyone who matters to me."

I swallow. *Except he's still putting himself in real danger. And there's a good chance he won't ever come back.*

"Kind of like you had to do with Rasha."

Is he—? I barely stop from smacking him. "I didn't choose to leave her behind."

"No, but you didn't fully fight it either. Why? Because you knew what had to be done."

I choke. "And what if we were wrong? What if Draewulf uses her to win this war? What if we're too late and her mother's right— that she could do more than any of the people I'm supposed to amass?"

"I'm not trying to be callous. I'm simply pointing out that choices have to be made. And just because you're suffering guilt over abandoning Rasha and Tulla doesn't mean you *did* abandon them. Nor does it equate to me abandoning *you* now. Our responsibilities are to our people, and sometimes that means we care for both sides. Just in a different order than preferred."

His gaze flickers down to my lips, my neck, my chest, and I swear hunger emerges in his eyes. He swallows and pulls away. "I have preparations to make."

I soften my voice and try one last time. "Wait to rescue your people until this is over. When I can help you."

He runs a hand along the back of his neck again. Over the scar. "I know you've carried the bulk of responsibility for so long it's like skin, Nymia, but maybe it's time you shared it. I'm technically in charge of myself and my people. So let me."

"You forget I was the one who—"

"I've not forgotten anything, love. I simply have to do for my people what you need to do for yours." He swallows and turns to stare me directly in the eye. "Look, I'm not ignoring your advice. But I *am* leaving for a few days and trusting you to stay out of trouble and Draewulf's clutches until I return. This is my way of keeping you safe. Perhaps trusting each other is the only way we'll keep each other safe."

"And what if you die?"

"Then I'll have died attempting to give you and my people freedom."

"I'm already free."

His expression eases. "Then perhaps it's simply safer this way."

Safer?

I frown. "What is that supposed to mean?"

He opens his mouth. Shuts it. And allows his gaze to slide down my small frame.

A heavy inhale. "I'm no longer your trainer, Nym. So like I said, you make your choices. I'll make mine." He lifts a hand to stroke my lower lip, then turns and strides for the door to hold it open for me.

CHAPTER 20

TANNIN WALKS ME BACK TO MY ROOM. I DON'T talk on the way and he, for once, seems bent on silence too. "Anything else I can see to?" he asks when I open the door.

I eye the steaming bath and cup of tea a maid must've just poured and shake my head. "But thank you."

He's hardly gone before I've slid off my clothing and settled into the warm tub. After swallowing the tea, I slip my head under water and hold my breath for as long as possible while the heat from the tea and steam from the bath seep into my aching joints and muscles and bone—into the soul place in me that aches with memories of a past being slowly revealed and frustration for the present. Frustration with Eogan—for leaving and for saying it was safer, whatever in hulls that was supposed to mean. Frustration with being back here only to realize we've lost more than we've gained.

Almost two weeks ago this Castle was full of celebration at the peace treaty declaring the war's end. Rasha and I even sat at the window celebrating with them as I grieved Colin and Breck. Now I'm here and Rasha's gone—and, good grief, I miss her airy, confusing speeches—and Myles has lost his stones and Eogan's walking into a wraith's nest and there's never a break. *Never. A. Bleeding. Break.*

My chest pounds the refrain: *I am so weary of war.*

I'm weary of Draewulf. Why couldn't I kill him on that airship? Why couldn't I take him out?

I scream beneath the water. Scream until my lungs are empty and I come up gasping for air that this has all been for nothing. I *swear it.*

The black itch beneath my skin flares and presses and introduces the reminder that I never finished carving the branch under the bird in my left arm. The little mugplant-tattooed bluebird I added to the rest of my skin etchings right after I first came to my owner Adora. Right after I first met Eogan.

My mouth practically salivates with the thirst to create another cutting in my skin.

I snap my jaw shut and refuse. *I refuse. I refuse.*

"*She's a miracle.*" My birth mother's words float through my vision.

I shake them away.

"*But what if she doesn't survive?*"

I pause. So what if I don't survive?

What will I do until then?

"*Hold it all lightly, my love.*"

Except I need control over *something.*

Over this war and my abilities. Over gathering an army.

Over rescuing Rasha.

I grit my teeth and pull my hair from the cooling tub water.

What I will do until then is the only thing I've known to do since the day of my birth apparently. *Continue fighting.*

Fight until we bring freedom to everyone. And destroy Draewulf before he can fulfill whatever part of the prophecy he thinks he deserves.

And if not?

I will defeat him the only way I know how.

With that in mind I climb out of the tub and grab a drying cloth to wring out my hair and wrap around my body as I go in search of a pair of blue leathers for tomorrow—or rather, later today.

They're in the armoire. I press my face to them and inhale the scent that smells good and normal. Like outdoors and fresh air and riding.

A knock on the door hits just as I'm crawling into bed.

"Pardon, miss, but . . ."

I open it to find Kel standing beside Tannin, looking tired and fierce and all kinds of lost.

"He was asking to see you."

"He can stay." I stifle a yawn and beckon Kel in. "Thank you, Tannin." And raise a brow at the child.

"They let me rest in my father's room while he's making arrangements for their flight. But I couldn't sleep." He runs a hand down his arm. "The floors and walls are too cold and everything smells strange here."

I yank a blanket off the bed and hold it out to him. "You're welcome here, but I can hardly keep my eyes open. Promise to amuse yourself and not disturb me."

He takes the blanket with a snort of insult and carries it over to plop down on one of the high-back fancy chairs nearest the window. I smile and crawl under my covers as he peeks out the drapery, and two seconds later I'm tugging the comforter over my eyes and ears and face in an effort to cocoon myself from the world and all thoughts of today and war and of whatever Eogan's irritable problem is.

"Nym?

"*Nym?*"

"Hmm?"

"Why do you have to go *ask* your people to fight? Don't they want to?"

I tug the covers down just enough so my mouth isn't muffled. "They've been fighting a long time and they're worn out from it. War's not been an easy thing on us."

"But we've been fighting just as long and we don't have to ask no one to do it. It's an honor. Why does your king give your people a choice?"

Is he jesting right now? I pull the comforter farther until my whole face is showing and peek at him through slit eyelids. "Each nation rules differently. Your people don't believe in castes but in uniformity, so while they have little autonomy, everyone is committed to the role of bringing honor to the entirety of Bron. My people believe in castes—and thus have slaves and peasants and upper class. However, they also try to value free will—in theory— and thus not everyone should be forced to fight."

Mercifully, the room falls silent again and only Kel's breathing and the breeze picking up outside tickle my hearing.

I've nearly dozed off when his small voice carries over again. "How do you know your people will fight this time, then?"

"Kel, I need sleep."

"Just tell me."

"We *don't* know."

"And what if they decide not to?"

I roll over and shove off the blankets enough to look up at the ceiling a moment. And sigh. "Then we lose."

"I'M COMING FOR YOU, PET."

The paper words float in my hand, in my dreams, in my mouth. Burning their sour taste into my throat until I want to throw Draewulf's words up onto his disgusting face as he lurches and leers in front of me.

That toothy smile gets closer as the blood-bathed valley behind him wavers through my vision. So do his claws. They still have the blood of the Luminescent queen on them. I gag as he reaches out to scrape a paw down my face, and suddenly I can't move, I can't slip away, because someone is holding me in place.

Lady Isobel. I wrench my head back to hit her only to discover it's Lord Myles holding me. His eyes have gone black and his face blank of anything but power and hate and fury.

Draewulf's claw slips down to grab my wrist so tight I cry out. Then he's carving through my arm, slitting my veins to reach the poison inside. He chuckles, and my entire spine stiffens at this monster who has left my people dead upon the field behind him. Who's torn the hearts out of Princess Rasha and King Sedric.

I glance over at Eogan, barely alive.

My blood ripples—then surges—as if that note or melody belonging to my soul has been released to rush through. Except this song's different. It's not a refrain of beauty.

It's a harmony of rebellion.

And it's burning through my skin.

I flip my wrist over beneath the beast's claw and press my hand against his, allowing the light and dark in me—the abilities in my blood—to go free. To thirst. To drain his to such a state that he will be weakened too.

"Nym, don't," Eogan slurs, but it's too late. The monster roars at the burn I've created—at the piece of him I've just taken. He slashes at me in fury, and as he does, I drop. Allowing the claw to connect with my throat. So that what was meant to be an impulsive wound to my chest is now my death warrant as it slices through the skin and tendons and a heartpulsing artery.

And I am bleeding out too fast for him to save.

His roar deafens the Valley, deafens my head, my hearing. All except for the words that keep repeating: "I'm coming for you, pet.

"I'm coming for you, pet.

"I'm coming for you."

A pounding on the door startles me awake. I yank the covers back to discover daylight is streaming through the sides of the emerald curtains and splaying itself in thin strips along the green tapestry rug and stone floor.

The pounding sounds again and something inside me says it matches the quick, heavy beating of my horrified heart. That dream . . .

"Who is it?" I gasp.

The door squeaks open, and when I roll over to look, Rolf, the Captain of the Guard, peeks his head in. "Would you mind coming with me?"

Now? "Why?"

His gaze falls to the foot of the bed where a light snore and movement are the only reminders that someone else is in here with me. Kel. He's curled up near my feet in the blanket I gave him. A tiny smile on his boyish face.

Rolf softens his voice. "The king's urgent request. We would not disturb you if we knew what to do."

"Sounds dire." I fail to keep the annoyance from my unsteady tone.

"It's Lord Myles."

Lovely. I rub away the sleep from my eyes, and with it the blasted dream, and then slide from the bed while being careful not to wake Kel. I don't even bother running a hand down my hair after pulling on a thin robe and boots before beckoning the guard to lead the way.

He discreetly hurries us to a set of chambers where a soldier unit is surrounding the door and speaking to one another in agitated voices, only remembering themselves when Rolf and I stride up. They straighten and salute, but I swear their eyes look confused. More than that, they look afraid.

The door has barely opened when the atmospheric wave hits and threatens to throw me backward. The entire bedroom has disappeared and in its place is a jousting yard outside the Castle with grass and horse stables and a perfect blue sky. And a host of young men playing at swords.

"What in litches?"

No answer.

It takes a moment to recognize the discomfort bubbling up in me isn't due to the incredible accuracy and strength of the mirage. It's the intimacy of it.

Whatever vision Lord Myles is creating is so far different from usual it's eerie. It's more personal. More vulnerable. Like walking into a dream you don't belong in, but you can't see clearly enough to find your way back out.

I peer through the images for the oaf, and it takes almost a minute to locate him huddled against the wall in the corner. King Sedric is standing a few feet away from him looking baffled as Myles's eyes are open but he's not responding to his cousin's coaxing.

Instead, he's staring at the people in his vision.

I follow his gaze to the room's center where a boy is playing with a group of young men, and I watch as the child's gaze keeps flitting over to a rather pretty girl on the sidelines. She winks and giggles, and the boy lunges his jousting blade harder at one of the taller youths to impress her.

Until a grown man strolls by, slim and sleek, with dark hair and pale skin. And a gait that tells me he's someone who's rather important and oddly familiar.

The young man is looking at him, and even without noise to the dream it's clear the other boys begin snickering. The gentleman doesn't give them or the boy the time of day, however. But as soon as he passes, the youths turn their laughter onto the child. They point at his skin, which is paler than theirs, followed by his eyes that have a reddish glint in a certain light.

Abruptly the vision becomes clear enough to see an expression flash across the young boy's features that is uncomfortably more recognizable than anything else in this mirage.

Hulls. It's Myles.

The other boys are goading thicker now—their lips forming the words *illegitimate* and *Cashlin blood*.

I want to turn away at how hard my chest wrenches. The look on Myles's face as he sits in the corner, a grown man temporarily out of control with his ability. He's accidentally revealing his deepest secrets for all to see. And here we are watching.

Focus, Nym. I firm my jaw and stare through the mirage until it wavers and fades from my view, then walk over to Myles—aware that, even as I do, there's a gasp from the soldiers for whom the vision is still very solid. Apparently I've just strolled through the young Myles's sword coming down.

Bending near him, I say, "Myles, stop this at once."

He doesn't respond.

"He's been at it for the past fifteen minutes," King Sedric murmurs. "Practically scared the hulls out of the guards."

I lean down and place my hand on his arm and not-too-harshly smack his cheek with the other. "Myles!"

He gives no indication he's heard me.

"One of my men saw Myles focusing on using his blackening hands to create mirages. The guard said it was as if Myles was doing it on purpose."

I glance at Myles's hands only to see they really are blackening, the veins popping up like roots from a thorn tree. They're so dark his skin almost looks scorched from his fingers to his wrists.

I rub my own hands as King Sedric waves at the room. "Except it appears he apparently lost control and it erupted into this."

The soldiers in the room begin swearing, and I flip around to find the vision has shifted to one of war along one of the southern Island Cairns from what I can tell. Was Myles in one of those battles?

Beside me Myles utters a low moan. He grabs his head, and the moaning turns to cursing as five half-dead wraiths drag their bodies across the floor toward the man who is him in the mirage. Behind him is a woman who clearly has the plague. She's weeping from the looks of it, but it's Myles's real-life screams I hear.

It's so horrific, so ear-shattering, I turn to grab him, to shake him, but it does no good. He's gone somewhere inside himself and all that's left is his body with eyes that have black around the edges.

Litches. Not yet. Not now. It's happening too soon.

I look up at Sedric. "Get Eogan and Lady Isobel *now*," I whisper.

"Lady Isob—?"

"We need both."

The king gives orders to his soldiers as Myles's vision ripples again and reveals his mirage-self hovering over someone. In this version he's clearly using his mind abilities to confuse a squad of Bron soldiers heading toward a hovel he's crouching beside. The soldiers scan the area, then move on. When Myles straightens, there's a woman and her baby staring wide-eyed and shaking. She looks almost as terrified of Myles as she is of the soldiers in the distance.

"That's Kendric," Sedric whispers.

I spin around. "Who?"

"One of the ladies at the Court who went to the Island Cairns with her husband, who was a general. He was killed there." Sedric looks at me. "I assume these are memories?"

I nod. Then tip my head toward the woman. "Did she survive?"

"She was sent to a convent asylum where she died last year from illness. As did her child."

The vision shifts yet again, but this time it goes back to the laughing boys and Myles's father ignoring him as he strolls by.

I want to be sick.

"I had no idea," Sedric says, more to himself than to me. And there's a measure of pity in his tone.

Three minutes pass and Eogan is walking through the image toward me. My chest shivers a moment as the butterflies inside welcome his presence. His calm. Even if the rest of me is still angry with him. "How long's he been like this?" he asks in a voice scratchy from sleep.

I glance at King Sedric. "Not long."

Eogan crouches in front of Myles and sets his hand onto his skin, and within moments the vision weakens and dims, then disappears. Eogan stands and mutters for the king's and my ears only, "Do we know what brought it on?"

"He was using the ability he consumed to try to strengthen them."

Sedric looks down at Myles, then back up at Eogan. "May I ask how your ability stops it?"

A tinkle of beautiful laughter ripples and it's the first indication I have that Lady Isobel has also been brought into the room. "King of a nation and yet hasn't the slightest idea how Uathúil abilities work? Shame, shame, Your Majesty. No wonder your Elementals were killed off in droves. Such lack of knowledge always displays itself in fear."

King Sedric glances from her to me.

"It appears Eogan's ability isn't simply a block but also has healing properties," I say quietly and peer up at Eogan. "Perhaps he'd like to explain."

"Oh, not just *properties*, my dear," Isobel chides. "I'd say he's quite good at many methods of touching, wouldn't you?"

My throat sours as Lady Isobel switches her stare back and forth between both kings. Although I swear it lingers longer on Eogan. My stomach coils in annoyance.

Eogan ignores her. "It does act as a block, but in this case I've merely replaced his overreactive sensitivities with something that soothes."

"I thank you for that." Sedric nods. "And if you don't mind, the lady raises a fair point. May I ask what exactly *is* your ability, then?"

Eogan glances my way, then stiffens and smiles politely at King Sedric. "Drat if I know."

Right. I frown and, ignoring them both, stride over to Lady Isobel, who's standing between four guards with her hands tied behind her back. "I asked you before how to help Lord Myles."

She shrugs. "You could ask the Luminescents. I imagine they pulled a tiny share out of me. Nothing of importance, of course." She flashes a sly smile. "Although, I wonder how willing they are to help an illegitimate like him."

The expression on her face says she's hoping to get a rise out of me, except her tone is laced with a roughness that sounds remarkably similar to insecurity. I raise a brow as it prompts an unwilling pity.

"The Luminescents could help him?" Sedric walks over. "*Is* there a way?"

She scowls. "Oh, there's a way. Maybe a few, in fact. But you won't like them."

I look up at the king, then at the Bron guards, and nod for them to take her since I was clearly wrong—she'll be of no help to us.

Two seconds later I'm turning back toward Eogan—my lungs hopeful, starving to speak with him.

Unfortunately, the Bron king is already striding out.

CHAPTER 21

WHEN I WAKE AGAIN, AFTERNOON HAS FULLY dawned and Kel is seated next to my head swinging his feet off the side of the bed.

"Finally." He jumps down. "I'm famished as a ferret-cat." Without waiting, he pulls the bell cord I showed him this morning before I returned to my beautiful blanket cocoon after Myles's breakdown.

To the boy's obvious delight, the maid appears within moments, carrying a lunch tray, which she sets up while I wash my face in a fresh bowl of water before forcing Kel to do the same.

"Pardon, miss," the pretty, brown-eyed maid says when I hand Kel a drying cloth. "But King Sedric was rather specific about your costume for tonight. And your hair." She eyes my white tangles I haven't brushed in more days than I care to count.

I raise a brow. "A costume?"

"The dress hanging in the right side of the armoire, miss."

Uh-huh.

"The Assembly starts in a little over two hours."

I chew my lip before nodding. "In that case I think I'd like to take a walk first."

"Very good, miss. Let me know if you need help." She gives a small curtsy and steps toward the door.

A costume? I shudder, turn to the window, and open it to let the breeze in before scooping up an orange and a cup of tea as I peer into the courtyard. The sounds of guard units being organized and banners for the Assembly being tamped into place float up as does the scent of good, old Faelen soil and sunshine. I inhale deep before finishing my orange.

Nine days.

Nine days to raise and equip an army we will likely be leading to death, rescue Rasha, and hope Eogan returns before all hulls breaks loose. I glance toward the Elisedd channel where we saw the single airship floating above the warboats.

Then I turn to catch Kel wolfing down an entire meat pasty.

"You have good food," he says around a giant mouthful. I snort. It's probably the first actual bread he's ever eaten. He shoves two inside his pocket and grins. "So where we going?"

"To get to work."

If I thought the courtyard was bustling with noise, the Castle hallway is even more so, but of a different kind. Weapons are being carried down the corridors in loads on top of carts already piled high with every piece of armor imaginable. And Rolf is giving orders to have more commissioned from the sound of it.

"Kings Sedric and Eogan?" I ask.

Rolf points down the stairs. "War Chamber."

"What do you want them for?" Kel asks while we walk.

"I just want to know if there're any further preparations needed for tonight." I swallow. "Or for Eogan's trip tomorrow."

"I hope he doesn't die."

I stall and stare at him, unsure whether to scold or laugh.

"But if he does—" He clamps his mouth shut.

I shake my head. "Then what?"

"Nothing."

"Kel, back on the ship you were bothered about him. Does this have to do with that?"

His face reddens brighter than a beet berry and his fingers get fidgety.

"Kel?"

He shuffles his foot against the carpet and looks down. "I just don't think he's good for you, that's all."

Right. I wait until he looks up.

"He just . . . he just better treat you nice or he'll have me to answer to." He spits it out all in one rush. His blush spreads down to his neck, and the next thing I know he's walking away from me. Oh.

Oh. I grin. *That's* it?

The poor boy has a crush.

I follow behind him, giving distance and a moment for his embarrassment to dim down, and by the time we reach the War Room, he's back to normal.

"If you're looking for either king, both are going over their joint speeches for this evening," Tannin says, exiting the room.

Oh. My shoulders deflate even as my eyes search the room for Eogan anyway.

"However . . ." His voice breaks off as he nods down the hall. I follow his gaze to find Gilford, the male Cashlin guard, striding toward us, flanked by three of our own.

The guard tips his head at Kel when he reaches us. "Young master." Then he turns to me. "The Luminescents are currently attempting to read Lady Isobel again, and I asked to come find you." He stops and glances around at the guards and Tannin before lowering his voice. "I was wondering what plans they have of rescuing Princess Rasha. Has it been discussed?"

I shake my head. "I brought it up last night, but they were still trying to catch up to speed on the war and bring the rest of Faelen on board. However . . ." I look at Kel. "I was hoping the information the Luminescents get from Lady Isobel might help us pinpoint where exactly to find Rasha. I have an idea, but if we can have confirmation, then we can request to pursue her."

He scowls.

"Or not request."

"And if they can't get it out of Lady Isobel?"

"Then I'm prepared to follow my hunches and do whatever I need to. Even if it means finding a few wraiths to interrogate and crossing the waterway back toward Tulla."

A glint of relief eases his features just as Kenan strides up, flanked on both sides by his own set of Bron and Faelen guards.

"Not gotten into too much trouble, I hope?" he says to Kel before giving me a nod. "I can take the boy now—we'll prepare for the Assembly this evening." His tone suggests he thinks Kel may be in need of more than preparation. Such as a good bath. I don't tell him I'm inclined to agree, but what is with seven-year-old boys and their smell?

"Miss," Tannin says behind me. "I believe you should be getting ready as well when you're finished here. I'm told you have a speech to give."

A speech? I turn to Kenan, who shrugs as if to say hulls if he knows.

I'm to wear a costume *and* give a speech. At least at Adora's home, things were always overplanned. This is ludicrous.

"M'lady?"

"I'd like to see Rolf."

"Very good, miss."

Rolf is exactly where I left him, inspecting a guard unit and informing them which sections of the Castle's banquet room he expects each to cover. I wait until he's finished before intruding. "Am I to give a speech this evening, Captain?"

His expression registers surprise that is fast replaced by an apology. "I'm sorry if we overlooked communicating as much to you, miss—"

"You did forget."

"Again, my apologies. His Highness mentioned it after you exited the War Chamber. I believe it is his belief that after his and Eogan's speeches, a positive word from you could add extra weight."

Of course they did. And of course it would. "Anything in particular he'd like me to say?"

"Something about how you're planning to lead them to victory?" His smile indicates he's only half-joking. "I'm sorry, miss, I'm not much for speeches. Give me a sword, though, and . . ."

"You and me both," I mumble. "I guess if you'll excuse me . . ." I head for my room and arrive just as the maid is leaving with our luncheon tray.

"Will there be anything else? Your hair, perhaps?"

"Nothing, thank you."

"I set the dress on the bed for you, miss."

I nod and wait until she's gone before I close the door and turn to the room. My gaze falls to the dress, and I actually choke on the air in my throat.

The thing is Faelen's ancestral color—a green so deep in the flickering candlelight it's almost black—with a corset top and jeweled back and lengthy taffeta skirt that is five times thick with material all cinched and bustled and looking very much like a dress my previous owner Adora would've killed for if it had a skunk-skin hat to go with it.

Oh, look. It even has a train for me to trip over.

I stare at the dress in all its flamboyance. I'll be lucky if I don't fall out the top. And what in hulls am I supposed to say while wearing it? "I hope you'll all join us in fighting—and some of you may die, but cheers!"

I groan and stride to the mirror to begin yanking a comb through my hair, in hopes that when I turn back to the dress, it won't look as gaudy as I fear. Five minutes into it, though, I'm thinking I should've had that maid help me after all, because I'm just as bad at twists and hair twirls as ever, which makes me miss Breck and Rasha something fierce.

I swallow and pile the lot of it into a massive, messy coil on top of my head that Breck would've been proud of. Maybe that'll diminish the dress's opulence a bit. Then I turn back to slip on the fancy dress, using my good hand to tighten the laces that are, mercifully, on the side of the corset. I finish it off by sliding on a pair of matching slippers and tying my new set of throwing knives to each leg.

A look in the mirror tells me I am exactly what King Sedric is hoping for. *Nice. Fancy.*

Influential.

I straighten my shoulders and firm my jaw in order to appear exactly as *I* am hoping. *Powerful.*

Finished, I stride for the door, running through fifty comments in my head that I could say to encourage the High Court members to fight. Unfortunately, the only things I can come up with are swears I've wanted to say to the lot of them far too often.

Tannin is waiting outside the door when I step out. He grins but doesn't say anything other than, "Feels familiar, doesn't it?"

I nod and try not to show my nerves, nor to mention that this is about as far from the other week's familiarities as possible. Because Eogan is no longer Draewulf. And Draewulf is no longer dead. And Rasha is not here to insult my life and clothing choices.

Once we enter the banquet room, however, it does, in fact, feel familiar, with its crammed balcony full of guests, most of whom are dressed in gorgeous silk layers and those silly pantaloon hats. The candelabras are illuminating the room, except rather than holding banquet tables and the noisy traveller's carnival, the place is barren—even of furniture. Only a few tables are set along the back balcony wall, holding weapons and maps and piles of scrolls that appear to have been already written on and sealed. For runners to carry to the villages across Faelen, I'm assuming.

"You look perfect." King Sedric's low voice carries past the councilmen and soldiers dotting the balcony.

He's smiling and bounding over in his rather unkingly way. I try to feel more charitable toward him.

"A symbol of victory." He gives a lavish bow. "Thank you for wearing it."

"I'll admit I'm not sure how my dress choice matters much, but if it lends to inspiring the Council to war, then so be it."

His grin widens. "You read my mind. These people—" He glances over the balcony's railing to the mingling High Courtiers below who are talking and, if I'm correct, looking a tad confused. "They respect the language they can speak. And whether you or I approve or not—that language tends to be style and power. Both of which you clearly wield tonight."

"Smart." I search the balcony for Eogan.

"Sire, I believe the Assembly is complete." Rolf comes up behind us.

"Good. Please tell King Eogan we're set to begin." Sedric starts to follow him, but stops and pats my hand. "Are you prepared to say something for the Court tonight?"

I nod. "Let me know when it's my turn."

"You have my gratitude for assisting us—assisting *me*—once again, Nym." With that he turns to go.

He steps toward the balcony's center and onto a slightly raised platform and gives a hand signal that prompts an instant blaring of trumpets, calling the room to order. A glare of light bounces off the wall mirrors to settle their glow on Sedric just as a bump against my shoulder alerts me the Cashlin, Gilford, is standing there along with both Luminescents. I nod to Mia and Mel and they smile politely back, their eyes lit up like red fireflies, before swerving my gaze away to scan the room again for Eogan.

"My friends." King Sedric's voice echoes across the banquet room.

"I have a request," I whisper to Mia.

Her reddened eyes are on the king as His Majesty expresses gratitude to the High Courtiers for assembling on such short notice before beginning a rundown of the horrific events from the past week. Although, from the sound of it, Sedric's only giving necessary details—and none that include Eogan's shape-shifter occupation.

"Let's hope it has to do with Princess Rasha," she murmurs. "For I confess my time here is beginning to feel wasted on Lady Isobel."

"I swear that will become part of it."

She grunts as King Sedric's regal voice continues to expound upon Faelen's dire situation.

"As you know, I am to visit the villages throughout Faelen over the next few days to rally volunteers for the war. I wonder if you'd be willing to join me."

"You're thinking to take Lord Myles," she says with only slight surprise in her tone.

"I suspect he'll become uncontrollable soon, which will lend a danger King Sedric and his men are unprepared to handle. Not that I feel much confidence to stop him, but—"

"Without Eogan's block for Lord Myles, you would be the best option for controlling him." She nods. "And yes, if you leave him here, he will end up endangering the palace. If your king is approving of my attendance, then I will come. As will Gilford. Particularly to act as a scouting party once we hit the northern region, as I assume that's what you're planning," Mia whispers. "To pursue the princess's whereabouts?"

I purse my lips but don't disagree.

"Might as well kill two birds with one stone," she says.

"Might as well give ourselves every last advantage."

She tips her head in agreement. "I agree you will need the princess to win the war—especially seeing the state Lord Myles is in. Your Uathúil ranks are already too few." She looks over at the other Luminescent, who nods. "Mel will stay to assist your king with Lady Isobel if necessary, as Queen Laiha intended."

I chew my lip and look back toward the king. Only to realize the audience is applauding and he is stepping down, his speech done, and from between a unit of Bron and Faelen guards, Eogan has emerged and is striding for the low stage.

His eyes spark green in the light, matching his pants and doublet that were clearly picked for him to wear to this occasion—to dissolve all hint that he is anything but in full support of Faelen. From the approving expressions on the sweaty faces of those around us, it's working.

"My friends," Eogan says as soon as the clapping has died down. "Nearly two weeks ago I stood before you, swearing my commitment to work side by side with your king and country as partners and brothers—both in times of peace and war. If I'd known then how quickly the latter would come upon us, I admit I may have been more inclined to hide out a bit longer during my recent trip to Bron."

His offered humor at a time like this elicits a roar of gratefulsounding laughter from the crowd. He gives them that half smile bound to make every person here swoon and makes that craving inside me for his company flare.

"However, as promised, I commit to you—to all of us—Faelen, Tulla, Cashlin, and Bron—what few resources are at my disposal at this time to help wipe out this scourge of the Hidden Lands once and for all."

The crowd's cheering forces him to pause, and for a second there's a hint of desperation in the sound of it. As if they know what we're truly up against as well as the strength that Bron can give. And the power that will be required.

"Tomorrow I will take my leave and return to my own people for a brief few days—to set things in order. My hope is to bring back more ships and troops to aide in your protection as well as in Draewulf's final desolation. However . . ." His voice deepens. "I confess I covet your prayers and well wishes for good speed, good winds, and good news upon my return." He nods and lets his emerald gaze flash in the mirrored lights, igniting his handsome face in a promise of confidence and peace.

I swear it also brings half the women near me to sigh, and, drat it all, I may have just sighed too. *Bleeding bolcrane.*

"Thank you." He steps back amid the rabid shouts and clapping of the entire Assembly.

"The people love him," Mel says near me. I tip my head in agreement as a swell of affection and pride and irritation blossoms to leave pink patches on my arms and heat on my face. I've rarely heard this loud of cheering from this Assembly of over three hundred councilmen and High Court citizens in any of my past months attending Adora's banquets. Eogan waves a hand at them, then casually steps off the stage and bows to King Sedric.

Sedric's gaze catches mine and he nods.

"I believe that's your cue," Tannin mutters from somewhere behind me.

"Apparently." I scrunch my cheeks and swallow. "Wish me luck."

"Don't trip," is all he says as I stride over to ascend and stand beside King Sedric.

A nervous energy runs down my skin and around the memorial tattoos on my left arm and the top of my chest that suddenly feels far too exposed in this tight bodice.

There are a lot of people.

They're all staring at me, waiting for what I will say that will empower them further than Eogan and Sedric already have. If that's even possible. I feel out one of my knives through the folds of my dress as Sedric leans in and raises his voice.

"My comrades and friends who've known my father before I was even born. I promise you that we *will* move forward against Draewulf in a show of force and fierceness. We will take Faelen's people of every class and ability and gender and show the monster that not only are we not to be trifled with, but we have not even begun to fight this war. We are about to unleash on him every weapon and person and ability that has been created through the greatness and passion of Faelen."

The crowd roars with approval. Whistles ring out amid the stomping of feet and cheers. And then the wall mirrors flash the candlelight on my face.

"Beside us will be our champion and salvation from our last struggle. I give you Nym."

It's like a bomb from one of the airships just exploded for how loud the audience cheers. King Sedric drops his arm and indicates me. Then steps back.

Suddenly I can't breathe in this dress, in this air, in this claustrophobic room of expectation. I swallow. *Shoulders back, Nym. And spit out something.*

How do I start? Do I call them "my friends" like Eogan and Sedric? Because they're not.

Breathe.

Do I tell them it will be all right? Because it won't be.

Breathe. And speak, you fool.

I peer around at their anticipating faces that are uplifted and glowing in the light.

"Good people of Faelen's High Court." I pause to firm my voice as the words continue to tumble out. "As one who has spent time among all classes and citizen castes of our beautiful kingdom, I have never been more confident in what we as a people are capable of doing."

Yes. Good. Both true and gracious.

"Nor have I ever been more confident of an imperative time to band together as one people, as one class and caste, than this time in our history. Do I believe that, in doing so, we will succeed at this war? I'll be honest with you—I don't know."

Lovely. The room just fell so quiet you could hear a beetle scuttle.

I clear my throat. "But what I *do* know beyond a shadow of doubt is that if we fail to come together and commit to fighting this evil, side by side, by utilizing *our* own energy—as politicians, leaders, and pontificates—rather than relying on those in the lower classes . . . then we will not survive at all."

I stop.

Only to realize after a second that there is still no hint of cheering. The crowd seems to be holding its breath, as if expecting more.

Litches. Um . . . "Also," I add feebly. "I will be with you at the front lines of this battle—should it come to that—doing everything

I can to slow Draewulf and ultimately stop him. However, I humbly admit that I can expend my energies better if I know each one of you is standing with me, lending me your strength. The strength that Faelen has been famous for since the creation of the Hidden Lands."

Now the cheering starts. Quiet at first but quickly building into a wave of hollers and shouts. Then bubbling over into a burst that sounds like fireworks.

I peer back at Sedric and find approval in his face.

Suddenly he's beside me again, holding up my arm like a symbol of victory, and the crowd's applause becomes a frenzy. Except my stomach is ill and all I can see is the desperation in their reaction, and all I can hear is my own heart whisper that just as I am a symbol of victory, I am also a symbol of death if we do not stop Draewulf. Because when he takes me, he will own all of us.

I swerve my gaze around for Eogan. And he is there. Ten feet away, watching me.

My heart's a sudden flare of aching to peel past that outer shell of kingly stiffness. To reach him. To tell him I'm sorry for my anger, but, good hulls, I'm still angry. To ask him why he seems frustrated too.

I swear there's a flicker of something—fear? nausea?—except the next moment it's gone and the look on his face says he's gone too. Restrained into his official mode that's meant to protect the world and me from himself.

I raise a brow and mouth, *Why?* Why hide yourself, Eogan?

He merely smiles, then turns to the people crowding around him.

CHAPTER 22

WITH THE SPEECHES DONE AND THE CHEERING fading, the room quiets a moment before coming alive again with a different sort of energy. It's like an eclectic mix of fear and anticipation smoldering through the atmosphere and pouring off the guests in waves so thick I can almost crash into them.

Servants move around the balcony serving hot ale and soft fruits as voices rise and high-heeled shoes *clip clip clip* their way to where King Sedric and I are stepping off the platform, their owners jutting pointy chins and fascinated gazes at us.

"Your Highness, when will the Dark Army arrive?"

"What is Draewulf coming for? And how will we know it's him if he can shape-shift?"

"Better yet, how do we know Draewulf's not already here? And if he's not, then, Nym, how about sending a storm north to deal with him?"

"What if the peasants refuse to support the war efforts?"

Sedric holds up his hands for quiet even as I'm edging backward to avoid their pressing hands and words. *Litches, I can't breathe in this dress.* I look to slip away, but rather than allow me, Sedric passes off the first three questions to me—as if I could answer better.

Why? I eye him and can almost sense the answer in my head. *Because these are my people.*

How well does he realize that? Whether he understands the history of Elementals, I don't know. He merely nods to indicate I should reply.

Fine. "As King Sedric said in his speech, we believe the Dark Army will arrive in nine days," I tell the first man wearing a poofed-up hat shaped like an oliphant. "It's why we're swiftly putting together as many tactical units as possible—to stay their hand until we can route an army to the coast."

I turn to the second questioner—a woman dressed more decently to the situation in a black mourning gown with glitter around her eyes. "We have Luminescents with us who, together, with effort, can see inside a person if Draewulf has taken them host. And we know he's still in either Cashlin or Tulla because that's where I last saw him, very much alive and in his shape-shifter wolf form."

"And what about attacking first with your storm abilities?"

I shake my head and shirk away from the gangly man's uncomfortable leer. "We'd risk destroying all of Cashlin and Tulla as well—or what's left of them. Plus, we've no guarantee my powers stretched that far would destroy Draewulf."

"But your powers *can* destroy him, right? When it's time?" The man presses closer, his face and damp breath invading my space.

I'm tempted to show him my powers to get him out of my face. I reach a hand toward his cravat and let the air between us crackle. He steps back with a muttered curse.

"She can absolutely destroy the beast." King Sedric jumps in with full confidence.

I give a caustic chuckle and drop my hand. And refrain from telling the poor man the method of defeating Draewulf may not be quite what he's imagining. Turning to run my eyes over the room again in search of Eogan, I let Sedric take over while more courtiers flock our direction. All hungry for answers from their facial expressions. My rib cage feels thick again with not enough air . . .

It's not until I rise on my tiptoes to peer above the sea of heads that I finally locate Eogan centered among another group who appear to be just as rabid as ours. Until abruptly the people in mine are growing louder, pushing for clarification from Sedric and me. Clarification about what, I don't know, because I've stopped listening. I'm watching Eogan's gaze flash around the faces in front of him and then over them to snag on mine.

My heart trips.

He smiles as if he, too, is bored as hulls. I stick out my tongue and his quirk of a smile turns into a full, gorgeous laugh. And for less than a second his gaze is open with a look so familiar and beautiful.

So . . . sacrificial.

I pause.

It's the same look he gave before he let me go that day at the Keep.

I frown as my caged chest squeezes my lungs that are crammed in there too small, too tight, and suddenly his expression is replaced with a flash of hunger—of wildness—and I instantly recognize that too. It's the desire to escape this place and these people and to inhale the open air, perhaps back at Adora's where there was more space and less obligation.

My mouth sours with how badly I want it, too, right now, and my desire must show because for a moment his gaze is all mine, sparking with suggestions and rebellion as that half smile he owns and works so well curves the full of his lips.

Bleeding oaf. My chuckle is loud enough that someone nearby slips an arm out as if to steady me—and effectively breaks the magic.

Eogan glances at him, then turns back to his conversation with the mob surrounding him.

For one hour.

Two hours.

Two hours and ten minutes go by and I am as dead on my feet as Sedric and Eogan look to be.

Sedric has spent the whole of the time ushering me from the balcony to the floor level and back again as we meet and greet and reassure the High Court members that yes, we believe this is our best course, and no, there are no other options, and yes, we're convinced we'll come out victorious.

And through it all I've watched Eogan.

Until Sedric finally seems satisfied with the work we've done and waves Rolf over to replace us. "If you don't mind," he says to the courtiers we've been speaking to, "I believe Rolf can answer the last of your queries. I need to speak with Nym."

I perk up at that. *Why?*

He beckons me to the side at the top of the balcony staircase where we're fully exposed to prying eyes, yet the space is open enough to speak privately.

"Can you still stand?"

"Are you asking honestly or figuratively? Because no to both."

He snickers. "Well, for the record, no one would've been able to tell—your speech tonight was smooth and your mingling with the crowd flawless." His grin is gracious. "Thank you for being here tonight."

"Of course." I look past him for Eogan.

Sedric starts to speak, then stops, and when I glance over, his brow is furrowed as if he's flustered. I wait.

He turns to scan the room, and something in his gaze says more than I want to hear. I can sense it, and it cowers my spine.

He says the words anyway. "It's as if you were made for this. You were made for *them*."

An internal shiver rolls down to skewer my gut.

I shake my head.

"I'm aware it's rightfully yours," he continues. "My position. Faelen and our people. It belonged to your ancestors."

He's wrong. I wasn't made for this. I was made for *them*, maybe. But not in the way he's thinking. *I was never meant to survive.* I study the fancy crowd in the fancy suffocating room and try not to snort. "Our people belong to themselves."

"You know what I mean."

"Yes, I do, and I know what Queen Laiha's letter apparently told you, but I don't want it, Your Majesty. So you have nothing to worry about."

"I wasn't worried; I was thinking. You've never had the option until now, but if we survive this war, you may find you feel quite differently." His voice softens, then firms as if he's making a decision. "I want you to know . . . I'd offer my support to assist you or join you in whatever way you need."

This time I do snort. "You'd give up your people so easily?"

"Not give them up. I'd help them. I'd help *you*. You could lead them in a way I might never be able to."

"I would say the same about you—except more so. The people need you, Your Majesty. Not a girl who has no experience, not to mention any interest, in ruling a country. Or even in *helping* to rule it."

He nods but his expression stays unperturbed. "Just consider that I am open to it. I'm not one to stand in the way of lineage." Then suddenly he's all smiles and looking up as Eogan and Kenan are walking toward us. "Ah, Your Highness, you survived—and quite well, I might add, by the compliments I heard from my subjects."

Eogan keeps his gaze on Sedric, but I can feel his emotions radiating all over me. That fear from earlier. Desire. Frustration. What is he so nervous about?

"I pray we have accomplished our purpose here this evening," he says.

Sedric steps toward Eogan and puts his arm out to show solidarity and gratitude and everything else politicians are so good at displaying. "Before you leave, I have a few more . . ."

Kenan tugs my arm to pull me aside. "May I speak with you a moment? I was wondering if I might ask a favor."

I turn from Eogan to study the large guard who looks so much like Kel. "I'm assuming you'd like me to keep your son," I say to relieve him of wasting his breath. When his eyes flicker surprise, I smile. "I can't promise he'll be completely safe with me."

"He'll be safer than with Eogan or me—and safer than if left here at the Castle."

Good point. I glance around, and as if in rebellion, my eyes land back on Eogan who's still speaking with Sedric. "Of course he can stay with me."

Kenan tips his head. "I'll speak with the boy tonight, then, and send him to you first thing on the morrow." He hesitates, then places a fist over his heart. "My thanks."

I nod as he steps away to go put a word in Eogan's ear, and a moment later it's apparent Eogan agrees with whatever Kenan's said without stopping his conversation with Sedric.

"You're collecting quite a band of misfits." Tannin's voice resonates behind me. He grins. "How will you control them while on the road?"

"Like this." I quickly touch two fingers to his sleeve, allowing a small shock of static from the air to jolt him.

He yanks his arm away. "Teeth of a—"

I let out a real laugh, and Eogan glances over at the sound. It hits me that I can't recall the last time I heard such warmth coming from my mouth. Probably at some point with Kel. But before that . . .

I allow the enjoyment of it to settle over me and let it loosen my muscles around my bones and lungs and heart. To ease the ache and frustration of the past two days.

When I look again, Eogan still has his head tipped my way, watching me, his expression amused and curious, until King Sedric says something and he's pulled back to their conversation.

"I may not approve of you going to his rooms"—Tannin casually waves a hand in Eogan's direction—"but I can see you might be good for each other."

My amusement catches in my mouth.

"My wife says opposites keep the attraction alive and the behaviors in balance. And in your case . . ."

"In my case?"

He shakes his head and smiles kindly.

If I'd begun frowning at him before, I'm quite certain I'm flat out scowling now. "Are you sure you're not Luminescent?"

Except . . . everything in me wishes he was. I look around for Mel or Mia. Would it be awful to ask them to read Eogan for me—to tell me what he's thinking and what his future might hold? And why he keeps distancing himself?

Tannin's grin splits his face, prompting heat like a blasted lightning bolt to ignite beneath my skin and burn through my cheekbones until I'm sure he's got more answer than he bargained for. He merely chuckles again, and I excuse myself to gain composure before strolling back over to Eogan, who's thankfully focused on Sedric.

"Should be no more than six days at the most," Eogan says. "Although I'm hoping for less if the wind currents hold."

"Our prayers will go with you." Sedric places his hand on Eogan's shoulder and tips his head in respect. In return Eogan thumps a fist over his own heart in the Bron offering of kinship.

Then they release each other and turn my way.

"Ah, Nym. I have a final few people I'd appreciate you speaking with if you don't mind." Sedric twitches a hand toward a group of old geezers I recognize from the War Room.

"In that case." Eogan nods politely to both of us. "Your Highness. Nym. I fear I must retire in order to get an early start tomorrow. So I will bid good night and good-bye to you both at this time." He turns to move off.

Pardon? "Your Majesty, I, too, must beg off for the evening. I fear I'm overly tired and won't be much help in carrying functional conversation." Without awaiting his permission, I stride after the beautiful green-eyed man who is a daft oaf. "Eogan, wait."

He stops. Turns. "Did I forget something?"

Like hulls you did. You forgot about a hundred things. Not the least of which is a decent good-bye. "I was just hoping to connect with you before you disappear."

He peers around. "I have a few minutes, but then I must make final preparations for the ships." He touches his fingers to my arm and leads us to a shallow alcove along the wall where it's a bit less noisy and a lot more private. "What did you have in mind?"

Hit you. Kiss you. Yell at you. Tell you I'm mad and confused and terrified you're flying to your death and this time I won't be there to save you.

"Nym?"

I shut my mouth and clear my throat. "I just . . . I wanted to know how you thought this evening went."

"I believe it went exactly as King Sedric hoped. Now we move on to carry it out and pray we all survive." He stares straight at me.

"And how did . . . I do—with my speech?" *Good grief, that's the best you can do? Do not blush do not blush do not blush at such a stupid thing to ask.*

He rubs a hand over the back of his neck while eyeing me. "Frankly, you performed perfectly. Not to mention you . . ." He stalls and chews his lip before eyeing my dress.

"Look ready to help lead us into war?"

"Something like that."

I frown. "What does that mean?"

He runs his eyes back up to my bodice, my neck, my mouth. "It means you appear ready for war in more ways than one." He glances around and smirks. "Between that dress and your speech, I'll wager you just declared war on half the men's hearts in this room."

I shrug like nervous butterflies are kicking at my chest bones. "King Sedric picked it out."

"I can see why."

I grimace. "He's not in love with me, if that's what your tone's implying."

"I know."

My stomach feels uneasy. Then why is Eogan acting odd?

"Sedric mentioned my rightful place as heir to Faelen's throne," I say after an elongated pause. "I told him I don't want the job."

"Don't you?"

I glare. "You know me better than that."

"I'm not saying you're begging for it. I'm simply saying that seeing as it is your heritage, perhaps it's meant to be, that's all."

I stare at him.

"You could do a lot for your people," he says quietly.

I stall and try to inhale the air that just left my lungs. *What is wrong with him?* I study his eyes in hopes he'll start making one lick of sense.

He merely gives that stupid, gorgeous, polite smile.

I scoff and look away.

He leans in. So close I can feel the heat from his body and the sweet clarity of his breath across my heavily exposed skin as he drifts his gaze over mine before it slides to my lips. And I'm suddenly back in his room with him, trying not to imagine him with his exposed broad chest and wearing only that blasted bath towel.

He opens his mouth. "Sometimes we give up what we want for the greater good."

I'm going to slap him. *Creator, help me. I'm going to slam the flat of my hand across his jaw because he is a bleeding bolcrane.* I bend in until the space between us is a mere breath. "Are you talking about for me or for you? Because I doubt I need to remind you I've given up *everything* for these people's good."

And I may give up more before this is all over.

I blink but don't drop my glare.

"And yet you're so anxious to run off and give up more. A bit ironic, don't you think, considering your anger at me for going to ensure your sacrifice for my people hasn't been for nothing?"

My stomach tightens. "What do you mean—anxious to give up more?"

He lifts a hand to a lock of my hair and turns it in the light, staring at it. "Going after Princess Rasha, of course."

I narrow my gaze. How'd he know?

He utters a dry chuckle. "Because as I said before, I know you. And I know you can't leave well enough alone. It's not enough you're helping put together Faelen's defense. You have to rescue your friends in the midst of it." He drops my hair strand and stares straight at me. "And I'm asking you not to."

I refuse to dignify that with a reply.

He twists his lips and nods. "Exactly." Then glances away again. "You should know I've given Tannin a map to the village where I last saw the two Uathúils living in the northern part of Litchfell Forest. If you happen up that way in your rounding up of armed forces, convince them this is a worthy fight."

I raise a brow. I recall him saying something about them amid all the noisy conversation in the War Room yesterday. "What kind of Uathúils?"

"One's a Mortisfaire, actually. Like Lady Isobel, though far less powerful. The other is a Terrene."

"Will they listen to me?"

"They will if you show them what you can do. Whether they opt to join after that, I don't know, but it's worth a try." His gaze falls to my lips again, and a second later he leans away and straightens. "And I'd strongly request you leave Princess Rasha until I return if—"

"If you thought I'd listen."

He snorts and looks away. When he peers back over at me, it's with his official kingly expression I'm just now deciding I officially hate. "Be safe while I'm gone, Nymia." Then dips his head and starts to walk away.

"Why is it safer, Eogan?"

He stalls.

"Earlier in your room. You said going to Bron was safer. What did you mean?"

The muscles in the back of his neck and shoulders tighten.

One second, ten seconds, twenty seconds . . .

He turns and his eyes are shadowed. Flecked with doubt.

"I was simply drawing a conclusion. That's all."

"About what?"

He swallows and his jaw clenches, mimicking the uneasiness behind his gaze. Then sighs. "About the fact that Draewulf was in my body. He left it, but that doesn't mean a part of him isn't still there."

He thinks a part of Draewulf could still be in him—could still have some control over him?

"It would make sense that if Draewulf now owns some of my blood, I, too, now own some of his."

"You're not Draewulf."

"No. But that doesn't mean I might not have a few of his tendencies."

"Do you?" I swear I feel my expression turn horrified.

"Not as far as I know, but . . ." He splays his hands. "I'm unwilling to inflict that on you or anyone else here. Good-bye for now, Nym." And for what seems like the hundredth time he turns his back to stride away.

My mouth drops open. *That's it?* The urge to grab his smoothly shaven cheek that smells like pine and honey and earth surges. Instead, I grab his arm and, without thinking, lean up and press my open lips to his. Allowing him to feel the frustration and refusal to believe what he just said burn through my own heated skin.

He stiffens beneath my fingers, beneath the caress of my lips, enough that I release him half an inch. And whisper against his mouth, "You told me once that if I was unsafe, you would come back from the grave and haunt me, Eogan. Well, I'm going to do the same. I know I don't own you, nor do I have any claim upon your life. But I *do* know you could never be Draewulf. And if you so much as get yourself injured while you're gone, I will come there and make you *wish* he'd killed you."

I slide my hand up to his neck, feeling over the top of Draewulf's scar there—over the wound that's healed and yet still so fresh in my soul. And touch my lips to his again in a final good-bye. His stiffness softens and his mouth opens as he puts his hands on my waist—and in that moment I can feel it.

His desire. His aching. His need for love and touch that hasn't faded in the least.

It's promptly followed by a different feeling—one just as familiar but no less aggravating.

I feel him willing me his calm. As if he could tame me—tame this moment—in which he is suddenly pulling away from me.

I blink. "If you don't want to kiss me, that's fine," I growl. "But don't you dare use your ability to try to steal my emotions."

His gaze cracks for one millionth of a second. But in that emerald crevice is the same hunger in him that is filleting the inside of me. Then his black lashes come down like a curtain, and before I can ask, he turns. "I didn't intend to anger you."

And suddenly Tannin is there, tugging on my arm, and Eogan is striding away.

CHAPTER 23

DAWN STRETCHES HER FINGERS THROUGH THE curtains to warm my chilly skin and the pillow my cheek is plastered to. I blink against the glare but promptly become aware of the droning noise overhead. The sound elicits a sensation of my body floating in the sky.

I frown and sit up. *Am I . . . ?*

No. My room is all stone and tapestry and wood—no metal or heated balloon. And the airship's humming is distant. In fact, there are two of them, if I'm not mistaken.

Litches.

Jumping from my quilts, I nearly tumble Kel from where he's sleeping on the bed's end again. He must've slipped in a few hours ago. I rush to peer out the window in time to see the expanded cocoon-shaped balloons of both airships bobbing up from the Northern Courtyard.

I grab my night cover and hurry to yank open the door—and run into the maid.

"Miss, I was just—"

"Have they loaded?"

"Yes, miss. That's why I'm here. I—"

I'm already stepping past her.

"I know you asked to be woken sooner, but the Bron king said—"

I don't catch the rest of her words as I race barefoot round the corner hallway to a flight of stairs and on through the two corridors that have become far too familiar the past two days. "Excuse me, gentlemen," I mutter when I reach the door leading out to the courtyard, then shove past the stationed guards who're promptly pushing it open for me.

I'm just in time to see one ship in the air and the second ascending in front of me.

No.

My throat goes dry. I move to the courtyard's center and look up, hoping for a glimpse of Eogan, or Kenan, or anyone other than the soldiers going about their duties of prepping the ship for higher altitude. The few men who are peering over the side to ensure they're staying clear of the Castle see me, because one salutes with a fist to his chest while the other eyes me warily.

I bite my lip and keep staring.

It's no use, though. Eogan's green eyes and onyx face don't appear, and after a moment I wave back at the soldiers. I keep my arm up while standing there with my night cover barely tugged around me and my hair flapping as all get-out in the breeze, until the ship is so high I can no longer see anything but the base of its glistening silver hull edged by the giant balloon billowing above it.

You'd better come back to me, Eogan.

"Nym?"

I don't look at Rolf. Just shake my head and stride by him to return to my room, forcing down the fear welling up with ridiculous intensity. *What is my problem? Why am I suddenly so scared? And of what?*

Of losing Eogan, my mind says. *Of maybe already having lost him.*

I climb the stairs and tell my soul to shut the hulls up. *Time to go raise an army and rescue Rasha, Nym.*

Tannin is waiting by my door when I arrive, and he's a welcome relief from my thoughts. "I believe the horses are ready and the delegation packed. All except your mare, that is."

My mare? I smile in spite of my mood. "Haven?"

He nods. "She won't let anyone touch her and the men are—"

"It's fine, I'll do it. Give me ten minutes." I knock three quick times before striding into the room where Kel is now awake and eating a breakfast the maid brought.

The servant girl grins. "There's some for you there too, miss. And I packed up a satchel of your leathers you mentioned you wanted along with a brush and some—"she glances at Kel before lowering her voice—"lady necessities."

"Thank you."

"Now, what about this dress? Does it need washing?" She holds up the green gown from last night.

"No need to clean it. I'm sure it's perfectly fine."

"No wine stains or food from what I can see," she murmurs more to herself as she inspects it.

"Or slobber stains," Kel mumbles around his porridge. "Might want to inspect it for those."

He wrinkles his nose. "Just in case she was kissing a king last night."

No matter how many weeks I've known Eogan, my skin still sets off like a fire. I frown at Kel. "Very funny. Finish your food."

"It's not funny, it's disgusting and—" He glances at the maid as if suddenly remembering she's there. And shuts his mouth.

"I'm sure whatever you did in it you were beautiful, miss," the maid breaks in as if to ease the awkwardness.

"You think?" I turn to size her up. She's about my height and weight. "In that case it's yours."

"The dress?"

"And any others in the armoire you fancy. I've no need of them and I'm sure you'll look lovely."

"Oh, miss, I couldn't."

"Yes, you can and will. I won't need them where I'm travelling to, nor will I need them when I return to the battlefield." *Nor maybe even after.*

"That's kind of you, m'lady, but I couldn't. King Sedric, he—"

"He has no use for them either, and if anyone asks, you can tell them I said as much. We're about to go to war, not a party. I imagine they'll fetch you a good price if you don't want to keep them all."

Her nod is hesitant. "Two of those would bring in more draughts than I've ever seen."

"Good. Then it's decided. So, did the boy come with luggage as well?" I ask, indicating Kel to keep her from going on about it.

"He did, miss. I've already sent both bags down with Tannin."

"Thank you." I turn to Kel. "Are you ready?"

He shoves a bite of honeyed bread in his mouth, then follows it up with a gulp of milk. "Nym, have you tasted this stuff? It's bloody unbeliev—"

"I imagine it is, but watch your language."

He snorts. "You swear all the time. So does my father and both kings." He hops off the chair to shove his boots on.

"Yes, but your father and both kings are not age seven and charged to my care."

He grins and grabs his cloak as I step behind the dressing curtain to change into my own blue leathers and black cloak. Their familiar softness and fit feel so much like home I'm near melting as, for a moment, that old desire to go back to Adora's, when everything was wrong and yet so much more right than it is now, overtakes me. When my position was set along with everyone else's.

Even if the woman was a mental crackpot.

Leathers on and hair braided, I emerge from the curtain and nod to the maid before beckoning Kel to follow me to the hallway where Tannin greets us. He leads us through the Castle corridors and past the beautifully carved gold-plate wood doors, then down into the lower quarters of the Eastern Wing. Outside of which sit the stables.

"The far one." Tannin points to the end of the row of stalls where the stable master is standing, hands on hips. Before I can issue a greeting to the man, a loud whinny erupts from inside the booth.

She smells me.

I smile. She also smells the meat I grabbed off the morning's breakfast tray.

With Kel wide-eyed and trailing behind, I scamper down to the stable master and Haven.

"She's all yours." He waves his hand at the man-eating horse that is at least five hands taller than even the largest purebred mare. "Let me know if you need anything."

I run my gaze over my beautiful lady. Her black, glossy coat and mane and that foaming mouth that says she was hoping for a bit of the older man's face to chew on. "How's my girl?" I whisper, to which she smiles wickedly in return. She snorts and nudges her nose toward me, sniffing me out as well as searching for the meat I've brought. I set it on the stall ledge and it's gone before I've hardly pulled my hand away.

"What the—? It eats meat?" Kel moves closer, his expression saying this is by far the most fascinating thing in the whole Hidden Lands.

I shove a hand out to ward him back. "She'll just as easily eat *you* if you get close enough. She doesn't understand the difference between strangers and food."

His round eyes gaze up at mine. "I *want* one."

"Um, no."

"Ah, c'mon. There's enough. Look, there're three more."

"Absolutely not."

He purses his lips and points to the other stalls housing a number of the other giant meat-eating warhorses from Adora's barn. Except those have muzzles on their mouths. Poor beasts. I wonder . . . I peer closer to find two of the beasts are familiar. Very familiar.

One is Eogan's.

The other was Colin's.

My chest swells with a wave of grief far too fresh, too raw, that about cracks me in half. As if the fissure Colin carved with his name on my heart can sense the weight of his spirit here. His memory.

"C'mon, Nym."

I shake it off and glare at Kel before looking back at Haven. "It would take too long to train you. Now move back while I step in to brush her down," I say with thick emotion.

Despite his grunt of annoyance, the boy obeys but shuffles back as close as possible once I'm in the stall. I allow Haven to inhale my scent proper-like in the way she prefers, while keeping a metal rope between her mouth and my hand, just in case.

She nickers and bucks and pushes her nose into my hand anyway.

I've finished brushing her down, and the stable master has helped me saddle her—something I can't do with my one hand curled in the way it is—and led her to the courtyard when ten Faelen guards emerge in full armor. Behind them strides Lord Myles, the Luminescent Mia, and the Cashlin guard. Tannin goes to help Kel onto a horse, a smallish mare to the boy's enormous disappointment, while I soothe Haven with tones and words Eogan used to use on her.

"Well, well, welllll. If thisss isn't a party." Myles looks around, and I note the sunken-in eyes and sag of his skin. Has he slept since we've been here? "Someone please tell me you brought ale," he mutters.

"Who thought it'd be a good idea to bring him along?" demands one of the guards.

"I did," I say without glancing up.

"With what he can do? He'll be a danger and a liability!"

I turn. "And if we leave him?"

The guard's face purses.

"Exactly."

"Besidesss, my good chap. Who wants a shot at trying to ssstop me from coming?"

My gaze drops to his wrists as he mounts a gray-speckled horse. They're untied. "I assure you," I say loud enough for both Myles and the guard to hear, "if he *does* endanger us, Mia and I will slit his throat."

Myles laughs, then winks at the guard. "Don't let her fool you, mate. She rather enjoys a good round of letting the mentally unssstable run around with her."

Despite my discomfort at his free state, I bite back a laugh. "In that case, why don't you ride beside me?"

Saluting the guards with mock respect, Myles nudges his horse to move forward as the rest fall in line and we move out.

The mist is still wrapping her tendril blanket across the High Court streets and over the hills and green grasslands farther out as we descend. I turn for one last look at the Castle and scan the sky for the airships, but of course they're long gone. Then I peer over toward the northern border—where the Elisedd channel sits with that third airship . . .

Clenching my jaw, I set my gaze onto Faelen's interior valley, to the main road we'll be travelling along and the people we're sup-posed to convince that their week of relief was merely a pause, and now they're needed for a bigger war with higher stakes. That they are no longer fighting just for their freedom, but for their very lives.

Eight days to go . . .

A rumble of thunder growls overhead, bringing the horses to nicker and shuffle their hooves. Unfortunately for them, it draws Haven's interest. She bares her teeth and snarls, then snaps for their haunches.

"Leave them alone." I pat her neck and prod her ahead. "You can hunt soon enough."

Except she's sensing it too—the tension in the air, of expec-tancy not yet turned to fear. It ripples down my skin and is met by another crackle across the sky.

I inhale and hope it stays that way.

When we reach the main cobblestone road at the base of the High Court's hill and gates, I pull Haven forward and allow her to take full lead. A few minutes into the ride, Kel strikes up his chatter, much to the early-morning annoyance of just about everyone by the sound of their muttered replies and groans, until Tannin joins in and begins answering. I grin as Kel drills him on all aspects of Faelen life and military and, eventually, on what types of animals he's seeing dotting the flatland the farther we get into the Valley.

I've been listening in on their conversation a good while when the odd awareness dawns. I can't recall seeing any animals in Bron. Do they not have them? Not only that, but from the view from the airship, I don't even know how they'd survive—or what they'd sur-vive on. Aside from their river, the place is as barren as a desert.

It's not long before the Cashlins add their own questions too and the stories begin flowing—of Bron, of Faelen, and of Cashlin.

They float from sea life to solstice traditions to food types to burying of the dead.

I twist backward to Mia. "Those chess pieces in the throne room—are they actual people in them?"

"Cashlin's most important ancestors—long dead now, but queens and kings as well as those whose abilities were exceedingly powerful." She encourages her horse closer to Haven until she turns with a bit too much interest and Mia's mare wisely thinks better of it.

"It's our biggest honor to be entombed in such a way," the male guard adds. "One day Queen Laiha will join them. As will Princess Rasha."

I raise a brow and turn back to the road, biting my tongue from mentioning that hopefully the queen hasn't *already* joined them. The thought makes me queasy. And anxious to get to Rasha.

"Let's hurry," I call to the group.

It's not long before we reach the first village—a small township we pass through without stopping. It smells of earthy peasant life and slaves and soil, as well as hope and hunger and cooling fires. I look in the faces of those who've assembled to watch us. Men, boys, women.

"Hoping for a glimpse of the Elemental who sssaved them."

"Clearly they've not been informed I didn't. At least not all the way."

"Oh, they have. King Sedric sent runners out yesterday to ssspread the word. They're just trusting you'll do it for real this time."

I look away from the expectant faces as small children watch from behind their mums' skirts and bigger boys run behind us.

"They'll be wanting a token from you, miss," Tannin says in a low voice.

I peer around for my satchel even as I know I have nothing to give, but five seconds later Tannin pulls a few draughts from his own to drop on the ground with a clink that sends the boys hooting and hollering. When he glances up, he merely smiles, as do the soldiers closest us.

"Thank you," I tell him. And I mean it more than I can say.

"How long until the first stop on this blasted trip?" Myles asks.

I snort. "Need some ale?"

"My dear, you know me so well."

I glance back to tell him, "Like hulls I do," when it dawns on me he may, in fact, need a sip of ale. He looks like litches. And he's scratching his arms surreptitiously.

He wags a brow at me and suddenly the air around him ripples, then displays an image of us all in Bron—in the War Room watching the boy soldier behead the man. Except for whatever reason the man looks like Myles.

Behind me, Kel gasps.

"Stick to reality, Myles," I snap.

The image fades, but he leans forward. "For now, perhaps. But imagine what I can do next time we see Draewulf."

"If you survive that long."

He frowns. "Just because Rasha's mum believes my . . . enhancements are fatal doesn't make it fact. Ask yourself, why would she want us to think such a thing, hmm?" He flickers another image in my face—the same one as always of me and him standing over Draewulf's dead body with the entire Hidden Lands at our feet. "Perhapsss it's the same reason she tried to wait out this war—her own survival."

"Not this time." I ignore him and pull out the map made in the council chambers in the dark hours yesterday morning. "We'll stop for rest and food in a bit, then keep on to our first destination."

Six places are marked, curving in a circular pattern around

Faelen, all central to each territory so the surrounding villages can attend. These would be the towns the repulsive tax-gatherers and pontiffs go to when reading off new proclamations or High Court decisions that usually have little to do with the peasants aside from costing them more—either in money or manpower for the war. I scowl. It will be a miracle if we can pull this off and convince them to fight again for the same masters who keep them underprivileged.

I peer at the names to see if I recognize any of them only to realize—

You've got to be jesting me.

I look again in hopes I'm wrong—that I read it wrong, that the dust and warmth from the road are getting to me. But the town's name is still there in all its simplicity and horror and curving hand-written strokes that make my fingers and throat clammy. Why was I not told this was our first stop?

I hold back a shudder and straighten as Haven tenses beneath me. And try not to think about what awaits us there.

Because it's the town of my ninth owner.

CHAPTER 24

THE VILLAGE IS JUST AS COLORFUL AND CHAOTIC looking in the evening light as I remember it. Yellow and green flags atop high poles wave in the breeze at the entry gate, and a rough fence still runs random lines down the unkempt streets and yards—attempting to keep out the goats and hens and unwelcome busybodies, but never quite succeeding. Patches of green grass and wildflowers interrupt the tan earth and cracked mud puddles where our horses' hooves tread.

I firm my jaw and keep my gaze away from the second house on the left with the run-down barn with the fields and sheep behind it. *Don't look, don't think, don't care.*

Just do what you have to and get out of here.

A shadow falls anyway across the dwelling as a cloud moves in front of the dying sun, and Myles glances over at me. "I believe your mood is showing again."

Blast the daft Elemental blood—even my emotions can't enjoy a bit of privacy.

I scowl at him and press on, only to catch Mia's tender gaze. Her eyes are glowing red around the pupils and I swear she's sensing the reason for my discomfort. I look away.

We've gone only a short number of paces when a low rumble of voices and hollers greets our ears. Five of the ten guards in our company automatically move to the front of us and draw their swords.

"Not sure that's going to help," I say to Tannin, with a nod to the guards' lifted blades.

"Is this type of greeting normal?" Gilford, the Cashlin guard, veers his mare too near to Haven, who promptly feigns interest in something his direction until I yank her back in line. She needs to eat.

"They're not upset. They're cheering." Mia's eyes glow even brighter as she points toward the town's center where the people are coming into view. From the number amassed there, it seems the entire community has come out to watch us.

I study them through the gathering dim. She's right. They're waving tree branches and flowers, and as we draw nearer, the words shouted make it clear they're embracing me as one of them, as having come *from* them, on my way to power and glory.

Apparently they remember I lived here.

I sniff and choke back a caustic laugh. How quickly some things change.

"Will we sleep here?" Kel is eyeing the run-down buildings that are so strangely different from his home of metal walls and warm baths in Bron.

"No," Tannin answers. "We'll speak to them in their common house and then be on our way. We can make camp halfway between here and the next stop on the map—that way we don't lose too many days."

"Or our livesss, depending how this goes," Myles says beneath his breath.

By the time we arrive at the town's center, the streets have become thick with bodies and noise and music. Even in the cool evening air, I'm starting to feel clammy from the heat they're giving off in the somewhat confined space. The guards keep pressing the people back with their horses, shouting over the crowd to give us room.

"You can come see the Elemental at the common house," they shout.

Such assurances don't stop them from trying to get by Tannin and the other guards to touch me, though. *"A magical token,"* Rasha had once joked. If only she could see how ridiculously serious some seem to be taking that now.

It makes my gut squirm.

The soldiers lead us to the back of the common house that is far too familiar to be comfortable. I keep my features straight and firm as we dismount and tie up our horses, posting Haven at a good distance from the others using the metal ropes Eogan made so many weeks ago. I pull out a squirrel she caught during our early-afternoon break and feed it to her, then with a pat on her flank command her to behave before following the others in through the common's back entrance.

The sour scent of ale and sweet herbed cakes leaks from the wall boards and floor and every inch of this place. I inhale and promptly clench my teeth when the song of a bard hits me. He's regaling the crowd with a tune about the origins of the bolcranes of Litchfell Forest and how some believe they used to be Elementals. Until their hearts got twisted with greed.

Lovely.

"Might as well get thisss over with," Myles says.

Kel looks at him. "Do you not like this place?"

"Not everything here is sssafe," he says softly to the boy.

I ruffle Kel's short black hair. "Stay near me, all right?"

He nods but peers around Myles and Tannin as the guards push open the back room's separation door.

A waft of musical notes and ale accosts us head-on as we enter the main space, and with it come memories—the part of my childhood I lost here, of the men I killed here, of the auction stand closer to the High Court where another bard was singing a different song. And of the last time I visited a common house with Colin and Breck.

I swallow and step in.

The singing stops with a jolt. The patrons' voices stop. All movement stalls.

Before they erupt into a roar.

"The Elemental!"

"One of our own!"

"From our town!"

"Make her stand so we can see her!"

Good hulls, I think I'm going to be sick. I turn to Tannin and Myles, whose face is damp with sweat. "Let's do this quickly."

Before any of us can address the crowd, though, we're all pushed into chairs at a table where food and drink are forced in front of us in overflowing bowls and foaming mugs. Myles sets upon it as if he's never seen nourishment before, as does Kel—at least until I take his ale mug away and hand him water, at which he grumbles something about never having any fun.

The crowd presses against the table and against the guards who're standing at our backs. They watch and wait as some of us eat and others of us try to shrink in our chairs. A few minutes of attempting to be polite and Tannin finally nods toward me and Myles, then rises to stand on his chair since the central counter is too far to reach.

"Good ladies and gents of this town, I implore you to quiet yourselves so we may speak with you on behalf of our favorable King Sedric."

He pauses and waits for the room to settle, which it does, although most people remain standing.

"We are here to share with you news only recently discovered of the dire need our great Faelen kingdom is in."

"Your runners told us," a voice from the back of the room shouts. "Draewulf's not dead!"

"And why should that concern us?" another yells. "We've paid our dues to war and he ain't done us harm in a hundred years!"

"Allow me to explain," Tannin says. Except he doesn't get more than five sentences into the account when the crowd boos so loud his voice is drowned out. He looks over at me.

"Clearly they need a delegate who holdsss authority up there," Myles slurs beside me. "Pardon." He stands, drags his chair near Tannin, and climbs onto it.

I raise a brow.

His silver tooth flashes in the candlelight, reminding me of the first time I ever saw him, in a place much like this, as he puts up his hands and waits for the noise to die once again.

"I asssume you know who I am. I'm Faelen's Lord Protectorate Mylesss, and cousin to King Sedric." He waves a hand around. "And *I* am here to inform you of *exxxactly* what is headed our way."

There's rustling and coughing, but the audience remains mostly still, listening with suspicion etched across their expressions.

"We all know of the existence of Draewulf. You've heard of his manipulation and his attack at the Keep two weeksss ago. Even better"—he points a finger at me, and for a second I think he might fall off the chair—"you've heard of how our own Elemental and the Bron king helped to defeat him."

"So is he dead or ain't he?" an old man shouts, but directs the question to me rather than Myles.

I shake my head.

"He'sss not. He survived by ssshape-shifting into another—and then hijacked Bron's airships and much of their kingdom. And now he'sss coming back soon with an army of *undead*."

Good grief. The way he says *undead* is so loud and dramatic, the audience responds with a gasp. Though I doubt it was as much Myles's intention as the dark power attacking his veins. He's scratching his arm and pulling the cravat away from his neck, exposing skin that is looking disturbingly splotchy and swollen.

Litches.

After a moment a sunburned-faced woman says, "Well, where's the Bron king been? He been working with the beast?"

"He's been working with usss, you fools. Now let me finish."

"Boooo!" A shout goes up, and within moments they all get in on it. Booing and hissing.

The air snaps and wavers out from where Myles is standing, and the next moment an image of Draewulf wreaking havoc upon the Tullan king appears. I watch as the king's body is torn open by the monster's wolfish figure.

Cries break out as Myles snarls, "This is what he'll do to every one of you if you refuse to join with us."

The image disappears as the murmurings continue, but it's not until food begins to fly that Myles apparently realizes they're not nearly as impressed with his ability as they should be. I snicker as an apple core hits his shirt, and the look on his face indicates he's never been so insulted or shocked. He glances at me and steps off the chair.

"Maybe you can talk sense into these peasantsss," Myles growls as I step by him to claim his spot on the chair.

I catch my breath.

There are a lot of them crammed in here. Local peasants— some of whom I recognize although they're quite a few years older,

209

a couple of protectorates and town watchmen—even some slaves are here, seated in the back. A few of their faces unnervingly familiar. I force down my nausea.

Don't think about them, just get on with this.

"Lord Myles is right." I firm my voice before raising it to reach the whole room. "Bron's King Eogan has brought me and Lord Myles back here to warn King Sedric. He's now flying back to Bron to loosen the hold Draewulf's wraith army has over his capital. If he succeeds, he'll return in time to help mount our defense before Draewulf descends."

"And if he's unable to? What if he's killed? We're to fight alone against an army that has taken Bron, Tulla, and Cashlin?"

"We'll be demolished!" another voice from the back says.

"No, Nym can defeat him!" another yells.

"Where's Draewulf now?"

I glance at Mia and her guard. "He's currently still destroying Tulla and Cashlin."

"Is that why you've got two Cashlins with you?"

"We have three actually, and they've come to lend assistance. They have more to lose at this moment than any of us. Their princess is currently in Draewulf's possession."

"Princess Rasha?" A tone of concern ripples through the crowd as they say her name. "She was kind when she came through here."

"I liked her."

"She gave out coins."

"Why are you telling us all this, m'lady?" a youngish man with three empty pint glasses in front of him asks. His dark hair reminds me of Myles's. "What do you want with *us*?"

"I'm here to ask you to join in the fight."

Wait for it . . .

And just like that the room falls silent.

I reach out a hand and style my tone in a way I hope they'll hear as honoring. It's the same one Eogan and Sedric have used more times than I can count in the past two days. "My friends, I know you've given much—more than was fair—and I know you're weary. So am I. But join us in this one last stand before he robs what is—"

There's a low creaking sound as the common-house door in the back of the room opens. How I hear it, I don't know, but my voice cuts off at the man abruptly filling the doorway.

Owner number nine.

His eyes are the first thing I see. Cold. Hateful. Instantly locked on to mine in disgust. I'm glad I didn't eat anything when they served us because it'd be coming back up.

My stomach heaves anyway and I can't breathe. I don't want to be here. Seeing the face of the beast who allowed his sons to hurt me, then punished me when my curse reared its head and tore them limb from limb . . . *I don't know how to do this.*

"What of the High Court officials?" a woman yells.

I blink and look away from the man I hate with everything in me.

"Them prissies in their fancy outfits having fancy parties," the woman continues. "We just got our husbands back and you want us to send them out again—and for what? So those upper classers can keep their pretty faces and lifestyles? No thanks. You can fight for Faelen—and I'll thank you for it. But I won't be stickin' my sons' and husband's necks out no more for anyone."

A round of cheers goes up as metal mugs thunk down on wood. "Hear, hear!"

"What she said!"

"They'll be fighting too," I say, finding my voice. "Every last one of the upper classes."

The crowd's noise dulls. "What'd she say?"

"They'll fight too?"

A woman spits on the ground in front of me. "Sorry, sweetie, but we don't believe you."

"Even if we did, it's high time they fight for *us*!" an older man adds, drawing the rabid approval of the audience.

I laugh louder than necessary until the room quiets. "Have you seen them fight?" I nod at Myles. "No offense, but he is by far the best they've got. If you're counting on the upper bloods to save your skins, you've sorely misjudged them. As you say, they're more used to parties and placing you on battlefields than fighting those wars themselves."

The expressions on their faces freeze. My words have connected with their pride. They begin nodding.

"If you leave them to fight for Faelen, none of us stands a bleeding chance. But if you fight alongside them, you will give them your hope—and hopefully some of your skills."

A few chuckles break out.

"And in return I will give you every last piece of me and my skill. I will give you all I can." I look around at their suddenly serious faces. "But I don't want to do it alone, because Creator knows, I'm scared as hulls. So will you fight with me? And will you stand beside me while I extend every last energy of my life for *you*?"

The silence is tangible. Until an awkward roar of forced laughter erupts from the doorway and owner number nine steps forward. The crowd parts, and I'm already cringing at his voice. At the guttural sound of it—at the familiarity that makes the blood in my veins bristle. "You'll give us all you can, eh?"

The beefy man looks around the room and guffaws. "Last time I saw this wench, she wasn't willin' to give all she could and ended up tearin' my boys apart. All for havin' a bit of teasing." He curses, then spits. "I wouldn't follow you to the pit of hulls even to save my own sons."

From where I'm standing I watch all drinking and twitching hands stop. And as the room pauses, so does my heart. Suddenly the lights are flickering, except it's not the lights, it's my vision, and I am abruptly twelve years old again, sitting in that blasted run-down barn with my bones and muscles and body paralyzed while my eyes can't stop leaking tears.

The lights flicker again and I shut my eyes a moment. Then open them and harden my gaze at him and then at Myles. Not that Myles has any idea what this man's done, but something in the Lord Protectorate's darkening expression says he doesn't need to. He smirks with lips gone too white as he mouths, *Make him pay for it.* Because he knows what it is to be different, and to be unliked and broken beyond cultural acceptance.

My blast of thunder ricochets above the common house and abruptly the tension in the air is increasing, snapping. *Warning.*

A few faces look around, then a few more, until a hush of whispers floats about the room asking what's going on. "Is she angry?"

"Why is she calling a storm in?"

A hand touches my arm. Tannin.

I ignore him and narrow my gaze at my previous owner. "If you are too weak to fight in this war with a woman, then perhaps you should join your sons. As I recall, they waged their own perverted war upon half the women in this village before I put an end to it."

A gasp goes up. A snarl from the man, and for a second I think he'll lunge for me except—

One, two, three women step between us. They're followed by a few youngish men—the expressions on each of their faces saying my accusation hit home deeper than I realized.

"But what about us?" another man's voice rings out. It's one of the slaves seated toward the back. He stands. "Why should *we* help any of you?" He looks around at the room full of owners. "So that we can, what? Allow you *your* comfort? So we can continue with life as you know it—as *your* slaves? I say in that case, perhaps Draewulf would be a better master."

The other slaves in the room lend their voices in support while the peasants glare expressions of insult or anger at them.

"I agree! Don't fight for *them*." I rise to the balls of my feet and make my voice louder. "Fight for yourselves. Fight for your land. No matter what, you'll be freed. But fight for your future."

"What does that mean?" a young mother whispers in front of me.

"King Sedric has given me his solemn oath that equality is to be given to peasants and slaves alike!"

Lord Myles sputters nearby as the place breaks into pure energy.

"What?"

"Is this true?"

"You have my word," I call out over their heightening voices.

"Did you hear that?"

"The Elemental wouldn't lie!"

Cheering mixed with shouts and drunken excitement explodes in waves throughout the space. I scan their faces. Most are pleased, from what I can tell. The clapping and approval grow louder until it sounds like the thunder I create. It's shaking the floors and ceiling and the very air around me until a tugging on my arm alerts me Tannin is trying to get my attention.

"Miss, we need to get you out of here if we're going to leave tonight. Otherwise they'll want to detain you for their own worship."

Or to burn at the stake. I eye owner number nine. Then lift my hand to give him a single, delicate wave and a smile that says he and his kind will never touch me again. And if they do? I scan the room. The people here will tear him to pieces.

Without looking back, I step down from the chair and turn to be immediately enveloped by Tannin and the Faelen guards.

"You can't do that," Myles snaps as we duck out the rear door and head for the horses before anyone realizes we've gone. "That decision hasn't been fully approved—it hasn't even been signed by the High Council."

"I told the council that was my offer in the War Room, and Sedric agreed."

"He may have, but approving it and deciding when to announce it are for the Court to do, not you."

I turn on him. "Why? So they can go back on it as soon as the war's over?"

His face pales.

"Just as I thought."

"You ssshouldn't have done it."

I give a caustic laugh. "Which is exactly why I did."

CHAPTER 25

THE WORLD IS FADING IN AND OUT, BLENDING INTO ONE OF MYLES'S visions. The same he fed me a million times last week when we were training. Images of bodies and blood and the almost-end of the war.

I reach out with a final lightning cut to destroy the monster who would own this world—would own all of us. Except before I can reach him, he shreds through Eogan's skin, and I don't have time to scream or feel horrified because I am slitting both their throats at once and they are falling falling falling dead at Myles's and my feet because we have fought and succeeded. We have saved the Hidden Lands.

And just like always, we are standing over the multitudes of people and they are cheering and screaming for us, their saviors. I shudder at the sound of it even as Myles steps forward to embrace it, hand raised, with a black mist swirling around his wrist and fingers. *What the*—? As he does, a movement beneath him snags my attention, but I'm too slow as suddenly Draewulf reaches up and somehow he's still alive. I catch the flash of an eye opening, its black pupil glinting in the sun. "No—"

My warning comes too late. Draewulf's hand flashes up and with it a knife that slides across Myles's stomach, slitting open his gut.

Myles's face pales and a gurgling sound bubbles from his mouth as he jerks from Draewulf, then swerves his gaze to latch onto mine.

Oh hulls.

He stumbles as Draewulf pulls himself up to stand at his full wolf height and peers down at me. His face ripples, as if his body is groaning beneath its skin—hungry, strengthening. His real man's form coming to the surface as his wolf image fades away. I watch the slit in Draewulf's throat mend and heal and seal itself shut.

He's healing? How?

I look down at Eogan's shredded skin.

Too late. Draewulf reaches for me and his hand is more sinewy and stronger than it ever was in wolf form. He leans over me.

I whip down a flash of lightning, but it's feeble and pathetic against the mixture of Uathúil abilities he's absorbed.

And I am the last.

His jaw opens to snap down on my neck.

I shove an ice pick against his skull, but it bounces off as—

Crack.

I awake to pitch black, drenched in sweat and shaking. I can't stop shaking.

The night fire's gone out and the cold is seeping up through the ground, making the embers smoke.

Crack-crack.

I freeze.

The sound comes again, but rather than indicative of Draewulf breaking my neck, my hazy brain recognizes the noise as branches crunching underfoot. Someone's walking. *Thieves?*

Worse. Did my owner stalk us?

I roll over and squint through the dark to where Tannin and both Cashlins are sleeping around the fire and near them five guards lay snoring. So is Kel beside me. I look farther in search of the other five soldiers standing watch, only I don't see anything but the thin trunks of a nearly stripped fir tree and the starlit sky beyond.

I slip my knives from my ankle belts, then slide out from the bedding and onto my haunches. Voices are muttering now to the right of me, talking to each other while someone kicks things around. *What in—?*

Two men come into focus, creeping toward the fire, arguing about something. I lift a blade as the first man stops right above Tannin's sleeping head as if unaware the guard is there. His face is set toward the second man, who's clearly upset about something. Then they're ducking down as a third body approaches.

I squint. This one has the shape of a man but—bleeding hulls, he's larger than humanly possible. I grip my knife tighter and prepare to throw it—at who I'm not sure yet. The two men near Tannin appear to be trying to scramble away.

I almost lunge to keep them from stomping on his head.

There's an odd roar, and the man stalking them emerges from the shadows. I see why his size is so strange. He's not a man—he's a wraith.

Litch.

I keep my body between it and Kel and aim for the undead's head just as the two men cry out—until it occurs to me the sound is coming from my right again rather than from their open mouths. Next thing I know they're falling and crawling over Tannin and the fire, but without disturbing either.

I am about to throw my knife anyway. Keeping my eye on the wraith just in case, I glance around for Myles. *Really? Again?* It takes less than a moment to locate him at the base of the tree, but when I do it's clear the cries are coming from him. And the cracking noises aren't from feet. They're him peeling bark off the tree.

Blast it all, Myles.

I stand and storm over to shake him, but although the whites of his eyes widen, he doesn't respond. I smack his cheek, which does nothing besides alert me to the fact that his body is shaking heavily beneath my hand. And he's burning up.

Placing my hand on his forehead, I blink and peer through his created visions to locate Mia.

"Mia!" My whisper is loud enough that the guards on watch outside the perimeter are promptly striding through the trees.

"Miss? Is everything all right?"

"It's Myles. Wake Mia."

The guards recoil even as I say it, and when I look to see why, the vision is showing the wraith gutting both of the frantic men now splayed out on the ground. I turn away. "Ignore it and do as I said."

One of the guards goes to get Mia up as I continue to press my hands against Myles's shuddering body and forehead.

Mia murmurs from her blanket even as her eyes light up red. She glares around until her focus locks on me.

"Myles is having another of his visions."

"Can you jolt him out of it?"

I allow static to rush down my skin from the sky and send the shock straight into his bones. He jumps and utters a cry, but the vision continues. Until a moment later, when he blinks and suddenly looks around. At me. At the Luminescent and the guards standing with their swords out.

"He was seeing his past again," the Luminescent says.

"Can anything be done for him?"

She gazes hesitantly from him to me. Then closes her mouth. She nods to Gilford, who promptly lifts his wristlet with the potion he used on us back in Cashlin.

"As I recall, that seemed to make my visions worse."

He shrugs at me. "That's a possibility."

"Will it slow the poison in his blood?"

He peers at Mia, who pulls her gaze from Myles to stare straight at me but says nothing.

"I encourage you to speak freely lest we lose what valuable time we have pampering him," I say.

"There is nothing *you* can do."

"That's not what I asked. Can anything be done *for* him? Lady Isobel seemed to think so. I had this power before he did and it was released. Can't he release it too?"

"Your body was made to handle strange and strong elements—hence the weather. However, with him, his body is rejecting it. Or rather, the more it attaches to his blood and becomes him, it is rejecting his body because his mind doesn't know what to do with it."

"You're saying it's going to kill him."

She nods.

"I mean no offense, but we already knew that. What I need to know is—"

"Lady Isobel is right—there is another option." Gilford looks at the Luminescent as he says it. As if prodding her to spit it out. "Two, in fact."

When she refrains, he continues for her. "A swift death being the first and most logical."

I shake my head as the words of my father slip into mind. *"Never destroy what simply needs taming . . ."*

"But otherwise, it is our belief that while he can't get rid of the dark ability consuming his blood, due to his Cashlin heritage he could possibly learn to control it. Because it's not his actual blood that's rejecting him. It's his mind that is fading and will lose control completely. When that happens, he will be gone and the ability will be all that is left. Until . . ."

"It kills him."

"Until it begins killing others through him."

Just like it would've through me.

The queen's words come back. *"Lord Myles stands on the edge of a decision. One choice will send him over a precipice and turn him into a lesser Draewulf. The other will most likely cost his life but will help the Hidden Lands survive."*

Mia nods.

"So he might survive because he's Cashlin—*if* he can be tamed. So how do we do that?"

She peers over at Myles, who's huddled up against the tree staring at us. Whether he's listening or not, I can't tell. He already looks more than gone.

The guard leans in and murmurs, "A stronger Luminescent would be able to help him learn to control it."

I glance at Mia.

"Not me. It'd have to be either the queen, one of the Inters, or . . ."

"Princess Rasha." I study her as if to say I'm no daft fool.

She nods. "The question is, how do we rescue her?"

⁓

At first dawn we pack up our bags and horses and leave for the next town. The fog has come in heavy, surrounding us so thick it's hard to see anything but the road in front of us—and even that is only visible for a number of feet. Thus, the pace is a bit slow, lending to our already quiet moods.

"Care to do anything about this cloud?" one of the guards asks after an hour of riding in silence.

I glance up. Oh.

Tannin leans forward from the other side of him. "It might help us move quicker."

Right. "Sorry." I whisper up a breeze to blow a clean path from us to the lights glimmering one by one in the far distance. Behind me Myles begins murmuring, but when I turn to see what his problem is, he's not directing it at me. He's not directing it at anyone. As if he's here but he's not, and whatever he's seeing is keeping him stuck inside his pale head even as he's looking around frantically.

Every once in a while a low moan escapes his quivering lips, indicating the images in his mind are of torment. And every so often a few escape to startle the horses and scare the hulls out of the guards and Kel. I shiver and glance away to Mia and the male Cashlin.

"He's getting worse," she says.

"How long?" is all I reply.

She shrugs. "The longer he stays in his visions, the more chance he has of getting lost in them forever. Until he ceases to function at all."

I nod and press the fog back even farther. "If I get us to the northern border . . ." I drop my tone. "Do you think you could get a read on precisely where Rasha's being held?"

"If we can reach the scouts. Or better yet, wraiths." She looks around. "But how would you even rescue her? You've no boat or airship, nor have you nearly enough people."

I don't mention the airship over the waterway. I merely glance back at Lord Myles, who's stopped muttering long enough to eavesdrop on us. "I'm working on that," is all I say and hurry us toward the next main village.

We're met by a similar crowd as before. And the common-house speech goes almost exactly the same, minus the disgusting ex–slave owner. It's a room full of doubtful then cheering patrons—only this time the people are edgier.

"We convinced them and that is enough," Tannin assures me as we rush out the back doors again, just like last evening, before the crowd overtakes us.

The same happens again at another village in the evening. But this time people are waiting when we attempt to leave the common house in an atmosphere that seems strange. It's the expressions on their faces. These people don't merely look admiring; they seem desperate. Like the people in the High Court.

A bump against me and I'm tripping into Tannin, who flips around and pushes his sword out farther. "Hold steady and do your jobs, men!" he yells.

They're too late, though. I already feel the knife against my tunic, slicing clean through it, and I'm reaching for mine in a flash as I push Kel out of the way and turn to shove my blade toward the man who's lunged for me, but he's already backing away, taking a piece of my cloth with him. And a lock of my hair.

What the—?

I reach up to grab at my thick tresses—still there aside from one chunk on the right side. When I look at the man, a fight has broken out between him and the other peasants who are bartering over it and the tunic piece as if they are good luck tokens.

Two guards fall upon them until I yell to leave them. It doesn't matter.

Abruptly I'm being placed upon Haven and all I can hear is Tannin's shouting at them to get us out of here.

We ride and don't speak of it because there's nothing to say.

At least until Kel decides there is. "Perhaps you should give them your undergarments too, Nym. Wonder what those would go for on the market."

A chuckle emerges from the soldiers even as Tannin snaps, "Young master, that's highly—"

I hold up a hand. "He's fine." And then a chuckle of my own is slipping out.

Soon the idiocy of such an awkward event and Kel's suggestion overtakes us fully, and our laughter is ricocheting through the Valley.

"Can you imagine?" Humor dances through the boy's eyes.

"No, and you shouldn't be either," I laugh back. "Perhaps Lord Myles might lend us some images, though."

"Ah, I would, my dear. But in my visions the poor men would give them back, I'm afraid."

Half of us flip around to stare at him and the fact that he's somehow coherent before the bursts of hysteria shoot even louder. He extends me a weary smile through the dim, and something about it—the smile, his humor, his bleeding insulting jabs—makes me miss him terrible-like.

Which might be the strangest feeling I've ever encountered.

"How are you?" I ask when I'm finished clutching my stomach from the laughter.

"Insane. Got anything to drink around here?"

Mia looks at me and starts to speak, but I've no time to react before a sensation hits my blackened hand veins and I feel a tug in them as I swear a wisp of black seeps from Myles's chest. It shutters around him like a fog and his eyes shimmer darkly.

Kel jumps. "Holy mother of—"

Myles's eyelids flutter. "No worries, young man, I've not lost my head completely. Soon enough you'll see the ability heighten my creative power. And that will give us the upper hand in this whole bleeding war."

I nod at Tannin to pull out a small flask of watered-down wine for the Lord Protectorate, who nods his thanks and sets to nursing it while I stare at his eyes. They're set and scheming, even if they look like hollow caves in his face.

After a moment he hands the wine back and goes back to watching the road, seeming unaware of the wisp clinging to him like death.

"Nym, what's—?"

"Not now, Kel."

We ride, and I continue to watch Myles under the stars until our horses are finished and we're forced to stop for another night. Haven makes her annoyance known as Tannin and I work to unsaddle her. She wants to keep going. I can feel her excitement in her tense muscles and neck. I can relate. Being out in the fresh air and the wind whipping through our hair and smelling her musky scent brings a whispered longing for freedom.

Freedom.

Ha. Everything seems to lead back to that word lately.

Something about it sparks the recollection of my father shaping my little sword with his big hands. *"The blade isn't to rule with, Nymia. It's to bring freedom."*

I bite my lip and cough at the weight it brings to my ribs. I didn't even know that memory existed. Bleeding Inters.

I place my blankets beside Myles's, then glance up to find Mia doing the same. She shrugs and tips her head toward him, indicating the images flickering around him so fast they're like apparitions. But ones he's clearly in control of. They are images of multiple ways Draewulf could die.

"He's calculating all the possibilities," Mia murmurs.

The horses are aware of the pictures too, which makes them spook and whinny. Myles is scratching his veins as pictures of himself holding a blade come in and out of focus. The guards draw closer to the visions before I notice Kel backing away as they portray Myles going through a room and slitting throat after throat of people tied up.

"Kel, close your—"

But Tannin has already slapped a hand over Kel's widening gaze for me.

Thank you, I mouth. And when I turn back to Myles, his face is dripping with sweat.

"Nym, this is incredible," he murmurs just before he lays his head on his mare's mane and shuts his eyes.

I glance at Mia and Tannin. "How soon can we reach the northern border?"

Tannin raises a brow. "That's not on our route, miss. The closest we come is our final stop in Litchfell, which—"

"How soon, Tannin?"

"Two days, tops. But are you saying we abandon the rest of your tour—"

"I'm saying we finish down here and then head for the border before entering Litchfell. If we can meet up with King Sedric's scouting parties or wraiths—"

"Pardon, miss, but I'm uncertain how they'll help. I'm aware you'd like to locate Princess Rasha, but Draewulf will have her more highly protected than any of our units are prepared to—"

"I'm aware of that, but I believe we already have an idea of where she'll be. Plus, we have the advantage of Lord Myles." I peer over at Myles who, even though still resting on his horse's mane, seems somewhat sane at the moment. Even if the veins beneath his facial skin are all blackening, making him look aged about twenty years. "Who I plan to put to good use."

"And may I ask how?" Myles slurs.

I purse my lips and unload my bag as the itching beneath my own wrist veins picks up.

After a moment Mia says, "She's going to use herself and you as bait."

CHAPTER 26

I T'S NOT UNTIL THE FIFTH MORNING AWAY FROM THE Castle—when my anxiety's been spiking along with my plans—that I notice it.

The fog is reeling back over the blue-gray hills to dissipate over the sea, and the sunrays are just beginning to warm the dirt. The guards are cleaning up breakfast while the rest roll up bedding, and I've begun to tie blankets to the horses, who're still acting jittery. Even Haven is shuffling and stamping her hooves.

I look up to fog-fingered mountains and sniff the air. I smell nothing and yet . . .

And yet I can taste something. The moment I recognize the sensation, it's like my blood comes alive with awareness of how deeply it's moving over the atmosphere.

I almost gag. *Draewulf's presence.*

"I'm coming for you, pet."

It nearly knocks my knees from beneath me, as if it's been moving in all along but so subtle, so slow, I failed to recognize the reek. I scan the purple horizon—searching for what? I don't know. His airships? Warning pyres? Wraiths?

Not even a flesh-eating bird trolls the sky or interrupts the song of a nearby thrush.

So why is a shiver curling my spine?

I glance over at the men and Mia, who've been so supportive, living, sleeping, eating together, and rushing me in and out at each of the five towns we've stopped at. And try not to think of what I'll be making them face tomorrow.

Just focus on the task at hand, Nym. Focus on today and the village marked on Eogan's map.

"We need to move out," I say to the group and, without further explanation, climb onto Haven and turn toward the mass of green coating the northwestern rim at the base of Faelen's Fendres Mountains. *Litchfell.*

It's not until I look around for Myles that the uneasy feeling comes back. When I don't see him, I turn to Tannin. "Has anyone seen the Lord Protectorate? We have to go."

"He's gone," Mia says quietly.

"He's what?" I spin around.

"He went for the princess," she says.

"He did *what*? Is he insane?" I almost laugh.

"Gilford tried using the wristlet on him, but we couldn't stop him in time." Her tone is beyond apologetic.

Is she jesting? "And you didn't wake us?" Why wouldn't she?

Mia grabs the reins to her horse and falls in line with the rest of us. "He'd already made up his mind." A rimming of red fills her eyes, indicating she'd read him. "He would've injured your men and still escaped. It seemed better to let him go."

I glance around at the group.

"He did ask me to inform you that his ability could exhibit enough for what needed to be done, so there was no sense in wasting your life as well."

I pause. He said that?

Mia nods.

Oh.

I shake my head. "He's an idiot."

"Completely."

"How does he think he'll make it across the waterway, let alone up into Tulla?"

"He is the king's cousin. It will take little convincing to get the Faelen captains to believe he's under King Sedric's orders. Or under King Eogan's, for that matter. I believe he means to hitch a ride on one of the airships Faelen's men have supposedly confiscated in the waterway."

"And will he actually make it to Rasha?"

"I don't believe so. But he feels it's his responsibility to try."

Of all the blasted—I pound my fist on my thigh and swear at him.

"Better he dies trying than destroy the rest of us with his disease."

The way she says it stops me in my tracks. I don't even have to look at her to know her eyes will be reddening around the pupils as she reads my intentions. The ones that are saying I don't know if I could've killed him had it come to that, and I'm quite sure her pacifist self couldn't have either.

I breathe out for only the humidity to hear. "So he's going to get himself killed."

"Yes. At least without our help."

"Will he even get close to Rasha?" I mutter after a moment.

"We'd have to follow him to find out."

I study Tannin's expression that claims he's been taking this all in. He shakes his head.

"I know you disapprove—"

"I only fear for your safety, miss. The king's cousin has made his choice, but you—"

"You know well enough I've already made mine too. We came

to rally the people and then find a way to rescue Rasha, if that's even a possibility." I glance at the horizon. "Now Myles has just given us a head start."

"Miss, I—"

"Either arrest me or follow me, Tannin. But we're only a few hours from Litchfell and we can follow that toward the border today if we start now. So what's it going to be?"

After a moment he tells the group to fall in.

Good. Thank you. I nod at him and set Haven free to ride for it, leaving the others in our dust for a while. Until it begins to mist so heavy the group swears at me to quit messing with the weather.

"I rather like it," I'm tempted to inform them but, instead, ease up and bring out the sun like a semi-decent person.

"As if following Lord Myles's tracks wasn't hard enough," one of the guards groans.

I bite my tongue and look away.

Maybe my nerves are due to Myles, or Eogan, or Rasha. I squirm in my seat and set my eyes ahead.

Or maybe they're due to the fact we're getting closer to Litchfell. I shudder at the thought of my last encounter with the bolcranes there. When Colin and Breck and I . . .

Sigh.

When they were still alive. Well, sort of.

"Up here," a guard shouts. "Tracks." He's taking a tradesmen's path that's heavily covered in brush between the Litchfell Forest on our left and the vast, green Faelen valley to the right. The sun is creating a ripple of heat waves across the surface of it. Warming the hovels and empty plowed fields and people who're even now deciding whether to fight for king and country.

I ride ahead to the guard to push on our pace. *C'mon, Myles, how far have you gone?*

It's not long until Kel strikes up his questions again as we wind our way up and down the path that leads to the slim set of foothills just before the ocean channel and the airship I hope is still there.

"And what are bolcranes like?" Kel asks after a good fifty terrameters.

"Deadly," Tannin mutters.

"How deadly?"

"They'll eat you in two bites."

"Neat." Kel's eyes are huge. "Will we see any?"

"Hopefully not." I frown.

"Well, what do they look like?"

Tannin clears his throat and shakes his head at me.

"Ah c'mon. I'll need to know in case I spot one, right? Probably be safer if I know what to avoid." Kel flashes his giant white teeth.

"They look like enormous lizards," I say. "Except with shiny black scales and crocodilian mouths that host sharp teeth. And they're bigger than the horse you're riding when they're full grown."

Kel's face is turning a darker shade of black, as if he's holding his breath. "And?" he finally whispers. "What are they from? How'd they get in the forest? How do they stay in there?"

Tannin puckers his mouth and looks quizzically in my direction.

Huh. Good question. I don't actually know. And apparently neither does anyone else in the group because they're suddenly all staring at me too.

And then, after a moment, "There's a legend," I say. I bite my lip.

"It claims they're descendents of once-powerful beings here in Faelen who lived in the most beautiful valley. Until they became arrogant and full of selfish, bloated hearts, and their Creator was forced to banish them to the forest. Where they've lived ever since." I kick Haven to move ahead.

"What kind of powerful beings?" Kel asks.

I don't answer.

Tannin clears his throat again.

"What? Tell me."

"Elementals," the guard says softly.

"Oh." Kel falls silent for a merciful minute. Until, "Well, is the story true?"

"I've no idea," Tannin replies—which becomes a common response during the next four hours, most of which the boy spends asking an inexcusable amount of questions.

"And what of—?"

A chill runs between my shoulder blades, so minimal I almost miss it.

Except it's followed by another.

What the—?

I try to shake it off, but even Haven is jittering beneath me as we reach the cusp of a hill that drops down into a forested trail blanketed in heavy shadow.

A noise ahead grows louder. Like Lord Myles's habit of hissing his words . . . but not.

Litches.

I flip around and flail a hand at Kel. "Shh!"

"What? Why?"

"Stop talking. Stop riding," I snap at the group. "Just . . . stay."

Tannin and two of the guards canter up beside me to lend their eyes and ears.

"I don't hear anything," one whispers after a moment.

"You don't hear the hissing?"

All three of them shake their heads. "Miss, are you—?"

I beckon Mia to join us. "Do you hear it?"

"No, but I see you believe wraiths are nearby."

"Are they?"

Her red-lit eyes scan the forest tunnel for what seems like far too long, until eventually she points a finger. "There."

A second later a wrinkle in the air erupts and the atmosphere comes alive with images, as if an unseen bomb went off and set the airwaves moving. At first it's hard to see them in detail—but then an army of Faelen soldiers is emerging from the forest.

The hissing noise spikes and is followed by the appearance of three wraiths reacting to the men. I sniff. Even from this distance their scent is floating up, permeating my nostrils with the stench of decay.

"Ugh, what is that?" someone behind us says.

"The wraiths," Kel answers. "That's their odor."

I wrinkle my nose.

"It was a wraith scouting party hedging along Litchfell," Mia says. "What are they doing this far into Faelen?"

Tannin's face is stalled in horror. "Looks more like it's an ambush on our men."

I study the way their limbs move through the brush and forest trees. "Those aren't our men."

He swerves toward me as do the other guards.

"It's Lord Myles."

His brow goes up.

"She's right," Mia says. "If I had to guess, I'd say he stumbled upon their scouting party and they ambushed him. He's creating an image to confuse them."

"We need to help him." I twitch the reins against Haven's neck. "Tannin, you and Kel stay here with four guards. The rest of you, follow me."

"But, miss—"

I ignore Tannin and twitch a crack of lightning toward the

234

forest's edge—away from where I suspect Myles is under siege, but enough to distract his attackers as I nudge Haven into a gallop toward the tunneled path leading down.

We've hardly gone one-third a terrameter when the hissing grows loud enough to fill the entire atmosphere around us. I crack the sky overhead with one, two, five more strikes, but don't allow them to touch down lest they hit too near Myles.

The next moment the forest is filled with black-cowled, ghoulish-faced wraiths, far more than merely the three. Dark wisps writhe around their gaping jaws and empty black eyes, and they appear to have been mainly pieced together from men, although a few have an extra appendage—one a snake tail, another the skin of a sea animal if I didn't know better. A third has the claws of a bolcrane on both hands.

"Bleeding litch!" the Cashlin guard yells.

"Of all the—" Myles yells from somewhere.

"Aim for their heads," is the only advice I give before racing toward them. By the time I'm close enough to the fray to see through the mirage of soldiers, I've impaled two of the wraiths with an onslaught of ice picks. I take out a third when Mia and our guards reach me. The guards have their swords drawn and hack away at the swarming beasts, while Mia looks on in shock.

"Myles," I call.

He doesn't reply.

A wraith jumps from the branches overhead and I've hardly time to move Haven out of the way before he hits the ground. His claws scratch up her flank, causing her to shriek. Next thing I know she's flipped around and bitten the thing's head off.

Except three more are right behind him.

Litch. Where did they all come from?

I snap lightning through the trees at them even as I note that one of our guards has fallen and Gilford is barely keeping the wraiths off of Mia. The poor thing. She looks absolutely terrified.

I take out another black-eyed beast only to realize that the party with me isn't experienced enough at fighting them.

They're going to get massacred if I don't do something.

I glance around for Myles—and I'm met with a claw in my shoulder. It wrenches me off of Haven before I can reach a hand around to freeze it. Two seconds later I've let an ice stream pool its way up the beast's arm and into his mouth, shattering his skull from the inside out. He drops.

I drop. I can't breathe. The air's too thick in here.

And that blasted hissing.

I look up just as two more wraiths lock their eyeless sights on me.

Hulls.

"Myles, where in blazes are you?"

Still no reply, but this time there's another shudder in the atmosphere and the sound of running, as if someone's crashing through the forest. The air around me ripples again and one, two, three mirage soldiers still standing abruptly shift into wraiths. The black-cowled undead who'd locked sights on me pause. One appears to focus his body toward me and I lift a hand to take him down. Except he tips his head at an odd angle, sniffs, then pulls back.

What the—?

A second later he turns to shuffle away and the other follows.

I glance behind me, then down to see what caused the reaction.

Oh litch. At my feet lies another version of myself, sliced open from stomach to throat and bleeding out in bright-red rivulets. I peer up and around in time to see the bodies of Tannin, Mia, Gilford, and the other soldiers materialize nearby—also dead, also bleeding out.

Nicely done, Myles.

"All of you, stop. Don't move." I keep my tone low, but loud enough for the group to hear.

The guards obey. "M'lady?" Tannin whispers.

"Look down."

Their exclamations of surprise say they see us as dead too.

"I believe Myles has them fooled into thinking their job is done. I'd suggest waiting until they've retreated to move, lest we show them different."

Tannin tips a finger to indicate he understands.

The sound of the final wraiths shuffling back into the tree line gradually dies away. Only a muted cry from someone farther out threatens to reveal us, but it fades as swift as it erupted.

I wait another minute before moving toward the group, and all but two of the soldiers, who take it upon themselves to search the area, stride back to where Kel and the others are waiting.

"Everyone alive?" I say.

"I believe so."

"That was terrifying!" Kel's eyes are as big as hornet eggs, but his grin suggests he wished to be in on the fight.

I shake my head.

"Miss, I recommend we return to the Castle. King Sedric should be informed immediately—"

"Sir!" One of the soldiers strides up from the direction of the tree line. "We can't find Lord Myles. There's no sign of him."

Bleeding hulls, Myles.

"Is he still after Princess Rasha? Even after all that?" Tannin's gaze narrows.

"Actually, it appears his tracks lead into the forest."

"Meaning either Lord Myles purposefully led them away from us, or . . ." I don't finish voicing my thought.

Or the wraiths have taken him.

I stare at the men, then Gilford and Mia.

"Are we going to help him?" Kel looks back and forth between the lot of us.

I swallow and run a hand through my hair. And sigh. And nod at Tannin.

"Miss, I—"

"Tannin, I'd like you to head inland a half terrameter or so and take Kel and four soldiers with you. I'll keep Gilford and the others." I glance at Mia.

Her face is pale, but she manages a smile. "As long as I'm here, I will assist you. That is why we were sent."

"But, miss, you saw what just happened. The danger you're walking—"

"Will be nothing my abilities can't handle. It's either that or leave Myles to whatever fate he's gotten himself into, and as much as I might be tempted . . ." I purse my lips. "Take Kel and go as quickly as possible. And under no circumstances is the boy to escape and come anywhere near the forest."

"What? I'm not staying outside the bloody—"

"Language."

"*Fine.* I'm not staying outside no daft forest just—"

"You are and you will," I say. "I don't need you dying at the claws of a bolcrane, and I certainly don't need you distracting the men."

"But my father said—"

"That I'm in charge of you." I turn to the guard. "Tannin?"

He nods. "I'd feel more comfortable coming with you, miss. But if that is what you wish, then we'll wait."

"But the bolcranes!"

I square a look at Kel.

Tannin turns to the boy. "Those bolcranes will devour you

faster than you can pull your sword. Nym won't be able to defend the rest of the group and you if the beasts come for them."

Kel purses his lips in disappointment but, surprisingly, doesn't push the point.

"And if you're gone longer than a few hours, what would you have us do?" Tannin asks.

"Then we're dead and you'd best prepare the king. But we won't be longer. Believe me." I eye the forest. "I have no desire to spend more time in there than necessary."

With that I click for Haven, and when she appears, I check her wound to make sure she can still ride, then pull myself up on her. The four guards and Kel begin making their way toward a better clearing that's farther from the tree line. "We'll wait a quarter ter-rameter from here, miss."

"We *won't* be long," I call after Tannin. And as soon as they're trotting away at a quick enough pace, I turn and take the lead toward the forest.

CHAPTER 27

I T'S MINUTES BEFORE THE SIX SOLDIERS, MIA, GILFORD, and I reach the spot where the brush is thickening and thistle trees are sprouting as if to claim more of the land for the forest. And right in the middle of it is a path recently beat down.

"Mia." I slow Haven and see her already pulling back with Gilford.

"Yes, miss."

"Keep an eye out."

I know it's unnecessary, but seeing as they're the least experienced and that nagging, clammy sense of Draewulf's presence is even stronger here . . . I scan the horizon and catch Mia doing the same, listening for any sounds of wraiths or airship engines other than our own. The only noise is the sound of hoofbeats carrying the rest of our group toward us and Litchfell's edge.

"Miss?"

I lick my lips. "It's nothing. Just . . ."

"Something's wrong with this place," Mia says. "I know that right enough."

I nod. "Good."

A wave of muggy heat slams into my skin as we get close to the forest's internal fringe, and I remember how it feels here. Where everything is eerily quiet and more dangerous than any other place in Faelen.

"Stay as close to me as possible," I say to her and Gilford before calling down an icy wind to keep the temperature around us cool.

When the Cashlins look at me, one of the soldiers merely answers, "Bolcranes hunt by sensing body heat."

Their eyes widen and they nod.

"Best not to talk either," he adds.

"And don't touch the trees," I mutter, at which the guards with us shiver but don't complain.

It's slow progress, following the scent of the wraiths and Myles's footsteps. We're working our horses past the spindle trees with their poisoned spikes and into the darker part of the forest path where the daylight is all but blotted out by thick moss that hangs down like leeches on all sides. Once or twice two of the soldiers veer too close to the edge and nearly wake the giant, bloated ticks nestled there that are as big as a man's chest.

One of the men is so disgusted at almost touching the vile thing, he actually leans over and throws up.

"Lovely," another mutters.

"No sign of Lord Myles or the wraiths yet," Mia says. "Is that a bad thing?"

"I'm not sure. But as long as their tracks stay fresh . . . Strangely enough, I believe we're nearing the place on the map Eogan gave me—where the Uathúils live." I don't mention that the coincidence seems more than odd. It's eerie.

"People actually live here?" Gilford asks in a shocked tone.

"They do."

"Why?" His expression makes it clear this is worse than any place he's thus far encountered in his young life.

"The same reason Cashlins keep to themselves. To be safe from other people."

"Forget that—what about from all these hideous beasts?"

"Oh, trust me, we've not encountered anything yet."

I keep up the cool air as we continue on until the growth is too thick and we're forced to walk, dragging the gradually resistant horses behind us.

"Your temperature control seems to be working quite effectively," Mia says at one point.

"I was just thinking the same thing." I don't tell her that more than that, I was noticing the lack of wraith appearances and bolcrane cries has actually got me unnerved. I'm not keeping our body heat perfectly hidden—and we should've attracted at least a couple of either by now. *C'mon, Myles, where are you?*

"This isn't making me like that man more," Gilford growls.

I snort. *You and me both.*

It's another hour before we finally stumble into a clearing that skirts a tiny village. One of the soldiers shoots me a look that says he's going to investigate for anyone hiding.

"How could someone live there?" his counterpart whispers. And when I glance over, the poor man's face is petrified. The muscles in his neck flex taut with every rustle of the surrounding trees.

Except suddenly my neck is flexing, too, because something's wrong. With my blood I can feel the *lap lap lap* of the ocean water not too far away, calling to me, but here . . . there is only silence.

And the smell.

I don't have to peer through the branches to know what we're about to find. It's the same as Colin and I had seen in another village much like this.

"Something's not right," Mia says.

I nod. Did the wraiths wipe out this village so fast?

No. It's not that. "The plague," I whisper.

The men start to fall back with curses, pulling their shirts up over their mouths and noses.

"The Luminescent can stay here with two guards and the horses," I say, "but the rest need to help us do a quick sweep for survivors."

They comply, though the whites of their eyes are bigger than their mouths. Before I can push forward, however, Mia slips up to me.

"I know you're also searching for the Uathúils here." Her eyes are lit up like red candle lanterns. "Only I don't believe they're here any longer." She swallows and stares, as if willing me to read past her words. Then, finally, "I'm not saying they're dead, but I'm not sensing them. At all. However, there's another presence I've felt since this morning."

"I've felt it too." I lower my voice. "Can you tell—is he in Faelen? Draewulf, I mean."

She shakes her head. "I'm not sure, but . . ."

"But?"

"But something is." She scans the area in front of us, then glances back. "I suggest we hurry."

"Agreed," I breathe out. And stride to the front of the waiting soldiers, who follow into the village of silence that grows so heavy I actually wish a bolcrane would come crashing through. For a moment I hear a hissing sound. Like a snake or like the wraiths we're tracking. Except before I can narrow in on it, it's gone, leaving me with the impression it was never there at all.

Bleeding hulls, Nym, just see if there's anyone left alive. And find Myles.

I keep the air cool around us even as the humidity picks up to near unbearable. And although I've yet to see any giant ticks hanging from trees in this area, the webs and mist are still thick enough to make the soldiers jittery.

"It's fine," I want to tell them, but I don't because we'd all know it'd be a lie.

We move across swamp holes that have logs laid across them efficiently enough to tell us people set them there and therefore we must be on the right path. Soon the hissing comes again, but after a few minutes it sounds more like buzzing. And when the trail nears a scattering of fallen trees, the air above them is black with flies.

"Well, that's despicable." A soldier waves a hand in front of his face.

I chuckle until I follow his gaze and realize he's not talking about the insects. He's staring at the bodies.

Bolcranes. Or rather, pieces of bolcranes are lying beside downed trees. They've been cut up just like the branches—but instead of oozing poisoned sap, the giant black, scaly beasts are oozing dark blood that looks and smells like oil. There are four of them, some missing legs or teeth from their bodies that are larger than horses and necks longer than snakes.

I peer away lest the temptation to vomit onto Gilford, who's tramping in front of me, overtakes me.

"What did this?" He peers back at us.

"My best guess is the people who live near here."

The Cashlin nods. Then, as if on second thought, says, "What do you think they use them for? And how in blazes did they bring them down?"

I shrug and try to ignore the ill sensation prickling every inch of my skin. And hope we don't have to find out. From the expressions on the soldiers' faces, they're hoping the same thing. I feel one of them pull back closer to me and lift his sword a little higher.

"Perhaps we should let the wraiths go," one of the men says. "I doubt they'll last long in here anyway."

"Neither will Lord Myles. Or the Uathúils we're looking for if the wraiths get hold of them." I let a film of energy ripple along my arms and neck, bristling the air around us as if to ward off any who might take interest as to why we're travelling through, and keep moving forward.

"Up ahead," a guard calls out. He's pointing to another clearing among the trees where it appears there's a small village. The only way I can see it through the murk and moss is by the shafts of sunlight glimmering off the branches and huts.

Despite the stench and sick feeling in my veins, the glow of light is warm, inviting even, over this town that appears to be located in a large circular earthen divot, about two feet lower than the path we're on. With hovels made from sticks.

Burnt sticks.

"You think the Uathúils are here?" Gilford moves closer to me.

I shake my head. "Eogan thinks so, but . . ." I stare around at all the burned-out hovels and dirty sheets hung over doors in warning. And the blackened forest dirt.

"There are signs of them."

I veer toward the soldier who spoke. "What do you mean?"

"The Uathúils. Or one of them at least." He points to the circular-divoted ground, then up to a section of earth that's been built up like a wall to surround the far side of the village. I assumed the people living here had built it, but when I peer harder it hits me that the dirt piled high is fresher than that packed along the edge. As if . . .

I stare at him. "A Terrene."

He nods.

My mind is playing games with me, because before he says anything further, I swear I see a flash of black cloak between the dirt-wall mound and a burnt home. But when I peek closer, nothing's there but the mist and dim. I shudder anyway. "Let's find Myles and get out of here. Uathúil or no Uathúil."

"Of course, miss." But the man is eyeing the soldiers behind us who've begun shuffling uneasily.

"I need you to hold it together another hour," I say calmly to them.

"Miss, over here!"

I trot to where three guards are standing over a pile of rot.

Not rot. Stopping three feet away I can see they're grown men with blackened skin and staring eyes and slashed-open throats.

One, two, three corpses. And more splayed on the far side of the clearing. Including what appears to be Lord Myles.

Oh bracken, no.

I can't help the gagging sound erupting from my mouth. I lean over in case bile comes with it, only to notice at least two of the soldiers have already lost their stomach fluid. After a moment the nausea eases.

"Myles." I beckon to the third soldier. "Is he . . . ?" I don't even have to wait for him to speak because I'm certain his set mouth matches my own. As if we both know what caused this.

The bodies aren't just rotting. Some of them are missing body parts.

I stare at the men just as that hissing sound picks up, and this time I know even if they can't hear it, they're sensing it. "Wraiths." I kick at one of the bodies before the soldiers draw their swords and Gilford nods to me.

"This is more than the plague," I say for the guards' benefit as I spin around to face the shadows that are suddenly emerging from the trees and hovel doors. "And, Gilford, that fancy ring of yours won't work on what's coming."

"What in blazes?" someone utters.

"They're only killed by impaling their heads!" I yell.

"But, miss, what—?"

Gilford's comment dies as the next moment it's like a tide of black mist and shredded gray cloaks is loosed. Fifty of them, at least, with hollowed-out faces and conglomerated bodies of humans and bolcranes heading our way and—

Litch. That's what they were using the bolcranes for. To make more wraiths.

Draewulf's been here.

CHAPTER 28

I GLANCE UP AND AROUND THE TREETOPS—ANYWHERE
the monster might be hiding—but all I see is a squadron of his
Dark Army descending.

"Nym!"

I duck just as a bolcrane claw attached to the bone-thin arm of a
dead man comes slashing down at me. Rolling around him, I touch
the monster's clammy skin with my hand and send a shock through
it all the way to its head. It falls, and before I can even think about
it, another has replaced it.

Four, five, six, I bring down ice pick after ice pick to slam into
their temples. Then, farther out, use a shred of lightning to tear
through the wraiths dropping through the tree line, lighting them
on fire along with what's left of the hovels in the clearing.

It doesn't matter, I tell myself. They're all dead. I eye the beasts
lashing at the guards with claws and swords and metal spikes.
These beings who used to be the people who made up this village.
From the looks of it, they've not been human for a week or more.

How could Draewulf have gotten here in time to create them?

I shove a bolt of static through the face of a wraith about to
decimate Gilford's backside, and the thing falls into a pile of dust as
the realization hits me.

Draewulf was in Faelen posing as Breck. And after that?

He was here for a week as Eogan.

I look around at the monsters crawling toward us in a slowly diminishing mass. And try not to be sick.

Eogan did this after the Keep when Draewulf was using him. He'd already started in on turning our own people to add to his army.

Litch.

A scream from nearby draws my gaze over in time to see one of our guards being gutted. *Thump thump thump*—a shower of ice picks impales the beast's brain and five others along with it, but it's too late for the soldier.

"Holy mother of—" Gilford yells from the right of us.

Suddenly the earth around me is grumbling, groaning, shifting as it ripples the rocks and dirt beneath my boots. I glance down only to hear another cry from another of our soldiers as in my peripheral he disappears. *What the—?*

There's a crack where he was just standing that's fast becoming a gaping hole, much like Colin used to create. In fact, exactly like Colin used to create.

Before I can see who's causing it, the crack enlarges to race toward me and the rest of the unit.

"Move!" a soldier yells, and we're promptly all jumping out of the way just before the earth crumbles beneath us.

Another shout—this one from a guard who scrambled straight into a wraith's snakelike teeth. *Bleeding hulls, we're getting annihilated.*

I take out two wraiths nearest us, then tell one of the men, "Hold them off!" before standing on my tiptoes and turning in a circle to get a view of who the Terrene is.

I don't see him at first.

In fact, I doubt I ever would have had he not lifted a hand right then to split the earth like a torn seam straight at me. The look on his face is unreal. Despicable. Heart-stopping.

Because it speaks of a power-intelligence that can only be of a Uathúil, or of one having *been* a Uathúil.

Litch.

Draewulf can turn Uathúils into wraiths.

The horror of that reality doesn't have time to sink in—I'm too busy trying to evade the disgusting dead Terrene's earth-moving prowess.

I send one, two, five blades of ice at his head, but he merely blocks them with clods of dirt.

My lightning strike at least makes him lurch and jump, and I catch sight of one of my men behind him, stalking to finish the job.

Except the wraith-Terrene seems to sense him—to sense something—because he bends down just as I'm drawing in a mist to shield the man and shoves into the ground so hard that everything outside a fifteen-foot circle begins shredding and crumbling into a chasm.

I stumble back but not soon enough, and as the earth beneath my boots gives way, I'm clawing, grabbing, grasping onto the pieces that are dropping into a thirty-foot pit. Bleeding hulls.

For a moment it stops, and my foot finds a chink in which to lodge. I hug the wall of dirt and catch my breath, thinking the soldier *has* gotten to the Terrene. But then the rocks I'm barely holding on to are moving again, and I know I am in the undead Terrene's sights. He's going to finish it.

I shut my eyes and call down flashes of hail and lightning to pelt the area behind me. *Please move out of the way,* I silently beg Gilford and the other soldiers. But while the snarling cries suggest I'm taking out wraiths, the earth shakes harder.

My foothold's loosening. My handholds are crumbling. Oh

hulls, I'm going to fall and this is not how it's supposed to be. This is how I'm going out? By a blasted Terrene-wraith?

I continue to clamber and climb until the whole space feels like a landslide I'm swimming through—

And then a snap in the atmosphere stops it.

The forest around me melts away into a wide-open space of green lawn and lights and party dancers. Even the crumbling cliff I'm clinging to appears to be gone, as does my body—and in its place is a pond of water and fish and starry lanterns reflecting off the surface. It's a scene from Adora's—one of her outdoor parties Colin and I attended. And Myles.

Myles. I gasp for breath and glance around for the oaf.

He's alive?

When my gaze finds him, he gives me a tipsy-looking wink as if to say we weren't the only ones he was fooling. I whisper a word of gratitude his direction, then strengthen my grip on first one rock, then another and slip my toes along the cliff wall until I find a space to fit them. It takes a solid half minute to haul myself up and onto the dirt that looks like grass. And another half minute to realize the sounds of fighting have diminished to grunts of confusion.

I peer around at the soldiers who are panting and attempting to see through the illusion, while the wraiths have begun wandering aimlessly. *Bless you, Myles.*

I stand and search the Uathúil out.

He's disappeared.

Hulls. I turn to aim at the wraiths.

I've taken out two when a human cries out. It's another one of our soldiers. The next second a wraith has found him and taken his head off.

I lift a hand just as Gilford utters a yell.

Spiders.

Crawling in masses toward us along the tree branches.

They look eerily like the spiders from my hallucinations when I'd ingested the dark power.

I swerve my gaze to Myles, only now instead of concentrating, he's merely standing, covering his face with his hands and pressing against his head as if he can tear it apart before the wraiths do. The spiders are dropping down around him and onto him. I begin to raise a hand to flick static at them, but something tells me it won't help. He's lost control.

Blast it, Myles!

I turn to the soldiers who're now not just lunging at the wraiths but cringing to avoid the crawling vermin as well.

"Ignore the spiders. It's Myles!"

"Ignore the what?" a soldier asks, shoving his blade through an arachnid that appears to have fallen on a wraith's face.

"The spiders! They're not real!"

"And the wraiths?"

Poor man, the soldier's voice sounds so hopeful, even as we both know the cut of his sword through their bones proves they're physical enough.

I call down a wind against the broadening mass of undead, and with it more ice picks than I've ever created. *Focus, Nym.* I hold them in the air, leveling them above the heads of the wraiths, until a tearing, burning, ripping sensation gouges through my back and down to my torso.

I cry out and fall forward, flipping over on moving earth as I do to lift my hands in defense against the bloody claws coming down to finish me off. I shut my eyes because I'm too slow, it's too late.

Boom!

What the—?

Boom!

The ground rattles along the tree line and up into the humid air. I open my eyes to see the Uathúil-wraith above me stalled midmotion, staring up at the sky. I scamper backward as the bombs' vibrations move beneath my feet. I peer up at the single airship. From the smoke behind it, it's dropped a bomb as it's flown in an odd, zigzagging line toward us, and by my calculations the next will hit our group. The wraiths are watching it too.

"They're heeeere. They've commmee," they hiss.

I flick a hand toward the ship and draw lightning to tear through it. Only the thing is more agile than I expected and it swerves just enough for me to miss. The bolt hits the ground and explodes to our right.

Litch.

I launch another and another, but the thing moves more strategically than any I've ever seen. As if the captains know where I'll aim next.

Before I've time to consider that further, my gaze has already snagged upon two more ships through the treetops, hovering over the northern waterway. They're so far out I'd be unable to see them if not for the sunlight reflecting off their hulls or the smoke rising up beneath them. What I assume were once our warboats have been struck and are now sinking, and those airships are headed for us too.

Blast it. I don't care who I hit or what boats may still be water sure inside all that smoke. I merely direct five strikes at those airships along with a strong gust of breeze to blow them in the direction I need.

They're in flames and dropping before the fifth hit lands.

"Nym, that one!" Gilford points up.

I squint but don't see where the ship above us went. Then— there. Dipping below the flash of the sun. Except by the time I get a good glimpse of it, the thing has already moved again.

Except . . .

I pause my hand in the air as something ripples in my blood. Whoever's captaining that ship knows every move I'm about to make. And before my thoughts have registered it, my mouth is already speaking: "That one isn't Draewulf's. It's Eogan." My realization is short-lived as a roar beneath me signals the crumbling away of earth. I jump aside just as another chasm opens up and pulls one of the soldiers into it.

I swerve toward the Uathúil who's no longer enamored with the ship—his focus is back on me.

One, two, three slashes of lightning explode near him, but he interrupts each of them with rocks that rupture into sand.

From the corner of my eye I see the airship's plank drop down approximately ten seconds before Eogan's beautiful self comes striding down it. It takes exactly four seconds more for a blade created from stone to slam into the ground next to me, skimming my arm and yanking a cry from my throat.

I shove five ice arrows at the Uathúil, but they hit a wall of stone that appears out of nowhere.

The wall crumbles as fast as it was erected, and the Uathúil is suddenly right in front of me, bending over. He tips his head with hollow eyes and sharpens a rock-blade midair.

From behind him Eogan dips his gaze my direction, then gives the slightest tip of his head.

I slam an ice pick through the Uathúil's face at the same moment Eogan shoves his sword through the beast's jaw, and together we relieve him of his half-mortal, earthly bone coil for the rest of eternity. Next thing I know the beast has dropped onto me, oozing out hot oil and slime onto my chest and skin, and I'm screaming at the disgusting beast crushing my lungs.

Eogan yanks the thing off me before offering his hand to pull me up. He peers toward the mass of wraiths and spiders and his soldiers descending the plank from above them. "You well enough to keep at it? Otherwise . . ."

He doesn't have to say it. I already know that *otherwise* we're not going to make it.

I lean up to slap a kiss on his chin, in case it's the last one I ever give him, then stagger forward as the bloody claw marks across my back from earlier burn. I call up the wind and ice picks again. This time Eogan guards my backside, which I'm only now aware is dripping blood and making me woozy.

Gritting my teeth, I let loose the ice. The pieces find their homes and ten wraiths drop.

I do it again and another dozen drop, except by the time I'm readying the last load, my arms are sagging too much. I let them drop lest I release ice picks on Gilford, who can't stop looking at the spiders on his legs, and the surviving soldiers who look nearly as confused.

"Myles!" I scream at the oaf. But it's no use. His blackening eyes are vacant.

I send a static shock over anyway, but it does nothing.

With a second, third, fourth static shock, I knock down the rest of the wraiths and, with Eogan, finish them off.

I grab Gilford and start running.

"Take the ship. We'll get back faster." Eogan is going for Myles. When he reaches the Lord Protectorate, he grabs his arm to simultaneously calm him and drag him with us. As he does, the visions cease.

"We can't. Mia and more soldiers are waiting with the horses. And Kel and Tannin are farther out awaiting our return lest they have to inform King Sedric we're dead."

The Bron and few remaining Faelen soldiers stare at us in shock.

Eogan nods at me and promptly commands ten of his men to go with us and the rest to reload and follow above the thick forest and wait for our signal.

Finished, he looks over. "What in hulls just happened?"

I shake my head at him. "Nothing good."

∽

When we arrive at the clearing where we left the horses, the soldiers are waiting for us, wearing expressions of terror.

"We heard noises." Mia's eyes grow large at the sight of Eogan beside me. "Your Highness?" The next second her eyes flash red and that's followed by a look of understanding. "You've come from Tulla."

"Yes, and we need to warn Sed— Wait, what?" I turn from her to Eogan, who hands off Myles to the waiting soldiers, then scoops me into his arms. "Eogan, what—?"

"We came just in time, too, from the look of it."

"Where are the other men?" One of the soldiers who'd stayed behind peers beyond us, as if waiting for the rest of our unit to arrive.

Eogan puts me down. "Dead. We've lost more than a few men today."

The way he says it . . . How many lives did he lose today? Doing what?

I peck a kiss on his cheek before glaring at him. "I almost killed you. What in hulls were you thinking? I could've shot you down! And what does she mean that you were in Tulla?"

"Aye, but you didn't. I knew you wouldn't."

"Okay." I stare at him. "But how did you know? And for that matter, how'd you know where we were?"

His tone is calm, but his emerald gaze is flickering from

adrenaline. "We were headed back over the waterway when I saw your lightning storm. I assumed you were in trouble or else some poor soul had seriously put you off. I came to rescue one of you."

"Uh-huh. And you came from Tulla?"

"He rescued Princess Rasha," Mia breathes, and she's suddenly searching the forest around us, as if Rasha's somehow been hiding there.

I frown. He did? And turn to search the forest too.

"She's on the ship."

"Above us?"

He smirks and walks over to pat Haven. "Hey, girl, how've you been?"

Haven whinnies and stamps her pleasure, bringing me back to the reality that we need to be moving.

As if reading my mind, Eogan says, "I'll explain on the way," and hands me Haven's reins. I cool the air as he helps Myles mount up, then turns to help me do the same. He murmurs to my mare while pressing his hand against my back, exuding a calm that flows over my skin like a healing balm. "You sure you're okay to ride?"

I suddenly don't have the energy to answer. The soldiers with us are climbing onto their own mares, but it's the sight of those few riderless horses that reminds me what we've just lost. Those men. I may have known going in we wouldn't all return—and they did too—but it doesn't make the guilt and solemn emotions any less.

I swallow. "Thank you," I whisper back in their direction.

I cool the air further and quicken Haven into a trot. When the forest has thinned enough for faster riding, we push the horses along the path, and Gilford pipes up. "Okay, so how? How'd you rescue the princess?"

"When I left Faelen I made my way up to Tulla through the mountain passes where the wraiths were less prominent. They can't run the airships without the Bron captains and soldiers—and it was those men's loyalty that enabled us to find the princess. She was being held on a ship in the center of the destroyed capital. Although, surprisingly, she was less guarded than one would think. It seems Draewulf's growing a bit too cocky." Eogan shrugs. "Or else Cashlin's giving him more fight than he bargained for."

Yet even as Eogan's speaking, there's a weight to his words, his tone, his expression that tells me it wasn't as easy as all that. As do the claw markings that are healing across his neck.

"You nearly died."

His jaw tightens.

Hmm. Good guess.

"Twice it seems," Mia says behind me.

"Why?" I glare at him. "What were you thinking? What happened to you going to Bron?"

He snorts. "So first you were angry I was leaving for Bron, and now you're angry I didn't? Good grief, woman—"

"I'm angry that you almost got yourself killed. Or worse, caught. You should've taken me."

Behind me Gilford clears his throat. To announce he'd like to hear the rest of the story, I presume.

"I did not almost get caught." Eogan's face is a ripple of insult. "I made War General at age twelve, so I'd appreciate a bit more trust in my prowess, if you don't mind. But regarding Bron . . ." His tone turns serious. "I sent Kenan with my seal in my stead. He'll have far more influence over the Assembly than them suddenly seeing me halfway through their war against Tulla. It would only add to the confusion and divisiveness, whereas Kenan will be able to communicate with the weight of my unseen authority behind him."

Oh.

His voice drops even further. "Either way, I agreed with you—

that what I accomplished in Bron wouldn't affect the outcome of what's decided here. So while—"

"Wait. Repeat that first part, where you said you agreed with—"

"As I was saying, while I am still afraid for my people and I still very much believe they deserve the presence of their king, I ultimately believed it wiser to rescue Rasha and prepare Faelen for war. And in doing so, give Bron and the whole of the Hidden Lands a fighting chance."

"So you lied to me."

"I did."

"And you let me argue with you about it."

"I did."

Well, at least the bolcrane admits it.

Behind me one of the soldiers has the gall to snicker.

"No offense, Nym, but you're a hardheaded, stubborn slip of a wench, and I actually hadn't fully decided—not until I saw the determination on your face at the Assembly the other night. Which is when I knew."

I purse my lips and wait. *Knew what?*

"I knew you'd want to follow me or insist on coming to find Rasha. Except your people need you to raise them into an army if they're to have any chance of surviving this war. And you are the only person to do that."

I snort.

"I also didn't think it wise to put us both in danger, lest things . . . didn't go as planned."

"You mean lest I get myself killed."

"I mean losing you is something none of us can afford, and you of all people know that."

"Look up." Mia points through the trees where a gap in the branches gives us a rare, momentary clear view of the sky above.

And the airship that must be tracking us as they're nearly right on top of us.

Mia gives a little yelp as Rasha appears at the railing. She looks down with the help of a Bron guard. I swear my face almost cracks in half with my smile stretching across it. My heart shoves against my rib cage as the Elemental in my blood sings a refrain that zips and flits through my veins. She's alive! And here!

I could kiss Eogan for this.

Until I see the Bron guard is doing more than helping her. He's practically holding her up.

She waves me off as if to say she's fine.

"Weak from exhaustion and hunger mainly," Eogan explains.

"But she's here. And she's all right." Everything in me wants to rush up there to wrap myself around her face.

"She will be."

Rasha smiles down on us, but the lines in her face that the past few days have brought on say it may be awhile. Oh hulls, she needs medical attention.

I turn to Eogan. "They need to get Rasha to the Castle."

He nods. "They're waiting until we reach the forest edge and then they'll take Kel, Lord Myles, the Cashlins, and us with them. The soldiers will bring the horses."

I swallow and nod. And force a grin before blowing her a kiss.

She returns it, then sags against the guard assisting her. Then the tree foliage turns thick again, blocking my view of her along with the sky and sun.

I lean over to Eogan to murmur, "Thank you," but it comes out more choked up than intended.

I'm rewarded with a half tweak of a smile.

Just then one of the soldiers rides up beside me. "Lord Myles isn't too responsive, miss. I think we should hurry."

I turn back to look and am met by the Lord Protectorate waving madly at the disappeared airship.

I set Haven to canter at a faster pace.

It's an hour of listening to the airship's muted drone and tediously avoiding ticks and trees and swamp water before any of us speak again.

"And what about the Uathúils? The ones you were searching for?" Gilford asks.

"That main wraith *was* the Uathúil," I answer before peering back to Myles, whose vision of spiders has popped up from time to time over the past half hour. They appear to be following us, to the chagrin of the last soldier.

The Lord Protectorate's eyes are flashing wildly, hinting at what's behind them in that head of his. *"He's on the edge of a precipice. He has a choice, but should he decide wrong, destroy him."* The words from Queen Laiha ripple through my mind. I glance away.

"But he was a wraith."

"Exactly," Eogan says as I push Haven ahead and let the silence fall as it may. Let the awareness sink in for Gilford and Mia, and even Myles who's slowly coming round, of what that means.

Because it means Draewulf can alter Uathúils. Which means the ones he finds in Tulla and Cashlin won't merely be killed . . .

"This changes everything," Eogan says.

Yes, yes, it does. I shudder and press harder to get us out of the forest as fast as our horses can carry us through the mist and heat and dripping swampy trees.

CHAPTER 29

H OW IN HULLS ARE THEY HERE AND ALTERING our people already?"

I'm waiting for steam to spew from King Sedric's nostrils the way he's been going on. I've never seen him this frazzled, even when he was facing down Eogan's brother, King Odion. Not only is his skin tight, I'm quite certain his hair has started graying in the past five minutes.

"I believe these people were turned to wraiths before I—*before Draewulf*—left Faelen. When he spent the week here in my body." Eogan's face remains firm as stone as he says it, but I sense the emotion underneath. The self-loathing.

The impression makes me want to murder something. I'm grateful Eogan doesn't remember most of what he did while Draewulf owned his skin because I'm not sure his pride could handle it.

"So you're saying there've been wraiths within our borders for over two weeks?" Sedric looks at Eogan and Rolf. "How? I thought Tannin said that group was just a scouting party. How could the men have overlooked checking them?"

"That group wasn't a scout party," I say. "They weren't smart enough for that."

Eogan tips his head. "Even Lord Myles had the gumption to fool them into thinking he was dead. They were merely minions—

wraiths with little intelligence to serve as part of the larger army. And it was obvious they were camped out there—waiting for Draewulf's orders, if I had to guess. It's just an accident Myles stumbled on them when he did."

"But our own scout parties—"

"Would've simply thought the stench and bodies were the plagues, Your Highness. I doubt they could've known Draewulf had been there changing them."

Sedric rubs a hand over his chin and swears while Eogan and I look on. "Yes, but how many others are there? If there's one village in Litchfell taken over, there must be more." He turns to his Captain of the Guard. "Rolf, I want three units to plow through that forest. Have them search out every last village and kill anything that's not alive. And by alive, I mean natural."

"But, sire, all our men are headed for the front."

"Well, now it's all except for three units. We can't afford to be taken from the inside of our own kingdom while fighting the border as well. See that the units leave immediately—and, Rolf?"

"Yes, sire?"

"I want a *thorough* sweep."

"Yes, sire."

"They'll be killed," I whisper, eyeing Eogan.

"Not if he takes our best soldiers who've entered that forest more times than the rest of us." Sedric frowns at me. "Do either of you have any specifics on how they make more of themselves?"

His tone suggests that if this is an insensitive topic for Eogan, he doesn't have time to care.

"It's my understanding only Draewulf and Lady Isobel are able to do such a thing," I say, without glancing at Eogan. "They use magic, and as I overheard them both say, doing so is a heavy drain on their abilities."

He cocks his brow. "Which may explain Draewulf's delay in arriving. With those airships, I confess I thought he'd have shown up by now to begin his assault. Instead, I've heard neither whisper nor holler from across the waterway. Perhaps he's adding to his army."

"In more ways than we thought." I inhale and glance at Eogan. *There's no good way to go about telling Sedric. Might as well just spit it out.* Eogan nods. "Your Highness, while there, we discovered Draewulf can turn Uathúils into wraiths as well."

When Sedric doesn't flinch, I add, "Into a sort of more magnificent wraith. Like a Terrene version."

There's the reaction I expected. Paling face. Muttered swear words. Glancing up and around until his gaze lands on Eogan. "Is this true?"

"It is."

"And Lady Isobel can do so as well?"

"I would assume so, yes. At least when she still had her powers."

"So we have wraiths in our midst—who knows how many— and Draewulf coming down on us with an army of Luminescent and Terrene-wraiths! What in bleeding's name—" He slams his fist against the giant map table.

"We do have the boat of Cashlins that came in yesterday," Rolf says quietly. "Perhaps we should ask them what they've seen on the altering-their-people front."

I raise a brow and stare at Sedric as behind me Mia gasps so loudly, it's the first time I'm reminded she's been in the room this whole time. "A boat? From Cashlin? Where are they? Why aren't we speaking with them?"

"Because we put them under quarantine until Lord Myles's and your return. Considering some were Luminescents and Terrene, we thought it best to wait until we had Uathúils of our own before we went too far with them."

"But Mel—"

"The Luminescent has been most helpful," Sedric says to Mia. "We've had her with Lady Isobel almost the entire past five days." He glances at Rolf. "And it's my understanding the Cashlins who arrived yesterday were more refugees than survivors of Draewulf's initial attack on their capital. What little information we asked them for, they weren't able to help much. Other than to say the wraith raids had spread to the southern borders where they came from—and they barely escaped before their homes were burned to the ground."

"But still . . ."

The king waves his hand at Rolf. "Go ahead and show Mia to her people's holding chambers and allow her to question them."

Rolf bows and escorts Mia from the room as her "Thank you" floats back toward us.

"Your Majesty, if I may . . ."

Sedric focuses on me.

I can't say it. That if Draewulf is truly changing Uathúils into wraiths, we don't stand a chance. We're biding our time against a lost cause. I nearly choke on the thought and instead smile. "Have we heard from Eogan's general Kenan?"

Sedric shakes his head.

"And the Faelenians?" Eogan says. "Have we any indication Nym's visits have spurred results?"

"Nothing so far." Sedric turns to me and smoothes his expression. "But we are hopeful. And I am grateful for your efforts."

I nod. "Of course."

"However, if we don't hear by tomorrow afternoon," a councilman says from the opposite side of the table, "the High Council is strongly advising a draft go into effect."

Sedric looks at me with an expression that indicates he will agree to it.

I nod again. Because I think I might just agree to it as well. "In that case, if you'll excuse me."

Sedric waves his hand and turns to Eogan. "If you'll stay, I'd like a word. And, Nym . . ."

I stop halfway to the door. Turn. "Your Highness?"

"It was brought to my attention that Lord Myles's extra ability may have been responsible for some of my soldiers' deaths."

"That was an unfortunate circumstance, I assure you. Had we been aware his abilities were displaying in such a way—"

"You would have what? Controlled them? You know I have long held my cousin at a personal distance due to suspicion he brought upon himself over the years. Rumors of where his loyalties lie as well as his time spent abroad. At this juncture I'm not decided on what to believe, nor on what precisely to do with him, but I cannot allow him to continue endangering any more of my people or missions. Thus, I am insisting he stay under guard for the time being. Whether he can't control it or in fact is using it on purpose, it is clear he is a danger. However, I will speak with you about him again when it's been considered how to proceed regarding his . . . condition."

With that he gives me a smile. "In the meantime I suspect you'll want to see Princess Rasha."

CHAPTER 30

OH HULLS. THE PEOPLE ARE DYING. FALLING IN MASSES AT THE CLAWS AND swords of the wraiths. And my powers aren't broad enough or fast enough or even focused enough despite Eogan's help—meaning I'm going to end up doing as much damage as Draewulf's army.

I look at Sedric. "I can't stop the army."

"But can you stop *him*?" Sedric nods toward Draewulf who has suddenly appeared in wolf form—from where, I don't know.

And bleeding litches. He's stalking Eogan.

I don't answer. I just break into a run for the beast who's got a lather worked up around his teeth as he lunges for the man I'm in love with. "Eogan!" I scream, just as he rolls out of the way and, as he does, brings his sword up beneath the monster's arm.

Draewulf roars in anger, then slashes a claw down so fast, Eogan doesn't have time to move again before his face is sliced open and blood pours.

No!

I bring down bolt after bolt of lightning, but they're absorbed by the black wisps emanating from Draewulf, protecting him just like they did at the Keep.

Flicking my wrist, I ram three, four, five ice blades through them.

Draewulf yelps just before he trips Eogan, who's rising to meet another of the beast's blows. This time the claws slash down far-ther, reaching Eogan's neck and shredding pieces from it even as the marks on his face have begun closing up.

I frown. *What in—?*

The next second Myles is standing behind the monster, rais-ing a blade of his own against Eogan, and when the beast slashes back at him, Eogan lands a clean jab that impales Draewulf's side. Then I'm there and telling Eogan to focus on Myles because the Lord Protectorate is no longer safe or sane or anything remotely human as I'm allowing the anger and energy in my blood to build into a force that will destroy the animal once and for all.

Except before it can explode from me, within me, Draewulf's jaw opens and lunges for Eogan.

Eogan's green eyes flash up as his sword jabs into Myles's gut.

I hear the sounds of battle around me—of my people dying. I see the flash of horror on my own face in Draewulf's black-eyed reflection.

His mouth comes down. I step in front of him.

I lurch awake with my face pressed flat against the cool window-pane I fell asleep against last night after meeting with Sedric and Eogan. I glance around for Draewulf at the same time I'm grabbing for my throat. Where is he?

It takes one, two, three seconds for it to hit me that it was just a dream. Or rather a nightmare, but unreal nonetheless.

I open the window and inhale the fresh Faelen morning air in hopes it'll clear my head. Then wince. If I thought the presence of Draewulf was tangible at Litchfell, the presence of fear is flat out suffocating here. At the moment, I'm not sure which is worse.

"Just enjoy it."

I twist around to find Rasha sitting at my feet, leaning her head against my leg. My squeal could wake a ferret-cat, it's so loud. It brings her to laugh and climb up on the seat beside me where I wrap my arms around her fragile frame. "How are you?" I search her face.

"Better." And she sounds stronger than yesterday.

"I came in here last night, but you were sleeping so soundly I didn't want to wake you."

"So you fell asleep on my window seat." She giggles. "Well, I'm glad you did. You were the first thing I saw when I opened my eyes this morning."

"I missed you."

She pats my arm and winks. "Of course you did." Then she looks around the courtyard below us as if it's barren of life. "Honestly, what have you even done for the past week without me? Boring as all get-out, I bet."

I chuckle. "All except for Lord Myles. He's been the life of the party."

"Lord Myles is the life of every party. As long as insanity is a requirement." Her laugh is airy and musical and oh-so-home-like, even with its faint hint of weariness. I rest my head on her shoulder and take it in. I swear I could sit like this forever.

"So have you seen him, then?" I ask.

"Oh yes. And he's a piece of work."

I sit up and study her. "Good work or bad?"

She shrugs. "He's humbler, so that's something, I guess."

"Did they tell you he left us in order to rescue you?"

"I may have heard something about that." She sniffs. "Doesn't mean I like him more."

I grin.

"What? Stop grinning. Why are you grinning?"

I twist my lips and look away.

"Seriously. Just stop. It's creepy."

"Or romantic," I say in a singsong voice.

She hits me flat across the face with the window seat's giant pillow and keeps hitting until I throw up my hands. "Okay, okay, I was just jesting."

"Humph. You better have been. But speaking of Myles . . . I was asked to go check on him again, but I wanted to see you first." She plants a kiss on my cheek. "And now that I've seen you, I must go deal with the blasted oaf."

I kiss her hand in the way that people kiss royalty. "See you in a bit." Then I wave and wait until the door shuts before going back to staring out the window. It's a good twenty minutes before I finally rouse again to find my way to my own room where hopefully breakfast is waiting.

When I arrive, Kel is practicing his throwing knives against the door.

They make a cracking sound every time they hit the veneer. *Good.*

"These are heavier than the ones we use in Bron." Kel balances one of the blades I asked Tannin to bring the boy—to keep him busy because it won't do for him to lose his edge. "I think they stick harder."

I nod and browse the food tray he's nearly decimated with his ravenous boy-appetite. And continue watching the maze of High Court streets beyond the Castle courtyards and walls. Waiting for any sign of new people, new travellers, peasants and villagers who've responded to our request.

So far nothing.

The sounds of horses being shoed and armor being moved echo off the white stone walls, as do the voices of the children and nursemaids who're slowly being moved up to find quarters inside the Castle gates. Carts of vegetables and cured meats follow them up while wagons full of ale make their way down toward the collections to be taken to the battlefield.

Priorities. I snort and scan the sky for airships—Draewulf's or Kenan's. But it's as empty as the roads leading to the Castle.

I wonder if Eogan's awake yet.

"What's wrong with that crabby one—Lord Myles?" Kel asks after a particularly fierce throw.

"You've seen him. He's suffering from a form of magic. Why do you ask?"

"'Cuz I heard him having another of those visions last night. It was . . . eerie. They had to summon Princess Rasha to calm him down."

Rasha?

Except the tone Kel's just said it in, I know he, in fact, believes it fascinating. I smirk.

"Could he always do that?"

"Since he was younger and his abilities began to show, I believe. But not as strong." I turn to look at the boy. "He enhanced them a number of years ago, and then recently enhanced them more, as you saw."

"But how'd he do it? The first time he enhanced them?"

"Don't even think about it—it doesn't work on non-Uathúils."

He juts his chin out, but the look in his eye proves my warning was well warranted. "You don't have to tell me not to do anything dangerous. I was just wondering, that's all. Like where did he get them from—how'd you and him absorb it?"

"A witch." I'm pleased when his eyes show a hint of startled fear. *Good.* "Draewulf's old wife. Not a very lovely person, if you must know."

He shivers and scuffs his feet over the carpeted floor. "You think he'll die soon?"

"What is with you and people dying?" I start to chuckle but stop when my throat softens and my gaze strays beyond him, as if I could see his thoughts drifting to his father.

"He'll be back soon," I say softly. "And he'll be safe."

The boy nods but continues to look worried. "But what about Lord Myles?"

Why does he—? Oh. He must've seen Myles suffering in his room. "You should really stop eavesdropping, you know."

At which he grins and sets down the knives he's retrieved from the door. "If I did, I wouldn't be able to tell you that Lady Isobel's powers might be coming back."

I stare. *Wait, what?*

And after a moment stand and stride over to put a hand on his chin. "What did you just say?"

He pulls away and widens his proud smile. "Just that Lady Isobel's powers might be reemerging."

"That's impossible."

He nods. "That's what the guards think too. But I heard her muttering about it, and when she didn't know I was watching, I saw her try to use it against a rat in her cell."

I freeze. "Did it work?"

"Couldn't tell. It might've. Or it might've just gotten scared to death by her personality. Either way, it squeaked loud-like, then dragged its body off like it was hurt bad."

Litches.

I swallow and run a hand over my memorial tattoos. Feeling the familiar bumps and lines fanning down my left arm.

"You think the witch enhanced them for her too?"

I frown. The witch? Then shake my head. "No. Her mother doesn't live around here and wouldn't have access to her anyway."

"I know. I meant when she was back in Bron with us."

Oh. "No. I think it's more likely the power that stole her abilities before entering Myles perhaps didn't actually steal them. Maybe it just blocked them like Draewulf did to my own. I don't know—maybe it even absorbed some of what Draewulf did to me and then mimicked it." I inhale and shut my eyes. Then open them. "It doesn't matter. I need to see for myself."

I stride for the door. "Stay here—"

"No way. I want to see this."

"Kel—"

"You're supposed to be watching me, right? Well, what if while you're gone I decide to . . . you know . . . get myself in trouble?"

"You little—"

"You owe me for not letting me see the bolcranes."

I swear I can't help my grin when he winks at me.

"Since when did I turn into someone who's bossed around by little boys?" I mutter as he follows me from the room.

"Since you met me, that's when."

I turn on him, but the blasted child slips his hand into mine and looks up so innocent-like I can only sigh and squeeze his small fingers. "Fine, come on."

Tannin is nowhere to be seen and neither is Rolf or Eogan, so I let Kel drag me to wherever they're keeping Lady Isobel.

The outer rooms aren't fancy but are still nicer than those the peasantry own. However, they're apparently for the guards' comfort since, when I look past them and through the inner doorway, the setting is more what I'd expect for a criminal. The room holds a large metal-bar cage with a stone floor and small slits for windows high in the wall. Although no one could say King Sedric is one to mistreat a lady. He's allowed her a velvet couch, a cot, and a cherry-wood washbasin.

Two guards step in front of us to block the doorway. The elder eyes Kel. "Back again, I see. Well, young master, like we told you the last time, you're not permitted near these rooms."

"And like I told you last time, I just want a peek."

The guard snorts, then nods at me in respect. "Can I help you, m'lady?"

"I wish to speak with the prisoner."

"Forgive me, miss, but while you are allowed in, the boy needs a letter of permission with the king's seal."

"He'll wait out here." I tip a smile to Kel.

The boy gripes but after a second slinks to the floor. "Fine."

"It's not as if you won't be able to hear us," I whisper.

I stride past the guards and straight to the center of the adjoining room, within a hand's reach of the metal cage. And thump on it with my fist.

Lady Isobel turns from her spot on the cot and sits up. And smiles a look I'm not prepared for.

"I was wondering when you'd get around to it." She flits a hand and stands. "Seems I've seen everyone else who's anybody in this place. I'd begun to think you didn't care."

"I was gone."

"And now you're here."

I hold out a hand. "Show me."

She giggles. "What, may I ask, are you wanting to see?"

"What you did to Eogan when he was younger. How you turned his heart to stone and yet kept him alive."

Her mirth reaches her eyes as she moves toward me until the bars are the only separation between us. "I'd love to, trust me. But I'm not quite certain how that would make a hulls of difference to you or him, or anyone else about to die."

"I want to know what he felt for you," I whisper, as if it's really true. But then, perhaps a part of it is.

She jerks toward the bars. "You want to know what he felt? Lust. Love. Hunger. All the things you only hope he feels for you. Except without being diminished by extended feelings for others."

I refuse to flinch at her words. I've no doubt they're true.

"If that's the case, then how is it you lost him? What'd you do that caused him to reject you so fiercely?"

She scowls and pulls away. And says nothing.

"The way he told it, he grew tired of your control," I say gently. "It's not quite love if you have to manipulate a man to keep him, now, is it?"

Her mouth tightens. "What is it you want?"

I reach a hand through the bars. "Tell me what made him so special. What is it exactly his ability can do? What did *you* want him for?"

"Ask him yourself."

"As you know, he's rather silent about certain things. But he must've had something you craved. Or was it simply love?"

She opens her mouth. Shuts it. Finally, "He was more my counterpart than you can imagine. Even in ability. Where I can destroy . . ."

"He can—what?"

Her lips clamp shut again in an expression that says I'll not get more. "At least help me understand what you and he had together."

She scoffs. "So you can have something similar? Or perhaps in your pathetic mind—better? Trust me, darling, neither of you will last long enough to find out."

I keep my hand through the bars as a sign I mean no offense. Because suddenly I don't. If anything, the only thing I feel is compassion. For the fact that every love she's known has eventually left her. Or is about to.

"About that . . . Do you think we're the only Uathúils left your father needs?"

"After the Cashlin queen, yes."

I lean in. "And that's what you think—that he'll come for me once he's consumed them?"

Her mouth twists along with her gaze, but there's a hesitancy behind it.

I swallow and continue holding out my hand. "Because it seems to me there's one missing factor you may have overlooked."

She turns and flicks a hand up as if uninterested in my speech even as her body tension says she's straining to listen.

"Your father needs each royal Uathúil from all five kingdoms. Except, who's the one from your land? Aren't the Mortisfaire tied to Drust?"

She stops and, from the side, I see her face pale so slowly I almost miss it, but the ash color emerges. Stealing the color from her cheeks, her lips, her throat. She turns.

I nod and slide a finger down the bars to her cage. "If I had to guess, I'd say that Uathúil was your mother."

"The Mortisfaire he consumed was head of our order. She was the first he took for power."

I shrug. "Interesting." And start to turn. "Only . . . don't you think—?"

"Don't I think what?" she growls.

I flip around. "I was merely wondering if he's ever shown you those abilities. Has he been able to do what you can do? Or what your mother can do, for that matter? Have you seen him turn a person's heart to stone?"

"Go to hulls."

But the undertone is so tight, so slick, she might as well be confessing I punched her in the gut. *Oh litches.* She's really never thought of this. I peer closer at her and see the fear slowly register. The confusion.

"I only hope for your sake he takes your mum instead of you."

She lunges at the bars, grabs my shirt, and shoves her hand against my chest. Then starts to yank away, but not before I feel the thing I've been probing for. Her ability. It's there. It's already reacting to my own blood in her attempt to harden my veins.

I don't move. Just let her sense the beat beat beat of my heart-pulse that feels nothing more than pity for her in this moment.

Her mouth goes straight as she pulls her hand back. "If my father didn't need you, I'd have killed you by now."

"I'm sorry," I say, and my voice cracks the slightest. For the life she's about to lose. *"Mercy grows hearts more than bitterness, Nym."*

Her face softens. Her hand against my skin weakens. She pulls away and looks at me with eyes full of fear. Of grief.

After a moment she turns and says quietly to the wall of her cell, "Have Princess Rasha focus Myles in on his innermost thoughts, not on interrupting the images. Those are merely the consequences, not the root. Tell her to train him at the root."

"Did you just—?"

"Yes, and you're welcome. Now please leave me."

I am about to reply with a thank-you when Kel's voice rings out above the steadily growing whirring sound of engines. "The airships are back! My father's returned!"

CHAPTER 31

KING SEDRIC, ROLF, THE LUMINESCENTS surrounding Rasha, Eogan, Kel, and me, along with a number of councilmen and guards, are waiting in the War Room when Kenan arrives.

He enters with a few soldiers. The air in my lungs catches at the sight of his haggard face. "Your Highnesses."

A quiet gasp beside me indicates Kel's seen his father, and then he's running for the large man who, rather than giving the characteristic gripping of the boy's shoulder, actually stoops to hug him.

I look away.

"It is with much relief and joy I find you returned and well." Eogan bounds over to pat Kenan on the back and, with that movement, expresses what the rest of us in the room feel. It's as if the tension hanging over us for days is given a slight reprieve and the men within visibly relax.

Sedric offers the room's available chairs.

"I'll stand, thanks, or I'm likely to fall asleep." Eogan's smile doesn't reach his eyes.

"As will I," Kenan says. "I assume the fact that we're all here means we each accomplished our missions." He's looking at Eogan when he says this and is rewarded by a nod from his king.

"We found Rasha," Eogan murmurs.

"And in good health, I see." Kenan bows to the princess. "And what of other airships? I've brought a few back with me, but have any more crossed the channel?"

"Only those Nym took down and the one Eogan returned on," Sedric says. "Although we clearly expect more now that they appear to have targets in mind and their forces in motion." He eyes me. "Although, aside from Nym's watchfulness and skill with the sky, I'm not sure what defense we have from them. If they will, in fact, be Draewulf's first offense."

"They will. I'm certain of it." Eogan peers over at me. "It's what I would do were I him."

"How much time do you think we have?"

Eogan glances at Rasha, to which she answers, "Three more days at the most."

He nods. "I know his forces were chasing me, but I assume they also purposefully took out our warboats in order to ferry his forces over using boats from Cashlin."

"Then Nym should head for the coast to stop them as they come."

"They'll have innocents in them." How I know this is beyond me, but my mouth goes dry at the awareness of it. I turn to Sedric. "It's what I would do. And Draewulf knows me too well."

Eogan nods his agreement. "We may not have much of a choice, though."

I raise a brow and stare him down. "There's always a choice. I believe you're the one who used to teach that."

"Eogan's right," Sedric interrupts. "They'll all be dead sooner or later if we don't act." He glances at Rasha for confirmation.

"I believe so, yes."

I bite back my comment. How could they be so matter-of-fact about it? At least show a little remorse before making such a decision.

"I believe the sooner we can get you to the coast, the better." Sedric waits for me to look at him before continuing. "Can you be ready to leave within a few hours? You should take whatever you'll need since . . ."

Since I won't be coming back.

I nod and try not to look at Eogan.

"However, before you go . . ." Sedric turns to the Bron king. "Can you brief us on the situation in Bron? And will there be more soldiers or airships on the way?"

His tone is so hopeful it almost drags the tension back into the room.

Kenan runs a hand over his unshaved face and peers across the war map at Eogan. "First off I should tell you that Lord Percy and Lady Gwen are still alive, albeit locked in small quarters. Aside from that, I don't know whether this is a positive or negative, but my going to Bron has set off an underground war."

He looks at Rasha. "I fear because of this I was unable to bring back anything more than the two extra airships and all the soldiers they could hold." Then he turns to Sedric. "My apologies, Your Highness, but if Eogan's people were to stand a chance at forming a resistance movement, they needed all the manpower they could get. I was able, through meetings and influential sources, to give them the motivation and freedom they needed to pursue such a task. But I could not in good conscience take more from their needed numbers."

"No apology necessary," Sedric says, and even I can tell he's trying to keep the sound of defeat from his voice. "Your people are your king's priority and it is as it should be. What will come will come."

Eogan bows his head, says, "Thank you, Kenan," then looks at me. "Any luck with gathering forces among Faelen?"

"Not so far."

"But they'll come," one of the council members butts in. "One way or another. We've just sent out runners and enforcers an hour ago."

I turn to the man. And again that sensation of being appalled while totally understanding his stance washes over me. It makes me feel ill.

I clear my throat and set a hand on the giant map before interrupting the kings. "In the meantime you should both know Isobel's ability is returning."

They stall midconversation and Sedric raises a brow. "It's what? How did you hear of this? How did you—?"

Eogan doesn't seem surprised.

"I believe it to be the case as well," Rasha adds, and behind her Mia and Mel nod.

"I was also able to discover that while we were still in Bron, Draewulf had his wife killed." Kenan's voice is quiet. "Presumably in an attempt to take her Mortisfaire power. Although I was told he was unsuccessful. Something about her having made too many alterations over the years . . ."

I freeze. And let the air build up in my throat before exhaling.

"Then Draewulf will need Isobel," I whisper.

The two kings and both their right-hand men swerve their attention my way. "And you know this how?" Rolf asks, not unpolitely.

I don't know how to explain it, but I've rarely been so certain of anything in my life. In my blood. In my head.

"In that case, it'd be wise to keep her as far from the battlefield as possible," Sedric says.

"Can we spare the men needed to watch her?" Rolf interjects.

"We'll have to." I look at Sedric. "Your Majesty, if you'll excuse me, I believe you can do without me now. I would like to pack and prepare for the coastal trip you spoke of. I'll be ready to leave when you send a unit to my room."

"Of course, yes. And thank you." The king tips his head, but it's clear he's still distracted by the conversation regarding Lady Isobel. He promptly resumes asking Eogan questions as well as inviting the Luminescents to fill in details from what they've learned.

I give Rasha's hand a squeeze and leave them to head for my room to pack two sets of blue leathers, extra boots, and a hair comb.

Once finished, I braid my long white tresses and settle in to sit by the window—to search the sky and landscape for more airships as Sedric requested.

After a half hour nothing new has appeared and I'm just eyeing the four airships being worked on when a knock on the door startles me.

"Come in." I stand to grab my bag for the soldiers.

Eogan walks in looking a bit unsure whether he's allowed to or not. The next moment he's shut the door and strides toward me with hands tucked into his pockets. "I thought you'd like to know I peeked in on Lord Myles a few minutes ago. Princess Rasha has been able to ease his visions enough to give him sleep."

I stare at Eogan. At this man who knows me so well that he's aware of how much I'd care about something so simple—about a man I loathe. More than that, Eogan's aware I'd want to know.

I swallow. "Thanks."

"From the sound of his visions, I take it your time travelling the villages didn't go quite as planned."

I look away.

"You saw an old owner."

I wave a hand toward the far-off forest that's melting into fog banks. "It doesn't matter."

"It does to me."

The tension, the fury in his tone, is simultaneously scary and severely romantic. I blink and force the heat in my neck down.

"That whole thing with rallying the people . . ." I look at the glimpses of empty roads stretching in multiple directions. "Apparently it's not what I'm cut out for."

He shakes his head, but before he can argue, I lift a hand.

"The thing is"—I swerve my gaze down to my boots—"I'm not sure whether I'm worried or relieved they're not coming." I run a finger over the itching vein in my wrist. The one that's still got the poison in it.

He steps closer until he's standing beside me, staring out the window too. "So you wouldn't be responsible for their deaths. Except . . ."

I nod and he waits until I glance up at him to continue. "Either way they're most likely going to die. Allowing them to participate in fighting for what they value is you honoring them, not leading them to their demise."

"I know."

"Would it make a difference to you? To be given the choice?"

"Of course, but I have abilities that—"

"No, you have honor. And free choice. Which is what everyone deserves." The way he says it—the way he looks at me—makes me wonder if we're still talking about war or . . .

He glances away before I can read more from his gaze. He runs a hand through his black hair, pushing his bangs back so they look gorgeous and his eyes greener. I inhale and curse him under my breath for whatever his hang-up is that is keeping us separated by so little distance and yet so much space.

"Why'd you really go back for Rasha?" I ask.

"I told you. Because we need her."

"Why else?"

He purses his mouth and stares at me a moment before uttering a swear. "Why are you asking?"

Because I want to know you. I want to know what's going on inside of you.

I want to know what you're still so afraid of.

I shrug. "Does it matter? Just tell me."

"I didn't want to expose myself to anyone else—my people in Bron, or you—without some assurance that Draewulf's . . . residual effects in me wouldn't result in harming others."

I bite my lip. That makes sense. "And?"

"As far as Rasha can tell, I'm fine. For now."

Meaning he's still nervous.

He drops his gaze to mine, then tips his head. "What?"

"Nothing, I just—"

"It's not nothing. You've got that expression on your face."

Lovely. I don't trust my voice so I shake my head.

"What's going on up there?" He reaches a hand out to tap the side of my head, making me smile, which then brings him to smile too.

Rather than pulling his hand away, he presses it against my hair and the side of my face as his smile slides away into something deeper, something I haven't seen in over a week, and it awakens every ache and thirst in me to fall completely into him.

I stare and feel the air deflate from the room. As if we've drawn it all in and left nothing but raw energy and emotion and— Oh hulls, why is he confusing me again?

He blinks and his lips open slightly. Then he's leaning in, my gaze wrapped in his, and I swear it's infused with static.

Thick inhale. Soft exhale.

His eyes flit past me to the window. And the next second he's clearing his throat and blinks before lifting his head. "Nymia," he whispers.

I could sink into his voice, at the sound of my name on his lips with that rich accent with which he's always murmured it. I shut my eyes because something tells me that's not why he's saying it now, blast him.

"Look."

Stupid oaf. I turn to look and the first thing I see is rain. Beautiful sunlit mist making rainbows against the green earth of the land I love almost more than anything.

I inhale again and relish the feel of his warm hand still on my arm. Thus it's one, two, three seconds longer before I notice what he wanted me to see.

People.

Loads of them. *Thousands* of them. Emerging through the fog along the winding roads as far as I can see, with nothing on their backs but clothes, tools fashioned into weapons, and a few pots and pans. Mothers holding the hands of their young; boys and even girls, not yet in puberty, walking with heads held high; old men, too feeble to walk without a cane, yet still strong enough to wield a scythe.

I blink away the heat, but the daft unbidden tears fall anyway. Why, I don't know—perhaps because I've never been so moved, so humbled at others' belief. At these individuals who're bringing their hope rather than expectation—I feel it like an offering they've just infused into me. These lives that will be lost along with mine too soon, too easily, too unfairly, and yet they come anyway.

I turn away to wipe my eyes before Eogan can see, except he's already seen. He slides a hand down my arm and grips my hand, pulling me to stand with my back against his chest as he leans over and drapes warm breath over my cheek, my neck, my hair. And points at the peasants and slaves and the entire Faelen population getting closer by the moment.

"*That* is your true ability. To inspire people."

I try to laugh it off. "Well, my words were pretty incredible," but the thickness catches in my throat.

"I'm sure they were," he says dryly. "But everyone in that War Council is also good with words, and they haven't inspired anyone to more than contempt in years. Your true ability is what I've always said it was. Your compassion and desire to protect. That is what you've extended to these people. It's what you've given them. And *that* is why they'll follow you."

"Even to their deaths," I whisper, watching the women, men, and children filing up the white High Court stone road.

Before he can answer, a pounding on the door makes me jump and pull away as his hand drops mine.

Then the door's opening and Tannin's head is appearing. "Pardon, m'lady and Your Highness. I was told to inform you there's been a change in plans."

CHAPTER 32

YOU'RE AWFULLY QUIET."

I glance over to find King Sedric watching me. And refrain from mentioning we've been on the road for an hour without any breakfast and a host of our Faelen people scrambling to keep up. "I suppose I am."

"Care to speak your thoughts?"

Do I care to speak my thoughts? Um, no, not exactly.

But after a moment, "Maybe I'm just feeling the weight of what we're heading toward—and that it's no small thing we're leading them to."

"Nor could we do so without you."

"So I keep hearing." *Litch.* I bite my tongue, but the words have already fallen out. "Sorry. I didn't mean to be uncharitable."

"Not uncharitable. Merely honest." He grins.

If he were Eogan, I'd hurl a blast of icy wind in his face. Bolcrane.

"Your sentiment's a fair one, Nym. I imagine what's intended as gratitude has placed a measure of pressure on your shoulders." He tips his head back at the mass following on foot and horseback and wagon.

A measure? I look away because I'm beginning to think this man has no idea.

And if I admit it, I'm fine with it being that way. I don't want him in tune with me—or sensing my thoughts and moods the way Eogan can.

I just want to get this over with.

"How long will Eogan be?"

He looks at the guards riding with Mia, Mel, and Lord Myles near us. Then at Rolf, who answers, "I believe he's merely a half hour behind, sire."

Sedric veers his gaze back to me. "I'll admit I'm quite curious what it was he went to retrieve from Lady Adora's old house. Most interesting."

"From the cottage," I correct.

"The what?"

"The cottage. Eogan lived in a cottage behind Adora's house."

"Ah, yes." He looks at Princess Rasha, who's riding beside a caged coach that contains Lord Myles, and I catch his glance, ensuring Myles's hands are still tied and the bar locks still in place. "You're looking better this morning, cousin."

"Thank you."

"No more visions?"

"Oh, plenty, but Her Highness has seen fit to *asssist me* from time to time."

Sedric nods in approval, but from the sheen of sweat covering Myles's forehead and the eyes that are blackening by the hour, I'd say he's struggling to keep up on those times. His pupils keep dilating and his hands are twitching to itch at the dark, spindled veins trailing up his wrists and arms and now around his throat. It makes the blood in my own veins itch.

I turn away. "You're certain you'd not have me ride ahead, Your Highness? To ensure more ships don't reach our shore?"

"According to last night's report, it's too late for that. Most had already landed by the time the runner reached us. And with that many already here and half our units having not returned . . . I fear we'd lose you too." He smiles. "Better to keep you within eyesight."

Like Lady Isobel and Myles.

I take a quick peek back at the woman being trundled along in a separate caged cart, surrounded by more guards than we can spare. Why Sedric felt safer having her beneath his watchful eye is up for debate in the wisdom arena.

I keep my lips pursed and scan the dark, clouded horizon ahead of us, then the road and the green, sheep-dotted hills we're trekking across.

Still no sign of Draewulf's airships. Nor of the sea.

I can feel it, though. The salty foam spitting and hissing and spraying, much like the wraiths crossing it even now. We should get a view of both any moment if the pricking in my blood and the growing, snakelike whispering in my head is any indication.

Although mercifully, the wraiths' hissing is quickly drowned out by a murmuring sound drifting forward from the ranks behind us. I yank Haven's wandering mouth away from Sedric's leg and look back again for Eogan, then at the people travelling behind the lines upon lines of Faelen soldiers.

My people.

Walking with a stride in their step that suggests pride and hope. I beg it to shore up the wavering in me that senses Draewulf's presence growing bigger, grander, more suffocating. Until it occurs to me they're not murmuring—they're singing, a melody as familiar as my own skin. It's "The Song of the Dreamer." Good hulls, I've not heard it in years, but I used to hum it every night before bed in the wee hours that were my own. It's the song of every warrior, homemaker, slave, blacksmith, and baker. My father taught it to me on his knee.

It's the song of freedom.

Something twinges in my arm. A fluttering, as if the bird carved into my skin is raising her head to chirp along with them. I grin and promptly join in humming. Until I'm singing it, and soon King Sedric and the troops are singing too, and in this moment, in this exhale beneath the Faelen sky surrounded by mountains and valleys and rich Faelen earth, we as a massive horde are the heartpulse of this land. And our voices together are her blood. My own voice grows louder at this thought until I swear it could reach beyond the atmosphere and rain forth victory.

A strangled snarl on my right is the first indication Lord Myles isn't so appreciative of the song. Then he's shaking and shuddering and his eyes are rolling back. There's a pop in the air around him, as if a suds bubble just burst, and suddenly a massive shift in the atmosphere ripples out from him, like a pebble tossed into a pond. As the rings spread, so does a vision of blood and soldiers beheading each other and death so horrific Mia begins to gag.

The next second it's as if his blood is calling to mine, his poison to my poison, and the bird that was just fluttering is now gasping a warning as the spidery hunger rears its head beneath my skin. It's hungry for the vision and the death it senses.

"Guards! Luminescents! See to the Lord Protectorate!"

It's all I can do to refrain from scratching my arm. Instead, I flip Haven around King Sedric while he's still giving commands regarding his cousin and allow Haven's teeth to warn the soldiers aside in order to ride up behind Myles.

I yank my blade out and flip it around to use the base of it on the back of his head.

Except before I can, Rasha's hand slides out to stop me. "Wait."

She speaks in a low tone to Myles, saying words I can hardly hear and can't for the life of me understand. As if she's doing a spell or a chant.

One minute, two minutes, three minutes go by and Myles's twitching lessens.

"Don't teach him to resist the effects—teach him to understand their causes inside of him," I say, recollecting Isobel's guidance.

Rasha's brow goes up, but she changes her tone and whatever it is she's asking, and then Myles's gaze clears and his hands firm around the cage bars. He's breathing heavy as if straining, hanging on Rasha's every word—as if they are all that is keeping him from slipping again.

Farther back, murmurs of confusion pick up, but it doesn't matter.

In a few minutes none of them will care—or even remember.

Because the hill we've been travelling up we're now cresting, and the Valley and rough stormy sea are splaying out below us.

And the sight nearly knocks me from Haven's saddle.

CHAPTER 33

M
Y HEART PLUNGES INTO MY KNEES AS A UNI-
fied gasp goes up around me.

"Bleeding litches," Kel mutters.

The valley below us is covered in a writhing, rippling mass of black, stretching from the northern coastline to Litchfell Forest on the west and the Hythra Mountain range in the east. There must be ten thousand of them, maybe more, all growling and moving and preparing to destroy us.

And above them hangs a heavy mist. Except . . .

It's not a mist—it's more vile. Like a film of evil lurking in the air, oozing up from the magic that created it. Same as what I'd thought were dark clouds hovering over the water and the boats littering the coastline—only these clouds aren't gray. They're black. Like the wisps Draewulf draws in to protect himself. Stretching far back beyond the normally visible mountain ranges inside Tulla and Cashlin.

The mist stirs and moves, like the wraiths it's guarding.

Litches. My skin crawls and it's as if I can physically hear Draewulf muttering his enchantments.

"Tell the soldiers to halt here and have the people set up camp," says Sedric in a voice as dazed as the look on his young, weary face. "At least we'll have the high ground."

I hardly hear the orders given for the troops to spread out and make camp. Nor the collective gasps of horror as more and more people crest the hill and see what awaits them.

What awaits *us*.

It's as if you can hear what we're all thinking. *We're going to be annihilated.*

"I see that explains why we haven't heard back from two of our soldier units sent out." Rolf points to the base of the valley below us where the road continues through to the coast.

It's a matter of strength that I tear my gaze away from the crawling mass of hissing undead to squint toward whatever it is he's looking at. Once I do, I'm suddenly grateful I was too nervous to eat this morning.

Ten stakes are on each side of the road at the base of the hill, like a hand-fashioned entrance gate to their encampment. Except rather than flags flying the colors of their land, the stakes have men impaled on them. Dead soldiers, to be exact, wearing Faelen colors. All except for one, who's dressed as a Cashlin.

Mia and Mel utter a cry at the same time as they see it too.

I force my gaze away—beyond the horror—and focus on those who committed it.

I swear I'll make as many of them pay as I can before I join them in their graves.

"Let me take some of them out now," I say through clenched teeth to Sedric.

"As much as I'd like to, I can't allow that. Yet," he adds in a tone that promises he's infuriated too. "You'd start the bleeding war too soon, before all of our people have assembled and prepared."

I scowl. "Then what about them?" I point to two warboats surging across the darkened waterway to join the five others moored to the Faelen shoreline. Above the boats float ten airships peeking out from the black fog—more than I thought he'd have after the destruction that happened in Tulla.

Sedric and Rolf both shake their heads. "Again, you'd start it before we're prepared to finish it," Sedric says.

Fine.

A sprinkle of rain begins to fall. Not on us, but on the massive horde below. My contribution to irritating the hulls out of the beasts without being accused of overstepping by the men in front of me.

I smirk. "If you'll excuse me." I turn to search for something that *will* make me feel useful. I promptly come upon Kel pulling bedding off a wagon to help lay out.

"Are these for the noblemen?"

"Nah. They can get their own litched blankets. These are for the soldiers."

I grin. "In that case . . ." I go to help him, and it takes little less than an hour before the cart's emptied and we've set up bedding for five whole units.

"Let's do another," Kel says, and it's only then it occurs to me he's trying to keep busy too. He won't even look in the direction of the wraith army.

Of course.

He's scared.

"Have you ever heard the legend of the bolcranes?" I ask after a minute.

His interest is immediate. I help him tumble off a roll of thin mats before hopping down from the wagon. "Some think they were from Elementals. Or rather, they are Elementals." I kick a mat toward him so he'll keep working.

"Ones that lived so long ago, no one remembers if it's true or not anymore. But legend claims they were the most beautiful beings on the face of the Hidden Lands—and the most powerful. Until over time they began to squander that beauty and power and started using it for their own gain and glory rather than for helping others."

I scratch at my wrist.

Then scratch it harder until I'm abruptly aware I'm doing so. I frown and glance around. And hear it.

I don't know what's just happened in the valley below, but there's a sudden spike in the wraiths' hissing, and it's not just from the rain I'm blessing them with. It scratches at my skin and inside my head, and for a moment I swear it sounds like, "He's coming for you, pet."

I flip around and stare down at the writhing horde that smells of death and decay and is worse than any bolcrane ever could be as a subtle suggestion hits me. Soon it's birthed within my chest bones and spine—*Draewulf has just sensed my presence.*

"Nym? What happened to them?"

What? I narrow my brow and turn to Kel, who's waiting with an expectant expression.

Oh. Right.

I shake off the eerie sensation and toss him another bedroll. "They became arrogant and selfish."

"Like Lord Myles?"

I bark a laugh and look around to see if the oaf heard. He didn't. He's too busy speaking with Rasha.

"Yes, a bit like Lord Myles. Except way worse."

"That why they turned into bolcranes? 'Cuz they wasn't acting human anymore?"

"You could say something like that."

He snorts.

"How about you? Any good legends to tell?"

Silence.

When I glance up, he's not even looking at me. His gaze is leveled on something to the right of me, and he's squinting through an air that hangs thick with what none of us are saying. "We will survive," I whisper.

When he doesn't reply, I turn to see what's got him so fixated.

"What are those?"

My gaze drops to where he must be looking and my breath clogs up my throat, my head, my heart. Wraiths have just lit the soldier stakes on fire, burning the dead men like they are fuel for light and warmth amid the sickly dark fog. Or food.

"Those are funeral pyres," I whisper.

"Not those. Those." He points closer to my right—along the ridge against the horizon. "There." He tips his head toward the shadowed sun. "Are they—? Ah, no way!"

Five giant oliphants are lumbering toward us, swinging their trunks between tusks that are larger than a tree. And riding on top of the first one is Allen, the Travelling Baronet.

"Anyone call for reinforcements?" the dwarf yells.

CHAPTER 34

MUSIC FILLS THE NIGHT AIR, SWINGING BETWEEN brassy pitches and soft, melodic voices that sing of wars and lovers and days of old. Of past queens I've rarely heard of and past kings who were dethroned.

One day left and then tomorrow we fight.

But tonight?

Tonight we celebrate life.

And love.

And freedom.

I grin and walk from my tent—an oversize white-linen thing provided to Rasha and me in spite of the fact I tried to decline it multiple times, until Rolf pointed out it had more to do with our safety than comfort. Tucking my hair inside my cloak for anonymity, I glance around for Rasha or Eogan before finding myself joining in the laughter as sweaty bodies wrap arms around waists and swing each other to the victorious notes. Squeals and shouts float into the sky and hang there above us, like the stars twinkling where I've blown back the massive black fog. As if the constellations are whispering, "Tonight we dance, for tomorrow, come what may, it will be as it should. It will be all right."

I shuffle my way through the growing crowd of peasants and soldiers as the scent of roasting meat and apples floats through the air and sends my stomach rumbling and my mouth salivating. I hadn't even realized I was hungry, but the food combined with the crisp smells of fire and earthen smoking pipes and ale has me making straight for the camp's center where great fires have been lit.

Around each of them someone's placed roasting spits loaded with meat for anyone to cut pieces off at their leisure. And beneath them, pots of boiling broths and stews.

I grab a bowl from a cart and help myself to one of the less-seasoned-smelling ones. Then turn to wander in search of Eogan, whom I've not seen all day.

A chorus of laughter draws me to the right where one of the travellers has brought out a panther-monkey and is entertaining the youngest soldier children by feeding it nuts. Which it throws onto their heads, bopping them and making them laugh all the harder because everyone knows panther-monkeys don't eat nuts. They eat dog.

On my left a young man has brought out what I suspect is double-lavka—an alcohol with a considerably higher content than the usual common-house fare. I grin as two elderly men challenge the young man and his friends to a duel of drinks because it's clear the old-timers are going to show them a thing or two.

Good for them.

I keep walking and farther ahead, around the biggest fire in the mix, someone picks up singing "The Monster and the Sea of Elisedd's Sadness." It carries low at first, like the hum of a death chant. Until another voice picks it up too. Then another. Soon the whole crowd around the fire is singing it, clear voices and tones rising up into the air and spreading to the rest of the camp. Until the whole hilltop we're standing on and the valleys below are ringing as one tragic song about the night Draewulf stole our identity as a kingdom.

The ocean, she's begging for our salvation. Begging for blood that will set our children free.

The song ends with a hush that falls so deep and heavy, it's like a blanket over the space. A blanket of grief and sadness.

"The fight will be loooong and losses will come," a child's voice pipes up to sing.

Every eye near me turns to see who it is, but I already know.

It's Kel. Adding his own ending to our Faelen anthem.

I smile and shove a gust of wind to carry his words over the entire camp as he continues singing.

But the hope of Faelen will not fail.
Because hope is in her people, in her brothers and children, in her friends who've come to fight beside her.
Lead us into battle, Faelen. And the other kingdoms will folloooow.
And Draewulf will fall through the power of unity.
Through the power of the Creator.
We will not fail.
We will not fail.

The farmer beside me lets out a choked gasp. Tears are filling his eyes and running down his cheeks. As they are on the weathered skin of every other face surrounding us.

The farmer's fist raises and thumps over his heart as Kel's song comes to a close. The Bron sign of high respect for this boy who has sung hope into our Faelen future.

The crowd moves as one to mimic the farmer's offering while Kel bows his head.

I sniff and wipe my nose on my sleeve because apparently I have been weeping too.

Until the music starts back up and this time it's a jovial tune—one often played before weddings or after the birth of a firstborn. Suddenly people are jumping up and hands commence clapping and, as more wood is thrown on the fire, dancing begins. Followed by laughter.

A hand slips into mine, and when I look down, Kel is there, smiling shy-like. "Want to dance?"

I nod. "Although I warn you I'm no good."

To our delight we soon discover neither of us is any good, which makes us a mess in the midst of what's already a rather poetic chaos of bodies and warmth and sparks from the fire lighting up eyes and faces filled with affection.

When we finish a round, I'm out of breath and laughing too hard. I glance around for Eogan, but I still can't find him amid the crowd.

"May I cut in?" Rasha's kind eyes greet mine.

I giggle. "Of course."

"Favorite part of tonight?" she asks.

"Um . . . Kel's song. You?"

"Petting the oliphants. Did you see their size?"

We burst into laughter, and words don't seem to matter in the midst of the music and energy and friendship. We dance until our hearts have opened broader than ever and our souls have emptied of everything but mirth and wonder at this moment. This time. These people surrounding us as family.

"Might I have a turn?"

I come face-to-face with King Sedric.

"Only if you give her back tomorrow," Rasha says in a tone of mock offense.

Sedric chuckles. "Will do, m'lady."

Apparently one doesn't have to be a great dancer—or even a

decent dancer—if one's partner has been trained in such a skill his entire life. The king has some incredible moves, I have to admit.

"How are you?" he asks after we've gotten our feet under us and are swinging quite neatly to the tune.

"Alive. How about you?"

"The same."

"We never finished our conversation from the banquet the other night. About you being the rightful—"

"Don't." I shake my head as, from the corner of my eye, I see Eogan. "I've made it clear I don't want the throne. And I don't even want to talk anything of it until after this whole thing is over. Otherwise I find it a bit like hoarding our goats before slaughter. We don't know which will survive."

"Meaning we don't know if I will survive," I almost tell him. Or if I *should* survive.

Or even if I *can* survive.

He nods. "Just know that I—"

"I know," I whisper. "Although I appreciate the offer, I really don't want to speak any more about it."

I sense him nod again, but I'm hardly looking. I'm watching Eogan watch me.

"Will you excuse me?" I say abruptly to Sedric. "I have something I need to do."

If he's startled I've cut him off in the middle of the song, he hides it well. "Of course. Enjoy the rest of your evening." Then he moves on to see about dancing with Rasha from the looks of it. Except from what I can tell, it appears she's slipping up to the cage where Myles is being kept.

Huh.

I make my way to Eogan, and when I reach him, I step close enough to feel his body heat and warm breath as I stare up into those brilliant green eyes that are taking me in even though his face is as sterile as ever.

"Care to walk?"

He smirks. "Depends. Where'd you have in mind?"

I point toward the outskirts of the camp, near where the tents are located, and beyond that, the Valley.

"King Sedric said you had a weapon left at Adora's you went back for," I say as we stroll away from the crowds.

He nods. "A few smaller versions of the bombs like those on the airships. With any luck we'll be able to use them at opportune times."

He stops as we reach the edge of the hill overlooking Draewulf's army. The valley they're settled into is pitch black. No lights. No fires. No celebrations.

And yet the magnitude of their presence is still tangible.

"There are so many and so few of us," I say.

"Ah, but you forget—we've got an Elemental on our side."

"Not funny," I mutter.

"No? Really? I'll clearly have to work on that." He glances back toward the party. "Did you have a nice chat with King Sedric?"

"Not overly. He offered me the same as before and I refused."

Eogan's already shaking his head. "You can't refuse before you've even tried your hand at it. For all you know it's what you were made for, and it may be exactly what your—"

"Do you want to fight tonight or dance?" I say far more gaily than I feel. I will not allow him to get on his soapbox about this issue. "I'm thinking we dance. So come on."

Tugging him to life, I grab his hand and force him to dance a good round to a rowdy and wholly inappropriate common-house song. A solid minute into it he's laughing and those eyes are relaxing.

Until a softer song begins and I get closer and our dance gets slower as our breathing grows heavier. Here on the edge of the world.

The music slows even more, and a moment later his hands are sliding to my waist. I gulp and try to keep my thoughts on the melody's words as his thumb moves up and skims along the edge of my jawline, forcing me to fail completely. I tip my lips toward his fingers before pushing his head back to gently kiss his throat.

His breath catches and his fingers move lower. Their warmth against my skin burns like a bleeding star.

I travel up his chin to his lips, and the next second he tips his mouth to meet mine, to meld with mine. And I swear a dam's broken loose inside me as every frustration and hunger from the past week pours forth into a single kiss.

Until his fingers gently tug on both wrists, untwining them from around his neck as he takes a retreating step and pulls away. "I can't."

"Can't what?"

"This."

I snort and open my mouth, but the torrent halts at his gaze.

"You're making me *insane*, Nym. As if this whole thing isn't hard enough. Can't we just . . . leave it alone for now?" His fingers loosen on my wrists as his eyes slip to my lips.

"*I* make you insane?"

"You're so bleeding stubborn."

"Stubborn? I'm stubborn? About what, Eogan? That I want to kiss you? That I want to speak with you? That I want to see you without you trying every single way in hulls to avoid me? For litches' sake—what is it? Have I done something? Or is it that you really think I want the throne?"

He shakes his head. "No. Don't even think that. That's not it. Let's just go back to the party and—"

"What the hulls is wrong with you?" I wrench my wrist away and stalk the fifteen paces to my tent.

If it had a door, I'd be slamming it.

Too late, he's pushing back the cloth opening and entering too. "Nothing's wrong with you or me. I'm just asking that we not do this tonight. We can wait until—"

"Do *what* tonight? I'm sorry if it makes you uncomfortable to actually confess what is wrong with me or why you can barely look at me sometimes. Or why every time I see you, your eyes say one thing while your fear says another. You know what? Forget it—yes, we *can* do this tonight. Because tomorrow we might be dead."

He runs a hand through his hair and I step right in front of him and let the sky rumble, prompting his lips to quirk as he stalls and this time looks down at me.

"This had better not be about whether you're still unsafe due to Draewulf's blood inside your body," I growl.

He opens his mouth. Shuts it. As if choosing his words is a force of will. Until finally, "I am trying to give you a choice, Nym. But you're making it blasted hard."

"I suggest you explain that."

He shoves fingers through his bangs again and peers around. "I'm trying to set you free so you can make your own choices. You've spent your life having things chosen for you, and never had the opportunity to explore true freedom yourself. Until now."

I think this is going somewhere.

This dratted well better be going somewhere.

He settles his gaze on me. "You're so blasted busy trying to help everyone else earn freedom, you can't even recognize it for yourself."

What is he talking about? "Have you been drinking?"

"Look. What I'm trying to say is that you and I met under . . .

rather different circumstances. And it would be wrong of me to hold you to a relationship status that was established then. You have your freedom, and I would be a very indecent person were I not to encourage you to explore how you'd like to live with that freedom. Thus . . ."

This is it. I'd bet my life on it.

"Did the queen tell you what I'd ultimately choose?" I say smoothly.

He raises a brow. "I asked. She said it's not for others to know a person's destiny unless that person wants to make it known."

She did, did she? "Well then, let me make it known." I slide my palms over his cheeks and pull his face down until those emerald eyes are level with mine. "You are the only man I've ever met who's both respected me and managed to make me hate you for keeping me in line. And you are the only man I've ever known who makes me feel safe enough to breathe and believe there's some actual good in this world."

I plant a kiss on his bottom lip. "*And* you are the only man who makes me believe that this world would be worth a pile of hulls if you weren't in it. So you can please stop acting like a daft fool and kiss me already."

He arches a half smirk and gives me a look that says he's still unsure.

"I'm waiting."

"Perhaps you need more—"

"Why? Because I've not made myself clear? Or are you unsure of your feelings for me?"

He chuckles. "Bleeding hulls, have I ever told you I love your temper?" Then leans in to obey.

The sound of a clearing throat rattles the atmosphere. I pull back, but Eogan won't release me. Just mutters, "What is it, Kenan?"

I glance over at the large soldier filling the tent opening.

"Your Majesty, King Sedric has requested your presence. I believe there's a question as to Lady Isobel's—"

A groan rumbles deep in Eogan's throat. I look up to discover his eyes are torn between annoyance and desire and it's all I can do not to tell Kenan to go to litches.

CHAPTER 35

MORNING DAWNS WITH A THICK, WHITE, blanketing mist rising up from the warm earth to greet the cool sky and blackened clouds. The sun is peeking between it on the eastern horizon, pale and dull and lifeless, as if it knows what today holds. As if it knows who will die today.

I step out of my tent fully dressed in my blue leather shirt and pants and boots. White hair braided back like I used to keep it when I was a slave. I pull my hood up. Like on auction day.

Oh hulls. That is the feeling I'm sensing—today feels like auction day, only it's not just me who's going. It's every person here.

"Don't let them die," I whisper to the Creator, hoping the spirit of him still resides in the Valley of Origin and can hear me, and care.

A sudden breeze rustles from that direction and with it the sweet scent of lake water carrying the melody that plucks at the strings of my soul, then it's gone and I'm blinking and left feeling a bit lighter, a bit stronger. I search around for Eogan and Sedric and the knights, whom I spot on a plateau surrounded by rank upon rank of our fellow countrymen.

It's only when I'm descending the slight slope toward where they're waiting that my breath catches. It's the first time I've seen our army assembled—and while they look tattered and patchworked together, there are so many more than I realized. My eyes warm and my throat hitches. They're all facing us—thousands of them—split into row upon row of farmers and mothers and soldiers.

But it's not until I get closer that I notice it. The silence. It grows as I move forward, and then the mums' and peasants' and soldiers' hands slip out to reach for me, like the words falling from their moving lips—whispers I can't understand but that cling to me anyway.

My heart constricts. *Oh litches.*

I swallow and force my face to display a radiant hope for them—a smile of promise for the victory we will claim—as the thought from two weeks ago in my room nudges its way into focus. An observation I've noticed a million times throughout my years but had never felt so real as on that night. And now, again, here. With them. The observation there is a moment before every storm when the entire world pauses. As if the atmosphere, in unison with the ocean tides, the wind, the sky's watery teardrops, is forced to hold its breath. A bracing against the violence it knows will come—the tempest that perhaps this time, this moment, might actually shred the world's soul.

I've been in that moment in a physical storm so many times before.

I have *been* that moment.

But today . . .

I look around at the few pitched tents and the bedrolls littering the open ground behind us as far as my eye can see. I look at my people—some of whom are dressed in fancy clothes too idiotic for a battle, while most are dressed in rags hanging off bodies that are too thin, too cold, too overworked. Soldier and farmer and nobleman.

Today *we* are that moment.

We are the storm.

And I have never been more proud of my people.

Nor more afraid for them.

No matter how hopeful my face may be, my stomach's performing flips so hard I'm wondering if my gut's just going to jump out from my spine in front of them all.

Keep walking, keep smiling, keep breathing.

When I reach the plateau, Rolf and King Sedric are finishing up giving a final exhortation to the individual generals, and Eogan and Kenan are speaking with Allen the dwarf who's hopping up and down on one foot as if he can't wait to get started.

A loud trumpeting from a meadow a half terrameter away shows why. Not only are his oliphants enormous, but at some point between late last night and this morning's dawn, they were fitted with giant, spiked leather strips along the sides of their bodies as well as down each of their hind quarters and legs. Long silver blades have been attached to their trunks so that anyone within twenty paces of their faces will get sliced in half with a single head shake.

Impressive.

A burst of laughter bubbles up at the sight of Kel on top of the largest oliphant. He's surrounded by a host of lethal-looking acrobats, and even from here I can make out his attitude. It declares he could own the whole Faelen island up there—the way he's sitting so proud and serious. Next thing I know he's waving like a madman at me.

I give him a salute and a whispered, "Creator, keep him safe," before turning to the kings who've stopped talking and are now directing their attention at me.

"Nym." King Sedric nods.

I return it, and the moment my gaze finds Eogan's handsome face, he breaks into that half smile I love. He extends his hand and I don't care what anyone will think—of who I am and who he is, or whether or not it's appropriate in the face of a war we're all going to die in. Perhaps it's the reality that we are *quite likely* going to die that makes me walk straight up to him, take his fingers in my own, and lift my face to his.

His lips brush my forehead. "Stay near me today," they whisper before he leans back to say to the others, "Gentlemen, it appears we are ready."

A rumble through the ground jerks the earth beneath my feet, drawing my attention to the fact that it's been building, growing louder like a herd of bolcranes. I'd been so overwhelmed by the sight of our people when walking down I'd barely noticed it. But now . . . now I release Eogan and stride forward to peer over the edge of the plateau. Down the steep hillside. Into the valley below.

My lungs shrivel.

If I thought the wraith army looked terrifying yesterday, this . . . this is beyond imagining. *Have they been multiplying overnight?*

"It seems Draewulf's magic has been busy," King Sedric says as if in answer.

I snort. "I think you mean out of control. This is obscene." The massive black horde that existed yesterday has grown to twice its size, which, given the land space they're occupying between us and the sea, seems hardly possible.

They're so tightly packed together down there, they look like a bubbling black oil slick. Always moving, always simmering. Always that blasted hissing that, though duller to my ears than a week ago, still makes my veins itch.

"They're moving, Your Highness." Rolf points to the front of the horde where the wraiths appear to be assembling in some sort of straight line stretching from the edge of Litchfell Forest to the eastern base of the nearest Hythra Mountain.

Oh hulls.

"They're simply going to march right into us," Kenan mutters.

"Like a wave," King Sedric says softly. "A tidal wave . . ." He doesn't finish, but I can sense the words anyway: *"of terror."*

"Stations!" he suddenly yells, so loud I about jump out of my skin. It immediately sets everyone in motion. The generals who're still lingering hurry off to their ranks, Kenan strides over to stand with a very large unit made up of archers standing right along the plateau's edge, and King Sedric and Rolf turn to mount the horses a soldier's just brought up.

I'm peering around for Haven when Allen the dwarf flips his hat and bows at me. "M'lady."

"Allen the Fabler, Travelling Baronet."

He grins. "May the sun shine on us by the end of the day. But in the meantime . . ." He winks. "May your storms kick their sorry wraith hind ends all the way to hulls." With that, he trots off to make the rather tedious trek for his short legs to his troupe of oliphants and what appear to be panther-monkeys and magicians.

I smirk and swallow, and the next moment Eogan is standing beside me.

"Where best can you battle from, m'lady?" King Sedric asks.

I look down on the wraiths just as a horn blare ricochets through the Valley. It's so loud, so eerie, it's clearly not from a natural horn. The sound has barely died out when a roar bigger than the sea waves at night, or the thundering of a morning storm, picks up and blasts across us—as if powerful enough to create wind in itself. And on it, I swear the seven airships are moving toward us.

Litch. "Right here." I glance at Eogan, who nods his agreement.

"You'll stay with her, yes? To increase her abilities?" Sedric's now staring hard at Eogan.

Wait, what? I frown and turn. "You don't have to—"

"I told you we stay together today."

"And what about Rasha?" I glance around for the red-eyed princess and her assortment of Luminescents.

"She's with Lord Myles and Lady Isobel, keeping them in line." Sedric indicates a group standing around two caged carts thirty yards away.

Eogan holds out his hand to Rolf, who is gripping two metal gear things. They're curved like an archer's bow, but the metal string crossing them is latched onto a metal spiked frame. Even with my limited knowledge of such weapons, I can easily see the tiny barbed arrows they shoot will go much farther and faster than anything the archers have. I raise a brow at Eogan, who chuckles.

"You don't have to look so impressed," he says. "With that expression, people will suspect you think I'm quite incapable of brilliance."

Despite the growing roar from the wraiths below, the airship engines beginning to drone toward us, and our own people's prayers and chants, I smirk.

Litches, I love that man's arrogance.

That eerie horn sounds a second time, and I feel it as strong as it shakes the air around us. Black mist that'd been sedated among the wraiths since last night filters up and around them, as if to block them from our eyes—or shield them from the morning sun casting its first rays into the Valley. Either way, the rumbling ground says the Dark Army's moving. And they're moving fast.

Gasps arise from our rows of archers on either side of us. Their view from the front line is the same as mine. Which means their stomachs have likely just fallen out the soles of their feet.

"We're going to get slaughtered," one of them murmurs.

"Hold your ground, men!" Rolf yells.

I glance up at Eogan and King Sedric. Then back at the ranks. They're starting to squirm, their nerves showing through.

I turn to Sedric. "Perhaps a word from you might help stay their strength, Your Highness."

He's beckoning a soldier, and when I glance over, the man's leading Haven to me.

"I've already spoken my piece to them this morning. They know what lies ahead. The time for words is past. Fighting for our kingdom is what we're here for."

I peer around at the nervous archers watching the wave of undead running toward them from a terrameter away—never swaying, never slowing. The archers' faces pale. Then I look to the rows upon rows separated into ranks—the farmers, the mums, the fathers who're holding everything from swords to pickaxes.

And I can see it in them. The sallowness starts in their arms and works its way up their necks and to their cheeks. Panic. Fear. A few are even inching toward the tents—as if that will save them from the death that's coming.

Death.

The air is thick with it. My throat is thick with it. Is that what I've led these people to?

Bleeding hulls. I grab Haven's reins and pull myself up. "Mind if I say something, then?"

I don't wait for Sedric's reply. I simply tug Haven around until I'm facing the masses made up from the individual faces of my Faelen countrymen.

"Brothers and sisters!" I shout above the disgusting, snarling noise growing louder behind me as the hordes approach. Thankfully it appears the people can hear me. Either that or the sight of Haven baring her teeth at all the other horses in the calvary a few ranks down from us has them distracted for the moment.

"Today we fight together for a freedom long owed us. A freedom from evil that has haunted our land, our history, and our homes from the very time Draewulf sought our destruction one hundred years ago."

Haven steps forward a few paces and I bring her round back, then pat her to stay. "Well, today . . . today we take back that freedom. Today we seek *his* destruction. And today we show the rest of the Hidden Lands what it means to be true people of Faelen—that we cannot, *will not*, be defeated!"

A cheer goes up so fast I feel the wave of it blast over me. I wait for it to taper a bit before holding up a hand.

"Fight for yourselves today. Fight hard. Fight strong. Fight as men and women who are alive—against a force that is but dead and empty shells. And for my part, I will promise you this." I raise my voice along with my hand so the thunder I create rattles in perfect time with my voice. "I swear to you upon my Elemental blood that if you fight for yourselves, then I will fight for you. And if needed, I will die for you."

CHAPTER 36

T HE ARCHERS ARE THE FIRST TO ENGAGE.
Their arms pull back the strings of their longbows, then release them to send arrows raining down like hail upon the black roiling, oncoming mass.

My knees weaken as I watch from atop Haven. The shafts fly in volley after volley, hitting their targets like hornets going in for a kill. Except the arrows only take out some. The wraiths who find a shaft impaled into their chest or arms keep going—only those whose skulls have been hit drop dead. Or rather, more dead.

"Continue," Rolf yells. "Aim for their heads!" And the archers begin another set of one, two, three releases.

It's effective, but not effective enough against corpses that feel no pain. Their hissing just grows louder and the black mist around them blows thicker.

"Nym?" King Sedric says from behind me.

I slide off of Haven and hand her reins to one of the soldiers assigned to me. "Stay away from her face," I warn and move to retake my place beside Eogan. And raise one arm.

Waiting for it . . .

The airships drone closer—enough so that I can see their decks are also covered in wraiths and they're carrying something attached to their hulls. I squint. *What—?*

"Bombs," Eogan says.

"Nym?" King Sedric says, and this time I hear the nerves lacing his voice as the archers keep their arrows flying. The look on his face says I should feel free to make Draewulf and his Dark Army regret they ever crossed that channel to reach us. "Have at it," he growls.

My lightning strikes rake across the hulls of a single ship but miss the others. The one I hit rocks and shivers and abruptly explodes into a fireball that is so far from natural it turns purple amid the flames. I jump back along with every soldier beside me as the pieces of wreckage drop down onto the wraiths beneath and take out as many as were on the ship itself.

"Bleeding litches," one of the nearby soldiers mutters. "What are those things carrying?"

"Let's not find out." I drag another two bolts from the incoming clouds and shred through the air, but just before they hit a second ship, that black mist reaches up and surrounds it. And I swear it's as if the sky's fire bounces right off.

Another attempt, but the same thing happens.

"He's fighting you," Eogan says.

"Question is, where is he?"

"Keep focusing on the ships." Eogan slips his hand over my owner circles and presses down until I feel my abilities respond to his and ignite. "Perhaps he's on one."

"He'd not be that idiotic." But with one flick of my wrist, I pull down the entire cloud cover and slam it into the dark mist. A charge of friction snaps through the atmosphere so powerfully, it knocks against me and heats up my face. "What the—?"

Eogan grins at me, and I yank the storm clouds down again and again, in hopes of rattling Draewulf, or at the very least annoying him.

They spark and shiver and fire goes every which direction, but when I ease them up the ships are still in the air and the black mist is as thick as ever. And my arms and hands are aching and sweating.

The awareness pricks my thoughts that Draewulf is simply playing with me. What is it he's waiting for? Why doesn't he just unleash his hellish abilities and attempt to end this all now?

Litch. That overwhelming sense of helplessness settles over my shoulders. I grit my teeth. *Fine, then.*

"Your Majesty, might I suggest we engage at this time also?" Kenan points to the diminishing gap on the hillside between the Dark Army and us.

"Do you need me?" Eogan asks.

I shake my head. "I'll let you know when."

He moves over two paces before lifting his arrow weapon and pulling back the metal string. Then releases it into the oncoming mass of undead. The machine he's holding is so powerful and sure, the arrow pierces three wraith heads before getting stuck in a fourth.

From behind me a number of men utter curse words, and I swear one of them is King Sedric. Ignoring them, I clench both fists and stir the clouds until they're swirling above the Valley, and as they swirl, I create hailstones. Large, hard, and deadly. And lower the clouds again onto the mist, where the static meets, then releases them.

From the sound of the horn that blasts, my damage has made it through, and I sense a pushing back on the atmosphere. As if Draewulf is physically lifting my storm back. I press in harder, fiercer, only casually aware of Eogan resetting his weapon against his shoulder. Nearby me he holds the undercarriage with one hand while pulling back the metal string with the other.

And that's when I feel it. Draewulf's presence creeping closer.

I create more hailstones and let them fly beneath the mist.

Except something's nudging in my head—something I should know. Something I should've realized.

Draewulf.

I glance around at the men surrounding me—at Sedric, at his soldiers, even at Eogan for a brief moment. Long enough to check the color of each of their eyes before scanning the faces farther out.

How fast can he heal enough to shape-shift from person to person? How many people here could he be inhabiting?

All he needs is one. *The right one.*

Rasha is standing stock-still with a sword in her hands, as if reading everything and everyone as fast as she can, while behind her Myles is studying the scene from behind his bars. I glance again at Eogan.

"You feel him too," he mutters before sending three cross arrows into the heads of ten different wraiths.

I nod and pull down a strip of lightning and rip it across the entire first two rows of wraiths rushing beyond the mist to close the distance between our army and theirs. The ground beneath them explodes in dirt and rocks and fire—throwing them into the air and ripping apart many of their bodies. Those who've not lost their legs or heads keep running though, until they trip over the fallen wraiths.

Suddenly a group of Faelen farmers is descending with a battle cry. King Sedric's sent them upon the rest of this first wave to finish them off.

I wipe sweat from my forehead and repeat the scenario four more times as more wraiths emerge from the mist. Perhaps there is a limit to Draewulf's magic if he's not stretching it after them to protect them.

Not that it matters, though. They just keep coming.

And my fire isn't fast enough, nor are the archers or farmers, because the growling, slimy, decaying wraiths have broken through our ranks and all hulls breaks loose.

CHAPTER 37

THE SURGE OF BODIES ERUPTING FROM BEHIND US is accompanied by a war cry that curdles the blood beneath my skin. For the few battles and skirmishes I've been near over the years, I've never heard the Faelen people do this . . . scream this loud, this furious, this scared.

Five seconds later they're shoving by the circle of grassy space the kings and I are standing in and slamming into the wraiths headed toward us, wielding their swords and hammers and axes with a fierceness that breathes hope and pride into my lungs.

My eyes warm as, in my peripheral, I catch sight of Allen the dwarf atop the largest oliphant with Kel moving toward us at a rapid rate along with his entire host of travellers. The smallest of which are blowing fire at the wraiths and the larger are performing acrobatics, leaping over and around the undead, their blades flashing as they lop off the monsters' heads faster than imaginable.

The sight is so gruesome yet so effective I'm tempted to laugh a bit crazy-like. Instead, I continue tearing lightning through rows of the Dark Army lower down the hillside. The bolts coming down are also keeping the airships at bay. As if there's an invisible line neither of us can cross—where Draewulf's magic protects them, and where my storm will destroy them.

I shove harder—

"Nym, wait."

King Sedric has turned from the beasts he's just annihilated long enough to point his sword drenched with black wraith blood at the next wave heading up the hillside toward us.

"I know, but I can't get through Draewulf's barrier!" Even as I say it, the sight makes me sick. There are so many.

My hands falter and I stop in my tracks.

Good hulls, there are so many.

I'd been so busy focusing on fighting and feeling proud of those fighting beside me I hadn't stopped to actually look at the effect we were having.

Which is none.

We are having no effect whatsoever compared to the hordes still waiting their turn to come against us. And as I peer around, I begin to see the bodies. My countrymen. Slashed and maimed by claws and teeth much sharper than any ax or dagger they owned.

Litch.

I aim icicles one at a time into the skulls of four, five, fifteen wraiths. But the people I was trying to protect are slaughtered anyway by the few who got through.

I look away and try not to vomit.

Our people are dying in droves.

I shut my eyes and feel Eogan and Kenan nearby, their weapons releasing arrows at whatever was just coming at them and me and King Sedric. I curl my hands into fists again and this time allow the dark ability in me to shiver. To swirl in just the slightest with my Elemental blood until the smallest hint of its hunger claws at my chest.

Good.

Slowly, carefully, so as not to lose it or let it take over, I push it out my lungs, my mouth, my breath into the sky above. Into the air hanging above that wretched black mist.

And begin to allow the ability-infused air to tug.

At Draewulf's magic. At the mist. At the mass amounts of dead souls housed inside those hideous, empty shells.

A crack—like one of the fissures Colin used to create—appears in my mind's eye, or perhaps in my Elemental blood, which is at one with the atmosphere enough to sense I've caused a disturbance in Draewulf's layer of power.

And it's all I need.

I slice lightning through the fissure and onto the wraith army underneath.

There it is. A smile forms on my face. This is how we might win.

"Nym, wait!" Sedric's voice comes more urgent this time.

I open my eyes and frown. He's pointing down again, and when I follow his gaze I realize I can see through the misty haze to the army below. Their black mass is interrupted by large patches of moving color. *Wait, what the—?* I peer harder.

It takes less than half a second to register what the colored patches are—and then for my lungs to dry up inside my chest. They are people.

Live people.

Wearing Cashlin and Tulla clothing.

Oh hulls. The wraiths have brought over innocent hostages from those kingdoms and sectioned themselves around them.

And surrounding them? Giant wraiths.

The Uathúils who've been turned.

"Eogan."

He tosses aside his used-up metal weapon and pulls out his broadsword from the sheath across his back.

"Eogan."

He looks up, then over, following my gaze to the beasts who're moving the earth and calling out magical chants and traipsing toward us as if all the world's elements are at their wicked disposal.

Litch.

And in that moment I sense it.

I let my fists fall and stare at the hostages and powerful wraiths. If I continue to fight with the elements, I will kill the people too. But it's not just that—it's something different about the atmosphere, about the scent of blood in the air and the smell of fear.

"Draewulf's using more of his magic." Eogan gasps and rips his sword up through the chin of a wraith's head before yanking it out and taking off another's.

"Yes, but for what exactly?" I yell back.

Eogan glances over long enough to bestow me with a sly wink. "To win the war."

"I'm not sure your attempt at humor is well timed, Your Highness." I yank two ice picks out of the air to shove into the heads of the wraiths about to lunge at us. And besides, this feels different.

When I turn back to Eogan, an enormous Uathúil wraith is moving in—from the looks of the way she's holding her hands, she used to be Mortisfaire.

This feels like the monster's done toying with us.

Eogan nods just as a splash of black blood lands on his cloak from the beast he's gutted, and I duck the Uathúil claw coming toward me.

But the claw wasn't for me.

It was for Eogan.

Hulls. I lunge at the beast to touch my hand to her head—to scald it with my bare skin and Elemental blood—and just as I do, Kenan steps in front of his king.

The claw comes down even as the wraith crumples beneath the ice from my hand.

Too late, though.

Kenan's cry is cut off by the spurt of blood tearing from his throat.

"Nooo!"

Eogan's yell is broken and more furious than I've ever heard him. He grabs Kenan as the soldier falls and presses his hands to the man's neck, trying to stanch the blood.

I lean over him and use the ice still on my hands to try to help seal up the wound, but with the amount of blood leaving his body and the way his eyes have already rolled back, it's all too clear.

Eogan's face is flushed in fury. In pain. And in the distance I swear I hear Kel screaming. And running.

I don't have time to respond to it, though, as a sudden, visible shuddering of the atmosphere ripples across my sight, my skin, my spine.

Lord Myles's ability has just been activated.

Bracken.

I release the cloud cover and turn to the cart where Myles is being held. Rasha is standing beside him with her hand on his arm. I can sense the fog parting above us and the shafts of sunlight filtering through. I wave a hand and press the storm back farther farther farther until it's out over the ocean and the daylight is reflecting off the thick, black mist now spread up almost to where we're standing.

With it appears a mirage of a giant dungeon—one that looks startlingly like the inside glass walls of the Cashlin Castle. *What the—?*

Luminescents are suddenly walking around, giant size, and I swear even the wraiths stop in their tracks and stare at the beings in confusion.

I squint enough to clear the mirage from my sight, and then

Eogan rises and shoves me aside to take another wraith's head off with his sword.

I flip around to him, but rather than speak he simply points across the way toward the caged carts.

Bleeding hulls.

Draewulf is standing there with Lord Myles, Lady Isobel, and Princess Rasha. And at Rasha's feet lie her dead Luminescents.

CHAPTER 38

"BLEEDING LITCHES," EOGAN MUTTERS, AND HIS tone is full of more malice than I've heard from him. "I'm going to rip his—" He grabs my hand and we start running—shoving through the wraiths and people alike toward Draewulf, who's leering down at Rasha from his over seven feet of height. Whomever he disguised himself as in order to make it up to the cage area doesn't matter—he's in full-gloried wolf form now. And seeing Rasha beside him, facing him . . . My chest squeezes.

She's wielding her sword—at first at him, I think, which he dodges adeptly and, I swear, appears to laugh. Except next thing I know the blade's hit the door of Myles's cage, then Isobel's.

I frown. She's freeing them.

For what?

I glance back at King Sedric and am relieved to see him still unaware of the monster's presence as he fights alongside Rolf and the guardsmen right in the thick of it. Good. Let us take care of this before he gets himself killed too.

"Nym, look out!"

I peer back just in time to see Eogan flip his blade around and stab at a wraith who's appeared from nowhere behind me, before turning to decapitate the disgusting thing. "Focus," he says to me.

I tear a strip of lightning down to eliminate the five monsters to the right side of us. "What about Kel?"

"I lost sight of him right after Kenan fell. But I know he saw it. His face . . . I'm sorry."

Bleeding hulls, please let Kel survive. My stomach clenches as the glimpse I get of Eogan's face before he's launching another attack says he's thinking the same.

I rip through another four with a hail of ice picks. They were headed for Draewulf too, to assist him by the looks of their size and rags. How I know this, I'm not sure, but they remind me of the higher-up general wraiths who entered the War Room first in Bron.

When we near the place where Draewulf is standing, the black mist is already curling its way along the ground and our feet. *As if drawing us in.*

I shake it away from my ankles even as the spider in my veins reacts in hunger. *Quiet,* I tell her, and will more freedom to my Elemental blood.

"Eogan, I'll go to the right, you—"

My voice cuts off with a guttural inhale as Draewulf shoves a claw around Rasha's neck and snarls. Then he stops and his gaze swerves to me, ten paces away. He grins.

"Ah, there you are, pet. I've been waiting." His eyes drop the briefest second to the body that lies at his feet.

Tannin. Or what's left of him.

I stumble back. How did he—? When did—?

It doesn't matter. At some point this morning he consumed the sweet guard and that is enough to know.

I let loose five shafts of ice so fast the first two pierce his arm before the mist surrounding him lifts into a shield. "You bleeding—"

He twitches a finger and Rasha cries out as if he's snapped

something inside her, and instantly Myles's mirage lessens. "You know she'll go just like her mother. Easier, in fact, now that I've got her mum's ability."

He licks his lips, but the next moment Lady Isobel's stepped between me and her father and grins at me. Then slowly turns her gaze to Eogan, who has just taken out two of her wraiths.

The lightning I yank down bounces off that curling, growing mist as Isobel holds her palm, face out, to me before turning to set it against Rasha's heart.

"No!" I lunge forward, but it's too late. Rasha's already screaming and writhing beneath Isobel's hand and Draewulf's grip. The atmosphere around us wavers, as if the magic veil Draewulf's wrapped most of the Valley in just expanded.

Except . . .

With an expression of indecisiveness, Lady Isobel yanks her hand back even as the air continues rippling. Growing. Rasha's head is thrown back, her shoulders stiffen, and her eyes turn a deep hue of red I've only ever seen on her mother. The air around her shimmers and bulges.

It takes another moment to realize Lady Isobel hasn't yet done anything.

She's waiting. Watching her father with an expression of displeasure.

And it's clear this is different magic.

This is Luminescent.

Oh. Oh hulls. This is what Rasha is capable of.

The expression on Draewulf's face says it's what he's been waiting for—to pit his newly acquired Luminescent ability against hers in a game of play.

Eogan's broadsword comes down on the beast just as he lifts

a claw to Rasha's neck. It's met by the blade of one of Draewulf's Uathúil-wraiths.

I fling ice stones at him and land two against his chest, but he doesn't even flinch. Just thrusts his weight against Eogan to push him backward into an earthen crevice he's just created as Princess Rasha screams.

I thrust more ice picks and then jump for her, but Isobel is abruptly in my face, smirking, holding her hand out—the indecision gone from her face. "Ready for your turn, dearie?"

I meet her palm with my own and a spark of friction explodes between them. My ability against hers. Reacting to hers. Her hunger reacting to the spider's thirst in my blood. They both reach out for each other and in that moment are well matched.

I yank out the blade from my bootie and shove it into her shoulder.

Isobel's scream is followed by a second change in atmosphere and a flickering of the mirage around us. Abruptly the dungeon image Myles has been exuding dissolves, and when I glance over he's frowning and blinking and staring first at Lady Isobel, then me. Until his gaze lands on Princess Rasha.

His face darkens and his mouth opens. I duck Isobel's swipe at my chest with my blade she just pulled from her shoulder and see Draewulf's body turn ethereal, as if he's beginning to dissolve.

And Rasha has stopped writhing.

Bracken.

I yank out the blade from my other bootie and slice out at Lady Isobel's knee. Miss. Swipe again. This time I catch her in the thigh and make her scream again.

Suddenly the mirage flickers back on around us. But this one's different. This one's of Princess Rasha in one of the hallways in

Bron. Then in the Throne Room. Then on the airship. Draewulf pauses and looks around at it just as Lord Myles steps forward.

His expression is so clear, so settled, I almost miss it. The affection.

What the—?

He's showing every image of every interaction he's ever had with Rasha. And in the moment of distraction—of confusion—Draewulf's grip loosens the slightest bit. Apparently the queen's ability to see through mirages didn't quite transfer all the way.

Myles steps in, pulls Rasha away, and shoves her behind him.

Good mother of— Does he—?

"He stands on the edge of a precipice. One choice will bring destruction; the other will help the Hidden Lands survive." The essence of Queen Laiha's words rings in my head.

Clearly he chose our survival.

Except there's no time to think about it because the next second Draewulf roars and Lady Isobel screams again. I look down to see that when I sliced at her leg, I cut deep enough to hit an artery. Draewulf jerks his head toward her, and before I can react or back away, he's grabbed his daughter and yanked her away from me.

"Father," she whimpers.

I allow the sky to crash above us as I bring down one, two, three strikes on them both—only to have the magical mist defuse each one before it reaches them.

Draewulf reaches out for Isobel and she folds into him.

Then he's slicing her open at the neck and his body is fading fading fading in front of me as he slips like a black plague into the wound and beneath her skin and takes over the Mortisfaire power of his daughter.

I think I'm going to be sick.

"Nym, look out!"

I turn at Eogan's words just in time to duck from the two wraiths coming at me. I shred ice from my hand into the ground and erupt it beneath them, causing both to slip and fall. I shove it forward to cover and crawl over them until the ice reaches into their mouths and noses and throats and hardens inside their heads.

I stand to turn toward Draewulf—to attack him with that same ice, to infuse it into Isobel's dead bones—when the sight below us gives me pause.

The war below . . . the war around us . . . the wraiths, the archers, the farmers, the mothers, the Cashlins and Terrenes . . .

Bodies of our people lie everywhere.

So thick and widespread and being run over by the black magic and wraiths that I can hardly see anyone who's still alive. Still standing.

My gut clenches. *Oh litches, what have we done?*

I open my lungs in horror at their lives spent on a futile struggle. Their last breath they've given for a nation that oppressed most of them. And I swear the moment I choke and gasp on my own grief for them, their voices are drawn into me. Their hearts, their beliefs, their courage. It permeates my lungs and mixes into my blood until it's churning churning churning and then it's abruptly coming up and, oh hulls, I don't know how to stop it, but when I open my mouth, it comes out as a song.

Their song.

The melody of old. Of Faelen. Of the original Valley.

Our song. The one I used to sing so long ago with my father.

My lungs expand and widen along with my mouth, and the force of the refrain comes out like a flood that reaches straight up through a hole in the sky and I swear it hits the sun. Because now it's as if the light is paused, the day is paused, and the sky itself is on standstill.

Only the people and wraiths and war around us keep moving.

The song ripples and threads through the air, across the expanse of black atmosphere hanging above this entire battle scene, permeating where my powers can't to the land and trees and hearts of the few people we have left.

I don't know that I would've noticed it if the rustle from the Litchfell tree line hadn't caused the trees to catch the paused sunlight just right. I squint.

The movement grows as the trees begin thrashing.

One, two, five seconds later the trees are snapping, and a herd of bolcranes pour forth in giant, horrific, slimy, black-scaled terror. As I watch, the beasts set upon the wraiths—and begin shredding through them like a tidal wave taking on the sand.

"Bleeding hulls," Myles mutters from somewhere behind me.

The next moment cries erupt across the plateau around us—cries from our own people, as if a quarter of their voices rose up in unison to join the song, but in pain.

I peer at them to see what I've done—where it's coming from—even as my own song continues to pour from my mouth.

I blink. Blink again. Because what lies in front of me, what is happening around me, is impossible.

Uathúils.

Many of the Faelen peasants are turning into Uathúils. Terrenes. Red-eyed Luminescents. And some types I've never seen before in my life—perhaps a blending like Lord Myles. The only way I know is because suddenly some of the people who were here moments ago have morphed, altered, *come forth*, and they're earth-moving and static-wielding.

I watch as they discover their powers and use them against the large wraiths attacking them.

The cries of my people turn to shouts as the realization sets in.

Whatever dormant power lay within much of the peasantry has just been called forth. And their abilities are greater than any physical weapon. They begin cutting through the Dark Army in batches rather than one at a time.

"Nym, here!"

I flip around to refocus on Eogan and Rasha and Draewulf-who-is-Isobel, except the monster has already erupted from his daughter's skin and is standing there, snarling over Eogan.

What in—? No!

Eogan raises his sword, only to have Draewulf's enormous claw smack it aside.

I step between them.

CHAPTER 39

N YM, DON'T!" EOGAN'S HANDS PRESS INTO MY side to shove me back, but I hardly feel them and they can't move me. If anything, my blood jumps at the magic they contain. The remnants of that dark ability itch in my veins and suddenly draw Eogan's power in, melding it with my own as my feet plant firm to the ground and my gaze fills with only one image.

"What in bleeding hulls are you doing? Move!" Eogan growls in my ear. But I'm no longer listening. I'm staring into the face of the wolfish beast that is looking more human by the moment.

His black eyes flicker, and for a second, I swear I can see the faces of Breck, King Mael of Tulla, Queen Laiha, and the tear-stained face of his own daughter, Isobel.

In my peripheral I catch sight of the world around us rippling, then altering into a bigger mirage than I'd known Myles could make. Rasha must be magnifying his powers as he projects images of wave after wave of Bron soldiers seemingly coming to our aid. Confusing the wraiths—even the Uathúil ones, from what I can tell.

Draewulf grins, and it's neither toothy, nor gaping, nor wolf-ish. It's simply the grin of a man who knows he's about to achieve the one thing he's lived his life for. The one thing he's destroyed everyone else's life for. He's taken what he needed from Tulla, from Cashlin, and from Drust. And he's about to take the rest of Bron and Faelen. And within that sly slip of a smile is no shame that I can find. No guilt. Nothing but pure, unadulterated greed for everything that is not his but soon will be.

The face of his daughter flickers across his features one more time as he grips his sword and points it toward me. "Move, pet, or I will maim you before I take him." He tips the point of the sword toward my belly.

I smirk and raise both arms straight out, my fists tightened to the sky as Eogan's hand is now fused onto me, my energies mixing with his, boiling the blood between us. My skin burns like fire where he's touching it, yet even the heat feels good.

Feels powerful.

Feels different.

I can do this.

I glance at the sky to where the dying sun is slipping away on the horizon and summon the atmosphere. Draewulf leans in, and the point of his blade cuts deep enough to make me wince the slightest moment before I sense the water from the ocean and air from the heavens respond with a burst of friction.

Flashes. Brief bursts of light overhead. They're enough to make Draewulf frown and look up. Because there are no clouds. No indication of a storm other than what is bristling in my veins as it connects with the energy around me.

The pull physically begins to tug at my sinew—from the ocean currents, the wind, the cracks running beneath our feet far under the earth, just as I feel the pull of Rasha and Myles's mirage they're sustaining.

Draewulf starts to step around me, but I move in front of him to the left. Then to the right. He barks and slashes a warning at my hip, drawing blood immediately and making me flinch. Even Eogan is trying to get around me. But whatever has fused his hands to my waist is also keeping him in place.

I turn my gaze again to the setting sun.

My hands begin shaking first. Followed by my legs, then torso, then neck.

I am summoning pure Elemental energy, which is more than any of his Uathúil-wraiths running around can do.

Next thing I know my back is bending and my chin is thrust toward the sky as the energy spirals up my spine and through my throat to burn its way from my mouth and tear, like a lightning strip, up to the sky. I blink, nearly blinded at the light. And suddenly it's not just pouring from my throat, it's shooting out from my fists, far and wide enough to shred through entire ranks of wraiths.

In my distant hearing I perceive a cheer go up, but it doesn't matter. I'm trying to focus the beams in front of me. Onto Draewulf, who's watching with sick fascination—as if enjoying a part in a theatre play he knows he is soon to take over.

And if what it's doing to my insides is any indication, once Draewulf consumes it he'll be intoxicated past any level of awareness when it fuses with the other abilities flickering in and out of focus beneath his overstretched, blue-veined skin.

Black wisps rise from around him and pour out of his mouth, and abruptly something's wrong. No matter how I move my arms to shove the energy at Draewulf and melt him alive, it won't reach him. He's deflecting it using the shadows as a shield around him.

I grip the energy tighter just as a voice, not my own, breezes past, causing my skin to tingle in its softness.

I ignore it and shove harder, only to watch the light from my fists bounce off his shield. At least it's keeping him from lunging for me or Eogan, and yet . . .

And yet it's not working.

Oh litches, it's not working. The dark ability is insufficient.

"Eogan," I gasp. "It won't—I can't . . ."

The voice comes again, and for a moment I think it's Eogan, but it's off. I listen closer, and this time I swear it's that of Queen Laiha. As if her ghost is whispering, reminding me of words once spoken.

I lean my ear toward it even as I summon every particle in the atmosphere above and around and beneath us until the light coming from me rivals the darkness surrounding him. And prepare to bring all of it into a shaft that will slice right through the beast in front of me, like the edge of a blade that has just been sharpened.

And then Queen Laiha's words come to me. *"Hold it all lightly."*

I freeze.

The static is now burning my insides so badly I'm forgetting that I am, or ever have been, anything but energy. But power. But fire.

"Hold it all lightly."

What does that mean?

I tighten my grip and the burn digs in. I glance around at the writhing armies below us, at Kel and Sedric and Rolf, fighting back to back mere yards away from us, and sense Eogan behind me.

But I suddenly know exactly what it means.

Hold it all lightly.

Because otherwise it's not going to work and we're not going to win.

I know that in this split second clearer than anything I've understood before. It's why I couldn't defeat Draewulf in Bron. It's why I couldn't defeat him on the airships.

Hold it all lightly.

Because it was never mine anyway.

This power. This gift.

These people.

I drop my arms and let the energy falter, then die off.

And turn round to face Eogan.

CHAPTER 40

TWO HEARTS BEATING TO THE MOMENT.

Two souls bleeding.

I press my lips to Eogan's in a promise that offers him all my hopes and wishes and joy that his life will be good. That his heart will be full.

That he will be loved.

Then I shove him off me and, releasing my shield, lunge forward onto Draewulf's outstretched blade as I grab his throat.

One.

Two.

Three seconds go by in which I can't feel anything but the atmosphere assembling around us. Building, condensing, creating static and energy and a mist filled with lightning and raindrops rubbing against each other. A crack rips across the sky and it's as if the sun is undone, unpaused, as slack clouds roll in to cover it. Suddenly they're bringing with them storms full of ice and hail and death. Storms this world hasn't seen in a millennia of Elementals.

Storms made of magic. Storms made of melody and beauty that are complementing Rasha and Myles's continued mirages. Threatening violence not just to these people near and far, but to this world. As if they are about to tear the entire earth apart at its seams.

The ground shakes, and from the mountains comes a rumble as if in reply.

Draewulf's not noticing the gathering storm, though. His eyes are too full of delight. He's staring at the blade he's just gutted me with, and he slips a long wolf claw against my skin. And slides it to the back of my neck.

That's when I feel it. My blood charged with the air, beating furiously to engage the coming storm. Except as fast as it's quickening, it's draining, flowing from my stomach in warm, red currents. *Like ocean waves*, I think as my gaze becomes foggy.

I blink.

A pain much sharper and more sickening pierces my skin at the top of my spine, and suddenly my vision's wavering and Draewulf is smirking. And then he's starting to dissolve into a thin black wisp that will invade my body for the few seconds it needs to own me.

"Nym! What have you—?"

I feel Eogan grab my arm. His fingers clamping around my owner circles to pull me away, to keep me from the beast whose black eyes are glaring greedily into my soul.

Eogan.

I blink again and refocus. Calling forth the one thing Draewulf will never own. The song of my origin in my blood and soul and quickly collapsing heart. It rises up, feeble and weak, but enough to create an immediate connection with the fire zapping back and forth between the billowing clouds overhead. With the people and beasts and heartbeat of the Faelen ground beneath that bore me to be this for them. To do this for them.

To free this world for them.

I hold tight to Draewulf's neck, keeping his blade tucked into my stomach even as my blood is draining out and the monster's face is becoming a fog. I clench him harder. As if by sheer will alone

I can keep him physical—keep him here in my fingers that are pounding with the slowing of my heartpulse.

Eogan's still tugging me back, but I can hardly feel it as I drop to my knees, bringing Draewulf with me. Instead, what I feel is Eogan's skin connecting with mine, sharpening the strength of my blood and ability.

I tap into it one last time.

The sky booms above us and finally prompts Draewulf to glance up. A flash of fear invades his face before he's looking back at me, and now his body is fully dissolving beneath my hands, and his claws and arms are stretching into my spine. I can feel the dark and hate and death as he begins to climb inside my skin.

I don't know why, but I start to laugh. At what? Maybe at him for being so pathetically desperate. Maybe for the people around me who've faded from my sight but are about to be free of him.

Maybe for myself and the fact that no one—not even Draewulf—can ever own me again.

A feeling of warmth takes over as the last of my blood leaks out.

And with one final utterance of the melody I was born into but never could quite grasp onto, before my breath leaves my body for eternity, I grab what's left of his neck and unleash the greatest bolt of fire and atmospheric light I have ever created into the beast in front of me.

Then I'm falling.

Suddenly the world is sideways and I'm on my back and my vision has faded to dark gray.

It's interrupted once by an eruption of light as the monster I was holding, the monster who used to be a man named Draewulf, explodes into a bomb of light that shoots out ten feet each way and shakes the ground I'm lying on. As if the sun I had paused has just exploded inside him. Next thing I see, he's still standing there but charred into dust. And, slowly, the pieces begin crumbling, trickling to the earth from which he came.

And he is gone.

Everything goes black.

CHAPTER 41

THE SOUND OF WAR DIMS AROUND ME. IT TAKES forever to open my eyelids again. They're so heavy. I'm so heavy. I can't move. My lids flutter eventually, and when they do, sunlight is spilling across a room of white curtains and windows, with a wooden ceiling much higher than my head. I frown.

I remember this place.

In a dream, I think.

Yes. A dream.

When I was losing Eogan.

I peer down at the bed I'm curled up on and trail my hands over the cool sheets before wandering them up to touch the sun particles the breeze is lifting through the air. I take a deep breath. The air tastes delicious. Like homemade bread and citrus.

Eogan moves from his spot against a door frame leading outside where he's watching me. The honeyed light slips down his messed-up bangs before shimmering along his black shoulders. The light that's coming from beyond him, through the door.

It's coming from the Valley. Beautiful. Lush. More vibrant than I can ever recall seeing it.

Enchanted. The word floats into my mind.

Real.

Something tells me it's more real than anything I've known in all my seventeen years. More tangible. More *thick.*

It makes me homesick, just like the melody streaming in and filling this space in my room, calling me, inviting me.

Eogan shifts in front of me, forcing me to blink and refocus. He smiles with relief. "You're here."

I frown. *Of course I'm here.* But . . . "It's beautiful out there."

"Can you feel?"

"Your hands on my arms? Yes."

His smile broadens suggestively, and my face warms before his expression turns stiff. He walks over as I slide my feet from the bed, but before I can stand he's bending over, taking my cheek in hand and willing my gaze to center on his. And suddenly it occurs to me that I really just did feel his hands in my hair a moment ago and sliding over my arms and pressing around my neck and chest. Except he wasn't touching me.

I try to sit but he says, "Don't get up."

But I want to. I want to be with him, and I would if my body would work. Blasted hulls, why won't my body work?

"I won't let you go. You'll be all right," he whispers into my hair.

Go? What is he talking about? Go where?

My eyes flicker toward the open door where the sunlight's pouring through. I squint to see beyond it, to the Valley that looks familiar and foreign. Sweet air emanates from it—that honey-blossomed scent—and entwined in it is that music again, wrapping its notes into the breeze and ruffling around Eogan's beautiful black hands and face.

My heart nearly jumps through the roof of my mouth with the

ache. That is where I'm to go—where I want to go—until every-thing within is aching to go—to explore, to find myself in that space, because answers reside there. What had Queen Laiha called it—not a person, but *something* exists there? A word.

Understanding ripples through my veins like the Elemental blood, pumping its way from my soul to my heart to my head. Bringing with it the thing I've always known but somehow, at some point, forgot. The word. The word that is life, that is in all things, that created all things. Like an existence all in itself.

The word that spoke life to these Hidden Lands of ours.

And yet, not a word as we know it.

I want to laugh at the simplicity of it. At the insanity. At the beauty and ache within me to become a part of it—to know the answers to this life and world and . . .

And to see Colin again.

Colin is there. I feel him in this moment, and I swear I hear him calling.

I reach toward the door.

"No," Eogan says. "You can't leave. Not like this. I will not allow it. I will not lose you this way. Fight it, Nym!"

I brush my fingers against his lips and inhale. Then try to yank away because I have to go now, but his hand grasps mine to hold it in place. I smile. "There are worse ways to leave, trust me."

He leans down and draws his lips across mine, his mouth caressing my own in a kiss.

It tastes of life. And death.

It tastes of good-bye.

"Like hulls I will."

Abruptly his face blurs as does the world, the air, the atmos-phere. Then he's swearing. "You survive this or I swear I will haunt your spirit with every last breath in me." His words begin to shudder, then slur. "Don't let go, Nym. Open your eyes. Open them, please. Because I refuse to let you go."

I will not let you go . . .

But he has to because this is my destiny.

And my whole journey has led to this place.

Eogan

Nym's body lies broken beneath my hands. I'm stopping up the wound, crushing down on her stomach to keep more blood in her body than is bleeding out on the rich, red earth and black dust that is all that's left of Draewulf.

"Nym, stay with me!"

I can already feel her spirit slipping. Feel it like the foreign emotion welling up within me. Grief.

I shove the emotion away and look around until I see Kel running over with tears streaming down his face. He's covered in dirt and blood. Good hulls, he looks just like his father.

"Eogan." His voice breaks as he turns and points back to where his father's body lies. But he keeps running.

When he reaches us, his face goes ashen. "No! Nym! Is she . . . is she . . . ?

I grab his hands and place them on Nym's bloody stomach. "Press down and don't let up."

He nods and presses down as I move my fingers to check her pulse. I face those blue, blue eyes that are glassy and glowing like the Elisedd Sea after a storm. She turns them my way and smiles.

"Oh hulls. I thought we'd lost you, love. I—"

It takes approximately three point five seconds for me to know she's not seeing me. Her eyes are there and her gaze is there, but she's not looking at me.

Her smile stays as her head tips slowly to the side.

In that moment, in that second, she is gone.

CHAPTER 42

Eogan

I PUSH HARDER AGAINST HER PULSE ANYWAY. "C'MON, Nym." Then I hit her chest as if to restart her heart. Restart her life.

Nothing.

I shove my hands onto her chest and hold them there. Willing whatever it is in me that's been able to heal wounds recently, to engage.

But there's no power. No energy I'm drawing out or shoving in.

Litches.

It's worked before on her—why not now?

I pound her heart again. "*C'mon*, Nymia! Do this with me!"

I pound again. Hours. Days. Years of her life and mine. I have no idea how long I shove at her heart. How loud I command it to work.

But at some point the awareness dawns that I'm pushing so hard I'm likely to break her fragile rib cage.

I lean back and let go.

Kel is still pressing furiously on Nym's stomach while tears and snot gush from his face onto her pale skin. He looks up at me as if to ask why I've stopped. "We both know why, kid," I almost mutter. Instead, I shove a bloody hand through my hair and try not to laugh painfully at the futileness of it all.

The caustic chuckle bubbles out anyway before I can stop it. It's followed by a prayer. A plea. A whisper. Whatever you bleeding need to call it—it's simply, "Please."

Because that's it—that's all I've got for the Creator. A pathetic, *"Please."*

I sag back on my haunches and stick one hand in my hair again and keep the other entwined around her long white strands, staining them red. Even at her death, I can't help but touch and tarnish her.

"That's enough, Kel," I finally say.

He stares up at me but doesn't obey. His face that looks so much like his father's is serious. Angry. Weeping. He presses harder.

Weeping for her and his father.

I squint and glance away, outside, to give him the honor of having this moment alone as the battle fizzles down around us.

Then I widen my eyes. It appears with Draewulf slain, his magic is gone. Leaving the wraiths weak from the looks of how easily they're being mowed down by Faelen farmers and noblemen.

As if to accentuate the duality of this moment—the victory for the Hidden Lands at the loss of Nym—a shaft of sunlight burns through the clouds and shoots down onto the scene. As beautiful as the day I first came to Faelen in hopes of finding restoration for my soul. For the man I wanted to be rather than the one I'd become—cold, hard, calloused.

As beautiful as the day Nym stood in Adora's room staring out the window at me. Not knowing I'd seen her white hair, white skin, and those blue eyes that could look through a person and sear value and hope onto his broken soul.

As beautiful as the day she stood in the Valley and called down the elements before splitting them apart in a rainbow. The same day I knew she'd forgive what I'd done to her family once I confessed. The day my soul became real and alive and hopeful. The day I almost kissed her again.

I'd like to think she is in that same Valley now. Reliving those moments, finding new ones, perhaps with people more deserving of her.

Perhaps with Colin. And Breck. And Kenan.

I drop my gaze away from the sunlit victory and let it fall back on her. The shock of her lying there lifeless hits me again because, bleeding hulls, I don't know how to do this alone.

I don't know how to lose her.

"Why the bleeding litches did you step in the way?" I want to scream at her.

Instead, a well of warmth slicks down my cheeks and jaw. I put a hand up to dab at it—to see what's happening—and when I pull it away, my fingers are wet.

I am a hard-hearted War General of a man, crying at the destruction of the woman who owns my soul.

CHAPTER 43

Eogan

I GROW AWARE OF THE CLOUDS HAVING ROLLED IN. Deep, dark, full of their own grief for this woman who owned them without ever abusing or bending them to a perverse will.

A flicker of lightning charges the sky.

Then another.

Then so many it's like the atmosphere's veins are exploding in yellow and orange in a farewell serenade.

My hand slides to her chest as if I can will the sight into her, feel the honor of it all for her, show her with my eyes and warmth what she's done to this world. The effect she has had.

What she's meant to it.

Abruptly something inside me breaks, like a bone snapping. I hear it as clear as I hear the absolute sickening silence of Nym, and a roar tears from my lungs, scaring the hulls out of both Kel and me.

What in—?

The Cashlin queen's words from last week come to mind—readings from when she interrogated me. *"Your forefathers misused the gift so long they forgot what it was. They've only known the cheapened version you've seen."*

I had frowned at her with no idea what she meant.

But I feel it. My power flows from my skin to Nym's—much like on the airship when her chest was torn open after the battle at Tulla.

And now I'm feeling it stronger.

Thump.

Thump.

Thump, thump.

What in hulls? A heartpulse. *Is it mine or hers?*

It's ours together.

Eyes widening, I stare at my hand. At the chest beneath it beating. So faint and slight—just like this slip of a girl. *How is this possible?*

It's getting stronger as the blood in my veins burns and singes and scathes the very flesh from my bones.

I cry out again as lightning above strikes and rumbles and my hand is fused to Nym's chest. The amount of power flowing out from my skin is terrifying as litches. As if it, too, was fully awakened by Nym's song.

Just like the other Uathúils.

The crystal shield with its diamond and light properties erupts from her skin and spreads across her body and up over my fingers.

In that moment she is here, breathing, heart beating, opening her eyes to stare at me with that irritable smile she wears all the bleeding time. I yank my hand from her in fear, in shock, as she reaches her own out to touch my cheek. And I can't help it—Kel and I swear out loud at the same time.

She is whole.

Tears catch in my mouth because, blasted hulls, I am a grown man crying again.

Because this . . .

This is more than I ever deserved.

CHAPTER 44

THE CLEANUP IN FAELEN HAS TAKEN JUST OVER A week. My healing took a little over a few hours, thanks to Eogan.

Draewulf's gone but his presence isn't. At least not all the way. And there are still wars to be won in the south—in Bron and Drust. Although rumor has it the people in both kingdoms have already started rioting. As soon as word reached the Bron coast, it spread like a lightning storm—the promise of freedom to the fragmented villagers of Drust seemed to prompt an especially quick reaction. They came out of hiding and began rounding up wraiths from what Rolf has said.

And without Draewulf's and Isobel's magic, the undead are weaker. Easier to kill.

"You're certain you and Eogan will come visit Cashlin as soon as you have a break in Bron?" Rasha asks for the five hundredth time.

"As soon as I'm finished helping, I'll be up to see you."

Her eyes glint red around the pupils, until she's apparently contented herself that I'm not lying, and throws her arms around my neck, squeezing so neither of us can breathe.

And it is the most perfect feeling in the world.

Her friendship. Her cheek pressed against mine as we both

pretend we're not crying even as the damp tears make tracks between us anyway.

"I'm going to miss you," I promise.

She pulls back and glares at me. "You better. Or I will hunt *him*"—she jerks her head toward Eogan—"down with every last blade at my disposal and skewer him dead."

Eogan lifts his hands in the air. "Whoa. Hey, I'm not the one in charge these days. She does what she wants."

Rasha snickers and winks at me. "Blasted right she does." Then leans in to mumble, "He's a good person, Nym," before turning to whisper something in Eogan's ear, to which his eyebrow rises.

"What?"

They both just smile as the airship starts up its engines, and I pull Rasha to me one last time for a hug. "You're a good person too," I whisper.

"Well, this is touching, but it's clearly time for you to go," Myles says. "So sad. We'll miss you. Now get out of here."

I turn on the man who is looking refreshingly like his old self these days, minus a bit of weight and his creepy obsession with hissing. And his blackened hands. Apparently the dark power within him dissolved along with Draewulf. How exactly, no one seems to know. Rasha's theory is that because it originated from Draewulf's early experiments—and then his wife's later ones—the minute they both were dead, the power died off with them.

I watch him actually extend Eogan a hug as he, too, winks at me.

"The door is always open." Sedric lifts his hand to grasp mine.

I grin. "In that case I suggest you find a wife and start filling the vacancy."

"Good advice." He laughs. "Maybe one of these days."

I squeeze his hand and give a small curtsy.

"Please don't do that," Sedric says with sincerity in his eyes. "Or I'll have to start doing the same to you."

I smile, then swallow. And look again at Myles, whom I've saved my last embrace for. Except he's not looking at me or Eogan or even King Sedric. He's looking at Rasha.

I frown, until it occurs to me she's looking right back at him.

I'm awkwardly aware I've no idea what happened between them this week other than Myles has been standing noticeably straighter, taller, and if I think about it, I could swear there's even been a dignified air about him.

He continues staring at Rasha with the strangest expression until I clear my throat. "I guess I should be going?"

He jerks his gaze my direction, and it's as if his mask goes back on even as he turns the slightest shade of red. I raise a brow and look at Rasha, but she's either acting or else impossibly ignorant to the fact that the man she despises totally just blushed at her.

I grin. I'd buy her ignorance if she weren't Luminescent, and the most powerful one, to boot.

"Don't you dare." She leans into me. "I still hate him."

"Uh-huh." I lick my lips and try to bite back my smile.

"I'm serious. He's despicable."

"Uh-huh."

"I hate you."

"Clearly. Which is why you still can't take your eyes off him," I say with a chuckle. Then, moving away from her, I interrupt their staring fest by lunging at him with a huge hug.

He stiffens, more in shock than discomfort by the expression on his face, before softening and wrapping both arms around my waist and squeezing me back.

"You going to be all right, my dear?" he murmurs against my ear.

I nod. "You?"

"She'll keep me in line."

"Oh, I'm planning on it."

I laugh. "It's the only reason I'm leaving you, you know."

He chuckles and kisses the side of my cheek. And when I pull away, he's blinking and his eyes are wet.

"Good-bye, Myles."

"Good-bye, Nym. And . . . thank you."

"For ruining your world-rulership dreams, I assume," I say with a smirk.

"Oh, my dear, I think those might still be in the running." He flicks a glance at Rasha.

"Ha. More like spouse to a world ruler."

He shrugs and grins. "Like I told you, a good woman's hard to find."

CHAPTER 45

W E ARE FLYING, SKIMMING SOMEWHERE between the Elisedd Sea and sky on our way to Bron. I hold out my hand and watch the buttery sunlight trickle through my fingers with the wind. Warming my skin as it spills across my arms and face through the airship window. Like the foamy ocean spray wafting from below.

The ship rises and dips on the air currents just as Eogan steps in front of me, blocking my view of the distant coastline as he runs a hand through his hair. "What do you think?"

"Of?" I crane to see past him at the rows upon rows of shimmery metal buildings that look like they're pumping out fire and steam on the horizon.

That self-assured look in his eye glints his amusement even as I swear his tone sounds nervous. "Of . . . us."

As if he doesn't know? "I don't know. Give me some time to think about it."

"Really?" The self-assurance deflates.

"No, you bolcrane, not really."

"Oh." He gives a lopsided grin. "Well, good." Then squints at me. "Are you sure you don't want some time to think about it? I mean, now that you have your freedom, perhaps you'd prefer—"

The crack of thunder that splits the sky three terrameters out the window actually causes him to duck. And laugh. "Just checking. But in that case . . ." He pulls me to him, lifts my arm with the owner circles, and caresses it between his fingers. "How would you feel about ruling a small kingdom that's half covered in wraith corpses and completely lacking in delicious food with me?"

I'd speak if I could, except my heart just dissolved in my mouth and my brain's no better. So I do what any normal, functioning person would do—I choke on my own spit, which leads me to cough and, in turn, causes the man in front of me to laugh a rich sound I love so much.

He kisses me once upon the forehead, then whispers against my skin, "Can I show you something?"

I raise a brow. "Is this the part where you give me a ring?"

He smiles and shakes his head and continues caressing my arm. "I was thinking more of removing them, actually."

And with that he presses his large fingers against my wrist, extending to me his calm and ability stronger than I've ever felt. And this time there's not merely a soothing, there's a rippling that sends goose bumps up my arm.

I look down. The next moment I'm gasping as the owner circles that have been the circumference of my world since the age of six—that have marked who I've belonged to and so much of what I've been—begin disappearing.

One.

Two.

Ten. They're dissolving. And in their place is fresh, smooth skin—as clean as the day before I was purchased.

My throat tightens and my eyes warm at this man who, even

in this moment, offers me freedom from everything—even the ties of my broken past.

"That thing Rasha told me back in the courtyard?" he breathes. "She told me who I am."

I flutter an eyelash against his cheek. "And? Who are you?"

"A Median."

I widen my eyes. "A healer?"

He nods and removes the fourteenth owner circle.

"How'd *Rasha* know?"

He smirks at me.

Oh, right. She read it.

I slip a finger across his. "And how does it work exactly?"

"Draewulf's blood. And your song."

I wait.

"You know the blood Draewulf took from me, and I was so concerned he left me some of his . . . Apparently he did. Not enough to damage but enough to reactivate what his daughter had blocked all those years ago." He runs a hand down my hair. "Then at the battle when your song broke out . . . I felt it. Like a breaking in me. My body isn't just made to block or calm. It's made to absorb and release wounds."

I plant a soft kiss on his chin. "Which is how you healed me."

He grows serious, more serious than I've seen him all day, and traces his hand down to remove the final. The fifteenth. The one he himself placed there.

I stop his hand before he can take it. "Not this one."

He raises a brow. "But it's—"

"It's the one you gave me. I want to keep it."

He frowns. "Why?"

I shrug. "You gave it to me out of protection, and it's the first time I can ever remember someone doing something to save me."

He leans in until he's mere inches from my face, my cheeks, my lips. "As I recall, it's you who saved me."

I smile at this wondrous person who is beyond the incredible power he possesses. Does he even know how unfairly attractive he looks right now?

He smirks and winks at me and swags a hand through his hair. Hmm. Yes, clearly. I snort. "Your arrogance is magnanimous."

"I was hoping you'd eventually accept it as one of my qualities." He chuckles and pulls me close and traces a finger over my memorial tattoos.

"Are you going to take those too?" I frown.

He shakes his head. "Those are yours. Your memories. Your scars. Your journey." With each word he leans down to kiss each one. "Your cutting." His lips land last of all on the little bluebird above my elbow. The one I carved in grief for the little girl my powers killed and in my hatred toward him for carving my final owner circle. And for once there's no itching. No ache. No hunger to carve up my skin.

"I swear I will never own you," he says.

"And what if my freedom means me wanting to be yours?"

He cups my cheek in his giant palm and traces a thumb down my nose, my lips, my chin, all the way to my throat.

"Silly Storm Girl. I will always be *yours*." And before I can say more he leans in close again, flashing me that unfair smile. To which I chuckle and present him with a kiss.

He raises a suggestive brow, causing me to laugh, and in that laugh to truly inhale a world of beauty. Every smile, every friendship, every bit of goodness I've seen. Every bit of goodness I've hoped existed within me. And just like the ship I am fluttering, dipping, soaring.

And then we are kissing . . .

Kissing . . .
And kissing . . .

.

.

.

.

.

Until a small boy's voice mutters through the ventilation grate, "Blasted hulls, are you two going to make babies now?"

The End.

MY POCKETFUL OF THANK-YOUS

DEAREST READER,

My earliest memory is of snuggling on my mom's lap in the late-afternoon sun while she rocked and sang to me in a giant, plush rocking chair. In that moment it didn't matter what the rest of the day held, or that I was too small to play well with friends, because she was rocking and singing and holding me.

My second memory is of waking up in my dad's arms as he carried me to the car on a dark, noisy night—and rather than feeling frightened I simply felt his strength.

That, above all, is the defining thread that has impacted my life. The continuum I will never recover from. The thread of incredible people taking time out of their worlds to hold my head up when I've felt so small, and to invest reassurance and strength when I've been at my most raw and vulnerable. Beautiful people who've gripped my hands, and even more so, who've steadied my heart and allowed me to mature into some semblance of the souls they all are.

This trilogy is for them.

This trilogy is for you.

If you've picked up these books and even attempted to put your face between the pages to see if I have anything remotely interesting to say—you've completely blown my heart away. Thank you for your time. Thank you for your e-mails and comments and kindness. More than anything, thank you for sharing this world with me. I am unbelievably humbled and honored.

And to my incredible husband, Peter, and my children, Rilian, Avalon, and Korbin. My heart gets all verklempt just thinking of you. <3

My parents, sister, brothers, and their families, as well as my in-laws and relatives who've been so exceedingly supportive.

Every friend, mentor, and fellow author who has continually fed and inspired me to no end.

Jay Asher for your friendship. And for editing the final chapters into Eogan's voice.

Marissa Meyer, for your beautiful soul that is such an encouragement and example.

My better-than-any-author-possibly-deserves Thomas Nelson publishing family, with extra special thanks to Daisy and Becky and my agent, Danielle Smith. Because you make magic happen. Again, and again, and again. I love you rabidly.

Lee Hough. I totally hear you laughing like a schoolgirl up there.

My Father's House family, youth, and leaders. I love you guys forever.

Every dear blogger who has written and talked about this series, and who's allowed me the honor of interviews and online chats and has given JUST SO MUCH KINDNESS. I adore you guys.

Jesus. Because you are all this heart exists for.

DISCUSSION QUESTIONS

Warning: Spoilers Ahead!

1. When Nym was a child, her father admonished her to "Never destroy what simply needs taming. Mercy grows hearts more than bitterness." What do you think he meant by this? What types of people in today's society often get labeled as "bad" or in need of "taming"? What about them is different? What would change if we viewed each other with more mercy and kindness?

2. Going off the previous question, it seems like the current culture we live in often revels in bullying and tearing others down (especially online). Have you encountered this? What do you believe is the cause? How could our world benefit from extended acts of compassion?

3. That said, there are also sometimes people in life who aren't the safest for our hearts to allow too close. Is there someone in your world who might not be the safest in their treatment or influence of you? Is there a safe person you know whom you can talk to about them and how they make you feel?

4. Throughout *Siren's Song*, Nym continually faces the reality that (1) she shouldn't actually exist, and (2) she should never have survived. And yet she did for a reason. Do you believe this is true for everyone—that, no matter how seemingly insignificant or great we feel we are, we each exist for a purpose? In your own life, what might that purpose be? Do you believe some people's purposes are greater than others, or do we all contribute a powerful part? Do you believe impacting just one person around you can have a bigger effect than being "famous" or "well known for your contributions"?

5. At one point, while Nym is in Cashlin, Queen Laiha indicates how the dark power Nym previously ingested still resides within Nym's blood. "You feel it," she says. "Because the choices we make have lasting consequences." Do you agree with this? What kind of choices in your own life have had (or could have) intense consequences? And what future decisions could bring about positive results for your life?

6. What do you think of the queen's statement: "No one escapes this life, nor do they escape war, unscathed"? Is it possible to grow stronger or become better because of those things? What would a person need in order to do so?

7. In *Storm Siren* (book one in the trilogy), Nym wanted nothing to do with saving Faelen. Partly because she saw herself as more destructive than the danger coming at them, and partly because the people needing saving were the same who'd enslaved her. However, by the end of *Siren's Song*, Nym sacrifices her life for those very people. What do you think brought about that heart change? What types of challenges or altered perspective might lead someone to defend a person who has wronged them?

8. At the start of the trilogy Nym privately struggled with self-loathing, fear, and self-harm. As she grew in appreciating herself and her abilities, as well as in developing healthy relationships, her confidence increased, as did her capacity to overcome cutting. Are her insecurities or struggles anything you or someone you know can relate to? Are there things that have helped you, or perhaps actually made it harder? If so, do you have a safe person in your life to talk to about them? There are incredible resources and hope available to anyone struggling with depression or self-harm, including To Write Love on Her Arms (http://www.TWLOHA.com). Just please reach out. I promise you are never alone.

Standing with you and cheering you on, because you are so extraordinarily precious.

~M <3

THE ORIGIN OF THE BOLCRANE

A gift for you, my preciouses . . .

THERE'S A STORY WHISPERED OVER THE HEARTH-stones of certain Faelen hovels on storm-squallish nights. When small children have curled up against the legs of their papas and the mums hold scalding mugs of tea. A legend that long predates Draewulf's own hideous history.

A legend about the bolcranes of Litchfell Forest.

"Won't the storm upset the bolcranes, Papa?" the son asks.

"Bah. The monsters are always upset. That is why they are monsters."

The father adjusts his legs as his little girl wilts beneath her blanket. "Will the monsters come here though?"

He smiles and leans down to ruffle her curled locks. "Not tonight, love."

"What do they look like?" Her brother's face flickers eager in the firelight.

"Like giant lizards," Papa says after a moment, glancing at their mum. "Black and oily and bigger than a horse, with scales for skin, strong poison for spit, and teeth as sharp as a sea dragon's."

"Are they so upset because they're so ugly?"

"Some believe so."

The mum clicks her tongue and sets down the mugs of tea. "Tell it to them right or not at all, 'enry."

He grins, then takes a swig of the steaming green liquid. "I am tellin' it right. The travellers say the bolcranes used to be beautiful beings. But they became powerful and twisted, so their souls turned from light to dark, and then so did their bodies. Although . . ." He leans down to the children. "I've heard if you listen close to the hissing breath of the beasts, you can still hear their voices. Asking for more power an' crying in grief at their cursed state." He sits back and takes another sip. "Or maybe it's hateful tears for what they've become."

The boy child's eyes widen larger than hornet eggs. "Was it the Creator who cursed them?"

"Your mum believes so." Papa looks up and winks at the woman, and is met with a biscuit in the face. He laughs and grabs it from where it dropped. "Well, at least the heathens from Cashlin do. They believe there was a great fallin' out, and the Creator banned the monsters from the Valley of Origin and forced them into Litchfell Forest to live. That's why they despise us Faelenians so much."

The father breaks the biscuit and passes pieces to the children. "But it's not true. The ancient spindle trees, which have watched the beasts roam and devour, claim it was the beasts who rejected the Creator. That their craving for more power was insatiable, and thus they cursed *themselves*."

"Is that why they have to live in Litchfell now?" the girl asks around a mouthful of bread.

After pulling the girl onto his lap, Papa dusts the crumbs off her cheek. "That, or they've simply forgotten how to live outside of it."

"But what were the beautiful beings before they turned to bolcranes?"

"The strongest Uathúils," the father murmurs.

"Elementals."

A rattle of shutters from the thrashing storm makes both children jump and the room falls quiet, until a moment later when the little girl looks up into her father's face.

"When they figure out how to be free of the forest, will they come for *us* then?" she asks.

ABOUT THE AUTHOR

PHOTO BY SARAH KATHLEEN
PHOTOGRAPHY

MARY WEBER IS A RIDICULOUSLY uncoordinated girl plotting to take over make-believe worlds through books, handstands, and imaginary throwing knives. In her spare time, she feeds unicorns, sings '80s hairband songs to her three muggle children, and ogles her husband, who looks strikingly like Wolverine. They live in California, which is perfect for stalking LA bands, Joss Whedon, and the ocean.

Visit Mary online at maryweber.com
Facebook: marychristineweber
Twitter: @mchristineweber
Instagram: maryweberauthor